W9-CBD-066

ME AND
THE DEVIL

ME AND THE DEVIL

A NOVEL

Nick Tosches

LITTLE, BROWN AND COMPANY

New York Boston London

Little, Brown and Company
Hachette Book Group
237 Park Avenue, New York, NY 10017
littlebrown.com

First Edition: December 2012

Little, Brown and Company is a division of Hachette Book Group, Inc., and is celebrating its 175th anniversary in 2012. The Little, Brown name and logo are trademarks of Hachette Book Group, Inc.

The publisher is not responsible for websites (or their content) that are not owned by the publisher.

The Hachette Speakers Bureau provides a wide range of authors for speaking events. To find out more, go to hachettespeakersbureau.com or call (866) 376-6591.

Library of Congress Cataloging-in-Publication Data

Tosches, Nick.
　Me and the devil : a novel / Nick Tosches.—1st ed.
　　p. cm.
　ISBN 978-0-316-12097-5
　I. Title.
　PS3570.O74M4 2012
　813'.54—dc23　　　　　　　　　　2012020006

10 9 8 7 6 5 4 3 2 1

RRD-C

Printed in the United States of America

To her who must here be nameless

If you bring forth what is within you,
what you bring forth will save you.
If you do not bring forth what is within you,
what you do not bring forth will destroy you.

—THE GOSPEL OF THOMAS

ME AND THE DEVIL

THE PAST IS A VERY BAD PLACE. IT IS NOT GOOD TO GO there. Not alone. Not like this. "Take a deep breath." They're always telling me to take a deep breath. But that deep breath does not come.

Somewhere along the line, something went wrong.

These words were supposed to have led to more words, to the beginning of what I cannot bring myself to tell.

Now, having got up, poured myself a drink, lit a cigarette, and stood awhile at the window—seeing night and rain, feeling nothing—I look at those words and realize that I've just written my autobiography, the story of my life. From beginning to end, that's it. Somewhere along the line, something went wrong. There's really nothing more to it than that.

But that's the easy way out, the easy way out of saying what I cannot bring myself to say. Yes, a lot went wrong. There were a lot of wrong turns. But this one. This one.

Let me drink.

The label on this bottle has a lot of words on it. Some of them are invisible: lies, truth, destiny, darkness, loss, shame, guilt, the sound and fury of the idiot's every delusion, sickness unto death of body and of soul. And courage for the coward. I have read and retched them all, these hidden things upon that label. They define what is in the bottle, and what is within me.

Courage for the coward. Yes, let me drink, so that I can say what I cannot. Even if in the end I let the flames consume it, and can then return quietly to my lies. This thought goes well with that coward's courage that I seek.

But can there be any returning? Any returning to anything? Now? From here, from this final somewhere? This final somewhere of endless wrong somethings and endless wrong turns?

Enough. Just drink. There, yes, that's better, that's it. Just drink and the words will come.

I T'S THAT THING WITH THE MONKEYS. THOSE MONKEYS, THOSE dead monkeys, haunting me for all those years, and me not knowing why.

Just the other day I was sitting on the bench outside the joint on Reade Street. Not on a barstool inside the joint, but on the bench outside the joint, not drinking. I mean a coffee from Dunkin' Donuts, that's what I was drinking. I was just sitting there, with that coffee and a smoke, looking into the clear blue morning sky. Looking for a way out.

"Here's for the guys that never came back."

My eyes moved from the sky to where the voice came from. Him again. Some stumblebum who passed this way every once in awhile. He was standing there, drunk and weaving, looking like shit.

"You know what I mean. You were there," he said as he poured some of the cheap whiskey from the pint bottle in his hand onto the pavement. This wasn't like a capful on the sidewalk for the boys upstate. It was spillage.

"Don't waste booze like that, you stupid fuck," I told him.

"We were there. We know," he rasped.

He was never there, I figured. He was full of shit.

"What was your MOS?" I asked him. Everybody had an MOS. Mine had been 2531, Ground Radio Operator.

"Communications is the voice of command." That's what

5

that fucking CO said. That's what he was supposed to say, but he said it as if he believed it. Worse: as if we were supposed to believe it, and that it was supposed to make our chests swell with pride. Sitting there nodding out in the middle of nowhere, conveying coordinates between one jackass and another on a nigger-rigged Prick-25. The voice of command.

Yeah, that's what I was fighting for. That's what I was defending. The American Way. Freedom of speech. But you couldn't use that word anymore. Shouldn't use it. No. The "n-word." Nigger-rigged. It was probably the one indispensable technological term in the Local 79 lexicon. Verboten.

It was all bullshit. But everybody had a Military Occupational Specialty number. I was somehow sure that this bum didn't even know what an MOS was. He looked at me, wove closer to me with that pint in his hand, grinned a big, drunken grin, baring dirty gums and a few dirty teeth. A mouth even worse than mine.

"If I told you, I'd have to kill ya," he said, hoarse with booze and bullshit, then laughed a laugh that was hoarse with booze and bullshit.

He didn't know what an MOS was. He didn't know that it was just a stupid fucking number for a stupid fucking asshole. I just turned away from him, and he saddened, took a swig from that cheap pint, and staggered away.

But the damage was done. He had brought back the monkeys. In the middle of all I was already going through, this fucking pain-in-the-ass, full-of-shit drunken bum had brought back those dead monkeys.

The Northern I Corps. The border of the DMZ, that stupid five-mile swath. The Dead Marine Zone, we called it. One day, atop a hill, I was standing around doing nothing. That was really my specialty, doing nothing, but there was no MOS for that. I was just watching the bulldozers, encircled by a bunch of artillery idiots—grunts, the lowest MOS, riflemen—raze the ground on the top of the hill to level it into a landing zone for helicopters. I walked off into the jungle to smoke a joint, hoping I might run into somebody with some smack.

The jungle was getting more and more bare and barren every day. That shit from those helicopters worked.

I was out a way when I saw them. These weren't just a bunch of dead monkeys. I had seen dead men, paused awhile to look at them, moved on, and forgot about them. But something about these monkeys affected me as nothing else ever had. It was beyond my understanding. I just stood there, transfixed, as a strange sort of horror overtook me; and breath must have stopped, or faltered, for the next heartbeat I felt came deep, hard, sudden, resounded within me, and shook my nerves with an inexplicable sense of vague, terrible presentiment.

Many years passed before I realized what I'd foreseen in those dead monkeys, and what about them had stopped, chilled, and seized me so. It was me that I saw. Me, my future, and my fate.

Those monkeys clung to one another in the throes of desperation, the throes of death. It was my end, your end, the common end of us all. Though the horror and haunting of those monkeys shot immediately into me and remained with me, only as age crept through me and over me did I come to see this and feel it full.

I was closer now in years to death than to youth, and I was desperate to cling to another. I felt it long before I knew it for what it was and could express it: the desire for mortal communion with the body and soul of one still in the flush of what had ebbed and was now lost to me.

It creeps into us, this desperation, without our being quite aware of its nature, when we enter our fifth decade of life. If we are fortunate enough to enter our seventh decade, its nature is clear to us. But society, thoughts of moral judgment, a sense of shame, even fear of public damnation and prison restrain us, and the growing compulsion devours most of us unslaked as we wend our way from life in silence and secrecy to our common end. Most of us. But I would not be one of them.

I felt more than thought that if I could not have youth again, I could at least slake myself in new life. Sustenance, moisture, deliverance.

If I could not bear the truth, I could at least close my eyes in the comfort of a lie.

MOST MEN BELIEVE THEIR LIVES TO BE SOMEHOW distinguished from the rest. But their lives hold as little interest as they do meaning, and are worthy only of being extinguished. As a writer I have encountered more of these men than I care to remember, indeed than I can remember. Though they do not read, except perhaps to graze on the mulch of an ill-written tabloid or the drivel on a handheld device or computer screen, they feel that writers might somehow be drawn to their drab and dreary tales of sameness. It is hard to escape them. They know nothing, least of all themselves. They go from cradle to grave seeking something. What they seek means as little to me as they do. They are a source of tedium and acid reflux, nothing more.

Do not think that I am setting writers apart from this majority. Most of them, in fact, belong to it. But they are not writers to be read, or countenanced.

I myself did not read much anymore. And I wrote even less. In fact, I had not written a book in years. Nothing seemed to matter. I felt that there was nothing left to write. I was a poet without pen or drum. Approaching a blank page, or even thinking of doing so, I felt disoriented and abstracted and my nerves went raw. Again and again I swore that I would stop drinking and resume writing. Again and again I drank. And when I did not, I sat and drank coffee and smoked and withdrew into myself. Yet I still called myself a writer when asked what I did for a living. Maybe I still thought like a writer. Or maybe, as George Orwell said, all writers are vain, selfish, and lazy.

"Writing a book," he said, "is a horrible, exhausting struggle, like a bout of some painful illness. One would never undertake such a thing if one were not driven on by some demon whom one can neither resist nor understand. For all one knows that demon is simply the same instinct that makes a baby squall for attention." Perhaps I had lost my demon. Perhaps other demons had overtaken it. Then again, Orwell wrote those words when he was in his early forties, and he lived to be only forty-six.

Exceptional men do not hold their experiences to be out of the ordinary or of interest to anyone else. Unlike the trodden fungus-men, they are not so ignorantly and presumptuously self-absorbed. They are nobody and they know it. They shun notice. They are exceedingly rare.

All in the way of saying that people are often drawn to writers. Not so much as to buy or read what they write, but simply as bothersome parasites. If you're not careful, they will drain you dry.

Women are not so bad as men in this regard. Still they too are drawn to writers, if only because this solitary and distressed way to make a living seems to them for some reason, or lack of reason, more alluring and more attractive than the usual occupations professed in bars.

And in bars, behind a mask that hides hatred or jealousy or fear or the unspeakable, everyone thinks he, or she, knows you, as you think you know them.

Where they knew me, where they thought they knew me, they came near, to drain what they thought to be my life force, or to cough up the dregs of their own on me. I was anathema, accursed and consecrated. Yes. They came near. It was easy.

We were all monkeys about to die. I did not want to die.

Though my inchoate and unclear desires carried the air of the forbidden, they stirred in me something like what I remembered the commingled feelings of love and lust to be.

THE OLDER WE GET, THE MORE THE GHOSTS CROWD AND claim us. Death does not deter the dead from living on within us and around us. We are under their spell. The world becomes irrevocably haunted.

It was she who spoke to me. I don't know why. I was old. My looks were long gone. Maybe it was because I did not speak to her. I was quiet. One of the fungus-men was trying to talk her up, and she escaped by turning to me and smiling. Some girls liked those guys. Girls seeking attention. Seeking their fathers. Those guys fell for it, bought them drinks, got suckered in.

All I had seen was her long blond hair. Now I saw a face and a smile, and I liked what I saw. I deliberated for a moment on what I should say to her to set me apart from the others in that half-lighted barroom.

I could not see her legs, but her breasts in her pale blue cashmere sweater seemed modest. This was good. No woman with large breasts has comely legs. I wondered if the cuffs matched the collar. She looked like a real blonde. But I was drunk, even if only I knew it. I wanted to bury my face between her legs. I could tell if the cuffs matched the collar, I could tell if she was a natural blonde by the feel of the hair between her legs, how soft it was or was not on my lips. Even drunk. Even in the dark.

Better not to make too much sense at first. Better to lure her with a gleam of inscrutability. Something that could be taken by her to mean and pertain to whatever she fancied.

"Thenceforth evil became my good," I said, hoping that the hair between her legs was cornsilk blond and that she did not shave it.

"Where'd that come from?" she asked. Her smile curled a bit and her blue eyes brightened.

"Milton. *Paradise Lost*," I lied. Milton said something like it, but he never said that. Maybe it was Mary Shelley. No matter. Better to quote Milton, even if it was a fabricated quotation. Had she ever heard of Milton? If she hadn't, maybe she had heard of his big fat poem. As I said, I was drunk. "The words of Satan," I added, returning to my drink.

"I think I read that in high school," she said. I figured that she was lying too. That was good. I wasn't expecting what she said next.

"Are you a Miltonist or a Satanist?"

"Neither," I said. "I'm just an old, old man trying to live while I can." Lefty Frizzell said that, or something like it; but she didn't ask.

I made love to her in my way later that night. An old man and a young woman who was to me little more than a child. It was not what I wanted. It felt good for a moment, then left me feeling emptier and more alone than I had felt before her smile and our desultory lies.

"How long is your refractory period?" she asked, with a giggle and a purr.

"Forever," I said. "Forever."

The shades of the night were endless. Maybe it was the booze, I told myself. But I had only been drinking beer. Maybe it was the beer, I told myself. But I knew that it was not. I had entered her, but she had not entered me. There had been no slaking. I had breathed no new life. Sustenance, moisture, deliverance were not mine.

The blond hair was real. My hands shook the next morning after she left. I have to stop drinking, I muttered aloud. I managed to make a cup of coffee and I sat there with it, smoking one cigarette after another. My stare was vacant, as if in mourning for myself. The last time I raised the cup to my lips, the coffee was cold. I took a Valium and exhaled. I do not remember her name.

A few nights later I was sitting at the bar at Circa Tabac with a vodka and soda and a smoke. My buddy Lee, who runs the place, sat down next to me with that inscrutable grin of his on his face.

"Happy Candlemas," I said.

"Is today Candlemas?" he said. "I thought it was Groundhog Day. What's Candlemas?"

"The Feast of the Purification of the Virgin Mary. Something like that. Lots of candles."

"Yeah? What do I know? I'm a Jew, and I don't even know Jew holidays."

"Also the first of the four traditional witches' Sabbaths of the year." I drank and drew smoke. "What I want to know is: how did Candlemas become the witches' Sabbath, and how did the witches' Sabbath become Groundhog Day?"

"It's when the groundhog comes out of its hole."

"Yeah?"

"I don't know." He drank and drew smoke. "You writing these days?"

"Next question."

"How are the girls treating you?"

My reaction was spontaneous. I don't know what my face looked like, but I think I uttered "Oh, God" and managed a laugh that ended in earnest with the words "It's sad" and a sound of a different kind.

At this he in turn managed a laugh.

That was the night I met her, right there at that bar on Watts Street. Her name was Sandrine, and she liked to be raped after bathing in warm water and milk and brushing out her hair. She was in her early twenties. If she had told me she was seventeen, I would have believed her. Maybe she was. I had not been with a redhead, not such a pretty one, in a long, long time.

I HAD NEVER READ ANY OF THE BOOKS, BUT I GOT A KICK OUT of the old movies. Bela Lugosi was a hoot.

I read a biography of him once. The only thing I remember from it is his craving toward the end of his days for a kind of oily peppery paprika bread that he had longed for since leaving Hungary. I remember this because I've been craving a kind of oily peppery paprika bread that a few of the old Italian-Albanian women in my boyhood neighborhood made in their black cast-iron ovens. I'm pretty sure it was called *zallia,* or something like that. The recipe seems to have died with the last of them, as I haven't been able to find it again in more than forty years of searching, and I'm beginning to feel that I never will. What they called *tarallia,* pretzel-shaped anise bread, I've found a lackluster echo of in *taralli.* And what was called—though the final vowels were never pronounced—*culliaccia,* the rich, buttery egg bread they made in glazed braided rings, I've found a more distant approximation of in what has been served to me as a dismal confection called Italian egg bread. But *zallia* remains a maddeningly tantalizing memory. When I read about the bread the Hungarian actor so longed for, I was sure it was pretty much the same thing; and in time all I retained from the story of his life was the mention of that bread.

In the pictures, they don't eat. And the mere sight of garlic can bring about a seizure. They react worse than a WASP school-

16

girl to it. It's ridiculous, not only to a wop but probably to Hungarians and Romanians too. Italy isn't the only place in Europe where they're big on garlic soup.

And what is this malarkey about the light of day? Are they all supposed to be independently wealthy? No nine-to-five working stiffs? It's like the nonsense about the cross. And wouldn't a stake through the heart do in just about anybody? I mean, come on. Think about it. Not at all afraid of rats, mind you; but afraid of garlic, daylight, and crosses. Who came up with this stuff?

I really get a kick out of the fangs. Hell, between Sandrine and the next of the four witches' Sabbaths, May Eve—yes, I've observed only pagan holy days, from Christmas and Easter to the four Sabbaths, for a long, long time—I had nine teeth pulled on a single day, and another had worked itself out of the gum on a day soon thereafter. As I had already lost a bunch of teeth before these ten, I was left practically toothless, with a loose, unsure contraption of plastic and wire to make do in my mouth.

How those guys on Bedford Street, on Sullivan Street, on Thompson Street shook their heads and laughed low and down at those Mafia pictures. A ban on dope dealing, mother love, a code of honor. Same thing. Garlic, light, crosses, and fangs.

It's not like that. It's not like that at all. Nowhere but in truth will you find the truth.

WHEN I BIT INTO SANDRINE'S THIGH WITH MY mouthful of plastic, wire, and the few real teeth that still cut, her moan turned to a jagged scream that slashed the night, and her scream turned to a wild sigh that was deep as the sea.

I tasted her blood in my mouth. It could not have been more than a few drops, a thin trickle, but it was as if I suckled on her very soul and the inmost mystery of her. That taste and the sweet taste of her flesh, soft and young, in my mouth were one; and the sound, which seemed to come from a distance, dreamlike and timbrous, of her surrender and her giving was a beckoning to enter more deeply into the strange black forest of lust on the edge of which we trembled.

She was mine, I was hers. We seemed to merge, I into her, she into me. I clung, quenching my tongue in the sweat and blood of her thigh. Sustenance, moisture, deliverance. I was lost, beautifully lost, breathing and feeling as I had never felt before.

I opened her lips with mine and had her taste what I had tasted, the taste of what she had given me, of what I had taken. We kissed gently. I collapsed, falling into a sleep without dreams, a sleep without hauntings, aware of nothing but a vague and comforting sense of enchantment.

This sublime feeling lingered when I woke. We did not talk about what transpired. Her presence was with me long after she left. I went more than a week without drinking. Then I returned to the bar where we had met. She was not there. I asked Lee if he had seen her. He told me that he had never seen her before and he had not seen her since.

I went home alone that night, not really drunk but feeling the old loneliness welling up in me.

She returned there a few nights later. I brought her home with me, but it was not the same. She seemed to regard me as a danger, as one who knew something unutterable about her, and it was as if the possibility that I might utter the unutterable put her on edge and made her ill at ease. I was not with the girl who surrendered and gave, the girl who had gone to heaven and hell when I broke her skin. No. I was with the girl who liked to be raped after bathing in warm water and milk and brushing out her hair. It was then that I knew her to be troubled. It was then that I knew her mind was not right. In the morning, when I walked her to the door and kissed her good-bye, she lowered her head and turned away and began to silently weep.

She had surrendered and given the heart of her youth to something far worse than I, who had taken her but for a single earthly night. She had chosen hell over heaven long before that night, and that night had not cured her.

We were to meet again.

I T IS ALWAYS EASIER TO SEE IN ANOTHER WHAT WE ARE uncomfortable with in ourselves. A few days after my second encounter with Sandrine, it struck me that when I felt that I was looking into her heart I was really looking into my own.

The blonde whose cuffs matched her collar had been the first woman with whom I'd had old-fashioned, missionary-style sex in a very long time. It had been years. I had grown jaded. My sex drive had evanesced and with it my virility. I looked like a man but I was not.

Once upon a time I had known the heat of passion every day and every night. The combustions of sensuality consumed me. Now there were only passing moments of lukewarm velleity. The prospect of being close to a woman, to anyone, repelled me. I could no longer bear a human touch without recoiling. Maybe this is what disturbed and haunted me about the prophecy of those dead monkeys. They had foretold not only my fate but my escape from it as well: an escape that involved the closeness to another of which I was ever more incapable. They had seemed to present a choice, unclear and unknown, between one terror and another. The terror had increased through recent years, as I grew more bound to the loneliness and desperation of my descending darkness and at the same time more loath to caress or be caressed by another.

I had embraced the blonde in my drunkenness. It had always been this way. Alcohol enabled me to do what I otherwise could not. The many lovers, remembered and forgotten, I had known in younger years were as much a part of my drinking life as of my love life. At times those lives seemed inseparable.

Why were they attracted to me? Not the women of my past. The blonde and Sandrine. What had possibly moved them? They were young and it was a young man's world. I was a toothless wraith of a man that once had been. It was not what they saw, I concluded, it was what they sensed. Was it a certain world-weariness that I evinced? The unrevealing nuances of a perverse vestigial cupidity? The hint of what they had never experienced? All of these, none of these? What beguiled them? Was the answer as elusive and ultimately unknowable as the parts of their souls that lay hidden to themselves?

Maybe I *was* different after all. They—the great royal they, who spoke from on high—had told me throughout my life that I was different. Maybe I had always been different. Not better. Maybe even worse. But different.

It mattered only that they were drawn to me. As empty and forlorn as I had been left by my night with the blonde, it brought back to me, I later realized, something of old, forsaken confidence, even of old, forsaken courage. Were it not for the blonde, there would not have been my night with Sandrine. Were it not for Sandrine, I would not have had my first lovely taste of what, as I clung to her and drew her into me, felt like deliverance. I had judged her to be a troubled soul. I would have judged Saint Teresa in her ecstasy to be the same.

Troubled souls or divine. Who was I to judge, and what did it matter? It mattered only, I told myself again, that they were drawn to me. And as they had been drawn, I now had no doubt, there would be others. Lost souls or holy intercessors, there would be others. All I had to do was lead them, go together with them, to where no one could go alone.

It was not sex that I sought, not as it was commonly conceived. I sought communion, sacrament, transubstantiation, the blood that brought redemption.

Sandrine had placed magic in my hand, in my mouth. It was the magic of herself, and it was mine. It felt good to be awakened, to be thrilled once again, like a child experiencing his first inkling of the illimitable.

The monkeys no longer anguished me. They became instead an inner sophia, an image of perception and veneration painted in indelible hues in my mind. They are sacred to me. They brought me to new life.

I would go headlong into the promise of this new life. This was not a conscious decision. There was no thought or deliberation. The momentum of exhilaration simply took me.

THE PART OF DOWNTOWN MANHATTAN WHERE I LIVE WAS once the quietest, least traveled, and most sparsely occupied area in town. Its stately old brick buildings, many of them dating from the middle of the nineteenth century, were from an era when buildings were built to last. The stonework of window arches and the loading platforms of warehouses, the narrow cobblestone streets and small shops evoked the atmosphere of a bygone New York. It was a place of lovely days and enticing hushed nights. The balmy summer breezes and brisk winter winds that wound through it from the Hudson were like familiar spirits that caused leaves, panes, and shadows to tremble in the lush silence. It was easy to imagine the elderly Thomas Paine idling here amid others to witness the hanging of a murderer, on the corner of Leonard Street and Broadway, as he did one day in the spring of 1804. Easy to imagine butter and egg traders still bustling within the old red-brick Mercantile Exchange, as they did a century ago and more, near to a Bayer heroin warehouse on Harrison Street. The bar I haunted occupied the ground floor of a three-story building that had been put up in 1852.

It was a wonderful neighborhood, a neighborhood of seclusion and friendly encounters and whispers, welcoming byways and odd purchases, peace and quiet, cosseting charm, and open skies above gables, chimneys, and trees.

Then, some years ago, in the closing decade of the last

millennium, everything began to change. At first the change was slow and subtle, barely noticeable. By the time it was perceived, it was too late. What had lingered on, so rare and so precious and so different for so long, was gone forever. New, ugly buildings of glass, metal, and cheap fabrication belittled the old structures and obscured the sky. I lived now in a valley of eternal scaffolding. Years before I had slept on my fire escape, rising with the soft light and stirrings of early morning. Now the night was a glare of artificial lighting and a blare of industrial clamor. Through the window that opened to the fire escape where I had slept so soundly, I now saw scaffolding that advertised Warburg Realty, where "Tribeca's cobblestone streets meet the information highway." The old and real cobblestone street beneath my window had been torn up and repaved with a new, quainter-looking surface: a stupid project that had brought with it a year of deafening noise. Forget about the sweet open-air sleep on the fire escape outside my bedroom window, back when an old florist had occupied the corner where Warburg now kept its windows brightly lighted all night. I now needed a blackout shade on the window just to sleep in my bed.

The whispering peace of the place vanished amid the obliterating noises of traffic, construction, demolition, street renovation, and above all and most abhorrent, the crowds that infested the place, blocking the narrow sidewalks with their twin baby carriages and strollers, whining shrilly into mobile telephones, professing a love for what had been as they ran amok and destroyed it.

Why had they come here? Because they read that it was the place to live. The school was good. Property values were rising. It was safe. It was a good investment. It was the perfect place to raise a family. So they came, and so they overcrowded the school, created a real estate bubble, attracted crime, caused inflation, shoved aside those who had been here before them, and remade the neighborhood in their own image, trumpeting their obstreperous entitlement over the vanishing remains of what had been and was no more.

Who were they? Emigrants from the Upper East Side. The rich white trash of Europe and Asia. Wall Street thieves. Speculators. Yuppies. The scum of New York and of the earth. I was becoming a racist. I was coming to hate white people. These white people.

I had seen their spawn grow into adolescent blobs of medicated hyperactive protoplasm. I had seen those blobs of adolescent protoplasm grow into the manic dusk of their teenage years, scorched, undone, and broken apart by privilege, free money, alienation, disorders of the mind, and congenital enfeeblement.

The doomed soul whom Thomas Paine had watched hang had comported himself tranquilly, attaching the gallows rope around his own neck to the crosspiece above. Not so these uneasy children of the damned, these blood blisters of entitlement and dejection.

I was surrounded by susceptible, impressionable lost young girls. Surely the magic in my hand and my mouth would not fail to bring longed-for grace to these trembling lambs. Even if they did not know it, they wanted me as I wanted them, needed me as I needed them.

It was better, however, to hunt elsewhere, was it not? The Lower East Side and other old pockets of character had also fallen, or were falling, to nothingness. Yes, better to hunt elsewhere, away from the eyes and tongues of these girls' parents and guardians. Such girls, after all, were everywhere in this fallen city, in these fallen days.

I thought of the girl-child, maybe sixteen, whom I had seen masturbating one morning, her eyes tightly shut, rubbing herself into a frenzy on the narrow arm of a bench in the little park nearby. (I had stopped watching her when two sanitation men, on their way to the bar, paused to watch.) I thought of the girl who offered me money to take her half-finished container of coffee into the bar and have it filled with liquor for her. I thought of the girl, thin and pale and hithering, who wore sheer black hosiery under the hiked-up plaid of her school skirt. I thought of the girl, a wisp older (the bars served her), who sang for me on a sultry late summer night but had never heard of Billie Holiday or the Jaynetts. I thought of the girl who asked me for a cigarette and smelled like freesia and dew when she drew close to the flame of my lighter. I thought of all the errant daughters, in their distress and in their dangerous desire. I thought of the blood like rainy lace on Sandrine's thigh, transposed to their thighs. I thought of many things.

IT WAS A TERRIBLE WINTER, THAT WINTER OF TWO YEARS PAST, that winter of my first, tentative steps into the passage of my resurrection. Frigid winds brought a barrage of storms, one fast after another. Icy sleet and rain transformed the deep snows into a treacherous mess of filthy black ice and slush that covered streets, pavements, gutters, garbage. Insalubrious gales of cold, humid air blew and slashed almost relentlessly, making the temperatures, which were most of the time below freezing, seem even worse. It went on for months without respite.

I did not succeed in my pursuit of the young flesh that I craved. Oh, they were young, yes, the girls I brought home those biting winter nights. But they were not virgin temptresses. They were in their twenties, even their thirties, and, on at least one occasion, over forty. It struck me that the younger these women were, the more willing, even eager, they were to indulge me as I descended on them—always gently at first, then letting my hunger lead me—to execute the rite of the dead monkeys, to cling to them, to revel in the taste and feel of their sweet thighs, to break open their skin and dainty tendril-like vessels, and to lovingly exsanguinate with my mouth the drops of their essence.

Yes, the younger they were, the more willing they were. I would have thought the opposite to be true. I would have ventured that the older and more experienced they were, the more ready they would be to experiment and accept. It was a pleasant revelation, what I learned from my encounters with these six or seven women over the course of that stormy winter.

I did succeed in finding my path to sobriety. The sense of new life I was beginning to feel, and the exhilaration it brought, were such that I wanted to be sober, I needed to be sober, because I wanted and needed to be fully there for these blessings. There could be no other way. Light now shone in the great cathedral of melancholy. It was as simple as that.

It wasn't easy. I recalled my father, lying in a hospital bed, telling me that he had been drunk since he was nineteen and that he was never going to drink again. At the time he was a few years older than I am now. They let him out of the hospital a few days later, and a few hours after that he was back in the bar drinking. I was not him, I told myself. I may have been like him in some ways, but I was not him.

For three or four days it was pretty bad. There were slight sudden seizures. I did not suffer delirium tremens, which I had in the past during severe spells of alcohol poisoning. But with every breath or abrupt frightened gasp my racing heart, mind, and nerves screamed with urgency for a drink. I put off taking that drink from one moment to the next, then from one hour to the next. Finally I slept. It was a troubled, nightmarish sleep, and I woke from it in a cold sweat. But it was sleep nonetheless. Finally I ate. A couple of runny soft-scrambled eggs, lightly toasted white bread with butter, a glass of milk. But it was food nonetheless. When I no longer feared cutting myself, I shaved. I took vitamin B, washed down Valium with more milk. I drank water. I drank tea. I ventured outdoors and inhaled deeply. After a week or so, my heart, mind, and nerves no longer screamed. I was weak, sickly, and on edge. My brain was not right. At times I quivered. But I was here, and I was sober. A few mornings later I wakened to a strength, clarity, and calm that had not been mine for a very long time. I made a cup of coffee, lit a cigarette, and listened to Arvo Pärt's *Litany*.

I tried to banish the self-torment and self-doubt that I had sunk into. Had I not been through this before, and had it not in the end led to nothing? Had I not, again and again, over and over, got myself sober only to get drunk again? Wasn't this just another suffering on the wheel of suffering? How could I feel so sure that I would succeed where I had countless times and invariably failed?

But recent events had filled me with belief—belief in a new life, which meant a new world, a new me. This was part of it all. It had to be. I whispered to myself the words from Isaiah that had always made me smile: "Woe unto them that rise up early in the morning that they may follow strong drink." I was not smiling.

Alcoholics Anonymous tells us to put our faith in God or a higher power. We are told to relinquish willpower and say, echoing the Lord's Prayer, "Thy will, not mine, be done." This theist dogma proves an obstacle to many. Such was the case with me until I simply learned to discount it. If the founders of A.A. could not see that it was folly to doubt the human will while at the same time propounding faith in a God that had been willed into being by man—so be it. To me it was the sort of nonsense that obscured the good of A.A. I had witnessed and felt that goodness, but it had never taken root in me. Some might say that my will disallowed it. But it was my will that got me there in the first place. It was their insistence on a "loving God," so indelibly fundamental to the precepts of A.A., and their Hallmark platitudes and cultish humbug that did the disallowing. Apologists and exegetes have stressed the importance of spirituality over religion in A.A., but that God remains. Not a god, not a godly force, but *the* God of man's stupid invention and enduring madness.

That there was good in A.A. I had little doubt. I had felt it and

I had seen it at work in those rooms and in what people took with them from those rooms. The times I had committed myself to hospitals to get clean, the cure that was offered in every institution, with no exception, was ultimately the same: A.A.

In all my reading, in fact, from E. M. Jellinek's *The Disease Concept of Alcoholism* to the present, I had come across only one credible author who offered an alternative. In *Heal Thyself,* an account of his own alcoholism, Olivier Ameisen, a medical doctor, advances the drug baclofen as the cure that saved his life and has since saved the lives of others. As baclofen is unaccepted as a treatment for alcoholism by the medical and pharmaceutical establishment, it is difficult to find a doctor who will administer it as such. Ameisen's book was published in the United States under the imprint of an editor and publisher I know, and she was kind enough to give me his private address. I wrote to him of my willingness and eagerness to undergo baclofen therapy; but he never responded. I wondered if he was laid out drunk somewhere.

Though published almost fifty years apart, Jellinek's book and Ameisen's book are companions on my shelf, along with two older books, Jack London's self-described "alcoholic memoirs" *John Barleycorn* and Charles Jackson's *The Lost Weekend.* (I was very late to discover Jackson's masterpiece, so stupid was the moving picture that prejudiced me against this book on which it allegedly was based.) Others, like Hans Fallada's *The Drinker,* I have read with some interest and at times admiration, then discarded. I like scary drunk tales, and the disparate three to be found together on my shelf are to me the best of them, each in its way. I blame it on myself that, alone or together, they did not scare me enough to effect a change in me. But it was very much to the contrary. I derived vicarious delight from reading in these tales during my fleeting periods of sobriety. I did not now draw down one of these volumes, but searched out my hefty little blue A.A. book, which I kept in a closet, separate from the others.

I had no trouble feeling the presence of, and believing in, powers greater than myself—the sea, the wind, certain sacred breezes that seemed to bear the lingering powers of old gods and old wisdom—but I knew that none of these powers gave a fuck whether I drank or did not drink. Only I did. It was up to me, only me, and my will—mine, not thine.

That Saturday afternoon I walked to the meeting in the basement of the Municipal Union Building on Barclay Street. "The only requirement for membership is a desire to stop drinking." I had read those words posted on meeting-room walls many times, and every time I read them I reflected that I did not belong, that I failed to meet this sole requirement for being there; for I knew in the back of my mind that I was intent on drinking again. I had brought men and women to these rooms who had fared far better in them, and in the program, than I. But I knew that this time was different. I had a desire, a very deep and real desire, to stop drinking for good. I felt that I belonged.

"Grant me the serenity to accept the things I cannot change, the courage to change the things I can, and the wisdom to know the difference."

I always loved these words: the mystery of their origin, the power and beauty inherent in them. Plain, straightforward, they invited no interpretation. Here, as often encountered in A.A., shorn of the God who was called on to do the granting when A.A. first appropriated it, and who remains when these words appear in the sanctioned literature of A.A., as do the closing words "Thy will, not mine, be done," was a prayer not only for drunkards but for every mortal soul. These words felt good coming from within me, my voice one with the voices of the others.

Her eyes, so sad, were the first thing I noticed. I watched after her as she hesitated then wandered slowly, alone, from the room.

She wore a skirt or a dress under her gray woolen coat, and under that, dark patterned tights. Her legs were shapely, very shapely. I imagined ripping open those tights, baring her thigh, and hearing her utter what wild and exquisite cries she might. I breathed the air through which she had moved.

IN THE COMING DAYS I DEVOTED MYSELF TO EASY INDUSTRY, shopping for groceries, cooking, paying bills, replying to correspondence, taking care of business, such as it was.

A woman named Irene at a publishing house called Errata Naturae Editores in Madrid had inquired about putting out an edition of one of my works.

"We do assure you," she wrote, "that we are fascinated with your text and that it will be carefully translated and printed into a beautiful book."

I fell for the line about her intention to produce a beautiful book, and offered to let her license the Spanish rights for a five-year period at an extremely modest price. I regretted my generosity immediately, but my word was my bond. But my price, she claimed, was all of two hundred dollars beyond her means.

"Unfortunately," she wrote, "Spain is a small country, with not that many readers."

The indignation I felt turned to laughter, and I dismissed the matter without another word to her. Maybe the name of the house—Errata Naturae translates from the Latin as "errors of nature"—should have served as warning from the start.

No wonder I didn't write anymore. To quote Tennessee Williams, from his final stage play: "Fuck it!" Nobody remembers Shakespeare's creditors.

So in my newfound sobriety I continued not to write. At least not consciously. Then early one morning something gave me start. I was sitting on the couch with my coffee when, from the corner of my eye, I noticed there was a pen on my desk, and beneath the pen was a scrap of paper. I was sure that these had not been there the night before. I went to the desk, looked at the paper, saw hurried-seeming words. My pulse quickened. The light and sounds of morning through my windows seemed to vanish.

I'm lying here dirty waiting for the undertaker to give me a shave. I shouldn't have put it off for so long.

The movement of my life was as the movement of my left hand. It stirred, reached out for the touch of another, raised the glass to my lips, and, when paralysis came, trembled occasionally, senselessly, vaguely, with no meaning at all.

Before that stirring I was a woman who spoke another tongue.

I was a leopard awaiting glance in bowering shade.

Remembered now: forbidden gods to whom I did pray.

Remembered now: the coming forth that awaits me into the light beyond day.

It is an electric razor. It is not what I would have wanted. There was no slow, measured scrape of the blade. Of course I should have known. Strange, the things we do not foresee.

I am risen now from what was me.

Eternal Savior, bear me unto thee.

Eternal Savior, rise.

Remembered now: the long dark passage without breath, the dark passage longer than life.

Eternal Savior, bear me.

Eternal Savior, rise.

Remembered now: what the lady and the leopard, the daemon-seeker and miller did know before me.

Eternal Savior, bear me.
Eternal Savior, rise.
Remembered now: it is not meant to be.

It was my written-in-the-dark scrawl, but I did not remember writing it. In fact, I felt certain that I had not, and that these words were not mine. But the handwriting attested otherwise. Had I written this while sleepwalking, or in a semiconscious state? What did it mean? I did not believe in reincarnation. But had I felt a sense of reincarnation when I wrote the lines I now beheld? Did my unconscious know what my conscious mind denied? Had something from within, or a voice from somewhere, spoken through me? What was I to make of this eerie incantation of everlasting life?

I read the words again, whispering them aloud to myself this time. I placed the pen in the center drawer of the desk with my other pens, and I folded and placed the scrap of paper in the drawer to the right. Something in me wanted it out of sight. I wanted to put it out of mind as well, but I could not.

These words were strange to me, yet at times uncannily familiar, as if they might be speaking to, or from, atavistic memories that were hidden, vague and veiled, unknown and unarticulated, in me. The phrase "bowering shade" meant nothing to me. But I have always loved and felt a deep affinity for leopards.

THE COLDEST MONTH OF THAT WINTER PASSED SLOWLY. Even the wolf moon when it arrived seemed frozen in the sky as I gazed at it through my kitchen window. It was there, to the west, looming high and big over the river, at four o'clock in the morning, and it was still there, seeming not to have moved, more than three hours later, after seven, when I went back to bed. The winds howled to gusts of fifty-five miles an hour in the wake of that moon.

More snow and frigid sleet came down upon the city. I took a taxi to the Lower East Side, telling the driver to let me off at the corner of Tenth Street and Avenue B. Leslie would be tending bar at the Lakeside Lounge that night, and I knew that she would accept, perhaps even be happy to see, that I was not drinking.

I liked Leslie a lot, and it was good to see her. She had a smile that always worked on me like mellow medicine, even when I encountered it through barely seeing narrowed eyes. But I was there for another reason. Whatever strays were out on a desolate night such as this, I figured, belonged to nights such as this.

"What brings you out?"

Leslie was one of the few people who ask this and elicit a thoughtful answer. It was the way she asked it.

"I feel like sucking a damsel's blood," I told her. She smiled that smile of hers, and I saw that she thought I was being merely glib and playful. "I'm serious," I said.

It was no use. I did better when I lied than when I told the truth, it seemed. She asked me what I was having, and I told her that all I wanted was a club soda with a piece of lemon. She brought it and pushed my money back to me. I looked around. It was dark, and it took a while to make out the animated or torpid forms at the bar. It felt good to be sober, to see and think clearly amid the slurred mutterings and the wailed descants of misery, complaint, and lunacy.

Leslie was talking across the bar to a girl several seats down to my left. When the girl laughed, I saw that she was quite pretty. She was alone and had a full drink in front of her.

I felt slightly demonic. It was a not unpleasant feeling. Old Nick or Nicholas the Ancient. Wasn't that it? No, no, no. Old Scratch or Nicholas the Ancient. And *ancient* was spelled in a peculiar, antiquated way. What was it? *Antient.* Yes, that was it. Old Scratch or Nicholas the Antient. Where had I found that? Something British, no? Seventeenth century, eighteenth century?

Maybe that explained the words on that scrap of paper. Maybe I had read them somewhere, and somehow they had come back to me when I was half asleep, and I had set them down and not recalled doing so. Or maybe I had written them long ago, completely forgotten them, and, yes, somehow they had come back to me when I was half asleep, and I had set them down and not recalled doing so. Memory and the subconscious could be very tricky.

But as I told myself these things, I did not believe them. I wanted only to solve that piece of paper and the words on it, to be rid of the uneasy strangeness they had left me with.

"Who's she?" I asked Leslie. "The girl you were talking to." Without turning I gave a toss of my head in the direction of the girl down the bar. Leslie followed my gesture with her glance.

"Oh. Melissa. I don't really know her. She seems like a nice kid."

"Give her a drink on me."

"She just got one."

"Back her up."

She went over, said something to her. They both looked my way. Leslie lightly rapped the bar in front of her.

Old Scratch or Nicholas the Antient. A leopard in the bowering shade.

I shook loose these words from my mind.

The girl finished her drink. Leslie set another before her and took money from me. The girl raised the drink to me, then drank.

I wasn't about to approach her. That was something that foolish young men did. I too may have once done such a thing. But I was a foolish old man now, and my folly was not without dignity. At the same time, I knew that she was not likely to approach me. I found myself walking toward her. After a few steps I decided to keep walking, to walk past her, as if I were barely aware of her, and to go outside and have a smoke. An inspired move. I made as if to be preoccupied and not to notice the curiosity in her eyes as I passed.

The awful cold and winds seemed not only to have rid the streets of people but also to have rid the sky of clouds. The moon had waned to a delicate falcated sliver, and stars were visible. As a child I had seen many stars in these night skies, but now it was rare to see one. Tens of billions of planets, suns, and moons in the Milky Way, and we had disconnected ourselves from them all.

Star light, star bright, first star I see tonight.

I flicked my cigarette butt at a parked car and saw the wind take it, red embers flying and vanishing.

I wish I may, I wish I might.

"So, Melissa, tell me. Can you control the tides by crossing and uncrossing your legs?"

She looked at me awkwardly.

"Do you like to drink strong drink, go mad, and dance with the apparition of freedom?"

She seemed about to say something but giggled instead.

"Do you like to watch old men masturbate and know that they too once were young?"

"Who *are* you?"

"I was asking myself that just the other day."

"Leslie says you write books."

"I used to."

"What do you do now?"

"I'm retired. I enjoy the fruits of my past labors and contemplate the pains of hell. What about you?"

"I'm a student. I go to school."

"What do you study?"

"History."

"How do you plan to make a living off that?"

"I don't know. I don't think about money much."

"I guess that's good. It doesn't think much about you either."

"That's pretty much the way I look at it."

Her voice was pleasant. She wasn't really drunk, though she was getting there. She was wearing pants, but they were quite close-fitting, and her thighs looked good in them. Her skin was beautiful. Her lips were full. Her dark hair was not all that long, and she wore it in a ponytail, which made her look even younger. Its end formed a sweet, lush curl that filliped amid the down at the nape of her neck with her every slight movement. She raised her knees to rest against the bar. It was a beautiful sight.

So strange to be like this, sober in a bar as midnight struck. Strange and exhilarating too.

She seemed as beguiled by me as I was by her. I did not know, and did not care, how much of her apparent beguilement could be attributed to the alcohol's warm, rising effect on her. The red lipstick she wore set off the whiteness of her teeth. I was lucky to have been mindful to put my teeth in before I came out.

When she laughed I glimpsed the tip of her tongue dancing on the pearly white crenulations of those teeth, and I felt a twitch and a throb in the vein that runs down the length of my cock. In that instant, it was all I could do to keep from placing her hand to it. The nails of her fingers were the same color as her lips, and touching her hand under the pretext of making a point of something I was saying, I felt how soft and smooth those pale fingers were. The unseen parts of her body would be even more so.

Her laughter and my laughter became shared laughter. Her talk and my talk became shared talk. Truth be told, I was starting to like her. If only I were younger, I thought. Much younger. But I was not.

I had the basic facts of her, as far as she had chosen to give them to me. Age nineteen. Born in Minnesota; this cold did not bother her. An only child. Father a medical researcher, but not a vassal of the pharmaceutical racket; and, no, she herself had never really thought of pursuing science.

She had come here tonight after walking out on a date with "this guy I met."

Why had she gone out with him to begin with?

"Because he was cute."

What was she doing wasting her time talking to me?

"Maybe because you're not cute. And you're not telling me how much money you're going to make and how to pronounce the dessert or how a single mother you heard about had her child taken away from her because she ate so many poppy seed rolls that she tested positive for opiates."

When I told her that I wanted to take her home with me, that I wanted to end the night with her, she gave me a look with eyes that seemed to demur, even to chastise. I did not further plead my desire but told her that I understood.

"Do you?" she said.

The taxi turned west on the corner of Broadway and Leonard. It was well after two. There was very little traffic. Furtive shadows seemed to appear and disappear in swirling blasts of wind.

"Thomas Paine saw a man hanged here," I said. Looking out the backseat window, I wondered which corner of this intersection the gallows had occupied.

"Who's he?" she said, glancing out the window.

"Friend of mine," I said after a moment, then smiled to myself. This was going to be a good one.

I placed my arm lightly around her, and she leaned her head just as lightly to my shoulder. She asked me if I had a cat. I told her that I did not. She told me that she did not trust men who kept cats. I told her that I did not trust them either. It was true.

The liking for her that I had felt come over me in the bar seemed to grow stronger as we rode alone through the night. If only I were younger, much younger, I thought. If only I were looking for, if only I needed, something other than sustenance, other than moisture or cure. But what had I always hungered for, even without knowing it? What did we all hunger for, in our way? I wondered what unknown thing it was that impelled her to me.

It took far less time to get her from the couch to the bed than it had taken to get her from the bar to the cab. I left the music on. Rachmaninoff's *Isle of the Dead*. To its grand thalassic echoes of the Great Dirge, I tongue-kissed her panties and the ankle from which they dangled so delectably. I did not hear the music end. I heard only her.

She uttered a little gasp. I felt her shiver and her flesh horripilate as I ran my nails down her hip and thigh. Her belly rose and she shuddered. I put my mouth to her breast. She shivered again, and shuddered more deeply, deliciously. Her panties were in my hand. I raised them to her face as I kissed the warm dew between her legs. Her mouth opened and her tongue rose through the sheer veil of the panties. My free hand grabbed her thigh above the knee. I breathed long and slow into her, then lowered my lips to her leg. I licked, sucked, lowered my jaw, felt her flesh between my teeth. Her hand was on my head, her fingers raked my hair, softly, then roughly, then softly again. She seemed to await the clench of my teeth, the pleasure of a suffering so sweet, and the release it would bring.

I bit her. She muffled her own scream. I tasted her blood in my mouth, in my throat. I felt her body relax, and I heard her breathe as if she were lost in a dream that would not be remembered.

I was not aware of how much time passed. I wiped blood from my mouth, licked blood from her skin. Then I felt her upon me, her mouth upon me, her tongue upon that vein that throbbed and that twitched. I worked her ponytail like a suicide clutch. I felt her hand stir. She raised it to my lips, and again I tasted her blood. I came violently, heard the sounds of her sucking become the sounds of her swallowing; heard the sound of her hand in a frenzy between her taut legs. Her mouth slowed but did not cease. I could take no more, and I withdrew from her.

Our breath slowed and we fell to sleep, closely entwined, her arm around me. It was almost as if, young and innocent as she was, she knew about the monkeys.

WHEN I AWOKE THAT MORNING I FELT INVIGORATED, as if I had taken some sort of root tonic that had cleared and cleansed me and set me aright. With Melissa still asleep, I rose quietly. As I entered the bathroom to piss and shave, I saw there was a calm and sanguine smile on my face. For an instant I did not recognize that smile as my own, that figure in the mirror as myself. It was good to see me.

I pulled on my pajamas and went into the kitchen to make oatmeal and coffee, enough for the two of us. It was not so warm in my place that bitter winter. My big old banging gas-guzzling HydroTherm MultiPulse AM100 heating boiler had finally broken down irreparably the previous year, and I had ended up replacing it with a fancy new wall-mounted, energy-efficient Lochinvar Knight. This was a nine-grand mistake. I should have had the old boiler rebuilt from the concrete up. But that would have taken brains. All I had was hindsight. The new boiler was so energy-efficient it didn't give off any heat to speak of. After Con Edison came to inspect it and I got my energy-efficient residential gas rebate and tax-credit authorization, I had the energy-efficient wiring disconnected, and the damned thing still did not work worth a damn. I got more warmth from the little twenty-buck space heater I kept on the end table by the couch than I did from my five radiators. The new could never replace the old. This was true of all things. But the old boiler had pulsed and clanged and banged its last. The concrete in the base of its tank and the cinder blocks beneath it had rotted clean through and the water that seeped through them flooded the boiler closet. How I yearned for the old antediluvian warmth that I had known. But on this morning the chill did not bother me at all. I didn't even feel it.

I sliced a banana into the simmering oatmeal, added some raisins, a nutmeg, a bit more cinnamon, stirred in buttermilk, stirred in butter, a little chestnut honey. She had crept up behind me, barefoot and wearing my robe. I asked her how she liked her coffee. Cream and a little sugar. I had no cream, only milk and half-and-half. Like most Americans who asked for cream, she meant milk. I asked her if she wanted a shot with it. Her "no, thank you" was enwrapped in a low sleepy giggle. I poured out the steaming oatmeal into bowls, the steaming coffee into cups. I turned on Rachmaninoff again. What's good for the dark of night is good for the morning light.

Who said that? Why did it whisper of ancient Egypt? Was it from the Pyramid Texts? The Book of the Dead? No, I had never read or heard those words before. Nor had I ever said them, written them, or thought them before.

She was looking at the wound on her leg, the red cicatrice of her broken skin and the livid swollen flesh around it. She seemed rapt by it as she ran her finger gently over it.

"Do you want to kiss it?" she asked.

I bent over her, lowered my lips softly to her thigh. This gave me no pleasure. I did it to please her. She closed the robe over the scar and returned to her oatmeal.

"Do you want to put something on it?" I said.

"Like what?"

"Peroxide. Ointment. I don't know."

She did not respond to this. Instead she asked me about the music. I told her what little I knew about it.

"I was fooling with you last night," she said.

I was taken aback. I asked her what she meant.

"Thomas Paine," she said. Her eyes danced with a sly playfulness. *"Common Sense."*

"Oh." I felt a sense of relief, and my spirits brightened again. "I should have known. History major."

"Ancient history," she said. "But I remember him from high school."

I gestured to the open doors of my library. "I've got a wallful of books in there on ancient history, ancient writing, ancient mythology, ancient everything. The shelves on the left."

My library had been carefully gathered together over the course of a lifetime, and in the course of a few years I had for the most part lost interest in it. Had I sent her through those doors, to those books, because I was experiencing the spark of a renewed closeness to them, a rekindling of my sense of their importance to me and to my life?

She went into the library, but, as I saw from where I sat, the cuneiform tablets on the wall immediately facing her caught her eye and she went directly to them.

"When are these from?" she asked with her back to me.

"They were put out to bake about four thousand years ago," I said. "Sumerian. Third Dynasty of Ur."

"What do they say?"

"They're an accounting of cult offerings to a god of war called Shara, from a temple in a Mesopotamian town called Umma."

"Can you read them?"

"No. Can you?"

"No."

She seemed transfixed by them. Only after some minutes did she turn to browse the shelves of books I thought might interest her. As she left the room, she paused to peer through the glass of the case that held the books that I had written.

"You've written a lot of books," she said.

"Yes and no," I said. "Most of the books in there are just different editions and translations of one book or another. Most of them I can't even read. Chinese, Russian, Japanese, Swedish, Dutch, this, that, the other thing. I can't understand a word of what's in most of those books. They just have my name on them. They just look good."

As I said those last words, I was thinking of how good she looked, standing there in the light of day that spilled from the northeast through the library window. Once again I was struck by doubt. Why had she come with me? What had she seen or sensed in me? Maybe I should just ask her. But not now. Not now. My questioning doubt left me as quickly as it had risen.

In our ways we all are gods or goddesses, even if we be forgotten in the end. Better not to dwell on our powers or attributes or the offerings and sacrifices made to us.

For a long time I had felt grim mortality closing in on me. Now, on this morning, in this moment, I felt that something lay before me, forthshining and resplendent. And in this moment, on this morning, that was all and enough.

I KNEW THAT I HAD NOT TAKEN A DRINK IN MORE THAN A month, but I was not counting days. And I was not going through the rigmarole of attending ninety meetings in ninety days. I had done this years ago, and in the end celebrated my success by going on a bender that lasted almost as long and landed me in the hospital.

I had asked people years ago about the significance of those ninety days. Why not sixty days, or a hundred days? Why ninety? No one could give me an answer. Someone suggested there were spiritual implications inherent in the passage of ninety days, but he could not expound further and in the end admitted that he really did not know what he was talking about.

I had also asked about the purpose of all who had fewer than ninety days of sobriety openly declaring their day count at the start of meetings. Someone suggested that it was to encourage others to open up more freely. I maintained the belief that it was for the entertainment of those who said such things.

The truth seemed to be that most of those in the program dealt with sobriety as they had dealt with alcohol, obsessively and compulsively. They did not liberate themselves from their alcoholic ways. They merely transferred them to a sobriety that seemed to me self-defeating and dangerously precarious, little more than a Pyrrhic victory over the torments and ill-being that had fucked them up and enslaved them in the first place. A sober invalid was still an invalid, a sober slave was still a slave.

No, I was not counting days. But I knew the importance of meetings and the inspiration and sense of fellowship I took away from a good meeting.

I decided that I would go on Ash Wednesday to Our Lady of Pompeii in the Village. With Palm Sunday it was one of the two days of the year when I went to church. Back when the old women—or their husbands, seeking free beer—came into Dodge's bar on Bedford Street with palms from Pompeii that they had taken home and woven into sprays as their mothers had taught them to do, Ash Wednesday was the only day of the year that brought me to church. The observance of these two days were all that remained of my Christianity. They were the only Roman Catholic rites in which I engaged, as I saw Christmas and Easter as good pagan feasts that had been co-opted by the early Church. I liked the ashes, the frond-leaves and little plaited crosses of palm. I had it timed so that I missed the Mass and arrived just as the ashes or palms were given out. I don't know what it was that I liked about them, but I liked them.

I would eat breakfast, take the subway to Sheridan Square, go to a meeting on Perry Street, then hit the church at the end of the nine o'clock Mass, when the lines for ashes were formed and moving rapidly. After that I would walk round Bleecker Street to Faicco's, buy some ground pork and sausage. Then I would go to Murray's and see if the *parmigiano* had the right shade of age to it in the half inch or so under the rind. If it didn't, I'd go down to Dean & Deluca. I had been craving pasta with the sauce that was better than my grandmother's, better than any chef's, here or in Italy. It was better because I had taken the best from wherever I encountered it, and I had blended the best together, and then had made it better. And I would make it tonight, and I would eat it tonight and for the rest of the week. There was already a big jar of stock in the refrigerator. I had boiled it up the other day. It was good to be getting back my cooking jones.

Perry Street was one of the places where I once had done those ninety meetings in those ninety days, where I had learned that this was not a good thing for everybody, that it was more important to be sober and serene without counting on a string of beads that might choke us when the last bead was counted. That was sixteen years before, in a different winter, a different springtime. I had encountered a lot of good people at those meetings. And a few arch assholes. When one chose to speak at a meeting, it was customary to introduce oneself by first name, followed by the phrase "I'm an alcoholic." Some people unnecessarily embellished this to "I'm a recovering alcoholic," or "I'm a gratefully recovering alcoholic," or some such thing. Among the habitués of the Perry Street meetings was a smarmy little putz who always wanted to speak and who always introduced himself as "an alcoholic and a sex addict." I was sure it was his way of cruising for cock. I couldn't stand him. And I had a hard time with the people who manifestly had little or no background of heavy drinking, who came to these meetings as others might attend church socials or coffee klatsches, solely to hear themselves talk. And talk, and talk. These people could and often did drive you to drink. I sometimes needed to absent myself from them or risk relapse.

I saw some people I remembered fondly, and it was good to see that they were still there and doing well. They looked older, as no doubt did I. But they all looked better, while I knew I looked worse. As I walked up the church steps, people marked with ashes were already leaving. I felt comfortable here, in this familiar old parish church, this church that misspelled Pompeii on its own calendars. I kept one of those calendars on my kitchen wall year after year. The local Italian undertaker was their featured advertiser.

The pale stone holy water font attracted me. I wetted my fingertips, genuflected, and made the sign of the cross on my forehead, where ashes, sprinkled with holy water, would soon be. I also liked holy water, the idea of it, the feel of it on my skin. I used to enjoy lighting candles as well, but the old votive candles and thin wooden candle-lighting sticks, with which you kindled one candle from the flame of another, had been replaced here and in most churches by electric candles with little toggle switches. So I did not pay to light a candle, and I did not light a candle. I put money in the poor box instead.

As always, my eyes were attracted to the statue of the Virgin Mary in the eastern apse. As always, I wanted to fuck it, wanted to rub my naked cock against the cool, smooth white alabaster of the Virgin Mary's ankle and face. I knew that this was a gratification I would never have. At its unattended sanctuary in Cyprus I had fucked the sacred black stone that is believed to be the oldest of venerated objects, the slab in which the Great Mother was first perceived. Not far from there, at the edge of the Mediterranean, I had fucked the hard wet sand of the shore near the big rock where Aphrodite was said to have first stepped from the sea. But city churches were no longer kept open through the night. I thought of all those reliquaries in the Vatican and throughout Europe that contained the true blood of the Virgin Mary. I wondered whose blood it was, drained from the dead or from kicking stuck pigs.

Holy water. Seawater. The priest before the altar touched ashes to my forehead and spoke.

"Remember," he said, "that you are dust, and to dust you shall return."

Like a phoenix, I thought, like a phoenix.

I ended up walking to Dean & Deluca, then walking home

from there. The cold winds were still bitter, but the knowledge that the spring equinox was only weeks away made them seem less unbearable. I stopped to buy a bottle of wine for the sauce I would make. I decided on a good Barbera.

This was something that many in those meeting rooms would not do: cook with wine. Some would not even go into a liquor store or wine merchant's. Some would even ask in restaurants if this or that dish was prepared with wine or alcohol of any kind. Such bits of stagy melodrama were usually affected or at best delusional. Who, having tasted both, could not tell the difference between the taste of life and the taste of death? Who could not tell the difference between the taste of good wine and the taste of dead-monkey juice?

I would use only about a cup of this wine, not measured but poured slowly from the bottle. It would be a shame to let the rest go to waste. I thought of Melissa. I thought of the rich red sauce. I thought of the deep scarlet wine.

It was all so much better when one was sober. All of it. I put on an album of Bach cello suites, sorted the groceries, took down a big enameled cast-iron pot and set it on the stove. I poured a glass of milk, took a ten-milligram Valium, sat on the couch, lit a cigarette, and relaxed. It would be a nice evening. And evening would become night. Yes. It was all so much better.

I T AROUSED ME TO SEE HER EAT. THE SLIGHT LOWERING OF her eyelids and full dark lashes as she opened her mouth. The movements, as she quietly chewed, of her nose, philtrum groove, and the perfect angel's cleft of her upper lip. The soft lissome undulations of her flawless smooth throat as she swallowed. It was more seductive than any slow forbidden dance.

"I love this," she said. "What's in it?"

"A little butter, a little olive oil. A lot of onions, a lot of garlic. Porcini mushrooms, cremini mushrooms. Ground pork, ground beef. A little stock."

"What kind of stock?"

"Pork on the bone, beef on the bone, veal on the bone, chicken on the bone. Onion, leek, garlic. Celery, carrot, tomato. Some parsley, a few black peppercorns, a few white peppercorns, a little sea salt, a bay leaf, a clove, water, an eggshell."

"Why an eggshell?"

"To clarify it."

I paused, then went back and picked up where she had first cut me off when I was trying to finish telling her what she wanted to know, which was what was in the sauce.

"A little tomato paste. Basil, parsley, oregano, thyme, pepper. A little salt. That wine you're drinking. San Marzano tomatoes. Sweet sausage, hot sausage. A bay leaf."

"It's really fucking great."

"Thanks," I said. I was glad she liked it. I didn't go by what she said, I went by how she ate. And I was glad she didn't say it was awesome. "It's missing one thing," I said.

The look in her face, and my undercurrent of arousal, allowed my imagination to sense a vague thrilling expectation of the unknown. But I saw a trace of unease in her look, and I wanted her to be rid of it. So I told her.

"*Parmigian*," I said. "I couldn't find any good *parmigian* cheese. It was all too young."

The trace of unease subsided, but it was not gone.

"Am I too young?" she said. Now she herself tried to hide that telltale trace behind a smile of sorts.

"Too young for what?"

"For what you want."

"And what do you think I want?"

"I don't know. Do you want to fuck me? Do you want to show me off? I really don't know."

"I don't want to fuck you. Not in the conventional sense. And no, I don't want to show you off." I looked into her eyes. I felt it strange that we were saying these things. We had only been together a single night before this. Then again it had been a night not quite like any other. "I want what we had the other night," I said.

"I'm sore," she said. It seemed, as soon as she said this, that she had not meant to say it, that it had just rushed out of her in a quick flight of breath.

I didn't say anything. It caught me off guard to hear a woman, or a girl or whatever it was that I should see her as, talk about her left thigh as if she might be talking about her breasts.

"You're not drinking," she said.

"No, I'm not drinking," I said, perhaps a bit defensively.

"You didn't drink the other night either."

"I'm not drinking these days," I said with a shrug, careful to give these words an air of casual insignificance. I watched her take a sip of wine. "I feel too good lately," I said. "I want to write a new book. I don't drink when I write. I can't." I was lying. I didn't want to write a new book. Maybe I didn't want her to know that I was trying to quit drinking forever, maybe because most people who drink don't like to be around people who don't drink, people who have quit drinking, especially people who go to meetings. And I didn't want to lose her. I had just found her, and I didn't want to lose her.

"I should probably cut down too," she said. "I drink too much."

Again I was caught off guard, to hear her, all of nineteen, talk as if she were hearing harps and harpies. I poured more wine into her glass.

"Oh, you're fine," I told her. "Here, drink up." I wanted her to relax around me. I wanted her to open herself to me. I wanted what I wanted to be what she wanted. It was good for her to drink the way she did. This wine would help her give me what I wanted. "Come on. You're fine," I told her.

"Do your parents drink?" she asked.

"My parents don't do much of anything anymore. They're dead. They've been like that for a long time." I smiled. "My father was a heavy drinker. My mother didn't drink much. She couldn't handle it."

I heard my own words. It was curious how I spoke of whatever it was, physical or spiritual or both, that had stood in the way of my mother becoming a drunk like my father; how I spoke as if it were a failing, a shortcoming, a disability. The words came readily, easily: *couldn't handle it*. How much more fittingly would they describe those who succumbed. It was drunks like me who couldn't handle it.

"My mom drinks a lot," she said.

I began to wash the dishes. She followed me into the kitchen.

"How old is your mother?"

"Forty-seven. No. Forty-eight."

At least her mother wasn't young enough to be my daughter.

"Let me do that," she said.

"You're the guest," I said. "What's the good of being a guest if you have to wash dishes? Thanks, babe, but no."

I thought of her legs. I thought of her ponytail in my fist. I thought of the taste of her. I thought of her tongue on that vein that twitched and throbbed. I thought of her stringent warmth entering my mouth, trickling down my throat. I thought of what ran in the veins of gods and goddesses.

"But sweeter to live for ever; sweeter to live ever youthful like the Gods, who have ichor in their veins; ichor which gives life and youth and joy..."

I shut off the faucet and turned around. She was reading some lines of poetry that were held by a magnet to the side of my refrigerator. I knew that she would ask me about them. I embraced her from behind, put one hand over her mouth and the other on her belly. I pressed her to me. Her buttocks felt good against me. I kissed the downy little hairs and skin on the back of her neck and slid my hand down the front of her pants, feeling her silky panties and, through them, the tussock beneath. I worked my hand farther, and she squeezed it with her thighs. I could feel hot breath from her nostrils on my fingers. She began to nibble and lick at them with darts of her tongue. I unbuttoned and unzipped her pants, moved my hand into her panties, then into her. I peered over her shoulder down the front of her sweater to the hidden flesh and shadow of her breasts in white lace, and farther, to the movement of my hand in her open pants.

She lay naked in my bed, her lower lip between her teeth, her legs spread, her eyes probing mine. Her labia were swollen and wet, rosy pink and glistening. I slipped the head of my cock, no more, into her and dallied a bit. She let loose her lip and breathed from deep within. I dimmed the light, grasped her hips, laid my head between her legs and stared at her hand on herself in the obscuring dark. I ran my fingers, then my tongue along the inside of her upper right thigh, which was unmarked, very close to the scent of her and the muffled accelerating sound of her hand. I opened my mouth, and I sank my teeth and tore. She exhaled with violence, like an ecstasy of storm wind through trees.

I felt a sudden thick rushing gush of blood that filled my mouth and would not be stopped. Even as I closed my hand over it, the blood rushed through my fingers. We scrambled to our feet in alarm. There was blood everywhere. And still it gushed.

I wrapped a towel around her thigh, tied the belt from my robe tightly above it. Nothing. The blood flooded and spurted wildly from her. She was pale unto fainting.

Saint Vincent's had been shut. I wouldn't bring a dog to New York Downtown. I called Lenox Hill, told them to send an ambulance. No cab would take us the way she was bleeding.

"What did you do to her?" the doctor asked me in a tone that accused.

"I bit her too hard," I said matter-of-factly. I did not look away from him. "She likes to be bitten. But I bit her too hard."

"You severed her femoral artery," he said. "You could have killed her." The doctor shook his head slowly.

They wanted to keep her there awhile after stitching her up. She needed more blood. I went out for a smoke, then went back in to be with her. She looked away from the blood going into her through the catheter in her arm. For a few moments she looked away from me. I stood there.

"They asked me if I want to press charges," she said.

I said nothing. I knew that if she were thinking of pressing charges, she wouldn't have told me this. Not the way she did, anyway. I put my hand on her arm and kissed her forehead.

She later told me that they also asked her if she wanted counseling. She told me that she had thought about it. She told me that she was still thinking about it.

Her color returned. She began to smile again, to laugh again. I enjoyed buying good wine for her. I wondered if, pouring it unseen and telling her nothing about it, she would find the bottle of Cheval Blanc I had hidden away for her to be special in any way. I wondered what might have happened if I had killed her.

I thought often of that terrible night in the days and weeks that followed. When I did, a shiver went down my spine and my eyes sometimes closed. That first reinvigorating billow of blood that had filled my mouth and overrun my chin and chest was like nothing I had ever known or imagined. The dangerous rush of blood from her artery had been for me a rush of life. After the events of that night and its aftermath had passed, I felt physically stronger than I had felt in years, and I enjoyed a sense of calm awareness that was utterly new to me.

On one of my bedroom walls, in a shadow-box frame, there hangs a Wolford pantyhose package featuring one of a series of photographs taken for Wolford by Helmut Newton. These photographs, which Helmut felt to be among his best work, captured some of the most erotic images I have ever seen. The most striking of these, to me, was the black-and-white picture used on Wolford's control-top Synergy packages. It was one of these rare, discontinued Synergy packages that Helmut inscribed to me a few years before his death, using a bold black Sharpie on the package's unopened cellophane, writing with a vertical flourish over the thigh of the central image beneath it.

It hangs above and to the left of a heavy mirror into which I rarely looked. One day, lingering before her reflection in that mirror, Melissa pointed to the shadow-box frame without turning her eyes to it.

"Would you like to see me in those?" she said. Her eyes looked to mine.

"Not those," I said. "But something like them. Yeah." I heard the pace of my words slow and turn soft and subdued. "I should like that very much," I said. "Very, very much. I really should."

"They would cover up the scar."

"That's not why. I want to see you in them because they're the only thing I can imagine that could make you even sexier than you already are."

And so I bought her some ultra-sheer Wolford pantyhose—the black Synergy, and others with improbably named shades: nearly black, anthracite, oyster, ecru—and a pair of Jimmy Choo black glossy snakeskin, Chantilly lace, and suede shoes with three-and-a-third-inch stiletto heels. Four packages of pantyhose cost over two hundred, and the shoes were almost nine hundred. It would have been worth it even for one night, even for one hour.

The sounds of her movements alone—the *scroop* of nylon as she crossed and uncrossed her legs, the click of stiletto heels and the sinister hushed squeak of welts and uppers—set my heart pounding. It was so innocently demure and so maddeningly lascivious at once. I did not speak, but only watched her and felt the effect of her symphony like a rising, slow-swelling crescendo within me. On this night I wanted to fuck her. I wanted to fuck every part of her, and I wanted to fuck everything she wore. I wanted to fuck the sound of her, the scent of her. I wanted to fuck her very soul, her very existence, her every breath. She was mine, and I was blest, and no god had created more than we had in this moment. Together with grasping wrenching hands and nails we tore open the crotch of those fancy overpriced pantyhose as the bed shook and creaked beneath us.

"Did you ever think of your mother licking your cunt?" I asked her. The words came deep on heavy breath.

"Yes," she said. "Would you like to see that?"

It was then that I realized she would say yes to anything that I asked.

"Yes," I said. "Tell me what it would be like."

Then my seed exploded from me like rain, and she moaned as if in grieving disappointment, or as if taking a blow to the gut. She said no more but only held me close and soon was asleep. There was no biting that night, though before morning I dreamt that I drank from her while she slept. I woke with a start, for in this dream her silent, tranquil sleep was revealed to be death.

It was good to see her stir beside me, stretching her arms in the early dim light, her eyes still closed. I got out of bed to make coffee. A few minutes later, as the water was starting to boil, she came into the kitchen with a sleepy smile and sat at the little table by the window. She looked out over the gabled roof of the old Mercantile building across the way. There were wisps of pink in a blue sky that grew heavy with gray. I brought her coffee to the little table and set it down before her.

"Maybe here," she said, still looking out the window, as if she were talking to the gathering gray clouds. She placed her fingers to where the back of her thigh and her buttock rested on the chair. "Maybe here. Next time. Maybe you could bite me here."

She took a sip of coffee. An extravagant wind whistled through a narrow breach in the window. A beautiful elemental sound.

"I don't think there's any blood to be had there in that sweet meat," I said, then slowly smiled. The coffee was good and hot. I leaned against the black granite countertop of the island in the center of the kitchen, facing the little table where she sat, so that we both looked out on the same sky, the same pink wisps and blue, all but gone now, and the gray clouds that grew bigger and began to roll, fuller and darker, in the wind.

"It's the blood, not the biting?" she said, and her voice seemed as lost in that sky as she was.

"Yes," I said. "It's the blood."

It seemed that she was waiting not for me but for the lowering clouds and umbrous sky to explain my words. She drank her coffee. There was another whistling through the window, and a rattling of the pane; and then distant thunder.

She asked about the lines of poetry on the refrigerator, and I told her.

"From Charles Olson's 'Maximus, from Dogtown'—*We drink / or break open / our veins solely / to know. A drunkard / showing himself in public / is punished / by death*'—and there's more, but those are the lines that mean something to me."

"And what do they mean to you?"

"I can't put it into words. It's hard to dissect or explain beauty or power." I gestured to the sky through the window. "Maybe if you can dissect or explain it, then it's not beauty or power. Maybe true beauty and true power defy reason and intellect and explanation by their very nature. They hit below the belt of those things. I don't know. To me they're like a light in the sky of a faraway star that died a thousand years ago. The light of Gnosticism. *'Solely / to know.'* The search for freedom through wisdom beyond learning. But the Leviticus of fear and morality cannot allow such a thing. As far as the poetry of it goes, you can see Olson's brilliance. Seven lines, and the central line, the fourth line, is shared by the Gnostic infinitive—*'to know,'* followed by a full stop—and the opening words of a killing law set against all that is inherent in that infinitive, the freedom and wisdom, no matter how high or how low, that fears, laws, and moralities must destroy. But that's not why I like it, not really. The bedrock of the thing—the rhythm, the meter—is majestic. It could bust a bronze Homeric pickaxe. But it goes so much beyond that. Like I said, I can't say because I just don't know. It's like that whistling wind, that thunder a few minutes ago. I can feel it but I can't explain why and what it makes me feel what I feel."

"Damn, you can talk."

"Yeah, I know." I smiled. "Without saying much of anything that makes sense."

"That's not what I meant. You talk beyond sense. You leave it in the dust. I like that."

"Maybe that's where it belongs, in the dust."

Was this her way of saying she understood about the blood? Her way of telling me I didn't have to make sense of it for her? Or was it just idle talk over coffee, to be forgotten when the cups were rinsed? I didn't know, I didn't care.

"I've got a paper due next week," she said. "I better go and get to work on it. Can I borrow that book you have in there, *Whom Gods Destroy,* I think it's called? There's some stuff in there I want to paraphrase."

"Don't paraphrase. Steal," I said.

Soon after she left I experienced a ravenous appetite. This was somewhat out of the ordinary, as my usual coffee and cigarettes left me with little desire to eat on most mornings, and breakfast for me was either desultory and meager or more often completely bypassed. But on this morning I feasted on a thick broiled pork chop, pan-fried potatoes with sage, thick smoked bacon, three eggs sunny-side up, and buttered toast to mop up the yolks, with two glasses of buttermilk and another steaming cup of coffee. And as I wolfed it all down, my mind dwelt on sausage, banana pancakes drenched in butter and real maple syrup, and a bowl of blood oranges, peaches, raspberries, and strawberries.

It was as if the sallow hollows and wormy protruding veins in weak sagging skin were demanding sustenance for what seemed like a regeneration of flesh and strength, a reversal of long, slow wasting away, a feeling of coming renewal of flesh and strength, a filling of the hollows and the sagging where muscle once had covered sturdy bone gone brittle. Even as my morning feast settled warm and filling within me and I lit another cigarette and drew deep satisfaction from it, I thought of the big, thick rib eye steak, sautéed onions, mashed potatoes, and sautéed greens and garlic that I would eat that night, the warm apple pie that would follow it, and the pancakes, sausage, fruit and berries drizzled with hundred-year-old balsamic vinegar that I would wash down with thick creamy milk and hot coffee tomorrow.

As startling as my appetite was, so was the heightened pleasure with which I indulged it. There was nothing of gluttony to my eating, nothing of idle displaced hunger apart from the good, healthy hunger of belly and body.

Substance and strength were in fact returning to me. Not only could I feel it, I could see it. My flesh, which had withered with the years, began to return to fullness. The atrophied musculature in my limbs subtly thickened to a former solidity that flexed beneath my skin and moved and performed tasks with greater ease and power. And even my skin itself, so loose and sickly for so long, seemed to tighten and glow with a newfound nourishment. When I lay very still I could feel a faint, pleasant tingling inside me, like the cells of my body blithely stirring after a long death-like sleep.

For most of my life the power that hung and hardened beneath my abdomen had been the sovereign of force and might at the center of my being. I mourned, hurkled, and entered my own shadow with the dwindling of that power, as it became little more than a weightless invalidity, a specter of what once had been; something in extremis that on occasion throbbed and twitched and weakly spat, but had for the most part been drained of force, might, and thews.

Now intimations of replenished life could be felt there, in that fallen temple, as well. Nerve endings pullulated anew. Brutal sinew thickened.

My balance was improving. I could get into my socks, shorts, pants standing up without reaching out for walls, doorjambs, the edges of tabletops.

I thought at first that these changes might possibly be attributed to my having quit drinking and the long-lasting effects of the alcohol beginning to leave my system. But this was a cleansing process that took months and did little or nothing to fix what permanent damage had been done. It brought remission, not metamorphosis. And it was nothing less than a metamorphosis that I seemed to be undergoing.

I felt whole. For a while I reveled in feeling as I had in my prime, when I rode the bull of this life into the crashing sea and wild woods of whatever might be. Then I came to realize that this was no lost feeling wondrously returned. For I had never known such a feeling before. Never.

If it was true that I was eating a lot, it was also true that I was eating well. More than well. One night I got hold of one of the last white truffles of the season, a beautiful firm fawny-brown nugget from a parcel of them flown in that day to my friend Silvano's restaurant on Sixth Avenue, the soil from the oak roots of Alba still clinging to them. The next morning I fried some thick, smoky duck bacon over low heat, dropped six quail eggs into the fat for less than a minute, removed them to a plate, covered them with truffle shavings, and ate them with the bacon, double-smoked Irish salmon with chopped red onion, Pantelleria capers, lemon, and dill, some good warm rosemary sourdough bread and butter, and a bowl of yellow, orange, pink, and red raspberries over which

I spooned fresh single-dairy heavy cream whipped with a bit of wildflower honey from Casteggio. The Lapsang souchong tea I drank with it was good, black, strong, and hot. Its faint smoky aftertaste of kerosene mingled perfectly with the scent of truffle that perfumed the kitchen.

As I ate at the little table by the window, I looked down across the street at those who scurried to their daily servitude, with their Styrofoam cups of bitter watery coffee, their dupe's containers of treacly Starbucks swill, their industrially dyed and flavored sugar-water "energy drinks," their assembly line donuts, their stale rubbery bagels, their tasteless doughy croissants.

I washed the dishes, took a Valium, poured a glass of cold goat milk, lit a cigarette, and relaxed. The day was mine to do what I would, or to do nothing at all.

It was a good feeling, an exhilarating feeling. I had long grown to despise this fallen, wearisome world. Now I sensed it held unseen timeless chambers yet to be explored.

Chambers of light. Chambers of dead souls awaiting release. Chambers of passage to what lay beyond imagining. Chambers of what the gods kept hidden. Chambers of wisdom proscribed. Chambers of experience and pleasure untasted for eternity. Chambers of stilled ageless magic breezes waiting to stir. Chambers to be unbolted by hieratic spell, or by a serendipitous movement of the hand—the swatting away of an illusory fly, perhaps, or the waving away of the world itself—that constituted unawares a mudra of primordial power, or by desire, or by the merest unconscious modulation of breath. And I became aware of the singular creeping suspicion that these unseeable but real chambers, which seemed to be secreted so far away, were in fact within me.

I looked down at the scurrying submissives, the divested. Some of them jostled for taxis. At this time of day, it took a lot longer to get anywhere by taxi than by subway. I figured they were too lazy to walk the few blocks to the subway station. They were fool enough to jog along the West Side Highway or on stationary treadmills, presenting a droll spectacle either way, panting toward their one true destination, which was nowhere. But they sat in taxis in traffic rather than walk, rather even than walk to the subway. Did they avoid the subway from fear of crime? Or from a fear of black people, even though they would never admit to it, even though the women they poorly paid to take care of their homes and chores and children, whom they themselves saw no more of than the designer dogs they paid others to walk for them, were invariably black? I think, in many cases, this was so. They were a funny lot, these white slaves of ignoble careers of lucrative indolence. To say that they were deserving of death would be to demean death. It would be without meaning as well, for they were in a way already dead. The jogging dead. Carbohydrate-conscious cadavers with frozen smiles of chilling insensate fake vibrancy on their dull scrubbed pampered faces. A slave who believes himself free conceives of no escape, for he conceives of no freedom beyond that which his station in life allows him. A slave who espouses the freedoms of slavery is a right good slave indeed.

If only they labored nobly, in fields or factories or mills, rather than abetting the masters of finance, whose only products were theft, usury, and lies, or masters of technology, whose only products were cheap and shoddily cobbled toys of degeneration. These slaves made nothing, except perhaps devalued money for themselves, and far more of it for those whom they served. For nothing was any longer made in this country. What did the financial sector produce that could be seen, touched, held, or put to use? Even the handheld devices made on the cheap far from any American workplace were only trifling toys, little more than electric rattles for the overgrown slave-babies in the vast playpen scrouge of their yowling, gurgling nervosity.

Servilia nervosa. They want children, they want dogs. But they seem to want to have little to do with either of these hideous yapping, shitting things, which they seem to regard as accoutrements of what they call their lifestyle—a ludicrous word invented quite fittingly by a psychotherapist.

When they buy inferior overpriced meat, they ask the butcher how to cook it.

On a recent day I had stood at a meat counter behind a woman who, while chattering into a cell phone, asked the butcher if the ground beef came from grass-fed cows. She believed that grass-fed beef was somehow preferable to grain-fed beef, which in fact is superior to it. But the notion of grass-fed beef was enjoying a cachet among au courant imbeciles. She did not ask if the ground beef was from a single cow rather than a mélange of scraps from many cows, which not only compromises the taste and freshness but exponentially increases the risk of taint. Worst of all were the uniform patties of ground beef, which were sliced from long roll-like loaves fashioned from cheap sources by industrial-grade suppliers. It was these patties that she was looking at and asking about, haughtily commenting that she wanted to make steak tartare. But the main event was when she turned around. She was about fifty, in leather pants, with desiccated hair dyed raven black, and a frightfully fallen facelift that could barely have been remedied by a linoleum cutter, a staple gun, a pound of putty, and a trowel. This had not prevented her from applying mascara, rouge, and lipstick in thick, bold, garish strokes, as if working from a palette with expressionistic strokes of a wide-bristled brush. I wondered who would be fated to share her grass-fed dog food tartare with her that evening.

The slaves and indentured laborers who made this country had their elderberry wine, their honeysuckle wine, their sorghum grain alcohol, their purloined whiskey when they could get it. The slaves of today, who raze what little is left with an empty greed that brings forth nothing, have what doctors with straight faces refer to as lifestyle drugs.

White Betty had a baby, bam-de-lam; white Betty had a baby, bam-de-lam. Damn thing gone crazy, bam-de-lam; damn thing gone crazy, bam-de-lam. Whoa, white Betty, bam-de-lam; oh, white Betty, bam-de-lam...

Baby's first lifestyle drug. Baby's first handheld device. Baby's first breakdown. Baby's first organic grass-fed beef. Baby's first step to slavery. Baby's first intimation of something like death.

If you want to make lobster fra diavolo as it should be made, you must forget the nonsense of sending the lobster to what you have been told is a painless sleep unto death in a pot of boiling water. You must hack the raw lobster to pieces in its shell. There is a merciful way to go about this, and that is by first severing the thorax from the tail of the living lobster. If you want to witness something disarmingly bizarre, lay the lobster on its back on a cutting board and bring down your cleaver hard and fast to separate the upper body from the whole of the tail. Then move the two halves so that there is a good inch between them. Touch one of the detached halves. The other half will twitch and stir.

This is how those slaves scurried and jerked, implausibly nervose, in their living death. From the vantage of my window, from a distance, I drew pleasure in a way from observing them. I detested their presence in the neighborhood, but their nature, and the cruel comedy of their existence, seemed a just punishment. When I was among them I drew no such pleasure. The lobster was undeserving of its fate. They were not. And the disturbing movement of the pieces of them was too loud, overbearing, invasive, and insufferable to allow either the mean entertainment or the malicious satisfaction that distance afforded.

Fuck them. Their lives, their death-in-life, their soulless devotion to mindless ulterior greed, the lowest of monotheisms, were the cast lots of their own ruin. Unlike them, I was free. If I could not cherish their inevitable demise, I could escape. I was resistant to the idea of fleeing from invaders. But I was not resistant to the idea of fleeing from pestilence. This city, once so full of life, was now little more than a necropolis. I could get away from this putrid stinking shit hole of Judeo-Christian perfidy. I could get a nice little stone house somewhere, in the countryside near some small town. An acre or two would insure peace, quiet, privacy, domain.

But these thoughts were unfinished. There was the matter of my desires, the matter of my continuance in the new world, the new life, that was just now opening to me. There was the matter of willing young flesh and warm blood, so plentiful in this city of night. Then again, maybe willingness was not of the essence. Maybe willingness was an unnecessary nicety. I shook away this thought. As I drank the last of my milk, my mind wandered through an entablature of images of bucolic solitary quiescence. Maybe someday, I thought. Yes, someday, somehow. Little more than a month ago I had felt that death was near. Now I could envision smiling at the late afternoon sun of my eightieth year and more.

Melissa returned the borrowed book that evening and placed it on the shelf where she had found it. As she did so, my eyes and hands savored the curve of the small of her back and her flanks.

I had a girl that other men—younger men and older fools too—would dedicate the sum of lies, sacrifice, and shifting purchase to have and to hold, to be with and to woo, to follow to where their dreams might come true. I too wanted to have and to hold her. And I did. But my dreams were not of the garden path variety. Since that night in the bar to this night, we had come to breathe in unison; and that breath gently blew away the years between us like so many feathery pappus harls from the seed head of a dandelion fondled by a sigh of soft summer air.

I more than liked her, more than luxuriated in her. I felt at times that I was falling in love with her. Was this a dangerous state of affairs? After so long in cold darkness of heart and soul, I had come once again to believe in love and happiness. Indeed, I now was beginning to feel their goodness banishing the cold and the dark with warmth and light. And the transformation from which the restoration of mind, body, and being grew, the miracle born of deathward desperation, was a rare and marvelous flowering. But it was a flowering not of the sun but of the moon. It was a flowering in the deep foreboding woods of night. A flowering not by spring rain but by the blood of those who, rambling lost in the springtime of their lives, chanced upon it and paused to wonder.

Melissa had paused and not turned away. She was one with the flowering. Her nectar and its nectar were one, and I alone drank of it, the nectar of new and full life. That she was still a child, sending into the air as a child might, playfully, the dandelion fluff of the years that imposed, did not trouble me. She was more mature in her ways, brighter and more intelligent, than many women twice her age. Her beauty was far from childlike. I could easily imagine living happily ever after with her. I had the means to provide for her, to lavish on her.

What troubled me, what quenched my moments of daydreaming, was the simple fact that there was not much blood in a human body. The three or so pints she had lost that horrible night when her artery opened had been very nearly enough to do her in. My flourishing would be her wasting away. The transfusions she had already received were bad enough. There was no knowing where that blood had come from. It could have come from that old bitch asking about grass-fed beef. I needed young blood, fresh and full of life. I wanted it to be Melissa's. But if it could not be—and it could not be, not without draining her, not without turning her into a ghastly anemic wretch, even if she were to allow it—then, to spare her, to save me, I would have to hunt. I would have to hunt as I had done not so long ago, before I even knew what I was hunting for.

I was living happily ever after right now, in this infinite moment, this present breath that was the sum of life's promise, the only ever after we really had. As Melissa stood atop the little library stepladder, stretching to replace the borrowed book, the curve of the small of her back that I savored was level with my eyes, and as she nestled the book into its place on the shelf, the waistband of her sweater rose from her low-cut jeans to reveal the dimples at the upper cleft of her buttocks. I put my mouth to those dimples, stroking her haunches and flanks as she lingered on the stepladder, her hands on the bookshelf edge, steadying herself as she flexed to enhance the curvature of her lower spine and swayed her pelvis ever so slightly, ever so slowly. Lowering one hand from the shelf, she pulled her sweater higher from the front, baring the scalloped satiny black back-strap of her bra. I was a sucker for the loose-librarian look. If only she wore glasses, I thought as I stepped onto the ladder behind her and undid the fastenings of her brassiere with my teeth. The ponytail more than made up for the lack of eyeglasses. I kissed the pink crenulations left behind by the loosened cincture of the bra.

Just as that lacy harness had bitten into her, so did I, but harder and more deeply. There was not much flesh to clamp between my teeth, and very little blood issued from it. I tasted more of her skin than of the red liquor that trickled thinly into my mouth. It was a taste that reminded me faintly of delicate Iranian caviar. Was it the trace of an ancient sea-magic, the pull of the moon on the tide within her as on the tides of oceans? Could I even have tasted what I thought I had: a scintilla of the suggestion of scented Caspian spray and roe of luscious life cut fresh from dead wombs? How had the taste of skin and droplets of blood brought such an imagining to my senses? All I knew was that this taste, this insinuation of a taste, real or imagined, left me hungering for more.

I drew a hot bath for her, lathered her and washed her all over with neem oil soap, lingering long not only on the cut on her back but on her breasts and the secret beauty between her legs. Her hips rose to the level of the bathwater as I lathered there until her hips sank once again and she quaked and there came from her a small deep sound, like a last gasp before drowning, or a first gasp after being saved from it. Only then did she seem self-conscious of the scar near to where I had lathered her to orgasm, the scar where she had been stitched. I felt that she wanted neither my hand nor my eyes on it, even clouded as it was beneath the soapy water and further obscured by the dimmed lights and steam.

I wrapped her in a big soft towel and dried her. I swabbed the cut with peroxide and rubbed some thick vitamin E on it with my fingertip. She smiled and raised her lips to mine. When I took her lower lip between my teeth, she stepped back and her smile did not return until she sat in my robe beside me on the couch, sipping Roquette 1797 from a pony glass. I had finally found some good *parmigiano reggiano* and had bought a hunk with a good deep tawny layer beneath the rind. I broke off pieces of it with a narrow chisel, put them on a plate, drizzled some unfiltered olive oil over them, ground some black pepper over them, peeled a blood orange, added the segments to the plate, and laid it down beside her glass of absinthe.

I wanted to talk to her about stone houses and rolling hills and sunlight and shadows in the pines. I wanted to talk to her about the difference between hunting and infidelity. But I said nothing. She was stroking my shin with her bare foot, and it felt good. I thought of the odd faint taste of caviar that I had experienced. I thought of the watery slightness of the blood, barely enough to moisten my lips and mouth and evoke that faint odd taste. There was not much blood, hardly any, to be drawn from the capillary vessels where I had broken her skin. There were not many nerve endings in that part of the body, either. You could stick a pen, an index finger, a comb, anything to that part of someone's back and tell them it was a gun or a knife, and they would never be able to feel that it was not. It was a trick that every mugger knew, the principal anatomy lesson of the school of crime. I wondered what she had felt when I bit her there. I wondered if she felt anything there now. It had been somewhat like taking a mere few drops of light, bracing aperitif or—that impossible taste—a mere smidgen of caviar from a dainty little mother-of-pearl spoon. Something that was so very deliciously satisfying while intensifying the appetite that rendered it satisfying. Something so wonderfully satisfying and so maddeningly unsatisfying at the same time. This effect was quite perversely pleasant, like catching sight of a wondrously beautiful bird in the instant that it vanished in flight from the visible sky.

In Vientiane one late afternoon, in the ghostly quiet before owl-light descended, I wandered through the winding dirt streets on my way back to the old hotel where I was staying. I had spent the day on my hip and on my back in an opium den, smoking and dreaming, smoking and dreaming, on the rotten wood-plank floors of paradise. A chicken crossed before me in the dust as I made my way. The moment I saw the chicken I knew why it was crossing that road. Utterly and truly and precisely, as if—no, not as if, but simply as—its mind and purpose were conveyed to me in a beam of irrefutable revelation, I *knew*. A life of "Why did the chicken cross the road?" A life of "To get to the other side." It was over. I *knew*. And what I knew, the inestimable truth of this sudden supernatural knowledge, was so overwhelming and life-altering that I felt that it would imbue my days and guide me ever thence. The knowledge filled me. I could never, would never breathe another breath that was without this knowledge that had claimed my mind and my existence.

By the time I made it to the next bend in the dirt road, maybe a distance of three or four yards, I had completely forgotten why the chicken crossed the road. The evaporation of this knowledge has tormented me ever since. I know that I will never recapture it. My only consolation is that I *knew,* if only for a fleeting, fated instant, why the chicken crossed the road. This great and mystical knowledge was mine. For that instant I had and I knew what no other human being ever had or ever knew.

For some reason, or from some idle misfiring of synapse and neuron, I thought of this now. Something so wonderfully satisfying and so maddeningly unsatisfying at the same time. The chicken that crossed the road, the sea spray and the moon and the tides, droplets from capillaries and gushings from arteries, living happily ever after, and the hunt without which there could be neither happiness nor ever after, even the dead monkeys and the exorcism and laying to rest of them. The more Melissa's bare foot softly stroked my shin, the more I felt myself falling into a shallow trance in which images and thoughts flowed in otherworldly harmony.

How I wished I could have opium again. The real stuff, the good stuff, the best stuff in the world. I could go out and find within a mile of where I lived a gun, heroin, crack, whatever I wanted. But not opium, not the most beatific of drugs. Not here, not in Europe, nowhere but in parts of Asia, and even there it was growing more rare as well, so much more profitable was it when processed into heroin. Everyone who had ever claimed they could get me opium in the city had turned out to be a liar out to impress with empty words or a fool who believed the hard black little pieces of foul matter he had purchased was real opium, and that, even if it were, it could be smoked in a hash pipe.

Yes, I wished I could have opium again, the sweet smoke of the one true heaven again. To cling to the young flesh in the heat of the vital flame, to draw from that young flesh the warm blood, *calidum innatum,* of new life, the rekindling of dying embers from the power and pleasure of that vital flame. To have this paradise and to enhance it with the paradise of opium too—it was a dream, this nocturne of blood and opium. Some dreams were not without a sublime magic of their own.

I imagined a long ivory pipe with a golden saddle, a lustrous yellow jade bowl, rich gold-edged cloisonné end bands, and shadow-wood tips; a blue and white Ming porcelain jar full of rich putty-soft chestnut-colored opium, its unique scent perfuming the air; a chased silver and cut-glass oil lamp, a layout of ivory-handled fine steel needles, scrapers, wick trimmers, spoons, tweezers, cleaning rod, and sable brush on a black lacquer tray inlaid with mother-of-pearl.

I imagined a small pool of fresh warm blood in a gold and enamel drinking bowl that bore the image of the protective spirit-creature, sword in mouth, beneath the octagonal symbol of the Chinese Eight Trigrams that was painted, its colors long fading, on a piece of wood nailed above the rickety door atop the rickety stairs at the entrance to the opium den.

I took a picture of that image with a cheap disposable camera and later sent it to ethnologists, anthropologists, scholars of Eastern religions, mythology, and symbolism, heads of Oriental studies at universities, curators of Oriental collections at museums, experts on the primitive magic, primitive art, primitive culture, and history of the region. None of them could identify the source and exact meaning of it beyond associating it with an animism of an ambiguous nature. They could not tell if it was good or evil. Only one of them, a professor at Columbia, quoted the fourteenth-century *Yü-li Tzu* of Liu Chu: "Can it be that what man regards as evil, the gods regard as good?"

I did not care if he was a god or a demon, that mad figure with the blade clenched in his mouth. And god or demon, I did not care of what. As for whether it was a numen of good or evil, the wisdom of Liu Chu had taken care of the idea that that there might be meaning in the answer to a question such as that. I gave a name to that image. *La beauté de diable*. It was a beauty, blessed and damned, that was everywhere, in every thing. Everything. And everything, the all of it, could no longer break the barriers of my mind. For my mind had no more barriers. It could flutter like a butterfly on a silent hilltop and devour the cosmos at once.

Everything. It was what I wanted. It was what I felt. It was what I would have. Everything.

The knife between my teeth, or what was left of them, felt good. The soothing, entrancing caress of Melissa's bare foot entered into my imaginings. Their still-life images took on life. Lost in the dreamlike flow of what passed behind half-closed eyes, I watched myself remove the knife from between my teeth and lay it down between the inlaid lacquer tray and the softly gleaming drinking bowl.

Sky. Earth. Thunder. Wind. Water. Fire. Mountain. Marsh. The Eight Trigrams. The everything. And the god-eyed, devil-eyed guy whose face looked out commandingly, angrily, all-seeingly beneath the suit of eight of everything. And the chicken, the giver and the taker of knowing; the chicken who crossed that dusty road.

There seemed to be music from very far away: the single piano notes, woven through deep silence, of Pärt's *Alina*, each note an evocation of myriads of subtle emotions, the subdued summoning of an ancient astrology, the slow bearing away of a

75

soul by the evening tide, a meditation on the dusk and decline of magic, a melancholy star in the black of the endless night before time.

But there was no music. It was in my head. Or somewhere in me. The very-far-away in me.

Blood and opium, opium and blood. And sky and earth, and thunder and wind, and water and fire, and mountain and marsh. Blood on the shadow-wood pipe tip as I sucked deep and long. The vapors and the blood entering my body. Animism. The body ascending to where the spirit beckoned. *Anima mundi*. Christ, I was dying for Chinese food. Not real Chinese food. It was good old New York Jew Cantonese food I craved. Shun Lee would not deliver downtown. Liberty View, which was downtown, would not deliver at this time, period. There wasn't a good old-fashioned Chink restaurant left in Chinatown since the old Mandarin Inn shut down a lot of years ago. There was always China Red on Chambers Street. No, forget about that joint. I thought of taking a taxi up to Shun Lee and getting a shopping bag of takeout. No, fuck that. I'd eat a couple of salami sandwiches and then I wouldn't give a damn about the Chinese food. My eyes were closed now. Near to the open porcelain opium canister, the pipe, the layout, the bowl of blood, the knife, there were open wire-handled Shun Lee takeout containers of roast pungent duck, steamed dumplings, prawns with garlic and scallions, twice-cooked pork, and dry shredded crispy beef.

I made the salami sandwiches, throwing them together on some dry, staling pumpernickel with slices of genetically modified tomato and the all but tasteless mozzarella that I had bought in a pinch at Glucoplastics. Never buy shrink-wrapped, Saran-wrapped, or any other PVC-wrapped food.

When I returned to the couch with the sandwiches on a paper plate, I saw that Melissa was bent over her big baggy black leather purse, which was on the easy chair across the room. She took from it a beat-up, dog-eared paperback, brought it to the couch, and sat down by my side.

I was pleasantly impressed, upon seeing the condition of the book, that she had taken such care with the book that she borrowed from me. It could have been worse. I knew someone who, if she liked a book, chewed on it like a slavering dog as she read it. Maybe Melissa had picked up the paperback used and on the cheap, and it was already pretty beaten-up when she got it. I didn't say anything. It was her book. She could do whatever she wanted with it or to it. I saw that the book was *Steppenwolf.*

Hermann Hesse. Every girl read Hesse. Him and Rumi. Between their first period and their first decent paycheck, even if they would never read another book in their lives, there were Hesse and Rumi.

"Do you like Hesse?" she said.

At least she didn't say his name as if it rhymed with *less,* or *yes.* A lot of people did. But then again I wouldn't have expected that of her. She pronounced it, like almost everybody who didn't rhyme it with *less* or *yes,* with a schwa at the end, so that it sort of rhymed with the way Simon, the black buggy driver in Faulkner's *Sartoris,* said "Yessuh," or the way Rochester, the black chauffeur in *The Jack Benny Program,* later said the same thing. This is how I said it for most of my life, feeling self-satisfied with this lint speck of presumed erudition. Then, about forty-five years after I advanced from the *yes* to the *yessuh* pronunciation, it was revealed to me that the final vowel of his name was really a Germanic long *e,* not a short one. Properly spoken, the name Hesse rhymed with *essay. Hes-say.* So I felt that I was in no standing to take it upon myself to correct anyone who was of the *yessuh* or even the *yes* persuasion.

"Yeah," I said, "as a matter of fact I do. I read *Siddhartha* and

Demian, and I liked them a lot. I wanted to read *Magister Ludi* but it seemed too long. But, yeah, I really liked the ones I read."

"How about this one? I found it in the garbage near school the other day, and I'm really getting into it."

"You know, to tell you the truth, I don't know if I read that one. If I took a look at it, I might remember. But I don't think I did."

"I bet you would remember this one if you had read it," she said with an inscrutable archness.

She skimmed the dog-eared pages until she found the dog-eared page she was looking for. It looked to be about a third of the way into the book.

"The main character is some guy about ten years younger than you. Some guy named Harry, and he's really losing it."

I didn't like where this was going. Younger than me. Really losing it. I chewed at my sandwich. Fuck those Chinks who wouldn't deliver downtown. Fuck Hermann Hesse. And that rhymed with *yessuh.* And fuck this Harry guy, this sputum from a sputtering pen and nothing more. And fuck Whole Foods too.

"And he writes this poem." She looked down at the dog-eared page. "I sort of wasn't paying too much attention when I read it. My mind was sort of wandering. Then this jumped out at me." She cleared her throat and, without removing her eyes from the page, read four lines aloud, as if rapt:

> *The lovely creature I would so treasure,*
> *And feast myself deep on her tender thigh,*
> *I would drink of her red blood full measure,*
> *Then howl till the night went by.*

I no longer cared where this was going. When verse and a salame sandwich vied, verse lost, no matter how much the salame sandwich left to be desired. How could they call this shit mozza-rella? How could they charge three bucks for a half-pound shrink-wrapped blob of it? How could I have bought it? I never entered that fucking Whole Foods without stealing something. I had a drawerful of Quince Body Moisturizer and other extrava-gantly priced Dr. Hauschka skin-care products. There were days when I had three pounds of Kosher Valley chicken under my belt and a pound of Health Valley butter in my pocket. This organic shit sucked, but you couldn't beat the price. I looked forward to the spring morel season, even more to the white matsutaki season in the late fall. The formality of waiting in a checkout line or paus-ing at a cash register was very rare. I even well worked the honor system in the coffee department, where you scooped your own beans from false-bottomed barrels and wrote the variety and price look-up code on the bag you put them in, whole or ground. I liked some kind of French roast, which I ground for a paper-cone drip into a bag whereon I indicated it to be some cheap shit, Morning Buzz or Café Blend or whatever it was, that cost a frac-tion of what was in the bag. It *was* an honor system, for few things were as dishonorable as allowing yourself to be played for a sucker. Yes, they may have been out to rip me off, but I was beat-ing them at their own racket.

My most memorable coup was perhaps the four-pound châteaubriand filet that protruded from my lower flank and hip like an elephantine colostomy bag about to burst all over the Ancient Harvest quinoa. Then there was that two-foot organic sprouted-grain baguette that, with one end tucked into my sock and the rest of it running hidden up my trouser leg, lent me a quite distinguished limp.

Natural. Organic. Dog shit was natural and organic. A puddle of piss left in the gutter by a drunken bum was natural and organic. Potassium cyanide was natural and organic (with a periodic-element pedigree, no less). And unlike the salmon at Whole Foods, dog shit wasn't artificially colored.

I remembered walking into Buccellati on Madison one day a few years back. There was only one customer, an elderly matron who seemed to be in the process of both croaking and buying about a million bucks' worth of jewelry. The armed guard must have gone out for coffee, and the lone saleslady was so wrapped up in catering to and reaping the fortune of the windstorm buying spree of the decomposing matron, that a bracelet of diamonds, sapphires, and rubies lay right there in the open, half on and half off its plush black-velvet display cushion, on a showcase counter.

The fat kike with the loupe I took it to in Newark offered me twelve grand cash, so I figured it was worth twenty-five. I was wrong. Another fat kike with another loupe gave me thirty a few months later. Yahweh only knows what he got for it.

From one end of Kosher Valley to the other. In the wrong direction. *Yea, though I walk through the aisle of the shadow of sugary death...*

So why had I paid for rather than boosted this misbegotten little ball of gypsum-like mozzarella? I chewed and swallowed, none too pleased with myself or my sandwiches. Goddamn fucking Chinks.

"What was it that made those lines jump out at you?" I asked.

A smile came over her face, and that arch look returned. "You're kidding," she said.

"So that made you think of me. Is that what you think of me?" I said. "That I'm some kind of monster?"

I was being defensive. She wasn't even Chinese. She wasn't even a team member of the Whole Foods cheese department. I took a deep breath, remembered what she meant to me.

"No," she said. "Not at all."

She was more than forty years younger than I, and her tone had the mature, measured, calm, and somewhat amused forbearance of a mother dealing with a recalcitrant child.

"No," she repeated. "It made me think of you, yes, but not as you say. It made me think of us. I read those lines over and over, and the more I read them, the more excited I became. I was on the subway, and I kept wishing more and more that I was with you, just the two of us, alone, together. I missed my stop. I got out and walked. I realized I had memorized the lines without knowing it, just by reading them over and over. I kept repeating them to myself as I walked. Every step I took, I became more conscious of the friction of my panties and my pants on my pussy. I felt my thighs rubbing together as I walked. It felt good. It felt too good. I just kept getting more and more excited, until I felt that if I were thrown down to the cold concrete and raped, it wouldn't really have been rape. It would have been part of the poem. The real rapist would've been me. And it was you that I saw throwing me down. You. I can't explain it. You raping me, and me raping you. But how could two people rape each other at the same time? Not as some silly game, but for real. How could that be? It wasn't what rape was. It was beyond that. It was everything rape was, but it was different. It was more."

She was no longer talking to me. The mature, calm, and forbearing mother had left the room, had left the night, had never been. And she was not talking to hear herself talk, or to ward off with words phantoms of torment that thrived on silence. No. What she was doing was trying, impossibly, desperately, to parse the inflections of feelings that lay outside the known grammar of feeling.

Communication is a shoddily cobbled shoe encrusted with the muddling sludge of time, trampling, and ill wear. We speak of

Isis, unaware that, in the vowel-less phonetics of Egyptian hiero-
glyphs, the symbols of the throne and the loaf that signified her
name give us not Isis but *Jst*. And we speak of Jesus, he of a later
mythology; but how many of those who yet kneel unto him know
that this is a name that he never would have recognized or
answered to, for his name was Yeshua? And we say of any of the
elemental turnings of nature that we can "smell it in the air"; yet
the word book we might use to more precisely express our per-
ceptions remains unopened by most of us, who with a single
word, *petrichor,* could describe the pleasing scent brought by rain
after long days of warm, dry weather. The word was welded from
two Greek words, the second of them being *ichor,* the ethereal
blood that ran in the veins of the gods and the goddesses. From
the first babblings of earliest childhood to the dimwitted preten-
sions of eloquence uttered in age, we pass most of our lives unable
to communicate effectively what we feel, think, or want to say.
Like trying to work wood or metal without tools, we can't even
articulate our worst stupidities, let alone the few worthy percep-
tions that attach themselves to us by accident. Unless helped out
posthumously by historians, how many of us can even string
together a cogent cheap platitude of parting on our deathbed?
The tired saying was all too often true: if you remain silent, people will take you for a fool; if you speak, they will know you to
be one.

But Melissa was no fool. I cannot say that I understood all of
what she was trying to say, any more than she herself did. Her
words, however, lighted on places in me where I felt that understanding slept and was about to wake. The more she spoke, the
more I admired her. She already knew what most people never
learn. It was what Homer knew: that words were for war, and not
for surrender. Even if she was unaware that she knew this, she
did. Like a rare and beautiful creature of an exotic vanishing spe-

cies who knows no others like itself but only the drabber beings that flourish in multitude around it, she may have felt herself merely to be different, and to be isolated by that difference. It was up to me to show her that what she might be mistaking as lowly difference from the flock was in fact the rare beauty that constituted transcendence, a difference of a very special kind.

"And what did you do when you got home?" I asked her.

She looked straight ahead for a moment or so, as if now trying to choose her words carefully. Then, seeming to discard any such attempt, she simply spoke the words that had been there waiting to be said:

"I raped myself.

"I masturbated like crazy. I bit my arms as I was doing it. I slapped myself. I snarled dirty things at myself. It was like there were two me's. It really did feel like I was raping myself. And I thought of you, and we were raping each other. And I felt myself beginning to come, and I told myself I was going to hold myself back and rush over here and rip open my coat and finish it here, in your face. All sorts of things. And then I just exploded. I came and I came again. And I fell asleep." Here she paused again. "And before I fell asleep, I looked around in the dark with my eyes open, and I knew you weren't there, and I said 'I love you.' And I was saying it to both of us."

"What did it feel like?"

"Saying 'I love you'?"

"No. The self-rape. You raping me and me raping you at the same time?"

"It was all in my head."

"But what did it feel like? What did what was in your head feel like?"

"It was almost too much. It was like being in a storm that was so bad I had to close my eyes. It was like I could feel the force of the winds and all these windblown things hitting me and flying past me, but I couldn't see what they were."

"When you say you closed your eyes to it, do you think that could mean you closed your mind to it?"

"I don't know. All I know is that I wanted to feel it a lot more than I wanted to see it. I didn't care what it was, I just wanted to feel it."

"And it felt good? You weren't afraid of what you couldn't see?"

"It felt more than good. It felt fucking great."

She seemed lost in that remembered feeling that was hers alone. She slowly stood, returned the beat-up paperback to her bag. She took a cigarette from my pack, lit it with my lighter, and sat back down. I had not seen her smoke before.

"What was really weird was that the whole thing, whatever it was, didn't even have a name. I never heard of any kind of sex, any kind of anything, that didn't have a name. That sort of shook me up a little. Like I had gone beyond what was known. Like I had gone beyond what was even imagined. I mean, they had words for guys who fucked dead bodies. Words for guys who got off disemboweling live children. I read a whole paper once on how Proust liked to jerk off while he stuck hatpins through rats. But there was nothing for this. Not a name, not a word. Bernini made a statue of Saint Teresa swooning while Jesus fucked her brain. They called it ecstasy. They called it—what's that other word they called it?"

I shrugged and grimaced indifferently with ignorance.

"Oh, come on, you know. You of all people. That word they only use when they're talking about her."

"I really don't know."

"Transverberation. Yeah, ecstasy, transverberation. And they put it in the Vatican. Nobody was going to make a statue of me raping myself, a statue of me raping you while you raped me. But it was ecstasy. And it was transverberation, whatever the hell that means. But it was way more.

"They say that if a fly flies too high it gets sucked off into space. I felt like one of those flies. Fancy words, dirty words, the whole taxonomy of sex and sin: it's all down there somewhere, and here I am, up here in dark space without any gravity to get my little fly-ass back to where it came from."

"Does that scare you?"

"A little. But this is all just—I don't know. If it does scare me a little, it's all just part of that other thing."

"What other thing?"

"That thing without a name. That thing, whatever it is, that feels so fucking great."

She then fell still. Though she was not looking at me, or at anything, I could see on her face the most serenely beguiling smile that I had ever seen, certainly on her, maybe on anyone. It made Mona Lisa look like she was taking a pleasant shit and nothing more.

"Do you want to rape me?" I asked her.

"I don't think I can." Only then did the smile on her face ease and become imperceptible. "I don't think it would work that way. I think I can only rape you by being raped *by* you."

Without thought, without hesitation, with nothing but a sudden white heat in my mind and body, I grabbed her by the neck, jammed my hand down her panties, and rammed my fist up her cunt. She screamed and clawed at me, and I tore down her T-shirt and sank my teeth into her breast without any foreplay of lip or tongue. She struck me as the blood, full and strong, entered my mouth. I smacked her in angry response. She pulled violently at my arm to remove my fist from her, and I drove it in deeper, deeper again, as I sucked the blood relentlessly from her. She punched my back. I wrenched my fist from her cunt, and with both hands pried open her clenched jaw and let loose a good amount of her own blood from my mouth into hers. I blocked her breath with my hand until she swallowed and gagged. As she made to strike me again I grasped her wrist and forced her to smear herself with the blood that still flowed from her breast. I shoved her aside. I was panting like a beast, and so was she. Our bodies loosened, our breath subsided. We looked as if we had overcome a wild boar and feasted on it raw with our bare hands. Glancing at each other, our bellies moved with mild, soundless laughter.

"I love you," she said.

How I had yearned to hear those words from her, and how happy it now made me to hear them. I felt blessed. I felt as if I could close my eyes and sleep in bliss in her embrace.

We talked awhile, wanderingly, softly, sleepily.

"So what do we call that? Me raping you and you raping me?"

"Do we need to call it anything?"

"No, I guess not, not really."

"Because we can."

She perked up, shot me a look, and said, "You mean this is something known after all? You mean everything I've been feeling and trying to explain, it's not something unknown? You mean it's not new? I'm not a freak? It has a name?"

"Not exactly. But we can give it one."

The perkiness ebbed. She looked quizzical and confused, then simply, deflatedly confused.

"You know," I said. "It's funny. Greek and Latin are such vast, nuanced languages. Especially when it comes to sex. I mean, there were words in Greek like *phoinicizein,* which meant to lick a woman's cunt while it was bleeding. One single word to say what it would take a sentence to say in English."

It occurred to me that I should have used a different example. Her own cunt might be sore and bleeding from the violence of my fist. All I could do was hurry on to another example that might throw a cloak on the one I had thoughtlessly given.

"We took the word *fellatio* from Latin. And, sure enough, *fellatio* meant sucking cock. But we never bothered with the Latin word *irrumatio,* which represented a fine distinction. With *fellatio* the mouth was active. It performed on the cock. With *irrumatio,* the mouth was passive. It got fucked like a cunt.

"But what's funny is that with all this sexual eloquence and precision, neither Greek nor Latin had a single word that referred specifically to rape."

I was too lazy, too tired, to go into the library to fetch my copy of *The Latin Sexual Vocabulary* or Forberg's *Manual of Classical Erotology,* or to lug out the big, heavy *Oxford Latin Dictionary* or the big, heavy Liddell-Scott *Greek-English Lexicon.* But I knew I was right.

"The Latin word *rapere* or *raptare*—they were both more or less the same—had a dozen or more different meanings, having to do with seizing, abducting, stealing, this, that, the other thing. But only one of those meanings came close to what we commonly mean by the word *rape.* It's a fucking mystery. Maybe you should write a paper on it for school.

"Anyway, *rapere* and *raptare* are all we got. That's where we get our word *rape* from. And also—and here's another pisser—also the word *rapture.*" I paused, recalling all the feelings that she had tried so hard to explain and simultaneously seeing a beam of light issue from what I had just said. "Rape and rapture. Linguistic twins. Maybe twins in ways that go far deeper than that."

I felt that I should have stopped there, but my weary mind maundered on, and my mouth along with it. I heard myself saying things about the shifting, sharing of roles of violator and victim, about "symbiotic ferocity," about "bilateral rape" and "equipollent rape." I had no idea from which yawning crevice of my drowsy brain that one came from. I had no memory of ever having used the word *equipollent,* and I wasn't even sure if it meant what I thought it did. I was sleepily aware once again of her search for a word, a phrase, a name that might bring her some sense of solace by lending definition to the screaming formless banshees of her inexpressible feelings. I muttered the words *"raptus aequus"*— equal rape. How stupid they sounded. I thought of what they called "the spintrian postures," traced to the endless pursuits of pleasure of Tiberius, and defined most wonderfully by Thomas Blount, in a manner that could but barely escape memorization, in his dictionary of 1656 as "pertaining to those that seek out, or invent new and monstrous actions of lust." Forberg's manual enumerated the postures to be ninety. But, as shown by Melissa and countless others through the ages, this list of erotic variations was far from complete. One that had always stuck in my head was *paedico paedicator,* "a pederast pedicated." As this posture was described as *spintriae tres,* involving three participants, there could be no doubt that the butt-fucker was simultaneously being butt-fucked while butt-fucking. There seemed to me a certain music to both the sound and meaning of this one.

"Raptor raptatur," I said, first whispering it to myself, then saying it aloud. The rapist raped. *Spintriae duo.* Perfect. I repeated the phrase again: *"Raptor raptatur."* Then, even though this phrase had never appeared in Latin, I said, as if it were a definition to be found in the commonest Latin dictionary: "A rapist raped while raping."

"Rap-*tor* rap-*ta*-tur," she said, pronouncing the words with a mock gravitas, in a cleverly understated burlesque of full and solemn imperial cadence. "I am she who rapes while being raped. I am she who rapes herself."

She looked to me, grinning crookedly. There was caked blood in her ponytail. The dried blood on her face was inescapable of notice all along, but I had not until now seen the dark glistenings that matted her schoolgirl hair. The rape of the lock.

"What about that part?" she said. "She who rapes herself. What about that?"

I immediately coined the word *autoraptus,* then just as immediately cast the coin into the gutter. The prefix *auto-* was Greek; *raptus* was Latin. It was an abomination to make a word by forcing a marriage of Greek and Latin roots.

What was the Greek equivalent of *raptare?* I couldn't remember. All I could remember, or seemed to remember, was that it was ungainly, unwieldy, and started with an alpha. Fuck it. Even if it worked, it would involve getting up off the couch. I was even having trouble remembering the Latin reflexive pronouns. I really was falling asleep. Ah, *sui.* Yeah. *Sui, sui, sui.* Self. *Sui juris,* one's own master. All right, then, so what was the genitive singular of *raptor?* Same thing. *Sui raptoris.* One's own rapist. *Sui-raptus.* Self-rape.

"Oh, that," I said, as if recalling something from a child's primer. "She who rapes herself. One's own rapist is *sui raptoris.* As for the deed itself, self-rape, that's *sui-raptus.*"

Somehow all of this seemed to make her feel better. And so I said:

"You're a goddess, baby. The goddess whose name is *dea raptor raptatur.* The goddess who rapes while being raped.

"Somewhere incense burns, solitary figures search the constellations, and the priestly and the low utter sighs of prayer without knowing why."

She wiped some dried blood from her lips with the back of her hand. She looked at the back of her hand. She looked at me. There were still stains of darkening burgundy on her mouth, and it was hard to tell if she was smiling or smirking.

"You just made all that up, didn't you?" she said.

"What part of it?"

"All of it."

"No."

"The part about the goddess."

"Every goddess is made up. Every god is made up. That doesn't detract from them. Look at Isis."

I had mentioned Isis not long before. But when I now said her name—or, rather, the name that Herodotus had somehow Greeked from what he had heard in Egypt in the Late Dynastic Period—I felt an uncanny consciousness of that mysterious and unsettling scrap of paper, in my scrawling hand but unrecognized by me, that I had kept secreted in a drawer since inexplicably finding it on my desk one morning not long ago. It had been for the most part out of mind as well as out of sight until this very moment. I experienced a quick wave of anxious unease.

"*Jst.*" The strange sound burst from her, a sudden glottal hiss, giving me a start and warding off whatever aftermath might have followed that wave that passed through me.

"Or however the fuck they said it. Look at her. The Greeks and Romans turned her into Artemis and Diana, Aphrodite and Venus. The Christians turned her into the Virgin Mary. All of them made up, just like her. But she's still there. Her beauty, her power, her magic—everything, undiminished. People die, but what they make up, what they wish to exist over them, what they make up to embody everything that they can never be, everything that can never be, period—that doesn't die. It's eternal."

"So you made me up. I didn't think they were making up any new gods these days."

"Are you kidding? Every breath, every breeze bears a god or a goddess waiting to be born, a theophany there for the taking. You know those lines on the refrigerator? In that same poem he summons the four hundred gods of drunkenness—'*The four hundred gods / of drink alone / sat with him / as he died / in pieces*'—which never existed until that very moment when he made them up."

Those lines had always scared me, and I had always wondered if they had scared Olson as he conceived and wrote them down.

"Not one god for him," I said. "No, four hundred of them in one fell swoop. There was a maker up of gods who thought big, all right.

"That statue of that saint getting transreverberated by that made-up Jesus. That other statue there of that made-up Virgin Mary holding the corpse of that made-up transreverberator. That painting *The Birth of Venus*. That stuff's pretty to look at, but it's just a bunch of stone and paint, a bunch of made-up stuff about made-up gods and made-up goddesses.

"At least you're real. You're right here, sitting right next to me. And what I said about making up that goddess. It's not true. You are a goddess. You embody what others can't be, what others can barely imagine. That beauty, that power, that magic. It's in you, and it's forever. All I made up was the name of the goddess. And I pieced that together from words made up by the same people who made up gods and goddesses. Every goddess has to have a name. Of course, you could always just stick with Melissa."

"I don't feel like a goddess," she said. But it was obvious that she was feeling pretty damned good.

"If you did, you'd be unbearable," I said. "And you'd end up in your arrogance like Jesus in his. Look at that fairy tale. Tormented for forty days and forty nights. All just to end up getting nailed to a cross in his diaper."

"The temptation of Christ."

"Yeah. As opposed to the temptation of Louie the Lug."

"I never got that. I mean, what was he supposed to have been tempted by?"

"By exactly what he wanted. Dominion over all earthly kingdoms. That was the main one, with the offer coming from Satan, the one guy who could probably actually deliver. There was a whole mess of other temptations, too, but they don't go into most of them." My eyes were closing again. I lit a cigarette. "I can tell you one thing. This salami sandwich wasn't one of them."

"Do I still have a lot of blood on my face?"

"It depends on what you mean by a lot."

Yes, I thought, as I drew smoke and let my eyes close for a moment: fuck normalcy and fuck the normal. It was death and they were dead. Dante looked down upon them as being unworthy even of entering hell, calling them *i vigliacchi,* the lukewarm, the cowardly.

I kissed the dried blood on her lips. I said the words I had so yearned to hear from her, and had heard: "I love you."

Her eyes were angelic. She rose silently to take a shower and prepare for bed. I sat alone, luxuriating in what I felt, which was all the more wonderful enwrapped in the comfortable warmth of deep and quiet drowsiness. The sound of the shower cascading behind the closed door of another room was soft and sylvan.

I went to her bag to get that beat-up paperback, so that I might read again the lines she had read me. I was surprised to find that, in context, the "tender thigh" and the "red blood" the character wished to drink "full measure" were those of a deer. Sweet self-raped Melissa had extracted them from the rest of the verse in a way that gave a very different impression and conjured a very different picture. As isolated by her, the tender thigh and red blood were those of a maiden; even, by the implication of her chosen and well-voiced reading, those of Melissa herself.

The discovery of this little deceit was an unexpected pleasure, like coming across a thoughtful gift that had been hidden away in anticipation of being given on a special occasion.

When I returned the book to her bag, I noticed a folded piece of paper on which the book had lain. I could see that it was a slim brochure of some kind. I took it out and opened it.

Printed on it were the words WHAT A DIFFERENCE A DAY MAKES. I was about to re-fold it and put it back where it was when

I saw that it was a publication of the American Foundation for Suicide Prevention.

The sound of the shower, which was no longer soft and sylvan, abruptly stopped. I sat on the couch in the dark and had another cigarette. Then I sat a little longer in the dark and had another cigarette.

By the time I went to bed, she was asleep. I did not wake her to mention the little brochure about what a difference a day makes. Nor did I sleep in bliss.

THE SUN THE NEXT MORNING WAS BRIGHT IN A CLEAR BLUE sky, but the cold could be felt through the walls and closed windows, and it was not hunger but a desire to generate and linger by heat from the stove that moved me to make a breakfast of sunny-side-up duck eggs, good fat greasy duck sausage, and toast, made of the last of that pumpernickel that was going stale the night before, smeared thick with dark apple butter.

Melissa swigged coffee and ate like a wolf. It was good to see. But I was still thinking about that little folded pamphlet from the American Foundation for Suicide Prevention that I wished I had not come across in her bag.

How to broach it? "What a difference a day makes," I might say, apropos of absolutely nothing. It was ridiculous. Here I was, sopping duck yolk with already sodden toast and shoving it into my mouth, mulling over asinine gambits instead of just asking her straight out.

And look at her. She was as bright as the sun in the sky, eating like it was going out of style, audibly enjoying it, seeming to be without a care in the world. Was this how a suicide started the day?

If I were drinking, I told myself, I would have no trouble at all asking her outright. Drinking did that. It washed away all the halting doubts, all the reservations, all the cowardices that beset and prevented communication. Liquor let the words flow freely. The trouble was that the tributaries of that river were the rivers of lies and of truth, and their influxes merged and were indistinguishable in the free-flowing current into which they poured. But a simple question like this, a simple honest question like this: liquor would loose it from the mouth and bring forth an answer in the time it took to raise or set down a glass.

What if she was seeking help? What if I could give her that help, or at least support her in her seeking it? All because I could not in this moment bring myself to ask.

How might she react to such a question? Would it strike her as condescending and presumptuous? As a felling revelation of how little I knew her, how little I esteemed her? As controverting evidence that all my talk of her possessing the nature and powers of a goddess was but cruel and idle entertainment at her expense? Might she berate me and feel violated? I did not know if such a question would bring us closer or send us headlong into estrangement. So I did not ask it.

I had feared that I might kill her through bloodletting. Now, obstructed by the constraining trepidations of my newfound sobriety, I feared I might kill her by a failure to inflict truthletting. There could be little doubt, I felt, that my sobriety was endangering her, that it might very well be standing in the way of my saving her life.

The coffee in my cup was getting cold. I lit a cigarette. Melissa asked me if I minded putting on some music. She still seemed bright as the morning sun. I asked her what she wanted to hear.

"That *Island of the Dead* thing or whatever it is."

There was whiskey in the cupboard. There was beer in the refrigerator. *We drink / or break open / our veins solely / to know.* Just one glass of whiskey. Or just a few bottles of beer. And I would ask. And I would know.

About fifteen minutes into Rachmaninoff's thanatopsis—just as the august processional cadences gave way to a rising, swirling storm of ambiguous emotion, then ebbed to silence and then a single plaintive violin—Melissa put on her thick cable-knit sweater, fleece-lined ranch coat, cashmere watch cap, scarf, and gloves, then slung her bag over her shoulder and was off to school, as all good little schoolgirls should be.

We kissed long and warmly at the door. Her eyes, which seemed to have taken on the golden sun and clear blue sky of the day, seemed also to express hints of the inexpressible.

I had read a biography of Cleopatra, out of which I retained lush descriptions of the rich colors of the sea beyond the city of Alexandria. They could not have presented an accurate picture of a sea that can be seen and known now only after two thousand years of dire sludging pollution, muck, and sullage, but they were well wrought and captivating in their evocative imaginativeness. Looking into Melissa's eyes was like looking into the magical beauty of the colors of that sea that may or may never have been.

When she was gone, I put away Rachmaninoff and blasted Chicago Jimmy Rogers's "Sloppy Drunk." I lit a cigarette. I stared at the knuckles of my right hand, as if expecting augury. I looked away, toward nothing: shelves and shelves of books that had been unopened in years, their contents dead and forgotten. I should have long ago disposed of most of them. It was not too late. They should be disposed of now, most of them, including most of the ones that I had written.

There was whiskey in the cupboard, I thought again. There was beer in the refrigerator. Just one glass of whiskey, I thought again, or just a few bottles of beer. And I would know, I thought again; yes, I would know. I was no longer thinking of Melissa, no longer thinking of what a difference a day makes. I was thinking only of my thirst. It was, I told myself, a thirst for knowing.

There are things that enter our minds that we wish never had. So deep-rooted is the opprobrium of them that we never reveal them, so that it might be to all but ourselves that they never occurred, that we would be incapable of such thoughts. And they never slip out, for our secreting of them is so very strong and the opprobrium beneath which we bury them alive is so heavy that they can never escape, and we are the only ones who can hear their desperate clawings and cries for freedom. So vile are they to us that we actually believe that they "enter our minds" and we are unable to see that it was our minds that gave them birth. Our minds are not the random innocent victims of a breaking and entry by assailing demons in flight. Our minds are the wombs from which the demons seek the escape we disallow them. Their vagitus, the vagitus of what is within us, the unspeakable and the inadmissible things that "enter our minds," is what we keep from being heard at any cost.

As I ground out my cigarette, I realized that if my goddess turned out to be a stupid little bitch, so stupid as to entertain taking her own life, I did not care. Fuck her. The only thing I did care about was that if she was going to kill herself, she didn't do it in my apartment. I simply didn't want the trouble. And reporting a teenage stiff—a fucking suicide, no less—in my home meant a lot of trouble.

I loved her. But if I was loving a girl who was suicidal, then I was making a mistake, and shame on me. And if she or anybody else saw me as a part of, or a symptom of, or a participant in her fucking self-ordained end, I wasn't buying in to that psychological bullshit for a single fucking instant. I was pro-choice. She wanted to off herself, so be it. Just not in my joint.

And I would just come out and ask her. "Do you ever think of killing yourself?" I would say. If she said yes, I would talk with her. I would do what I could. If she said no, I would say, "Then what are you doing with that Mickey Mouse bullshit in your bag? 'What a difference a day makes.' It's a stupid shit song and it makes for a stupid shit advertising slogan. So why are you carrying it around?" If she asked me how I knew about it, I would just tell her that that didn't have anything to do with anything. And it would be the truth.

As I say, I loved her. I wanted to have her for whatever remained to me of forever. But you got right down to it, there were other goddesses out there, other beautiful, magical young broads to have and to hold, and who would let me drink their blood full measure from their tender fucking thighs.

I would have a drink. Fuck everything. Have a drink? What did that mean to me? It meant I would get drunk. It meant I would likely stay drunk. Yes, fuck everything. But did I want that? Did I really want that? No. Fuck it. I would go to a meeting.

As soon as I stepped outdoors, I felt different. It was barely above freezing, but the cold did not bother me. With the passing of the years and the dwindling of my weight and substance, I had grown more harshly affected by the cold, which set me to trembling and tightening into myself. But on this morning I did not even feel the chill entering me. I did not even feel it to be cold, really, but instead found the wintry air to be brisk and refreshingly bracing. I drew deep breaths of it into me, feeling calmer and more clear with every vigorous inhalation.

It went beyond the pleasant invigoration of the cold that only a month or so before would have stricken my frail body like an icy lashing, a punishment that would have reduced me to shallow breath and numb shivering. I felt physically strong and hale in the cold of this day. I felt as I had felt in the seasons of my youth: impervious to the elements, enjoying them, thrilling at the sensations brought by their extremes, moving through them as if I were intrinsic to them and they to me.

I felt great, not only strong but with a sense of heightened awareness of which I became more and more conscious as I strode the winter streets. A sparrow lighted on the stark branch of a nearby tree, and I heard it—the almost soundless flutter of its little wings—before I saw it. To my ears came the sound of an easy wind rounding a corner almost half a block away, newspaper rustling by in the gutter across the street, the all but weightless sound of its movement crisply distinct amid the louder noise of the street's traffic. I could see greater distances, more sharply, more clearly. When I flicked a cigarette butt, it flew more than two yards against the breeze to strike the moving car at which I had aimed it. I descended the steep stairs of the Franklin Street subway station with sureness and alacrity, making no use of the side-rail.

I was sure that all of this, or most of it, was the effect of the blood-passion of the previous night. I relished the memory as I flexed musculature in my calves that seemed not to have been there, except as atrophied and weak tissue in wrinkled skin, a few weeks before.

A middle-aged black man in a cheap suit, bowtie, derby, and overcoat approached me on the subway and presented me with a leaflet. I glanced at it and was surprised that I could make out what it said without my reading glasses. The man looked at me a moment, as if he were awaiting a gratuity or a knowing response, then ambled off as if on his solemn way to a cheap snazzy funeral, handing out his leaflets on the way.

THE END OF THE
WORLD IS ALMOST
HERE!
HOLY GOD
WILL BRING
JUDGMENT DAY ON
MAY 21

JUDGMENT DAY is feared by the world and
is the day that God will destroy the world because of
the sins of mankind. The world is correct in believing
that Judgment Day will come. The Bible gives us the
correct and accurate information about that Day.

The Bible is the Holy Book written by Holy God
who is the creator of this beautiful world. The Holy
Bible is without question a very ancient book....

The fucking thing unfolded to eight pages and went on for
fucking ever. Who published this thing? I turned to the last page,
where there was a listing of fourteen states and the call letters and
frequencies of the radio stations in them where Family Radio
could be heard, and the note that "Family Radio is a Bible-based
Christian broadcasting ministry with no church affiliation." The
local station that carried Family Radio was WFME, 94.7 on my
FM dial.

"Why didn't you let me know before I paid my taxes?" I
wanted to ask him, to see if the features of his face were motile,
but he had already passed on to the next car.

I got off the subway at Sheridan Square and walked west to
Perry Street.

Rachmaninoff's gloomy roving tone poem was in my head. It
was the music we had listened to on the night when I first tasted
her blood. And she had wanted to hear it again this morning.
When was that night, that holy night, when I first brought her to
my bed? I could not remember, other than that it was not long
ago. The full wolf moon had just begun to wane. And the full
crow moon was now a few days off. Less than a month. Yet it
seemed that we had lived through long seasons of the heart in
those few weeks—new and different seasons from any we had
ever known or imagined. Had she wanted to hear the Rach-

maninoff this morning because of the first-month anniversary, just two or three days away, of that night when these new and mysterious seasons began? Could that mystical ferrying to the Isle of the Dead have been for her not an evocation of the death-ward tide of timeless night, but an evocation of romance, a sea-lapped stone in moonlight that marked the memory and celebration of that romance?

And what of that suicide-prevention brochure in her bag? I myself was now walking down the street with the end of the world in my inside coat pocket. Had suicide been handed to her on a subway car by a derby-hatted negro of fixed features, as Judgment Day had been handed to me?

I was seeing, thinking, and feeling lucidly now. I had put myself through all that torment about being unable to ask her because it was a way of working up to drinking. Alkies are the most ingenious and expertly devious people in the world. The simple truth is that they never apply these qualities to anything worth a damn, and, worse, can't even tell when these ingrained traits are working independently of them, and against them.

It was nice going to Perry Street. I liked the morning meetings there. I liked the quiet little corner of the Village where the room was, and had been for over half a century. I liked many of those who attended the meetings there, a varied bunch of characters who seemed unconcerned about the presence of any good-book God, loving or otherwise. I liked the venerable age and history of the place. I liked the tales that were told about the guy who confessed to a murder, was ratted out by a few who heard him and broke the bond of confidentiality ("what's said in these rooms stays in these rooms") so integral to A.A., then had his manslaughter verdict overturned on the grounds that his confession had been part of a constitutionally protected religious activity and could not be used against him. I liked the tales that were told of the so-called treasurer, the guy entrusted with the gathering, tallying, and banking of the donations given at each meeting, who one day cleared out the room's little account and rode off into the sunset, giving rise to the enduring and instructive Perry Street apothegm "a sober thief is still a thief." Yes, I liked the meetings there, when the morning light still lent promise to the day to come. And when I didn't like one of those meetings, I could, as at any meeting anywhere, simply get up and leave.

I felt like sharing this morning. Sharing. That's what they called it. A very big A.A. word. As if unloading your bullshit was a gift unto others. Then again, if it inspired somebody else to do the same, maybe it was. I wanted to tell of how, earlier that morning, I had woven myself with tortuous knots of circumpressure in a camouflaged attempt to cogitate myself into drinking without even knowing what I was doing. This was how insidiously the alcoholic mind worked. It was like the snake in the fable of the Garden of Eden. That snake was so good at what he did, such a consummate master of deceit, that few even noticed his coup de grâce of transferring the blame for the fall of man from himself to Eve. You could talk about Satan all you wanted. But that snake shot straight out of an alky's skull.

When I thought of Eve, I thought of Melissa, upon whom I indirectly laid the blame for the fall I myself had very nearly brought about. I got ready to raise my hand. The chair of the meeting acknowledged another raised hand. Then I heard him, before I even saw him. "Hi," he said, drawing out this simple syllable into a lofty arc of the longest possible duration. "My name's Peter and I'm an alcoholic and a sex addict."

Shit. The little cocksucker had not succumbed to AIDS or age. Fuck him and fuck this. I wasn't going to sit here and listen to him and the gumdrops of self-pity that he dispensed while adjusting himself as if heeding the requests of a photographer but careful always to keep intact the curl of his prissy, shit-eating Chessy-cat grin. And I wasn't going to talk to an audience that included him. Better a bunch of filthy, stinking, sick and contagious bums who had come in off the street just to escape the cold. I got up, put a cigarette in my mouth, walked out, and let the door slam behind me. I had already once today barely escaped driving myself to drink. I wasn't about to risk being driven to drink again, not by somebody else, and surely not by someone like him.

I walked over to Patisserie Claude on West Fourth Street. That was another thing, the proximity to this little place, I liked about the morning meetings on Perry Street. Claude made the best, maybe the only real, croissants in downtown Manhattan. Rich, soft, buttery, flaky, hot from the oven. I got two to go and a cappuccino. I crossed Sheridan Square to the downtown station.

Sometimes I made it to a meeting just in time. Sometimes I escaped a meeting just in time. Today I did both. And I still felt as great as I had felt when I first stepped outdoors this morning. With every breath, in fact, I felt better, stronger, more perceptive. And now I had in one hand a couple of hot croissants in a little bag and in my other a cup of hot cappuccino. I could smell the butter in the pastries, the thick froth in the coffee. I could smell them as if I were tasting them. Never before, in fact, were the scents of such simple pleasures so full and satisfying that I could only wonder with anticipation at the possible new heights I might experience when actually tasting them. I descended the subway stairs with greater agility than I had earlier; adroitly juggled the bag and the coffee, and swiped my card through the turnstile without a thought or a moment's hesitation as to the movements involved.

The coffee and croissants were still hot when I bounded from the Franklin Street station, quickly walked the two short blocks to my place, and set them down. Three subway stops, some wintry air, and they were still hot and the spume on the cappuccino had subsided a bit but was still thick and foamy. I had been eating Claude's croissants for twenty, maybe twenty-five years, and they were always good. But now, as I bit into the first of them, my taste buds bloomed as never before, and my tongue discerned everything in that croissant, the traces of milk, egg, sugar, and especially butter, individually and in sublime concert. I remembered walking most mornings to one of two bakeries not far from where I lived in Paris, on rue du Dragon. These two bakeries sold the best croissants I had ever tasted, and I knew precisely when they came out of the oven. I could not remember those croissants tasting as good as the soft delicious croissant that I stood in my kitchen eating right now, washing down mouthfuls with coffee as if they were the savorous consecrated elements of an unimagined Eucharist of earthly delight.

I thought of the movement of the sparrow's wings, the faint faraway wind, the flimsy sheet of newspaper in the gutter across the street. I thought of the cold that did not enter me except through deep pleasant breath, the assured musculature in my legs as I moved nimbly, the natural ease of my maneuverings. These croissants, I then realized, were not special. In fact they were, they had to be, inferior to what they had been when I purchased them, and almost certainly not as fine as those superb morning croissants fresh from the ovens of the two patisseries I favored in the sixth arrondissement. The magnificence of these croissants, good as they were, was not in them. It was in me. As I could hear the near-silence of the unseen sparrow's subdued fluttering wings, the hushed murmur of a wind I could not feel, the faint, almost soundless stirring of newspaper in a gutter not near to me; as I could see and read clearly without my eyeglasses—so I now could taste, relish, and discern the morsels and draughts of what pleased the tongue with a new acuity that raised the mundane pleasure of these simple croissants and coffee to the sensuous Eucharistic delight I was experiencing.

Last night I had taken a long hot bath and cleaned myself well. Beneath two of my fingernails, however, there remained, almost unnoticeable, slight dark traces. I raised these fingertips to just beneath my nostrils. I could smell the scent of blood. More than that. I could distinguish it as the scent of her blood.

The heightening of my senses and the strengthening of my body, of which in recent weeks I had at times felt passing intimations and inklings, were real. My dulled mind and senses were growing ever more delicately and sharply attuned to every subtlety of every sensation in me and around me. My tired, worn-out body grew ever more kinetic and vigorous.

My body. My soul. My life. I had discarded them. But now I was regaining them. A sound mind in a sound body, as Thales of Miletus, one of the Seven Sages, is often believed to have said in the sixth or seventh century B.C., and as the Roman poet Juvenal, whether or not he stole it from Thales, said in the second century A.D. A sound mind in a sound body. All my adult life I had mocked this definition of a well-tempered and happy life. What, I thought, was a sound mind in a sound body but a plain and pretty flower in a plain and pretty vase? The world was full of such parlor-piece lives, I thought. But things were different now. Old dogs sidle with lowered heads and dragging tails toward that at which they once had snarled and bitten. A sound mind in a sound body. This is what I felt myself becoming.

I took a Valium, poured a glass of cold milk, and brought it to the couch. I found myself looking at my forearm. The skin seemed to be tighter, less parched, less cross-hatched with the witherings of age. The thin, frail veins and the large, wormy veins that visibly pulsed were less protuberant, as if the skin was not only younger-looking but also more solid and substantial. I did not understand what was happening, but I knew myself to be blessed, to be reentering the realm of rosy health. The deterioration of my flesh and faculties was in remission.

Remission? No. What was happening went far beyond that. The god within me was coming forth. This was not remission. This was apotheosis. My apotheosis. I was becoming a god.

I looked away from my forearm. I lit a cigarette. I looked away from everything. I very slowly nodded, then just as slowly smiled.

THE AIR BROUGHT AUGURY ON THE AFTERNOON PRECEDING the night of the full moon, the eve of the vernal equinox, the spring harvest festival of Isis.

The winds were strong and the sky was overcast, but the weather was otherwise balmy and pleasing; and that morning I had opened a few windows slightly to let in the air of the day. The afternoon light through the gray cloud cover was beginning to diminish when I saw it resting on the sill beneath one of the narrowly open windows. A dried pallid tawny-brown oak leaf.

Living six flights up, with not a tree in sight, I could not recall a leaf entering my home, not even in the late autumn gusts. And the branches of what trees there were in the neighborhood had seemed to be starkly bare since the harshest days of this harsh winter. And the windows I had opened this day were ajar hardly a hand's-breadth. But there it was, resting and still, awaiting me. The last leaf of winter, on the last full day of winter, on this afternoon preceding the night of the last full moon of winter, this eve of the spring equinox.

The full moon now rising was a rare one, a big and full perigee moon, raising tides as it drew closer to the earth than it had been in eighteen years. This powerful perigean effect on tides and other natural forces had not been so strong in all the years since that long-ago night. Melissa then was in her infancy. Perhaps she had howled at the light of that moon as she lay in her bassinet.

I knew it was an oak leaf. I found its likeness in my little Golden Nature Guide to trees. The oak was sacred to Zeus, god of gods. I seemed to remember that, according to one cosmogony, Zeus and Isis were the true parents of Dionysus. I looked through some books to find confirmation of this, and found that this belief was based on a fragment of Ariston. While looking through the books I searched, I discovered that the grandest of the festivals of Dionysus, the great Dionysia, was held in Athens in late March, at this same time of the Egyptian spring harvest festival of Isis.

In a fleeting reverie of whimsical imagination I envisioned the oak leaf wafting over ocean waves for thousands of years, from ancient sacred grove to the here and now of my windowsill, passing through the veil of time but showing its antiquity through that strange dry pallid tawny-brown that made it appear as delicate as it was enduring.

This was mere dreamy fancy, of course. But the presence of the leaf was not. I placed it carefully on my desk and I looked at it awhile. It was just a fucking dead leaf. But the convergence of all that surrounded it—moon, equinox, gods and goddesses, hallowed tree and hallowed turn of hallowed days—evoked a sense of magnitude, like a precession of some vast unexplored astronomy, of which this leaf was a silent betokening.

As with the return of my youth, I did not understand what was happening. Less so, in fact, because I was at least sure, or believed it to be sure, that my rejuvenation was being nurtured by my physical and spiritual immersion in, and merging with, the vital youth embodied in the vitally youthful flesh of another. I was, so to speak, being born again in the flesh. And in the blood; for I knew, or believed I knew, that this most intimate of acts was at the heart of it all, the most powerful and the highest aspect of our merging and the sustenance I received from that merging. It seemed like magic, but maybe it was nothing more than simple, science-based physiological cause and effect. The better part of medical knowledge—the better part of all knowledge, scientific or otherwise—lay unknown in plain sight, waiting to be known. Postulate precedes theorem, the empiricism of natural law precedes the formulae of its laboratory explication.

But this, the appearance on this day of what I felt to my bones to be a sign of the supernal, this leaf of augury, was to me a greater mystery. A mystery to whose meaning I had not a clue. Yet I somehow knew that, whatever it was, whatever it meant, it was good. Very, very good.

A new season of my life was upon me. And it would be like no other season of any life that had ever been lived. That's what that leaf said. And that's what I knew.

I SLEPT THROUGH THE EQUINOX THE FOLLOWING EVENING. I had been awake the previous night, gazing at the big silver moon until early morning, then had slept only a few hours before waking with a feeling of auspicious currents flowing through me. In the late afternoon I drank a cup of coffee, began to feel sleepy, and shuffled to bed to take a nap. It was still light outside. When I got out of bed, it was almost eight o'clock and dark. I had fallen asleep in winter, woken in the spring.

There was still some coffee, quite cold now, in the cup. I drank it, enjoying the subtle changes in taste that time and temperature had brought to it. Hot coffee turned cold had never tasted so good. It also made me aware that this first night of spring was colder than the last night of winter. I turned up the thermostat, but my new boiler, which had failed me through the worst of the winter, gave off no warmth.

Spring was now here, and with it the promise of warmer days to come. But the long winter's end still lingered in the air. I made more coffee and dug out the boiler manual and specification sheets. The crowded, complicated diagrams and the dense technical terminology concerning the intricacies of the machine's plumbing and electrical elements were so immediately and overwhelmingly daunting that, before the first sip of coffee, I almost returned the stuff to where I got it. Then I took that sip of coffee, lit a cigarette, and calmly stated to myself the words of Terence: "I am human, and nothing human is alien to me." Now of course the boiler was not human, nor were these pages of impenetrable diagrams, charts, and undefined specialist terms. But they were the convoluted product of the convoluted human mind. The alarming sound and fury of an idiot gizmo on the blink, and nothing more. With newly heightened perception, my own enhanced mind raked the detritus from what confronted me.

My coffee was still hot when I figured out how to fix my boiler. I needed to disable what was called the night-setback function. And that was that.

Next year, I told myself. I would have sufficient heat next year. It was good to feel that there would be a next year.

And it was good to know, as that leaf told me, that the passage of breath and seasons between now and then would unfold and resplend with the fulfillment of a mysterious promise so profound that it and its fulfillment were one and unnameable.

My coffee and my cigarette brought me great pleasure. I felt a stirring that also brought me great pleasure. For the first time in a very long time I raised pen to paper with a sense of purpose, a sense of desire.

Purpose, yes. Desire, yes. But, so strangely and beautifully, not a wisp of prescience as to what was to come when the pen touched the paper. And yet there was no hesitation, no doubt that something was to come.

I pray to a memory
I kneel before a weathered stele
I invoke the stars of an ancient blessing
I utter the names of phantoms
I carry within me the soul of the savioress
I know the way to the sea
I open tombs

I seek the air
I know the colors of breath

Only then did my hand and pen pause. And only for a moment. Then once again they moved.

May the gods without names redeem me

I put down the pen, gently pushed the sheet of paper along the surface of the desk, away from me. The sense of purpose and desire that had brought me to raise that pen to that paper were released from me, and had released me from them. I felt as I had felt just minutes before, when I figured out that I needed to disable the night-setback function on the boiler. I felt good.

With no reason, for no reason, I placed the leaf on the piece of paper. It was where it belonged. There was no reason involved. No reason at all, no thought at all. It was simply where it belonged.

From the couch I looked toward the sheet of paper and the desiccated leaf. My mind wandered, to the familiar, and to the curtain-partings in dimmed lights of what might or might not be.

"Hi. My name's Peter and I'm an alcoholic and a sex addict."

I had always detested that face, that voice, that presence. But in years past, when I first came to know the cumulative vileness of that face, voice, and presence, I found it almost as often to be a source of perverse entertainment as I found it to be a repellent that drove me at times not only from the room but very nearly from A.A. itself. While I would not have minded seeing violence done to him, I had never felt an urge to inflict violence on him. Now I realized that this was not so the other morning. I did not flee from him in abhorrence. I fled from my urge to squash him as one would a relentlessly annoying insect. It was, however momentary, an impulse to kill. But it was as real and impelling as it was momentary. As my brain flashed white with rage, I could see nothing but his destruction at my uncontrollable angry hands. That is why I rose and left the room. It was not he, but a new and terrible rising in me, that caused my flight. And among the marvelous heightened senses of that day, from the fluttering of that sparrow's wings to the Eucharistic feast of those croissants and that coffee, I had not thought of the intensified new sense of brutality that I had also experienced. What if my increased sensitivities toward and receptiveness to all that was good and pleasant in this life were accompanied, by the very nature of that enhancement, by an increase in all that was evil and monstrously pleasurable? What if the new dimensions of this new existence allowed me to taste of heaven while at the same time consigned me more deeply to the unexplored regions of the private hell that had darkened and defined my old life?

These thoughts gave me unsettling pause, but I turned away from further pondering on them. I could not turn far. What had brought me to that meeting in the first place that morning? It was my inability to speak to Melissa, the self-deceiving that led me to believe that alcohol would enable me to speak what I could not speak. I had been fortunate to see this self-deceit for what it was. Now I thought of the night I met her. There had been no compunction as to biting into her flesh. And now I loved her. Why then, the other morning, should there have been any faltering or unwillingness to open my mouth to gain entry to her mind and soul, which might have been in need? And even when I realized it was a matter of my wanting to open my mouth to nothing but drink, I blamed her, damning and cursing her in my mind, as if she were the Eve to my serpent. Was this only a passing disorder, an outrageous tumult of confusion and derangement, or was I the serpent, seeing and feeling himself forever an angel forever wronged?

If I were turning into a god, it was a god most strange.

THEN AGAIN, BECOMING A GOD AND BEING A GOD WERE not quite the same. And even gods knew madness at times.

I wanted simplicity and serenity without interlude. But this could not be. I decided to go to another meeting, a different one, where there would be little or no chance of encountering the bane of the self-adoring sex addict.

What I did encounter was a young, tall, thin, sexy, longhaired, flat-chested girl in skintight blue jeans. There was a time when I did not like them thin and flat-chested. But time changes everything.

"You're doing what I should've done," I said to her after the meeting. She looked dead straight at me. The light of the cold sun settled in her long straight chestnut hair.

"What's that?" she said.

"Coming here in time. Quitting in time."

"'Do as I say, not as I do,' is that it?" she said.

I couldn't tell if the look on her face was antagonistic, suspicious, or good-natured. This is probably because it was all those things, a vacillation to and fro of all those things.

"No. I mean, I've wasted my life."

I felt that these words flowed honestly from me and had much truth in them. Then I thought of the books on shelves, the ones I had written, the "postcards" of my life that attested that I had been more than a drunkard wasting away in bar after bar, drinking bottle after bottle, the postcards that attested that I had accomplished things, more than most, and that what I regretfully saw as a life of discarded years, shiftlessness, and drunkenness was in truth much more than that. Maybe that was why I kept those books around. Maybe I needed those postcards.

These thoughts shot through me in an instant. There was no noticeable pause between what I had begun to say and the words that followed: "You have yours still ahead of you. All those years to live."

"You've got a face like a map," she said.

Again, antagonistic, suspicious, or good-natured. Again, probably all those things.

I tongued and sucked my false teeth into place for what I wanted to say and I said it: "Terrestrial or celestial?"

"Both."

Good-natured. No ambiguity, no vacillation. A good-natured look.

"Thank you," I said.

I smiled, then she smiled too. Her teeth were pearly and perfect. I hated her for them. I wanted her for them.

We ambled from the room together. I was careful to speak calmly, easily, casually.

"Have you been coming here a long time?" She knew that I was referring to this specific meeting, at this particular room.

"Oh, for about a year or so," she said.

That was good. It meant that she wasn't a newcomer to the program. There was an unwritten law that there should be no interaction with newcomers in their first ninety days of sobriety that did not relate directly to the program, and especially no interaction of even the most vaguely romantic kind.

We walked slowly south on Sullivan Street. She said she was

returning to work. Even in her old-fashioned Keds Champion sneakers, she was as tall as I. Wanting not to force foolish conversation, I fell silent and waited for her to say something. I was curious as to what, if anything, it would be.

"This has been the worst fucking winter," she commented idly.

I nodded slowly, deliberately, before adding my words to hers. "Yep. It sure has." A brief pause. Then, ruminatively: "But, then again, I guess it beats six feet under."

Her quiet laugh was like the hint of a cough that did not come to pass.

"You live around here?" she said.

"Yeah, down a ways, below Canal."

"Tri-Beh-Ca," she said, in a manner that served as an open indictment of real estate agents.

"Tribeca. Treblinka. Whatever."

This time her laugh escaped her thorax, and she smiled. "It's nice there," she said.

"Yeah. Springtime in Treblinka. It was a lot nicer before they ever gave it that cutesy-poo name."

"What did they call it before then?"

"Nothing."

"That's a great name," she said. "They should've kept it."

"Where do you work there?"

"On Greenwich. The Tribeca Film Center. The Treblinka Film Center."

"Do you know Chiemi Karasawa? She's got an office there. Isotope Films."

"Oh, God, Chiemi. I love her."

"I've known her more than twenty years. She's the best."

"Really? What's your name?"

"Nick. Just tell her you met her friend Nick."

"My name's Lorna. Yeah, Chiemi's one of the few people in that building that actually care about making movies. Real movies. The kind without the 3-D glasses and the pre-production merchandising deals. Not like the people I work for. I think she's on the fifth floor. I'm on the fourth."

I was in. I knew Chiemi. I was no longer a stray pervert set only on getting into those skintight blue jeans. I mean, I was. But not in her eyes, not now. I hoped.

"And what do you do there?" I asked.

"Bookkeeper. Every bit as boring as the movies they make."

She asked me what I did, and I told her, adding that I hadn't been doing much of it lately. She said she had heard of two of the books I had written. She didn't say she'd read them, only that she'd heard of them. That was good enough. This was getting better as it went along. I suggested we stop for some breakfast on the way.

We managed to get a quiet corner table at Locanda Verde. I never used credit cards and I never made reservations, so I never got mistered by name in these joints. But I guess they knew me by face and could match the face with the tips, so they treated me all right. I got the *uovo modenese*. She got the oatmeal with grappa-stewed fruit, and we split an order of garlic potatoes. She asked for a cup of coffee and was surprised when I didn't.

"I thought everybody in the program was a coffee junkie," she said.

I told her that I drank more than my share of coffee, too. But I never drank it unless I could smoke with it.

"Cross-addicted," she said with a smile.

"Cross-addicted? Vector-field-addicted," I said with a smile of my own.

As we ate, we talked about this and that—How did she like

the potatoes? Did I come here often?—with the customary reserve and politeness of two people conversing for the first time.

I mentioned something that Johnny Depp had told me about the movie business, being sure to use his name but being also sure to glide smoothly and glibly over it, as if the name were nothing more than the equivalent of "somebody" or "this guy."

"You know him?"

"Yeah. I'm the godfather of his son."

"What's he like?"

"He's a good guy. A really good guy. I liked him better when he was living in France, before he moved back to Hollywood. Probably that's because I saw more of him then."

"I didn't know he had a son."

"Yeah. Jumpin' Jack. He's got a birthday coming up. April ninth, something like that. Getting big. Probably wouldn't recognize me if he saw me. It's been that long. Too long."

I had eaten the same thing for breakfast here many times before. But never had it tasted so delicious. It was another Eucharistic meal. My newly heightened senses had lost none of their keenness.

With my fork I moved some cotechino hash through some egg yolk, raised it to my mouth, chewed it slowly—my only option—then said what I wanted to say. She was in the movie racket, even if she was just a bookkeeper with few kind words to say about the racket. But you never knew with these people. Still, I wanted to say what I wanted to say. In a way, I needed to say it.

"L.A. is a fucking disease. It's the land of death. It's like the Egyptians said. The Western Lands. Death."

I imagined the taste of her blood. I would get no closer to it than that, I was sure: imagining it. That's why it didn't matter saying what I said. But who knew? The writer angle. Chiemi. Johnny. The garlic potatoes. Who knew? It was a good breakfast, if nothing else. I was ready to order a cappuccino to go, take care of the check, walk her down the block to where she worked, make a left, and go home.

All of a sudden I saw that she was looking at me—into me—in a way that left it all far behind, as if the morning until this very moment had never been. The writer angle, Chiemi, Johnny, the casual reserve, the breakfast, everything that had transpired or been said. It was as if a mask had suddenly been torn from me, revealing someone, or something, that had lurked behind it. That may have been true. But when my heart slowed, I saw that it was she who had torn the mask from her own face. The beauty of that face was still there. In fact, she looked more beautiful. But her now unsmiling beauty reminded me of the beauty of a big cat in the wild: a leopard daring any other creature to peer into the irresistible splendor of its eyes, at which fatal instant, the instant of eye contact, it would by nature pounce and kill.

The one with magic of her own saw into me and shocked me:

"Do you want it?"

I didn't know exactly what she was talking about, but I knew that it was drenched with sex. My "yes" remained in me, unsaid. It seemed that neither of us knew quite what was going on here, other than that we were wading in a voluptuous but perhaps dangerous pond away from the light.

"Want what?"

She wasn't talking about her lithe lovely body. Or rather she was. But her question cut more deeply—devastatingly, astonishingly so—than that. I could sense her looking at me as if she knew my words of ignorance were false. As if she were waiting for me to replace them with truer words.

A thousand things I might say whirled, sped, crashed through my mind. But as I dared a glance into those fatal leopardess eyes, I heard myself say only:

"How did you know?"

"There's a look," she said. "It's haunted me all my life. It was the look in my father's eyes. I was twelve, almost thirteen, when I first saw it. Maybe it was there longer, but I didn't see it until then. The night he came into my room, tickled my belly until I was thrashing with laughter, then threw up my pajama top and sank his teeth into me. That was the night I saw it. Fourteen years ago. And every time I see his face in my mind or in my dreams, I see that look on his face.

"He died young. Killed himself. I saw that too. I mean, after he did it. I came home from school, and there he was. Looked sort of like this." She gestured to what was left of her oatmeal and stewed fruit. "His brains or whatever the hell it was. What a fucking mess.

"I thought it would change then. I thought it would die when he did. But it didn't. You know what's funny? I never, ever had a single nightmare about finding him that day. How he looked and all. Nothing. Every time I see his face in my mind, every time he comes to me in my sleep, there it is. That look.

"What he did to me—and it was more than just a few bites— fucked me up good. I've never been with another man since him. I've tried, but I can't do it. That's where the drinking and the drugs came in: to help me break through, to help me break out. But all they really helped me do was drink more and take more drugs. I'm still a virgin. I'm still afraid of that look I once saw for real. It's haunted me and fucked me up ever since. But at least I never saw it again in real life. Until now."

I did not know what to say, so I said nothing. Then she asked again:

"Do you want it?"

Those dangerous leopardess eyes now seemed so limpid and vulnerable as to be about to well with tears.

"It shouldn't be about what I want. It should be about what you want," I said. "It should be about what's going to help you."

I meant every word of what I said. I really wanted to get out of there and have a smoke. I really wanted to feel my cock in her mouth. I really wanted to press myself to that little-girl's flat-breasted body and be enwrapped in those big-girl's long lithe legs of hers. And I really wanted the taste and life of her blood. But I meant every word of what I said.

"Help me," she said, throwing aside the words as if they were rat-ridden refuse of worthless derision to be discarded. "Umpteen kinds of fucking therapy. God knows how many medications. Years of counseling. All this fucking sharing-and-caring program bullshit. Jung. Vibrators. Hypnosis."

She threw away the phrase "help me" again and slowly shook her lowered head as if grinding the words underfoot. When she raised her head to speak again, tears truly were welling in her eyes.

"That look. You have it," she said. "But on you that look doesn't scare me. You seem like a nice guy. I feel some sort of intuitive trust in you. Don't ask me why. None of this makes any sense." Then she sniffled, gave a cursory little laugh. "Yeah. You seem like a nice guy who wants to drink my blood. Just like that. The usual stuff at the Norman Rockwell soda fountain."

I smiled gently, and for a moment we smiled together. I wished I had a clean snot rag to offer her to wipe her eyes and blow her nose. That's what nice guys do.

"Maybe you could get it all out of me," she said. "Maybe I could break through with you. What could I lose? At this point, not a goddamned thing. The worst thing would be that I ended up running from you. Running right back to where I've been for all these years."

I reminded her that I lived pretty much around the corner

from where she worked, and I suggested that she come over when she got out this evening.

"It has to be at my place," she said. "There are certain things. You'll see what I mean."

I never visited anybody. I had got like that slowly over the years. I simply never visited anybody. But something in me stopped me short of laying down this law to her.

"What do you mean, 'certain things'?"

"Just certain things. I can't have you bite me. I just can't go there. So I need certain things."

"I don't want to take a blade to you or anything like that," I lied.

"No knives. But there are certain things that I can enjoy. Certain things that I need. You'll see."

"I didn't think I had any special look," I said.

"Look at yourself in the mirror," she said. "Take a good long look. Look at the size of your pupils. No, forget about that. Never mind the size; forget about the size. Look at the color. Your pupils don't stay black. I mean, yeah, sometimes they're black and sometimes they turn iridescent, like black pearl. And your irises. Who has eyes that change from blue to brown to gray to green to amber in the course of, what, half an hour? Nobody, that's who. And it's what I see in those eyes. You don't look at me like you're looking to get into my pants. I know that look like the back of my hand. Men don't pick up on it. They don't know there's no entry. You look at me like what you really want is beneath my skin. I'm not talking about any of that 'real me' bullshit. I'm talking about the blood in my veins."

I did not respond, but simply allowed my silence to let her know that she was right.

"That thing with the eyes. What's that all about?" I said when my silence was done.

"A lot of molecular stuff. I tried to learn about it once. All I can remember is pigment polymers. Molecules. I'm no doctor. I don't know. But it's all molecules. And your molecules are going crazy."

I ordered a cappuccino to go, took care of the check, lit a smoke as soon as we got outside, walked her down the block to where she worked. We exchanged lingering smiles. I made a left and went home. I was anxious to peer into my own eyes. I thought of the feeling of currents flowing through me that I had experienced lately, and the physical changes I had recently undergone. I thought of her.

I turned on the overhead lamp in my bathroom and pushed to its highest limit the slider on the dimmer switch that controlled the halogen lights to the left and right of the big medicine cabinet mirror. I looked into my eyes.

She was right. Even in the bright artificial light, my pupils were dilated, and I could see them turn from black to an iridescence that was like the shimmering of lustrous clouds in a moonless sky, then once again turn black. But it was the slow-shifting circular rainbow reflected in the membranes of my irises that first frightened then fascinated me.

Sunglasses, I thought. I had a few pairs lying around. I should start wearing them. A shame, I thought, because my eyes seemed less sunken, and the dark bags under them and the wrinkles around them seemed fainter. I mumbled words from one of Ezra Pound's cantos: *"Pull down thy vanity, I say pull down."* But vanity seemed part of the pleasure of my restoration to youth.

Those eyes, those fucking eyes. Had they got like this with the improvement in my sight? Molecules, as she said, molecules. All interrelated. There were no eyes like these. Prismic eyes. Magical eyes. The eyes of a fucking god coming into being.

I shut off the lights, sat with my cup of coffee, and lit a cigarette. I reflected on my fine fortune, to have had this new aspect of my metamorphosis, the radiant wonder of my new eyes, brought to my attention not by one of the flotskies at the Reade Street bar, but by her.

It was at that moment, more than three months after I had written him, that I had a call from Olivier Ameisen, the author of the book *Heal Thyself,* with whom I had been so eager to speak about the power of the drug baclofen to cure alcoholism. Having not heard back from him, I had wondered if he was laid out drunk somewhere. Quite to the contrary, he was in fine fettle and busy as hell, lecturing and trying to raise money for sanctioned testing that would provide the medical establishment with clinical proof of baclofen's efficacy. He was up against a lot. Baclofen was an old drug, first synthesized in 1962 and long used as a treatment for muscular dystrophy before Olivier's discovery that it was a cure for addiction. The trouble was, its patent had run out, so the pharmaceutical industry, which controls most of the funding for drug testing, stood to make no money from baclofen, no matter how miraculous-seeming and far-reaching its ability to suppress addictive cravings might be. It was a matter of life or death or the cash register, and the cash register was all that mattered. This problem was compounded by the tendency of those who call themselves "addiction specialists" to wish to perpetuate rather than cure their patients' addiction. Again, this was simple economics. An addict who was cured of his addiction had no need to weekly feed the pockets of an addiction counselor, who thus preferred prescribing far less effective medications, such as naltrexone and topiramate, or even medications such as acamprosate that have been shown to be no better than placebos. Baclofen had an astounding success rate, well over ninety percent, better than the failure or relapse rate of any other known treatment.

My desire to take baclofen was now somewhat less compelling than it had been when I first reached out late last year. I was, after all, no longer drinking. And the dysphoria—a part of the underlying chemistry of addiction also alleviated by baclofen— that once had darkened my days had also been lifted by my regeneration. But at the same time, I had just witnessed and knew how deeply and insidiously alcoholism was ingrained in me. If I wanted to enjoy my new life, I must remain sober. Baclofen could do me no harm. It could only enhance and protect what other, more mysterious if no less complex chemistry had already brought about.

We talked a long time, and I grew more and more impressed with him, his knowledge, and his goodness as our talk went on. He was calling from Paris, on his own dime and time; and he spoke more like a human being than a medical doctor, and communicated scientific and other unsimple matters so well that I had to remind myself that English was to him a second language. We concluded by discussing the best way I could go about getting a prescription for baclofen in New York, this city he knew well and in which he had practiced cardiology, this city whose medical establishment was so inimical to baclofen as a treatment for addiction. Was there some hospital, some institution, some doctor he knew? He asked me if I had an internist, a personal general practitioner, whom I trusted. I told him that I did. He said to go to him, and if he cared about me, if he gave a damn whether I lived or died, he would give me the necessary prescription. I told him that I would make an appointment with my doctor and send a copy of Olivier's book along with a letter via FedEx overnight. I promised to call Olivier after the appointment to tell him how I fared.

I called my doctor's office and asked for the next available first appointment of the day. I never visited doctors unless it was their first appointment of the day. I was lucky. There was one open in less than two weeks. I got down my copy of Olivier's book and hastily wrote a letter addressed to my physician:

I am hoping that you will have a chance to look at this book.

I had a long transatlantic conversation yesterday with the author, Olivier Ameisen, who is presently in Paris.

Since reading this book, and especially after speaking with Olivier, I have been convinced that the baclofen treatment he propounds is the only effective treatment for alcoholism.

He told me that if I had a personal physician whom I trusted and whom I felt cared about my fate, I could then easily obtain the necessary prescriptions.

There has never been an adverse reaction to, or negative effect of, this drug, which is believed to be safer than aspirin, and whose dosages are simple to establish.

I sent Olivier a detailed list of the medications I take, including the Valium, and their dosages, and he assured me that there was not the slightest risk of interaction with any of them.

Olivier said that if you should have anything you should wish to ask him, you should feel free to do so. He can be reached at the number you will find on the inside front page of the book. He also said that you could find his papers online at PubMed.

I have an appointment to see you a week from this coming Friday, and I am hoping that by then you will have had ample opportunity to review this material.

I apologize for the length of this letter, but this is extremely important to me.

I wrote down Olivier's number where I said it would be, then read through the letter as hastily as I had drafted it. The grossly grammarless phrase *"whom I trusted and whom I felt cared"* was set aright, to *"whom I trusted and who I felt cared,"* and the *should*-dense mess of *"if you should have anything you should wish to ask him, you should feel free to do so"* was recast so that only one *should* remained. There was a time when I would not have made such slovenly mistakes, not even in slipshod haste. I had gone far too long without writing. Far too long. I felt like an imbecile, and I denounced myself for it. Then the god in me rebuked me for this, telling me that I had caught and fixed my errors as quickly as I had committed them, and negligences such as this had probably always crept into my writing without my even being aware of them. At least this time my awareness was sharp and quick. I would err no more. My heightening sensibilities would see to that.

I signed the corrected letter, folded it, placed it in the book, prepared a FedEx form, put the book with the letter into a package, and made it to Mail Boxes Etc. on Greenwich Street in ample time for the last FedEx pickup of the day. On the way back, I bought a banana from the vendor on the corner of Chambers Street and ate it as I walked home, wondering about the night to come and the nature of "certain things" to be made known.

My haunted virgin angel, long, lean Lorna, lived up in Hell's Kitchen, or Clinton as they liked to call it now. A third-story walkup in a decent enough old building on West Forty-ninth Street. Night was just beginning to fall when she buzzed me in. The three flights had no effect on my pulse or breath.

I gave her a bunch of yellow roses with red-edged petals. She seemed truly surprised, truly pleased. She was wearing an unbuttoned shawl-collar beige cashmere cardigan over a man's ribbed white athletic undershirt. I wondered for an instant if the sweater had been left unbuttoned for my sake, to show off that irresistible flat chest in that tight, thin boyish undershirt. But I figured she had not. Flat-chested women, no matter how beautiful, do not very often believe just how sexy their barely-there breasts can be.

My eyes were then immediately drawn to a doorway draped with thick black velvet. From beyond that doorway a dark ruby light emitted a peeking blush that was dimly discernible at the hem folds of the heavy black curtain.

"I almost asked you if you wanted a drink," she said.

"Old habits die hard."

"I didn't have a chance to shop after work. I really don't have anything here."

Oh, yes you do, my dear, oh, yes you do.

"We can order something if you like."

I wondered aloud if Shun Lee delivered to West Forty-ninth Street. But I wasn't really hungry. No, that's not quite true. What is true is that my hunger for Shun Lee was eclipsed by a different, deeper hunger.

"I'm good," I said. "Maybe in a little bit."

"You're sure? You don't want anything?"

"I want to know what's on the other side of that curtain." I smiled.

She seemed oddly hesitant, as if she had been living here with this red-lighted curtained-off room of hers and nobody had ever before been curious about it. And come to think of it, why was that red light on if the drape was drawn as if to hide it?

"I want to show you," she said. "It's just that since we were talking this morning, I..." Her words trailed to silence.

"I just want you to feel comfortable," I lied. Or maybe it was the truth. I did want her to feel comfortable. But it wasn't the only thing I wanted. "I want you to feel better." More sweet truth with the peach pit of a lie at its center.

She took me by the hand, led me to the big black velvet curtain, and drew it aside. The room was small. That dim red light came from a single bare overhead bulb. And there it was, overwhelming and oversized in this underwhelming, undersized room.

It was the big X of a Saint Andrew's cross made of two planks of wood bolted together diagonally.

My first thought was: how does she keep that fucking thing upright? Then I saw that it was not upright. It was leaning against a wall with the bottom, about a foot from the wall, fixed to the floor with big fat galvanized nails, and the top fixed to the painted brickwork of the wall with big fat masonry nails. It looked as if it stood upright because the incline was so slight. At the top and bottom far-corner ends of the two planks were big fat old-looking steel eye-lags. Hanging from the top lags, one from each, were pairs of old-looking Smith & Wesson chain-linked handcuffs. Hanging from the bottom lags, one from each, were pairs of old-looking Smith & Wesson chain-linked leg irons, with the chains knotted to reduce their length.

I put my hand on the cross as if assaying its integrity. That's when I saw the three or four whips of different sizes in a supple heap, like dead snakes, in the corner of the room. Real whips. Leather whips.

"Did you make this yourself?" I asked, moving my hand and my eyes over the grayed and slightly cracked and warped two-by-twelve lumber.

I suspected that she was indeed its maker. Whoever did make it wasn't a carpenter. It was nigger-rigged. No notching of the beams where they traversed. No real joinery. No knee-brace struts. No joisting. Just nails, no screws except for the threaded eye-lags, which had probably been driven in, somewhat crookedly, by hammer blows followed by turns of a screwdriver shank or some other rod-like object placed through the eyeholes. Then again, nigger-rigged or not, it was one hell of an imposing piece of work.

"Yeah."

"You want to show me how you use it?"

"Sure. Let me go change. You sure you don't want anything? Coffee? Anything?"

"I'm good."

"All right. I'll be right back."

Standing there by that certain thing, I realized that I might be the one who was supposed to get spread-eagled and cuffed to it. That would fit in with the father thing. The humiliation and punishment of the father-surrogate. Ah, yes, the Reverend Thomas Fuller, who gave us the adage "It is always darkest just before the Day dawneth." In the same seventeenth-century book in which he said that, a book about his travels in Jerusalem, a book whose title I recalled only as a strange one, he also said, writing of the good old days of crucifixion—and why did I remember these things, when at the same time, entering a store, I could not remember what I had come there to buy, or to boost?—and I believe these were his exact words: "Hereupon a substitute or surrogate was provided for him to bear his Cross."

Could the same be said now of Lorna's father? Did she think that I was to be his provided surrogate in her longed-for freedom from the haunting he had inflicted on her? There were moments this morning when she could have been talking about anything. The thirst for her blood that she saw in me might have meant that I was the right and ordained sacrificial victim. "Maybe you could get it all out of me," she had said. That could have meant anything. For all I knew, her father had turned her into a lipstick lesbian with intent to kill. She said she had gone to change. What the fuck was she changing into? A cuirass, mail gloves, and an executioner's hood?

She returned barefoot and naked under a transparent vinyl raincoat that reached to just above her knees. She went to the cross. She positioned one bare foot then the other, so that, bowing down, she could adjust and clasp the leg irons above her ankles. She braced herself and stood. With one hand she handcuffed the wrist of her other hand. She raised her free hand to touch the opposite set of cuffs. She spoke over her shoulder to me:

"Could you do this one for me? I can do it myself sometimes but it's a bitch."

I handcuffed her wrist and stepped back to look at her and the way her long, slender limbs were stretched to form an open X that conformed to the X of the Saint Andrew's cross to which she was shackled and pressed hard against its slight incline. The tautened curve of her spine and the tension clench of her buttocks were visible through the clear raincoat. I began to like the dim red light of this room.

"Why the raincoat?" I asked.

"A long time ago I read that the cops used to throw raincoats over people before beating them with rubber hoses because it left no marks or scars. It turned out to be true. I don't like scars."

She spoke with her face hanging slightly forward and resting sideways on the brick wall in the cleft between the cross-beams.

"Why a clear raincoat?"

"I like the way it feels. I like the way it exposes me." Without a breath of transition, she said, "Get the blacksnake."

"Where is it?"

She moved her head a little in the direction of the nest of whips. I didn't know one whip from another. She seemed to sense this.

"It's the biggest one."

I lifted it by its thickest part. Its narrowing braided leather, a good deal of which lay on the floor as I held the thick handle near my hip, appeared to be about six feet long.

"I clipped the fall and cracker," she said, as if making clear to me something about this. I had not the vaguest notion of what she was talking about, but I asked her why.

"Too much. They hurt too much. Way too much."

I instinctively moved farther from her with the whip in my hand. She sensed this and she asked me to go farther, to just within the doorway.

"All right," she said. "Go for the center of the raincoat. Stay away from the legs."

When she said that, I looked at her bare slender ankles and bare arched feet in the dim red light. I wanted to rape her.

I raised the whip and cast my arm forward to let it unfurl. It was not as easy as I thought. There was not enough force. The end of the whip did not even reach her. It just drooped awkwardly to the floor in midair. I thought of the summer days when I was a little boy trying to perform lariat tricks and lasso dogs with a length of old clothesline.

I reeled the narrowing plaited leather into a loop, which I hooked with one finger of the hand that grasped the girth of the whip's stock. Unhooking my finger and heaving forward with a much faster and more violent pitching motion, I heard the loud smack of the whip against her vinyl-covered body, seeing it strike her at the small of her back. She uttered a sound that struck me as being more an expulsion of anticipation than an expression of its fulfillment. I struck again, with even faster and more violent movement. This time she cried out as the lash struck her hard below the shoulder blades. Her cry was intense.

"Get me something for my mouth," she said.

"What should I get?"

"A facecloth. A wet facecloth. Anything."

I looked for the bathroom and found it. On my way there, I passed her bedroom, looked in, and saw her pretty pink cotton panties lying on the bed. I wanted to put these in her mouth instead of the facecloth. I ran them under cool water, wrung them in my hand, rolled them somewhat, and took them to her open mouth. I watched her bite into them, and again I wanted to rape her. Maybe I had not stopped wanting to rape her since seeing her bound ankles and arched feet.

When I next cast the whip, it was as forceful as an act of rape.

I was aiming for her buttocks, but the end of the whip passed hard and with angry noise across the backs of her thighs directly below her buttocks. I heard a muffled yelp through the dampened panties that were jammed in her mouth.

I was getting used to the physics of it. The power of the propulsion had to extend not merely from the shoulder of the arm that whipped. It had to begin in the heel of the foot on the side of the body that whipped. I felt the strength and velocity of my strikes, as well as their accuracy, increase. By the time I finally hit the meat of her ass, my upper arm was growing sore and tired.

This was strenuous shit. I could see how doing it with any regularity would give you biceps like a those of a pickaxe ditch-digger, but probably also the back ailment that came with the muscle.

It was a good cardiovascular workout as well. Fuck those assholes who went to the gym every morning. What was that stupid fucking country song? Well, fuck that. Whip an angel good morning. That was the way to go.

Yes, I was sore and I was tired. But what I saw made it all but impossible for me to lay down that whip.

The restrained writhings and jolts of her body drove me more wild with lust than if they had been allowed free rein and unfettered abandon. And her juices, which I had earlier noticed trickling down her leg in thin tendrils of chrism, had become a cascade that spilled to the floor from between her outstretched legs.

Her muffled screams grew less fierce. They became merely low muffled groans, as if she were spent. It was then that I decided that I would in fact rape her, in my way. I walked to the cross and ran my hand up her raincoat to the heat of her drenched cunt. She made a sound that I could not interpret. She seemed unable to spit the panties from her mouth. I worked the lower part of her raincoat up to her waist, and I bunched it tight and fast in the close cranny I forced between her and the center of the cross. I beheld her like that, and I backed away and shot the whip through the air with all my gathered might, slashing one of her buttocks and the back of one of her thighs. The sound was like that of a loud sudden hiss from hell. Something worse than a muffled scream shot from her gagged mouth.

I stood and watched the slashes on her raw flesh begin to bleed, slowly and slightly at first, then more copiously. I tossed aside the whip and knelt behind her. I sucked the warm running blood from her buttock and thigh. The more freely it ran, the more deeply I sucked. It was delicious. I drank until the flow was greatly diminished, than I ran my tongue down her legs, stopping to lick, kiss, and savor here and there along the way, following the lacy trails of blood that led as far as the slender ankles and heels of the lovely arched feet of her captivity.

We were both spent, she draped on her Saint Andrew's cross, I lying at its base on my back, looking up through the dim diffuse red light. For a moment it occurred to me to leave her there. I had done what she had asked me not to do. I had lashed open her bare skin. I did not know what hostile censure was to come if I yanked those cotton dainties from her mouth. But I had to do what I had done. I had to open her skin to let flow the sweet warm ichor from beneath it.

I lay awhile longer, then rose. I was ravenously hungry. I was thinking of Shun Lee as much as of the damnation, exculpation, and calls for expiation I faced. I removed the saliva-drenched panties from her mouth. Her face was flushed, her eyes half closed, strands of her long soft hair clung to her sweating forehead, cheeks, and neck. I asked her where the keys to the cuffs and leg irons were. She seemed too exhausted to speak. This was a good sign, at least for now, I thought. She gestured with her head to a small round wooden end table in the corner of the room near the heap of whips. There was a little crochet-lace doily atop it, and the keys were on that doily.

I unlocked the handcuffs, gently massaging the reddened areas of her wrists, to show that I cared. I unlocked the leg irons, stroked the reddened marks above her ankles, again to show her that I cared, but really because it gave me pleasure to fondle the tendons near the base of her slender calf muscles. I did not touch her where I had slashed her, as I felt that any show of caring here would only serve to bring further attention to my misdeeds. She remained silent, and I took this, though awkwardly, to be a good sign.

"How about that Chinese food?" I said.

"Sure."

"What do you want?"

"I don't care," she said. "You pick it." Her voice had a vague, lifeless, bereaved quality to it. She walked very slowly to the bathroom. I heard water running. I knew that she was washing blood from herself, maybe from her raincoat as well. Then I heard the shower running.

By then I had ordered the food. I lit a cigarette and looked for something I could use as an ashtray. In the kitchen cupboard I found a pair of two miniature Asian bowls, like the ones they give you to mix the cheap soy sauce with the fake wasabi for sushi in Japanese joints. Fuck it. Function follows form. I would be sure to wash it out good before I left. To show that I was a nice guy, and that I cared. If she didn't end up throwing me out before I got around to it.

I felt wonderful. Even the soreness and tiredness induced by my exertions were giving way to a balm-like inner restfulness. Even my anxiety over the wrath of Lorna became dreamlike and inconsequential. My communion with her, and my fill of her succoring blood, had brought new rejuvenation, new life; and with every renewal this rejuvenation and life became stronger and more magical within me. I looked forward to the Chinese food and my next breath with greater anticipation and appreciation than the wretched and the self-appointed inheriting meek of the earth look forward to the envisioned glories of their eternal paradise.

She appeared clean and lovely, in flannel pajamas, her lovely long hair freshly towel-dried.

"How do you feel?" I asked her calmly, as if we were two souls merged and lingering for a single infinite breath. Her wrath would fall unheard and unfelt on one, a god coming into being, who would use it only to rinse and refresh his palate before the Chinese food got here.

"I feel fucking great," she said.

She smiled beatifically. At that moment I respected and cherished her with all my being, and her happiness was my happiness. I was proud of her, and I was proud of myself for making her feel as she did.

"Don't worry, I'll wash this," I said, grinding my cigarette butt into the little Asian bowl thing.

The Chinaman came. As usual, I had ordered too much stuff, almost everything that I had been craving from that joint for a long, long time. Roast pungent duck, steamed dumplings, prawns with garlic and scallions, twice-cooked pork, dry shredded crispy beef, and more. She got us cans of Caffeine-Free Diet Coke out of the fridge.

As we ate, we talked. As it should be, the talking was secondary to the eating, but on this night they went together well. The talk was natural and easy.

The red light was still leaking from the edges of the drawn black curtain at the doorway of the room where we had spent the last hour. I asked her if she always kept that light on.

"Sometimes," she said. "Like a night-light, sort of."

"Who usually does this?" I said.

"Buys me Chinese take-out?"

"Whips you."

"Sometimes I pay somebody. Usually a chick. Sometimes I do it myself."

"Why do you pay?"

"Anonymity. I like the anonymity. They don't know me, I don't know them, and that's that."

"And why usually a chick?" Maybe she was a lipstick lesbian after all.

"They're gentler. And they seem to understand more what's going on."

"And how do you manage to do it by yourself?"

"It's easy. That free right hand after I lock myself up, I use the crop. That's the short, stiffer one. It's got a popper, a little leather loop, on the end, but the popper doesn't really hurt because it's pretty hard to crop yourself hard over your own shoulder. Same with the Rose whip, the other short one, the one with the separate leather thongs, the one that's sort of a candy-ass cat-o'-nine-tails: softer leather, no knots in the lashes. Though I guess you could knot them if you wanted to. I don't know. The leather strips on that one may not be strong enough for knots that would last."

"I'd like to see you do that. Whip yourself with that crop. I'd like to sit there and jerk off and watch you do that."

"Not tonight. I'm beat."

"Do you come when you do this? I couldn't tell."

"I don't know if I've ever come in my life. The nuns told us that women didn't have orgasms, only men had orgasms. I know that's not true. But I still don't know if I've ever had one."

"You had something going on there when those juices were flowing."

"I had something going on there when you pulled up the raincoat and cracked me. I had something going on there when I felt you sucking the blood from where you cracked me."

"I couldn't resist. This morning, when you were talking, saying you knew what I wanted—then tonight I just, I don't know, I—"

"It was perfect."

"What you were talking about, breaking through, getting rid of that haunting, that curse you were talking about, I was afraid I might be doing more harm than good."

"No," she said, slowly, ruminatively. "I'm pretty sure you did more good than harm. We'll see. I feel great now, but I don't know how I'll feel later, how I'll feel tomorrow night, or the night after. We'll see. Right now it's better not to think about it."

"I'm sorry about the marks."

"It's nothing. It already looks like just a couple of nasty scratches. And I've got so much vitamin E on them that I'm stuck to the seat of my pj's. But, no, I really don't like scars. If we ever end up fooling around again, we've got to keep that in mind and figure something out."

We ate awhile in silence. It was amazing. It was like the Eucharistic croissant raised to the realm of golden heavens.

"What does it feel like?"

"Whipping you?"

"Drinking blood."

"It feels like I'm closer to the beauty and fresh-blossoming life force that I crave than I could ever otherwise be. It feels like I'm one with it, drawing it into me; drinking everything beautiful about it and being transformed and renewed by it. Like a miracle. Like a sweet, delicious, transporting miracle. Lust, love, and life all at once, with an intensity that's almost ecstatic. It's great."

"And what about those eyes?"

"What about those eyes? Like you said: molecules. The blood

is regenerating me. I feel younger, stronger. That intensity, that ecstasy. I have your blood—you—in me now. There's bound to be some kind of molecular change. And it all feels good. It all feels great.

"The most renowned scientists alive don't even know how many trillions of cells there are in their own bodies, in any body; and every single one of those unknown trillions of cells, every one of them, has hundreds or thousands or millions of molecules. You've got almost three hundred million molecules of hemoglobin in one single red blood cell alone. Platelets, plasma, this, that, the other thing. Nobody really knows what the hell's going on in there. These scientists can talk about molecules all they want, but they don't know shit. At least I know that whatever's going on with the molecules in me is good. It's better than good. It's great. I can feel it."

"The way you describe it, you make me want to do it," she said.

"But that's the thing. You've already got it. You don't need it. The essence of that young flesh and soul, that blue sky, that spirit of illimitable youth. You would just be drinking from yourself. Maybe you don't feel it now. Maybe you need to break through and let the light out, like you say. But it's there. It's in you. It's you."

"I sure don't feel it."

"You will. That stuff you do in there. You're not punishing yourself. You're trying to drive something out of yourself. And it's the dark, not the light, that you're trying to expel. Some people cling to their misery. You're not one of those. Believe me, you gave me more of you tonight than you give yourself. One of these days, you'll feel the magic that's in you, and you'll know what I'm talking about. You'll know the gift in you."

"Does it feel like—I mean to you, what you're talking about—does it feel like anything I might've ever felt?"

"Well, it sure ain't like booze, I can tell you that much." I ate and I thought if there was anything to which I could compare it, even remotely. "Love, maybe. But a kind of love you can't imagine." This sounded stupid. It sounded vague and senselessly airy. We ate a little more, saying nothing. Maybe it was the ethereal play of the food on my senses that brought me to say what I said next.

"I used to think that opium was the greatest thing in the world. It turns the world and every breath of this finite life to a poetry so pure it's wordless and soundless. There's nothing like it. Nothing comes close. Yeah. I used to think opium was the greatest thing in the world. In fact, I'd love to be able to smoke it again. The real stuff. I hate to travel these days. The only way I want to travel is internally. The only places I want to go don't involve crowds or security checks. None of that. If I never saw the inside of another airport or airplane, that'd be good by me. But if I ever do travel again, it's going to be to smoke opium."

"You make me want to do that too, the way you talk about it."

"Well, maybe you will. Maybe we'll do it together one of these days."

"So, that's what drinking blood is like?"

"No. I said I used to think it was the best thing in the world. I used to think it was *la chiave d'oro,* the key of gold. Now I know that blood is. The right blood. Blood like yours. Smoking opium can let you dream of youth and love and the magic and poetry in the air. Drinking blood can give it to you. For real."

"But those eyes," she said. "They're otherworldly. They're beautiful, amazing; but they're so otherworldly."

She had said that morning that she had seen in her father's eyes what she saw in mine. I did not want her mind to be drawn back to the ruinous darkness into which her father had long ago cast her. So I said nothing. I offered her some of the pork that I had just begun to eat. Her senses would not discern the subtleties of flavor or experience the synesthetic evocations mine did, but it was downright delicious enough to thrill any palate. An antidote for any wayward ramblings through the dark. She loved it. She was letting out light every time she opened her mouth, and she didn't even know it.

At home, blissfully sleepy, I brought to bed with me a book I had purchased some time ago but, as much as I looked forward to reading it, had not got around to it: the first volume of *The Letters of Samuel Beckett*. Although Beckett was one of my favorite writers, I was not as interested in these early letters, from 1929 through 1940, as I was in those of his later years. But still I was sure that there would be much here of interest and illumination; and it was always better, or so it seemed, to start at the beginning. Besides, when you got right down to it, I had no choice. Cambridge University Press had not yet published the second volume in this daunting undertaking.

It was the wrong book to bring to bed. I don't know how much this hard-bound book of almost nine hundred pages weighed, but it made for highly unwieldy reading abed. I laid it aside, shut the light, and let myself drift off. While drifting, I encountered good old Keith. At first I wondered what he was doing in the passway through which I drifted. Then I remembered that I had been listening earlier to "Let It Bleed":

> *Yeah, we all need someone we can bleed on,*
> *Yeah, and if you want it, baby, well, you can bleed on me.*

Then I remembered the day's reveries and talk about opium and eyes, and how on the night we met, at a dinner one spring night about a dozen years ago at the Closerie des Lilas in Paris, he politely asked someone sitting between us to tell me that I had "the most beautiful opiated eyes" he'd ever seen. I may have been directly back from Asia at the time. I don't recall. What I do recall is that when I left Keith's suite at the Plaza Athénée at dawn, I had met one of the most remarkable gentlemen I have ever encountered, and this esteem for him, and my fondness for him, grew steadily over the ensuing years as we grew closer.

Though he had spent much of his adult life seeing the world through hotel room windows, albeit the windows of very nice hotel rooms, he did not accept the fate of a prisoner of fame. To the extent that he could get away with it, he did and went as he pleased, wherever and whenever. There was a good deal of common ground in our far-rambling conversation, but there was little doubt that fortune and circumstance had afforded him a greater worldliness and ability to indulge it than me, though he never flaunted it or seemed even to look upon it as having much value. I liked the fact that he considered the library in his Connecticut estate to be one of the very special comforts and chambers of his home and life.

I thought of those old tales, though I knew they were not true, of his having full blood transfusions in Switzerland to renew and detoxify himself. I also thought of an article I had seen in a popular health magazine a few years ago titled "Why Is Keith Richards Still Alive?" I did not bring it to his attention, feeling it to be a reprehensibly vulgar and mean-spirited question to put forth about anyone but a detested personal enemy or a politician.

As these thoughts merged with my slow, soft descent into slumber, I felt that I should talk with someone about this sublime but strange matter of new life and the blood of blossoming young beauty. Someone who was not judgmental. Someone who had been around, who had done, seen, and learned of things that most were unaware of.

That person would be Keith, I told myself as I slipped into the sweet untroubled sleep of the debtless, wantless, and sinless.

There was no telling how long I slept in this deep and dreamless state. When I woke, the morning light was rising full and the telephone was ringing. It was Melissa. She wanted to know if I felt like getting together tonight. There was nothing I should like more, I told her. She said she had to put in an hour or so at the library, then run a few errands, and could be down here by half past six or so. That would be great, I told her. She lingered on the telephone awhile, as people often do, without having anything of consequence to say. She spoke of the weather, of how it was now spring but it still felt like winter. She spoke of a documentary film she had seen the night before at the Film Forum. She asked me what I had done last night.

"Nothing," I told her, seeing in my mind that dim red light and that Saint Andrew's cross, tasting in my mind the feast of that Chinese food, tasting in my mouth and throat the residue of Lorna's blood. "I started to read the collected letters of Samuel Beckett, but the book was too damned heavy to read in bed."

"I've got a surprise for you," she said. "Something I think you'll like."

"And what might that surprise be?"

"You'll see. If I told you, it wouldn't be a surprise, then, would it?"

"So you'll be keeping me in a state of anticipation all day."

"It's nothing really. It's something that has to do with my legs. Something I think you'll like."

"Ah, now you'll be keeping me in a state of excitement all day."

"I read Beckett's *Stories and Texts for Nothing* last year."

"Great stuff. 'The Calmative.' What's the other one? 'The End.' Yeah, 'The End.' Great stuff. Unbelievable stuff."

"Did you ever see *Waiting for Godot,* or did you ever read it?"

"I hate that shit. His plays suck. All of them except for *Krapp's Last Tape.*"

"Why does writers' worst stuff become their best-known stuff?"

"Because people are fucking idiots. The stupider it is, the more they eat it up. With the highfalutin idiots, the more they're told it's art, the more they eat it up. Stupid shit, stupid people. The secret to success."

"So I'll see you later on."

"Have you noticed anything weird about my eyes lately?"

"You have great eyes."

"I mean the way they change colors."

"Yeah, it's really something. Isn't that what they call *pers* in French? *Pers* eyes. Eyes that keep changing colors."

She was as good with that one as she was with Hesse's name. She didn't pronounce the *s* at the end. But she didn't know what she was talking about.

"*Pers* eyes change between brown and green, or like the colors of the sea, or something like that. You haven't noticed anything *weird* about the way my eyes change colors?"

"Are you stoned?"

"No." I laughed. "Weird guy, weird eyes, I guess."

"Who was that saint that carried around that plate with his eyeballs on it?"

"Oh, man, I forget. Those guys were always carrying around platters with some part of them on it. The broads too. Come to think of it, the only one I remember is Saint Agnes. I read this book once, some sort of sex manual from the late seventeenth or early eighteenth century. *The Mysteries of Conjugal Love Revealed.* Something like that. And the guy who wrote it started talking about women afflicted with Saint Agnes syndrome or something like that, and I couldn't figure out what the hell he was talking about. Then years later I found out that Saint Agnes carried around a platter with a pair of tits on it, because that was the way she was supposed to have been martyred, by having her tits cut off. All this just to say a woman was flat-chested."

I thought of Lorna, my beautiful virgin flat-chested leopardess and her cross of Saint Andrew's martyrdom. Then I realized I had the wrong saint.

"No," I said, "not Saint Agnes. It was Saint Agatha. She was the one with the tits on the platter. Saint Agatha of Sicily, not Saint Agnes."

"And oh yeah, the eyeballs, that was a female saint too," Melissa said. "Saint Lucy. She was the one with the eyeballs on a golden plate."

"Who came up with this shit? Who were these sick fucks who concocted these stories? It's like some fat kike Hollywood mogul or something: 'All this martyrdom shit is getting tired. These martyrs are getting to be a fucking dime a dozen. We need some pizzazz. We need to sell some popcorn. That blonde. Let's cut off her tits before we kill her. And that other one, what's her name, that bitch with the bedroom peepers. Let's rip out her eyeballs before she gets it.' Is there some kind of art historian at school you could ask? I really want to know. The first Christian blue plate special. I want to know which saint and what was on his or her platter."

"You're on a roll. What did you have for breakfast?"

"I just woke up. Slept like a baby. I'll probably just go with a Mexican breakfast, cup of coffee and a cigarette. What about you?"

"A bagel."

"We're livin', kid. So before you run off to find that tits-on-a-plate professor, tell me more about this surprise."

"No."

"Come on, just a hint."

"It's something you can sink your teeth into. Something you can sink your teeth *through*."

"Oh, man," I said, then gave up.

She was in a sprightly mood, and I was feeling great. That cup of coffee was just a few minutes away.

"Did you ever think of killing yourself?" I said. The words just came out.

"Are you serious?"

"Yeah."

"No. Have you?"

"Never?"

"Maybe once when I made a cake for a school bake sale in the fourth grade and it fell apart and I tried to put it back together again with toothpicks and it came apart again even worse than before and everybody laughed at me. That may have been my suicide moment. I was saved by the intervention of my mom and dad buying me a cake with buttercream frosting at the corner bakery, which I palmed off as my own, blaming my previous failure on a faulty oven knob. I didn't really think of killing myself. I just cried to my mom that I wanted to die. Which was pure schoolgirl melodrama. I was no good in the school play, either."

I made a sound between a grunt and a laugh.

"Why do you ask?"

"I was wondering what you were doing with that suicide thing in your bag the other night."

"What suicide thing?"

"That brochure. That what-a-difference-a-day-makes thing?"

"A friend of mine at school. She's getting pretty spooky. She doesn't talk it, not directly. But it's getting to where it seems like just a matter of when and how. I really like her. She's a really good kid. But as it turned out, that brochure was just a plug for an overnight walk to help prevent suicide. Something like that. Don't ask me how a bunch of people marching down a street at three o'clock in the morning is supposed to help somebody a mile away not commit suicide. But there was also something in there about an informational meeting, but you had to register, your address and phone number and everything, which means they'll probably drive you to suicide by bugging you for donations. I did learn that, according to that brochure anyway, suicide is the third biggest cause of death among teenagers and the second biggest cause of death among college students."

"What's the first?"

"They didn't say. That's probably a different brochure."

"A lot of broken cakes out there, I guess."

"You'd like her. She likes cutting herself a lot."

"Bring her down sometime. I've never made a cocktail of two bloods. Is she pretty?"

"Shut up."

I was smiling, enjoying the fact that she couldn't see it over the telephone as I hung up. Actually it was an idea not without appeal. Two girls, four thighs. A nip from one, a sip from the other, long drinks in the dark from soft young legs entwined.

This brought to mind the fifty-milliliter sample vials, decanted from bottles of rare liquor, I had ordered from Oxygénée in England. A pre-ban Absinthe de Ville Chabrolle. A pre-ban Absinthe Gempp Pernod. And the one I really wanted, an extinct tea liqueur that was older by far than the century-old absinthes: a pre-1850 Crème de Thé from the cellars of Badminton House.

Why would a sober man, a man who intended to remain sober, be making exorbitant purchases of uncommon booze? I could tell myself that it was the collector in me. I could tell myself that I was making investments. There were, in fact, in my closet bottles of great-vintage Margaux and pre-ban absinthe, even a bottle of 1811 Cognac Napoléon Grande Fine Champagne Reserve, all of which had remained sealed and undrunk through numerous mad and mindless benders. But the three little vials of rarest booze I had ordered, as well as several wine futures I had bought, were not purchased, like the bottles in my closet, when the idea of sobriety was nothing more than an occasional fancy. These, the little vials and the futures, were bought in what I felt to be the full and never to be sundered embrace of sobriety. The snake in the alky's skull. The self-deceit so consummate. Was I methodically, meticulously planning, as if in somnambulance, a bender to end all benders? In a few days I would be seeing the doctor, and was glad that I might likely be leaving his office with a prescription for baclofen. If it was not in my pocket when I left, I would go to one or another of those walk-up doctors' offices in Chinatown and get a prescription there.

I relished a smoke and the hot strong brew lightened with half-and-half of my *petit-déjeuner mexicain.* I relished looking forward to spending the night with my sweet Melissa. I relished the little quiver of boyish excitement the prospect of her "surprise" presented. I relished the slow serene progress of drifting from this morning to this night that lay ahead of me, each breath of it a relishing to come. I relished the eidetic image of Lorna stretched and gagged in ecstasy on her Saint Andrew's cross in the dim red whorehouse light of the poky black-curtained sanctum of her Hell's Kitchen flat. I relished the sense of strength and renewed life and peace that ran through me like a soft current of spring brook water, reflecting the glistening twinkling light of godliness. I relished the very relishing of it all, and the growing sense of the all within me.

I placed a pair of old Ray-Ban sunglasses—more than thirty years old, in fact, in a style no longer made—on the kitchen counter beside the plastic cup that held my fake teeth. Two things now, instead of one thing, to which to attend before venturing out into the day: one to put in, the other to put on. I wondered idly if the color wheels of my irises were any more noticeable to passing observers than the fake teeth in my mouth. No one, after all, had commented other than Lorna, in her talk of "that look." What if on Friday morning my doctor should cast the ray of his penlight into my eyes? What would he see and what would he say? Would it matter? Would it mean anything? There were biochemical "laws" that supposedly governed and explained muscle tissue growth. But none of them applied to the recent growth, the recent resurgence of my muscle tissue. And regardless of what might be seen in the narrow beam of a penlight, I knew my eyesight to be sharper and more acute than it had been in years. Was I outstripping the bounds of accepted medical science, which, for all its advancements and its posturings of understanding what it did not, remained not so far removed from its medieval antecedents?

Paeon, the physician to the gods, carried no stethoscope or disposable wooden tongue depressors.

There is a large black jagged rock that juts from the sea close to a secluded cove on Levanzo, an island off the western coast of Sicily, in the ocean waters off Trapani. The natives have a name for this eternal large black jagged sea-presence: Faraglione. In warm seasons of many years, I used to lie naked on the solitary little stony shore looking at it from early morning to sunset, immersing myself in the tossing blue waves between me and it, watching the sun turn from gold to fiery red, increasing in size as it did so and descended. It was easy to see how this great perfect circle of the red sun descending was a god to those who once dwelled in the caves in the high rock above where I lay; easy to see that while theologies and religions die, true gods do not. Since I felt cured of everything when I left that place and walked the long distance back over the hills to the island's little hamlet, Cala

Dogana, in the chill of nightfall, I had my own name for Fara-glione. I called it *il dottore,* the Doctor.

I don't think I knew about Paeon then. I had likely read of him in Homer without either awareness or memory. No, I did not know of him, but I felt his being there, nameless and unknown to me, all the same, whispering into the wind to me, or through the voices of the birds that flew overhead: "Someday, you who see and long for and worship what is right. Someday." Paeon. *Il dottore.* The Doctor. It was when I stopped pilgriming to him and lying naked all day before him in the sun that my darkness fell and claimed me. Paeon. *Il dottore.* The Doctor. He was ready to see me now, by name, and I him. I felt him to be with me. I felt him everywhere. The only true value of his lessers lay in their prescription pads.

I could still faintly taste the traces of Lorna's dark blood as the hot coffee going down liquefied them and drew them into its brew, to which they added an exotic enticing hint of something like angelica or dandelion root. It was delicious.

Looking out the window to gauge the weather by seeing how passers-by on the street below were dressed proved fruitless. A few women wore heavy winter coats, but it was impossible to tell if they wore them against the cold or only to flaunt their luxury. A few young fools wore T-shirts, certainly not because they were warm in them but to flaunt their biceps or present a show of self-imagined toughness to the elements. There was even someone with a raised and open umbrella, though it was clearly not raining at all. This umbrella at least served from my vantage as a decent wind indicator.

I put on an old heavy leather Schott jacket whose zip-in lining had been lost for about the past twenty years, and which I still expected to somehow reappear. I put in my teeth. I put on my shades, I ventured out.

It was not that bad out whenever the wind eased. The sun was high and the breaks in the rolling grayish-white clouds came often. I walked south, intending to pick up another coffee at Dunkin' Donuts and then stroll back to the Reade Street Pub and, if it wasn't crowded, occupy a barstool while I drank it. The chill was still such that enjoying the coffee on one of the benches outside the bar was not an open choice. I did notice, however, that the fruitless pear tree across the street from the bar was beginning to bud. I took this to be a sign that warmer fresh air— as fresh as it ever got, anyway—might be soon coming to narrow, shaded Reade Street. And with it, as we cigarette-smoking malingerers and over-the-hill roués called it, good bench weather.

But after leaving Dunkin' Donuts with my container of coffee, I decided to wander instead over to Uncle Mike's bar on Murray Street. The barmaids there would be scantily clad. Instead of shooting the shit with Mike Hickey, the bartender, and random members of the usual cast of idling miscreants, barflies, and good-hearted buddies at Reade Street, I would whet my appetite for this evening's pleasures. As always it was dark in Uncle Mike's. I removed my shades. No one there was going to be looking at my eyes, not with those bartenders in those baby-doll negligees and come-hither smiles.

I didn't know either of the girls working that day, so I put down a sawbuck next to my container of coffee and slid it toward the gutter of the bar so that they knew it was a tip for the privilege of taking up space while I drank the senior-discount buck-seventy-five coffee that I had brought in with me.

I was drawn to one of the girls, a plain grisette type who exuded an uncaring sensuality. I stared at her breasts, her ass, especially her thighs. She was fleshy, but not buxom. I imagined biting into those breasts, that ass, especially those thighs. What sort of sounds might she make as I drew her blood into my mouth through the broken skin of that flesh? She seemed blasé. Maybe she might make no sounds at all. What a delicious imagining. I would never know. But it did inspire me to the imaging of something else. An imagining that could be realized. Would Melissa play dead for me? The thought thrilled me.

I finished my coffee, gave a parting glance to those fleshy thighs, rose, and left, hearing her thank me as I did so. I slipped my shades back on and walked to Korin, the Japanese knife store around the block, on Warren Street. For some time I had been enticed by a one-of-a-kind hand-finished Togiharu *gyuto* knife, about nine or ten inches long, with a handle crafted from mammoth tusk. At about two grand, it was a steep price to pay for a kitchen knife. But every time I looked down at it through the glass of its display case, and the times I had asked for it to be removed from the case and held it, I became more enamored of it. Maybe it was the gleaming heavy steel beauty of the blade. Maybe it was the brown-streaked rocklike heft and beauty of the prehistoric fossilized bone handle. Probably it was both. Every time I hesitated, I knew that the day was drawing nearer when this unique knife would be gone, and that there would never be another quite like it. Tomorrow, I told myself, tomorrow, as I told myself whenever I looked at it. Maybe that's what I subconsciously hoped for: that it would one day be gone, and that I could then no longer desire it, for it could then no longer ever be mine. For I never fully understood the hold of its beauty on me. I never fully understood why I so wanted it.

When I removed my sunglasses to gaze at the knife, I noticed that the elder of the two shopkeepers was looking at my eyes. More than that, he was looking into them.

Did he see the eyes of one who had grown different? The eyes of one who had become transcendent? The eyes of one whose way of seeing had become rare, even unique? Was he now comprehending at last the attraction of those eyes, and what lay in and beneath them, for the rare deadly beauty of this thing that was also unique? In the past, we had exchanged friendly and easygoing words, and I had learned much from him about the arcane ways of traditional Japanese blade forging. Now he was silent and said nothing as I put on my shades and left. I wondered awhile what his silence meant.

Back home, I thought to call Lorna to see how she felt. I decided that I should, but not now, not today. It was better to wait and not to rush. If there was an emotional change for the better, and I hoped there was, it would need time to settle in. The years' ghostly treadling at the loom of darkness could not be braked and stilled so easily.

Should I begin to write again? Was there a tale left in me to tell? How had Thomas Mann recognized and plucked from the air so that it might germinate in his hand the seed of the sublime, simple, and elegant tragedy that we know in English as *The Black Swan*? Could the sediment of unused words and rhythms be stirred to rise and dance once again in the distillate dregs of an alembic left so long to gather dust and grime? Of course it could, I told myself. The neglected alembic and the sludge of what years ago had danced and sparkled and sung, they were in me; and I was new, and they too could be as new. I decided that, yes, I should begin to write again.

I felt strong, and I took from the drawer the piece of paper with those words so strange that I had found on my desk that cold early morning in February. "Somewhere along the line, something went wrong." Those words so unrecognizable, yet written in my hand, on that piece of paper that seemed to have appeared from nowhere, which had so unsettled me that I had hidden it— words, paper, the whole thing of it—away from myself, in a drawer where I would not see it. Now, holding it in my hand and reading it once again, I realized that I had hidden it from myself, yes, but why, I asked myself, had I not simply got rid of it, this eerie thing that still struck me as some sort of spirit writing, written by an unknown hand, which must have been my own, and left for me by an unknown hand, which must have been my own? What, for all the unease it brought me, had made me want to keep it?

I placed it down in open sight on the desk. Beside it I placed down what I had written on that equinox day when that leaf had appeared on my sill. I glanced at them. I just left them there, and I made up my mind to leave them there until—until what?

I shaved, took a long hot bath, changed into fresh clothes, took a Valium, poured a glass of cold milk, put on Arvo Pärt's *Alina,* and sat and sipped my milk surrounded by its mystical simplicity. And still the answer to the question I had posed myself— *until what?*—did not come.

Instead of an answer, Melissa arrived.

"That Herman Hesse thing," she said. "I got the original from the library."

"That's my surprise?"

"Hold your horses. It's all connected. Like the Buddhists say. Everything's connected. So just hold your horses."

"I didn't know the Buddhists talked so much about horses."

"Shut up." She unfolded some photocopied pages and a sheet of handwritten notes. "Do you know any German?"

"I know enough to know that the name of the guy who wrote that is pronounced *Hessay,* not *Hessuh.* And I can say *danke schön,* and *Fräulein,* and *Gemütlichkeit.* And *sauerkraut.* I can say *sauerkraut.* And *die Betrogene.* I can say *die Betrogene.*"

"What's that?"

"It means 'the black swan,'" I said.

"Quite a vocabulary you've got there in German," she said.

"And *Deutsch*. I can say *Deutsch*."

"Why didn't you tell me before?"

"That I can say *Deutsch*?"

"Oh, come on. About *Hessay*'s name. Why didn't you correct me the other night?"

"Because I didn't want to be pedantic. Because you were saying it like everybody else says it. You were saying it better than most people. Because that's the way I always used to say it, and so to correct you would've been like being a pompous asshole. Besides, fuck him, he's dead, call him whatever you want."

"You would've been sharing your knowledge. That's not pedantic. Now I can say it right. And everybody will think I'm saying it wrong."

"That's another good reason. And, hey, I checked out those lines, and you edited them. You took them out of context. He was talking about the thigh of a deer, not gal-meat. The sick fuck was in love with a goddamn doe."

"All I was doing was giving you the essence. The essence of what you seem to share with that sick fuck. And I'm probably the sickest one of all. At least the deer didn't know what she was in for." Her voice grew softer. "I thought I would make it special for us," she said.

Her words made me feel slightly humiliated, humbled, and touched. I let my face relax in the calmed, loving openness I felt. She showed me the lines in their original German:

> *Ich wäre der Holden so von Herzen gut,*
> *Fräße mich tief in ihre zärtlichen Keulen,*
> *Tränke mich satt an ihrem hellroten Blut,*
> *Um nachher die ganze Nacht einsam zu heulen.*

"It sounds pretty cool in German. I listened to a recording of it. And see this thing here." She placed her dainty finger below the ß in the word *Fräße* and looked at her notes. "That's called a *scharfes s,* or an *eszett.*" There was slow care in her saying of this: "*ess-tsett.*" Her eyes rose from her notes. "And this one's for you, smarty-pants. You may know how to pronounce his name, but I bet you don't know how to spell it. You spell it with one of those things. She pointed to her notes, where she had written large: *Heße.* That thing, it's the German double *s.* It sounds sort of like a snake hissing.

"But here's what's really cool. This word here: *Keulen.*" She said it, again with care: "*Koolen,*" with a slight accent on the first syllable. "It means the hip and the fleshy area of the buttock and thigh below it. Is that some kinda word or is that some kinda word? *Keulen.* And get this. It's also the real name for the city we call Cologne. The city of the hip and the fleshy area of the buttock and thigh below it." She grabbed this part of her body with her right hand, and with great mock enthusiasm and pride announced: "*Keulen!*" Then she looked at me with a mischievous, kittenish grin. "Well, buddy," she said, "are you ready to go to Cologne?"

"I certainly am ready to go to Cologne, *mein Fräulein*. I most certainly am."

She rose quickly from the couch and scurried with her bag into the bedroom.

And where had Hesse got *Steppenwolf* from? These Krauts were pretty fucking good at grasping seeds from the wind. It was spring now, the season of wind pollination. The pear tree on Reade Street was already budding. Soon it would blossom full and white. I looked at my hand, opening and closing it, then opening it again. I looked over to the sheets of paper on the desk.

Then I heard the commanding seductive click of those Jimmy

Choo stiletto heels, and I looked only at her, and all thoughts vanished, and there was only lust.

There were moments in recent days when I had begun to take
her beauty for granted. But what an extraordinary beauty it was,
superlative in itself and enhanced by those touches—the ponytail
and the insouciant curl at its end, the demure shapely curvature of
her lips, the shimmer in her eyes, the natural glow of her
complexion—that made of her the very picture of innocence
inviting defilement. Now, as she stood before me, that picture
had been raised to salacious perfection by the sort of masterly
sable brushstrokes that belonged neither to skill nor to practice
but to inspiration alone. She was purity poised for the brutal taking. She was the Virgin Mary casting from her lap into the dusty
dirt the burden of that dead diapered thing and opening her
chaste mouth to suck the cock of the next bestial passer-by. She
was gorgeous. I had told her she was a goddess, and she was.

The smack of her hand on her hip was as commandingly
seductive as had been the slow, louche click-clack of her approach.
I was speechless. She wore, fitting her superbly, like a second skin
of exquisite sinfulness, a corselet of black batiste lace and silk-
satin. It looked as if it had been made for her, painstakingly, exact-
ingly. The rich fabric that cupped her full sweet breasts was not a
millimeter too loose, not a millimeter too tight. The garters that
extended from the open lace bottom of the corselet were hooked
into the welts of pale beige stockings that were so sheer I could
not imagine the fineness of their denier. The one thing I did
clearly discern, from their gleam, was that they were pure nylon:
the real thing, stockings as they were meant to be, stockings as
brought forth into the world by DuPont and the gods in the holy
year of 1939, antecedent to the holy year of 1959, or A.N., *Anno
Nailonensis,* in the Year of Nylon 20, when pantyhose followed
them into this world. The black satin over-the-elbow gloves she

wore, her fingers and forearms snug and well defined in them, delivered the finishing touch. I imagined the feel of them around my naked back, those satin fingers caressing my breasts and neck, clutching my cock, stroking it, drawing it to her mouth.

She wore no panties under the corselet. She drew closer. I buried my face in the soft ringlets above her cunt, moved my hands over the tactile Eden of her nyloned legs, kissed the bare skin between the lace of the corselet and her stocking-tops, ran my tongue along the taut garters, sucked at the hook-and-eye fittings half exposed and half veiled through the lush nylon welts.

My cock was risen full and rock-hard in resurrection. There was no end to this renewal, this rejuvenation. I had a hard-on like an eighteen-year-old.

"Where did you ever get these?" I whispered, one hand on the nylon at the bend of her knee, the other moving slowly on the nylon that ever so thinly covered her shin.

"I found some place in Leesburg, Virginia. I was on the computer in the library, looking for a chronology of Predynastic Egypt. I ended up in Leesburg, at this place called Secrets in Lace. They had a Bettie Page Collection in their Leg Salon section. A lot of cool stuff. I got these stockings. I got these gloves. This"— the corselet—"I got at a fancy-pants place up on Madison in the Sixties. What a store. Learned the difference between a corset and a basque. Absolutely no relevance to Predynastic Egypt, but then again. Agent Provocateur or something like that. Splurged. Check from daddy."

As much as I wished I could savor her as she stood before me, I could not. My hands trembled, unable to relax and luxuriate in the lavish delights of her. Seeing her like this was too much. Restraint did not present itself as a crescendo of pleasure, but only as an unbearable torture. There was no fending back what surged within me. I felt like a madman with a knife in my hand. Savage consummation was the end, the means, the all.

What had she said? "Something you can sink your teeth into." Yes, those were her words. They shot now through the fire in my brain. "Something you can sink your teeth *through*."

I sank my teeth through the nylon into her thigh as she stood there. It seemed for a moment that the shuddering of her body as she gasped would take all balance from her and cause her to fall. But, clutching my shoulders as she swayed a bit, she remained upright and gasped again.

The first mouthful of her blood quenched me. It was divine replenishment. Consummation. The violence of my sucking eased, but I could not stop. I chewed on the sheer nylon, reached down to grasp her ankles and the heels of her shoes, as I drew her blood into me, more and more gently, as if sipping sparingly of one of those wines gathering the subtle nuances of increasing grace in the dark of my closet.

I coaxed a bend into her left knee, raised her leg as she clutched my shoulder all the more for support, brought her foot to rest on the edge of the couch between my legs, the toe of her shoe nudging at my crotch. I worked my cock and laid it on the black rat-snake skin, Chantilly lace, and suede of the shoe's upper. Bending round, I brought my mouth to the flesh below the haunch of her upright leg and bloodlessly kissed and sucked as I slowly stroked my cock against her raised shoe. Grabbing her buttock to both steady her and fill my hand with her, my mouth still to her flesh, I began to fuck her shoe. The thrusts of my hips grew harder, faster. I bared my teeth. The bloodless kiss was bloodless no more, and I grasped her ankle and watched my cock twitch in a fierce spasm, as the white stain of its eruption spread, darkened, and penetrated the nylon where her shin flexed in response, raising and tilting the heel, snakeskin, and lace of her shod nylon-shimmering foot against my crotch.

At that moment she uttered a sound, low but clear, like a whispered hiss: *"Jst."* Her breasts undulated as she breathed, looking down at me through half-lowered eyelids. She repeated it, accenting and lingering long on its sibilance: *"Jssst."*

Then I recognized it. The true name of Isis, uttered as if it were she, the goddess herself, announcing her presence and dominion.

She let down her raised knee to the couch, then brought her other knee to the couch as well, straddling me as I sat there, spent. She leaned forward, pressing herself to me, my face to her breasts. Then she arched her back, so that there was between us freedom to breathe more easily.

"You don't want to get blood on that thing," I said. She knew I was talking about the fancy batiste lace and silk-satin that clung to her. She caressed my face with black satin fingers. Already my cock was stirring again, and again I imagined the clench of her gloved hand.

"Blood," she said low, almost whispering, as if to dismiss my mention of it. "Phoenician purple, the dye of royalty, the most coveted dye of empire. Reddish-purple slime from the slimy glands of slimy crawling mollusks. One slimy ounce of it worth far more than its weight in gold, and far more coveted."

She smeared her satin fingers in the blood that had run down her outer thigh from the haunch of my bloodless and bloody kisses. She put the satin fingers to my lips, anointed them, then to her own, opening her mouth to them and sucking them.

"The true dye of empire," she said. Her voice was trancelike, so different from the voice I knew. "More precious than gold and Phoenician purple together. Caesar had all of both he could ever want. But this was the dye"—again she ran her moist satin fingertip across my lips, again she put it to her mouth and sucked it—"that turned out to be the one true dye of his imperium. The dye of himself. The dye of his fate. The dye of his immortality. The dye that blotted out all the gold-threaded Phoenician purple of that—what's the word I'm looking for?"

"Toga?"

I felt so comfortable, so glutted, so full, so dreamily relaxed. I knew the pattern now. First this, the becalmed lassitude, then the serene rest, then the renewed and ever more heightened vitality, the waking to new life.

"Yeah, but the all-purple one. All Phoenician purple. The fabulously extravagant thing that Caesar took to wearing as his regular everyday street clothes. Toga something-or-other. Come on, help me out here. You know Latin."

"I don't know Latin," I said drowsily. My cock was no longer stirring anew. I was floating in placidity, white clouds and soft light flickering through leaves and boughs above. "I can bluff Latin, that's all."

"Well, bluff me what I'm trying to think of here."

It was good to again hear the voice I was used to. No more of that trancelike stuff.

"Toga picta," she said.

"See," I said, "you're the one who can speak Latin."

"No. I've been thinking about this. I looked it up. Then I forgot it. Now I just remembered it again."

I had never heard the expression before. I wasn't about to get up and look in the *Oxford Latin Dictionary*. I wasn't even about to get up. Merely lighting a cigarette seemed something like a labor of leisure.

"The dye of fate. The dye of life. The dye of death. The dye of immortality. The dye that blotted out and obliterated all the gold-threaded Phoenician purple of that *toga picta*."

What the fuck was she talking about?

The foul smell hit me. I had lit the wrong end of a Parliament. I let it fall in the ashtray. I repeated this labor of leisure more attentively. I looked at her. Those satin gloves. Lace and nylon. That ponytail. I almost wished she'd put on my robe. But that would never cover all of her, and even if it did, I would know what was under it. My cock, which I did not want to stir anew, stirred anew.

Blood. She was talking about blood. That's what she was talking about.

I thought of the girl in Uncle Mike's. The blasé one. The one who might make no sounds at all. The dead one. I took Melissa to bed. All that satin and lace. The nylons, the shoes. The bared flesh. I laid her out on top of the bed and arranged her. She was pliant, asked no questions, said nothing. I shut off the lights and lit a candle.

"Be still," I whispered. "Like you're asleep."

I kissed her on the forehead, on the lips, ever so gently on the forehead once more. Extreme unction.

She drew a deep breath and closed her eyes. I knelt over her, took my cock in my hand, rubbed it to the lace, the nylon, the bare flesh. She mewled faintly.

"Sh-sh," I whispered. "Like you're asleep."

She lay still beneath me as I knelt between the open unmoving legs. I worked the swollen end of my cock slowly into her wet cunt. She made not a sound. She understood.

I fell to sleep that night like a rock falling deep into the cradling sea, feeling her arm close around me.

IN THE MORNING SHE WAS GONE. SOMETHING IN ME HOPED that she had left behind a note of love or endearment or light-hearted fondness. But the dark stains of her blood that here and there mottled my skin were all the billet-doux I found.

As I bent slightly forward, bare-chested, to look at them in the mirror, I saw that the flesh of my chest extending to my arm-pits no longer sagged. The tissue of the pectoral muscle beneath the flesh was fuller, firmer. The same was true of the skin and tissue of my neck.

Then I caught sight of my eyes. I had forgotten to ask Melissa to look closely at them the night before, and she had remarked nothing. But it seemed to me that their courtly minuet of chang-ing colors was becoming a sprightly galliard of shades and nuances, like the mingling fluctuations of unearthly dawns and sunsets set awhirl.

I shaved and showered, using the Dr. Hauschka Blackthorn Body Wash that Melissa had left on the edge of the tub for herself some weeks before. It felt good, and I enjoyed the notion that my skin might have the scent of her skin.

It was raining softly, silently. I stood near the kitchen window, watching it, lost in it, feeling good as I drank my coffee.

The pattern was becoming familiar to me. The ravishing, the lassitude, and the deep rest; the renewed strength, the rejuvenation, the increased sensibilities, powers, serenity. Lust and beatitude, blood and being. I would never again feel or fear the desperate fate of the dead monkeys, or be shaken by the foretelling memory of their final, fatal clinging.

The frieze of the dead monkeys would remain forever to gaze upon whenever I looked up to the architrave of the temple within me. But the image would be nothing more than that. A mysterious icon of a mystery religion, born in the cave-temple of myself, its meaning unknown even to the initiates and celebrants chosen to enter into it by me, a god without name who drank of eternal nectar dew from the very blossoming of those initiates and celebrants.

I got down the *Oxford Latin Dictionary.* The adjective *picta,* the feminine form of *pictus,* meant painted or colored. I went to the long entry for *toga,* where I did indeed find *toga picta,* defined as an embroidered toga worn by triumphing generals, perhaps originally by royalty. Neither the definition nor the chosen illustrative quotations specifically mentioned Phoenician purple, but I was willing to go along with her on that one. Impressed, I returned the stately weight of this volume of more than two thousand pages to its place on the shelf.

Ogni giorno è la scuola, I told myself with a degree of satisfaction at having fulfilled this good Italian saying. *Every day is school.* One learns something new, or should learn something new, every day.

My mind was again on that carved mammoth-handle knife. I walked to the shop on Warren Street, stopping off at Dunkin' Donuts to pick up another cup of coffee on the way.

I rested the container of coffee carefully on the glass showcase and sipped from it as I looked at the knife, slipped off my shades, and asked for it to be removed so that I could study it more closely. I had not thought of it before, but it now occurred to me that most fossil wooly mammoth tusk bone came from Russia, and I suspected that the mammoth bone from which the handle of this knife had been carved was from the earth of that place so close to Japan.

I despised Russians, a loud, gaudy, overbearing, smarmy, and obnoxious people. They could make the most elegantly faceted blue-white diamond look like a cheap zircon simply by wearing it. The legacy of their literary greatness, in reality based on little more than the pomposities of a bunch of lice-ridden beards, was as fraudulent as they were; and the only good thing at all that could be said about them was that they paid to translate and publish my books. I refused even to eat Russian caviar, though it probably often came from the same sturgeon that swam off the Iranian side of the Caspian Sea.

My suspicion about the source of the mammoth bone was confirmed. To me this tainted the handle of the knife, as beautiful as it was.

I saw not far from it in the glass showcase another one-of-a-kind Togiharu *gyuto* that had previously escaped my notice. The blade was similar: hard, strong, gleaming steel, about nine and a half inches in length, hand-forged and hand-finished by the revered Seki sword maker Hiromune Takaba. Its unique handle was fashioned by the same master craftsman, Koji Hara, who had made the mammoth-bone handle.

How I had overlooked this one I do not know. Perhaps it was because the handle, which far surpassed the other in its beauty, also far surpassed it in the subtlety of its beauty. It was of rare petrified blue maple. The delicate grain and veining of this wood-turned-to-stone was an infinity of deep colors and a penumbra of shades and hints of shades thereof. As if with black magic, the slight strains of storm blue with the rock-wood seemed to emanate intimations of every color and every hue, an effect brought to perfection by the understated luster brought to it by the seeing brilliance of Hara-san.

It was like looking into my own eyes.

These knives arrive from Japan with their blade edges at seventy to eighty percent of their maximum sharpness. After buying the knife with the black-magic blue maple handle, I had the shop's knife-sharpening master, Chiharu Sugai, hone its blade to a razor edge. At the sunken basin of water at which he squatted, he worked at the blade with expert movements on a series of wetted sharpening stones of increasing fineness.

As he did so, I went to a farther glass showcase in the little shop. Set off by themselves, near a variety of folding knives designed by Koji Hara—handsome blades in handsome handles of stag, abalone, exotic hardwoods, silver inlaid with mother-of-pearl—were a couple of stranger and much older-looking knives.

The blades of these knives were about three inches long and remarkably slender, narrowing to sharp points from a maximum width of barely a quarter of an inch near where, with a small flourish of twenty-four-karat-gold symbols laid into the steel, they were set into thin ebony handles not much longer than the blades. Each had a fitted sheath of wood, with a removable metal ring to which were attached braided colored cords intended to be fixed to sash-belts. These knives, I was told, were called *tosu*. They were among the last made by the last of the master *tosu* craftsmen, Uegama Nobuyiki, who retired some years ago, bringing to an end the long history of *tosu* artisanship that began more than two thousand years ago.

"What are these used for?" I asked.

Young Keisuke smiled his friendly smile. There was in that smile now an element of implied but unspoken knowledge that he seemed to suspect I already shared.

"You could use them, I guess, to open letters," he said, smiling still. "Maybe to eat fruit."

They were assassins' knives. So deadly, so beautiful. The one of the two on which my eyes were fixed had a sheath of snake-wood with a hand-wrought silver finial and an elaborately embroidered woven-gold Nishijin storage pouch.

So deadly, so beautiful. And so much more costly than the best of the cutlery that New York's most celebrated chefs came here to buy.

We got past the letter-opening and fruit-peeling. For the last few hundred years, I was told—there seemed to be only the merest hint of warning, the merest hint of advice—*tosu* were used only as part of ceremonial or decorative dress, or bought only as collectors' items.

Sugai-san had finished with my big magic-handled knife. It was being placed in a sheath of light magnolia wood and arranged in a hard black felt-lined, silver-clasped carrying case.

The assassin's knife, I knew, was also to be mine. I asked Sugai-san if he could restore the *tosu* to its razor-like cutting edge. He was a knife-sharpening master. A blade was a blade. I was told that the relatively fragile nature of the *tosu* blade was such that I should make careful use of tsubaki oil, derived from the camellia plant, to tend it well.

I was still sipping coffee, though it was cold, when I put my shades back on and left the shop, a few grand lighter, but pleased with my black magic knives. Words came to me from nowhere, and I said them as I dumped the empty Dunkin' Donuts cup into the trash on the corner of West Broadway:

"One for the kitchen, one for the killing."

S O THERE I SAT IN THE CROAKER'S OFFICE ON THE UPPER East Side. He was a good guy, a general practitioner who specialized in gastroenterology, whom I had inherited as my internist from my previous doctor, Allen Yanoff, who was the greatest man of medicine and one of the greatest human beings I have ever known. The two doctors had adjacent offices and shared examination rooms on East Sixty-third Street. Yanoff had always spoken highly of his colleague, and so when Yanoff, who did not smoke, died of lung cancer, I began seeing his friend and fellow doctor.

I had once gone for more than thirty years without seeing a doctor, except for an Italian-Swiss guy in the Village, also now passed on to the Hippocratic beyond, who simply asked me what I thought I should be prescribed and then gave me the prescription for the drug that my self-diagnosis had been calculated to call for.

What had brought me to Dr. Yanoff was the inexplicable loss of more than thirty pounds within barely three months. I figured it was the end. But how to find an actual good doctor? I knew that good, honest physicians were as rare as good, honest grease monkeys or good, honest lawyers. It was my old friend Richard who, when I told him of my quandary, provided me with the sage advice that led me to Allen Yanoff.

"Ask a healthy person," he said.

The healthiest-looking and best-preserved person I knew at the time was my dentist. I asked her who her doctor was, and she told me it was Yanoff. I went to see him. I later came to suspect that I did so only to hear the worst, which would have given me full license to drink myself to death forthwith. He took a good long look at me, told me it was not what I thought, drew some blood, and—I was impressed that a physician would be so caring as to do this—called the next afternoon, which was a Saturday, to report that the results of the blood tests, on which he had placed a rush, revealed that I had diabetes. The woman with whom I was living at the time told him that I was not there, that I was drinking at a nearby bar. "Tell him not to drink beer," he said. She came to the bar with this message. I turned to my drinking buddy Hoboken Jerry, who lately had been given to spewing blood but refused to see a doctor and lived not too much longer.

"You believe this?" I said. "The doctor just told me to drink Scotch instead of beer."

"I want the name of your doctor," he said.

Having just met me, Yanoff had no way of knowing how much of a binge drunkard I was. I went back to see him again, and then again. Sometimes I wondered why. Maybe there remained in me, even at my darkest, a grain of hope that if I did what I could to lengthen my wretched existence, there might be a day when light would come. Then there were times when I thought it was only the Valium prescriptions that kept me coming back. Only after he was gone did I appreciate the fact that it was he who kept me coming back.

"How do you feel?" he asked me one day.

"The words 'I don't give a fuck if I live or die' keep rising to my throat. I don't really mean them. I don't want to die. So I don't say them. But they keep rising in me, like a part of me really doesn't care about a single fucking thing in this world."

I saw that he was smiling benignly, as if I had made him happy for me and thereby for himself. I didn't get it.

"That's great," he said. "You're free. It means you're free."

What I had felt to be something fatally bad within me I now felt to be something very good. It was an illumination. In a few minutes he had performed, off-the-cuff, greater good than psychiatry could or would perform over a lifetime.

He was like that rock in the sea off the coast of that Sicilian island. He cured. Body, mind, and soul. He cured. Like the jagged black rock called Faraglione, he could not be replaced. Only after he was gone did I fully realize this, and my sense of loss was great.

But the new guy, the new croaker, his buddy, was not bad either. On his desk as I sat with him in his office this day was the copy of Olivier Ameisen's book and the letter I had sent him.

We talked about the baclofen I sorely wanted after reading Olivier's book, corresponding with him, and speaking with him.

"One man's opinion," he said of the efficacy that Olivier claimed for baclofen.

As is your own, I thought.

He told me that the American Medical Association placed what is called a "black box" around baclofen. This, he explained, was a sort of warning regarding certain medications with potentially severe withdrawal symptoms or otherwise adverse drug reactions, which the AMA referred to as ADRs.

While he had me there, he wasn't going to let me go without a complete physical. In the examination room, he asked the usual questions. How frequently did I wake up at night to urinate? How were things in the erectile department? Was I coughing up much phlegm lately?

"Yeah. I figure it's good to get it out."

"What color."

"Oh, it depends on the day."

And so on. He examined the inside of my mouth pretty thoroughly. Then out it came, that penlight. I watched his eyes narrow and his brows rise.

"Any change in vision?"

"If anything, it's getting better."

He muttered something. It was as if he were asking himself a question that he expected another part of himself to answer. Did he say it just to hear himself say it?

"Have you seen Dr. Chang lately?"

Dr. Chang was the eye specialist whom I saw every year or so for retinopathy examinations.

"No."

He put his little penlight back in his pocket and said no more weird words, seemingly satisfied with having passed the buck to Chang and thus got himself off the hook.

My pulse was a bit fast, he said, but my blood pressure and blood oxygen level were perfect. He put his stethoscope to my front and my back. I lay down on the table. He pressed, poked, palpated my lower abdomen, my upper abdomen.

"What's that?" he said. "Does that hurt?"

"What? I don't feel anything."

He took my hand in his and placed it to my lower left belly, where sure enough one of my guts was protruding hard under my skin like a fat dead snake in rigor mortis.

"Has it been like that all the time?" he asked. "You haven't felt it before?"

To tell the truth, I had felt some occasional cramping and stiffening there, but it had always passed. The same occurred, with more intensity and more frequency, in my lower legs. But I was not in the mood to tell the truth. Whatever it was, it would go away, and I didn't want any further tests. I rolled sideways, my upper knee raised, and he finger-fucked his way to my prostate.

The nurse came in. She gave me an electrocardiogram, drew blood, and wheeled out the spirometer. I was untrusting of this new spirometer, which factored various data into its breath-capacity readings: age, height, weight, and how much you smoked. Why should my lung power be measured differently from that of a twenty-year-old? Shouldn't the spirometer's results be independent and indicative of how much I smoked, rather than being influenced, one way or the other, by this information beforehand? My antagonism to the device made me blow the required three times to the absolute fullest of my wind power, as I was supposed to. She took me into another room for a chest X-ray.

When I was called back into the doctor's office, he told me that the electrocardiogram and lung capacity readings were fine. The X-ray hung over the light box on the wall to his left.

"You broke a few ribs, I see," he said. He had been saying the same thing every time he looked at my chest X-rays for the past two years, ever since I had cracked three ribs falling down drunk one night. It was always as if he were noticing the healed cracks for the first time. This is one of the things that made me leery of these guys. They seemed never to remember anything about you that wasn't in your medical file, and even then only if the record lay open before them like a cheat sheet. There was no human or personal element. You were not a lost mortal creature with a life with which you had entrusted them, but only a mess of test results from an impersonal, unknown industrial-suburban laboratory with which they had a sweetheart deal. If you told them your wife passed away, they would probably ask you how she was when they next saw you, if they could remember that you had ever had a wife.

And so I was thankful for those cracked ribs, which served as a constant reminder that most of these guys neither knew, cared, nor remembered anything about you no matter how many years they saw you.

"Yeah," I said, looking at the familiar marks from the cracked ribs that showed on the X-ray. "That was awhile back."

He asked me if I needed prescriptions for Valium and dandruff shampoo.

"I think I'm doing all right with the dandruff shampoo," I told him. Then I added aggressively: "What about the baclofen? Are you giving me the baclofen?"

"Reluctantly," he said.

Yeah, I thought, the same way I'm paying that eight-and-a-half-yard bill on the way out.

"Call me next week for the test results."

He had sent the baclofen prescription electronically to my pharmacy, he told me. Modern times. The prescription had already been filled by the time I walked to the E train and got back downtown. In the bag with the baclofen there was also a container of anti-dandruff shampoo.

A few days later I saw my endocrinologist. I had also sent him a copy of Olivier's book and a letter. I wanted two sources, my internist and him, for all my prescriptions. I liked to remain stocked up.

Much to my surprise, the endocrinologist declined to give me a prescription. He spoke of unknown possible side effects. He said he did not trust a drug for which it was claimed that there were no known side effects. "Even aspirin has side effects," he said. He was doing this, he said, because he cared for me.

The aspirin reference. The caring about my fate. My own words were being used to deny me what I wanted. The business about concern over possible side effects was what really got me. What about the fucking ADRs of booze, including death not only from the shit itself but also often from the withdrawal from it? Where the hell was the AMA's little fucking black box there? You would think that medical doctors, who collectively have a higher rate of addiction and suicide than any other profession, would better understand these things. But it did not pay to think. As the old Hippocratic writings tell us: what drugs do not cure, the knife will. Yeah. The knife of suicide.

Fuck these doctors. Fuck them all. With Yanoff gone, Olivier on my side, and Paeon in the air I breathed, the rest of these arrogant venal frauds could go to hell. Prescriptions could be had more honestly and cheaply from Chinatown croakers, or from the Hindoo who had a storefront practice just a few blocks from me.

I walked out onto Fifth Avenue and spit on the sidewalk. I didn't look to see what color my phlegm was. It's the thought that counts.

I turned east, walked down Madison to Lobel's, the best butcher in New York, to get a nice slab of kurobuta pork and a great big dry-aged steak. Besides the Valium, the proximity to Lobel's was the only other reason to throw money at this schmuck. A good butcher was harder to find than a good doctor, and far greater and more valuable as a healer and a man.

A bit farther south on Madison, at the Christian Louboutin boutique, I blew seven hundred bucks on a pair of black leather pumps with red-lacquered soles. The stiletto heels were even higher than those of the Jimmy Choo black snakeskins.

As I walked to the Lexington Avenue subway line with my bag of swine and beef in one hand and the bag of high heels in the other, I felt myself in possession of goods of true medicinal value.

PALM SUNDAY, WHEN THE GRASS MOON WOULD RISE FULL, was nearing. Two days later, Mars, the bringer of war, would enter into conjunction with Mercury, the messenger, in retrograde, with folly of all communication, all sense, moving backwards. We were under the force of the warrior.

I believed in none of the astrological bullshit presented by any of this. But I was enamored of the mythic poetry inherent in the idea of the sky of these nights belonging to the bringer of war. I slept well under that sky. I was beginning to notice, however, that the grand rebirths of my mornings were more fleeting, and less grand, the longer I went without communion with the flesh and blood of those life-giving goddesses whose dew rose not only with the coming grass moon but with every moon.

Lorna was all right, she told me when I called her, and she sounded all right. We met for breakfast on a morning when the chill at last seemed gone from the air. It was good to see her. Looking at her, I could not help but think of her long slender limbs stretched bare and on that Saint Andrew's cross, the lashes striking her through the transparency of the vinyl raincoat as the panties in her mouth gagged the screams of her pleasure and pain. Her juices dripping to the floor.

I asked her if she had gone to the meeting on Sullivan Street that morning. I purposefully took off my shades and laid them on the table.

"Christ, I haven't been to a meeting since that night I was with you."

"Is that a good thing or a bad thing?"

The waitress came and we ordered. In declining coffee, I managed to get in my line about never drinking coffee when denied the freedom to enjoy a smoke with it. Useless words, but if I had a credo by which I lived, this was it, and I was going to affirm it whenever the opportunity arose.

"I don't know if it's good or bad. How about you? Have you been hitting the rooms lately?"

I shook my head in the negative. I said that I just hadn't felt like it lately. I wasn't going to say what part of me believed: that I had got all I was ever going to get out of A.A. when I got her. I told her that I had no desire to drink, however. I told her about the baclofen that I had been taking now for several days.

"A pill that cures addiction?" She followed her words with a little laugh of disbelief.

I told her about Dr. Ameisen's discovery, about the ways it had been suppressed.

"Rimbaud said morality is a disease of the brain," I said. "I think he was right on the money. Of course, a lot of people disagree. But I don't think anybody disagrees that alcoholism is a disease of the brain. I think that's a given. Baclofen alters the brain chemistry so that the underlying causes of addiction are eradicated. I forget the science, all the scientific words. But it's all there in black and white, for anyone who can understand it. The thing is, it doesn't really matter. All that matters is that it works. The science just explains how and why. Some guy who won the Nobel Prize for medicine came right out and said it. He said, 'Dr. Ameisen has discovered the cure for addiction.' The thing is, there's no money in it for the pharmaceutical companies because its patent has expired. But companies like Novartis are trying to play with the molecules so they can come up with something like it that they can patent."

"So you're cured?"

Again she followed her words with a little laugh—no, not really a laugh this time, but a wry, mischievous smile—of disbelief.

"I have no fucking idea," I said. "I just started taking the shit." I put a forkful of eggs in my mouth, chewed, swallowed, took a drink of water. "We'll see."

She took out one of those handheld-device gizmos, asked me the name of Ameisen's book and how to spell his name, then put the gizmo back in her bag.

"How about you?" I asked. "Have you felt like drinking lately."

"No," she said. Now there was a different sort of smile on her face, an almost plain and happy smile.

"And how do you feel otherwise?"

I hesitated following my question with another, the question that seemed naturally to follow it. And she hesitated in her acknowledgment of understanding what I meant, even without that unsaid second question being asked. So I went ahead and asked it:

"How about the spooks?"

She looked into my eyes. Who knows what they looked like. Who knows what she saw. But she looked into them quite easily.

"They're still there," she said. "But"—she knocked on wood—"they seem to be receding into the shadows."

She fell silent for a few moments, and I took care not to break that silence.

"That night."

Then she fell silent again, and again I let the silence be. It was a silence so heavy that what little noise there was in the restaurant on this quiet morning seemed to fall into silence as well.

"I don't know how to say this," she said. "I don't know how to say this without it sounding melodramatic. Without it sounding stupid."

I took a sip of water. I looked at her lowered eyes with my own, waiting for those eyes to rise, to meet whatever it was to see, or whatever it was that she might see, in mine.

"You took something out of me," she said. Then, as her eyes rose, more words followed quickly: "I mean that in a good way." Then the words slowed again, to a normal if slightly halting pace. "You took something out of me that needed to be taken out. It was like some bad thing inside me, some kind of growth, some kind of disease that needed to be removed. I don't know if you got all of it. I don't think you did. But you got some of it. You got a lot of it. I could feel it. I can still feel it. Something was taken away and something was given back. Something bad was cut out, or let out, and something good was let in. I really don't know how to describe it. I really don't."

She began to eat again. A good sign, I figured. I finished what was on the plate. She drank some coffee.

"Don't dwell on it," I said. "Don't try too hard to figure it out. The way you describe it, it makes sense to me. I don't know exactly what you feel. That's something nobody can ever do, get inside somebody else and feel exactly what they feel. But you sound like you feel a lot better than you did. You seem like you feel a lot better than you did. It's probably better not to even question it."

She nodded slowly in agreement. I couldn't tell if it was truly a nod of agreement or merely the simulacrum of one. I smiled at her. She smiled back, and there was no doubt that at least this was real.

"So," she said, "when you went to the doctor to get those little magic pills, that Booze-o-Fix or whatever it is, did he say anything about your eyes?"

"He mumbled something and moved on to my prostate." I did not want her to fear my eyes. That is why I had removed my shades. But I did not want to lead her back to the eyes of her father, either. For her to see my eyes as beautiful without even a thought of her father—and this was what I really wanted—was to want far too much.

"Do you want to get together tonight?" she asked.

How could she think I would not? How could she think I would not have asked her before we rose from this breakfast table? How could she not know that she was irresistible to me? Why would she even ask?

I got a cappuccino to go, lit up in the street, walked her to work, kissed her good-bye, squeezed her hand, and told her I'd see her later. Before entering the building, she turned and smiled to me. It made me feel good.

I passed a new store, on Hudson Street, a sort of day care resort for yuppie mutts called Biscuits & Bath. It offered grooming, transportation, natural foods, puppy kindergarten, classes in basic manners, exercise programs, and socialization services. This neighborhood really was fucking going to hell. It was getting embarrassing just to live around here.

I stopped by the joint on Reade Street, finishing my coffee and tossing the cup into the trash on my way. It was good, the coffee. It was really good. But there was no denying that the Eucharistic euphoria wasn't there. It was good to know that it would be there again tomorrow. My night with Lorna would see to that.

I still couldn't get used to the television sets in these joints. News, baseball, commercials for dick-stiffeners and hair-sprouters. Half a dozen customers and three satellite television sets going. Some of the guys in these joints would rather stare at a soap opera than drink alone and face themselves and their drinks and the screaming emptiness and desperation inside them. It was as if they had forgotten how to talk, even if it was to talk only the nonsense of their shambled brains. Only when there was enough booze in them did they give voice to the empty, desperate screaming inside them. And still the television sets droned on.

From the bar I went to the knife store. I did not know why, but I wanted to pursue the possibility of having made for me a dagger with a leopard-bone handle. If it had been suggested to me an hour ago that I might be entertaining such a pursuit, I would have responded with a blank, nonplussed stare.

It was a short dagger that I wanted, I explained. A *hishu,* a *tosa,* a *hishu-gatana.* But I would also take a longer dagger, a *tanto,* or an old-style traditional hunting knife, a *yamagatana.*

Whatever the type, I wanted a knife that was at least about eight inches and not much more than about a foot in length. I suggested that the dagger should have a modest *tsuba,* or hand guard, of hard metal, maybe good silver or good, strong-alloy twenty-karat or twenty-two-karat gold.

To craft a knife with a leopard-bone handle, a true master craftsman, or two master craftsmen, one for the blade, the other for the handle, would have to be found.

A leopard-bone dagger, carved from treated fresh leopard bone or from petrified leopard bone, must be made by a true craftsman working with his own hands, not by a mere big-business designer who oversaw a modern assembly-line company.

The question was: could there be found a true traditional master? A true, old-fashioned knife-making artist?

Sugai-san knew real Japanese blade-forgers well. One of them was Keijoro Doi, an eighty-four-year-old master of masters. Sugai would be going to Japan at the end of the month. The more precise an idea I could convey of the knife I envisioned, and the amount of money I was willing to pay, the more likely it was that the very special knife I wanted could be made for me.

I knew that leopard bone was difficult to obtain here in the United States, but that it also was not too costly. Not long ago, a friend in Texas, where the remains of protected and endangered species can be sold legally to Texas residents by licensed dealers, bought me a leopard skull. As federal and local laws prohibited its interstate transportation, it was more difficult to get it to me in New York, where dealing in poodle skulls is probably a capital crime, than it was to purchase. And the price had been under four hundred bucks for a fine skull with all its teeth. It sat now atop my cherry television cabinet. I also knew that endangered-species bones, as I had seen firsthand, were far more easily and openly available in Asia, where I'd had many chances to buy leopard pelts but no way of getting them back home. So the cost of the bone would be the least of the expenses.

The problem was that I had no idea how durable or workable leopard bone was, or how it aged, treated or untreated. Could it, for instance, be gold-riveted in two identical simple, striking pieces to both sides of the tang? Could it be ornately carved, even carved out, *katabori*-like, for a hollow center, to be affixed to and expose glimpses of hard, dark-brown ebony or black onyx beneath it? And I had no idea what petrified leopard bone looked like, or if it was an available or desirable material. Without this information, it was hard to arrive at the more precise details of the leopard-bone handle I envisioned.

Would it be possible to obtain this information, so that I could then know the limits of my envisioning, the extent of possibility, and thus the extent of craftsmanship available to me, so that I might then be able to explain in more precise detail what I wanted, and how much I would be willing to pay for it? There would also be the *saya,* or wooden sheath. Leopards spend much of their time in the boughs of trees. I wondered if they had a favorite type of tree. If so, it was wood from that type of tree that I wanted. If not, any one of many dark and beautifully grained woods lay open to me. Or perhaps, going against tradition, a sheath of fine-tooled strong dark leather.

One way or the other, considering the blade-forging alone, I knew it would be an expensive proposition. The one thing I had going for me, I told myself, was that this knife would present a new and most enticing challenge to any true master. An elder master of masters might see in it the masterpiece that could prove to be the end note of his long years of workmanship.

I figured I would be willing to go the price of a bottle of great Cheval Blanc. Yes, the price of a bottle of great Cheval Blanc. Maybe even as far as a 1947. Why not? I would drink the bottle, and it would be gone. The knife would be forever.

I caught myself. Sober, on baclofen, and still calculating according to the wine standard.

Old habits die hard. And—an uncomfortable thought—all too often they die only when we do.

Standing on the pavement outside the store, I lit a smoke and wondered for a moment whence this yearning for a dagger with a leopard-bone handle had pounced. I had always loved leopards, which held for me a mysterious power that spoke to me in ways that went far beyond their surpassing deadly beauty. The leopard skull I possessed was a totem, a symbol of that power. I had wanted such a skull for a long time, and I drew much from its presence. But never before did I think of a killing knife whose grasp-hold might offer that same elusive power.

Heading north on Church Street, I stopped at We Are Nuts about Nuts, stepped through the storefront door, and inhaled deeply for the scent of a current or very recent fresh roasting. The scent was thick in the air. The roaster had been shut, and I asked which nuts had come from it. I was led to the big covered plexiglass bin of cashews, placed my hand to it, and felt that it was hot to the touch. Before the cashews, almonds had been roasted. I placed my hand to the bin of almonds and felt that it was somewhat warm. I asked for a quarter pound of each, took the two small brown paper bags, one hot and the other a bit warm, to the counter, laid down three dollars and seventy-five cents, and left. The aroma from the little bags was delicious.

When I got home, I put the little bags of nuts on the end table beside the couch, took a Valium, poured a glass of cold milk, and returned to the couch. As I did so, I paused to look at the two sheets of paper on the desk, the one with words I remembered writing and the one with words I didn't remember writing.

I was a leopard awaiting glance in bowering shade.

I read the words slowly, silently, then simply stared at them awhile. My eyes moved farther down the sheet of paper and once more paused. Again I read slowly, silently, then simply stared.

Remembered now: what the lady and the leopard, the daemon-seeker and miller did know before me.

The lady and the leopard. The daemon-seeker and the miller. Why had I spelled it—"daemon"—in this archaic way? There was no doubt that this was my scrawl, but were they my words? The idea of spirit writing, in which I did not believe, insinuated itself once again in my mind. And the "miller"—could this be Blake's "Miller of Eternity"? And who was "the lady"? Or what was "the lady"? And what, or whom, did this particular leopard represent?

And that phrase: "Awaiting glance in bowering shade." What

of that? Yes, leopards were given to lounging in quiet stealth on the boughs of trees. I had heard that this was what made the leopard so exceedingly dangerous. You could pass unawares beneath a leopard looking down on you from a great tree limb above you. But if by chance, distracted by a bird in the sky, or the sun receding or emerging from behind a cloud, or the first pale star of dusk, or anything that set the eyes to wandering upward, your glance met with the eyes of the leopard, in that instant the leopard would leap upon you and you would be dead. Your eye contact, though inadvertent and brief, would not be suffered by the leopard even in its most lulled and sated quietude. This was why, by comparison, lions were such easy game. They lay hidden in path-side gullies, and hunting guides tossed stones lazily into those gullies until one of them hit a lion, which would instinctively rise and run, an easy target for the shot. Leopards, however, did not run, and if in coming upon one, your glance met the glance of the leopard, you were no longer the hunter but the prey, and you would be dead before you had the slightest chance to raise your gun. Your first trembling of fear would be your last.

I looked up "bowering" in the *Oxford English Dictionary*. Bowering, embowering. Participial adjective of "bower," to enclose or shelter in leafy covert, or in seclusion overarched with the branches of trees.

I was a leopard awaiting glance in bowering shade.

I didn't want my milk to get warm. Sometimes I wondered why I even took the Valium. I felt nothing from them. I once had told this to Dr. Yanoff, seeking something stronger to relax me. He said that the Valium did have an effect on me; it was just not a drastic one that I was conscious of. But still I wondered about this. There had been times when I had taken as much as eighty milligrams over the course of a day and a night, while drinking wine, and still nothing. I had come to more or less believe that it was the ritual, not the drug, that relaxed me: the Valium and the cold milk taken together in respite. I no longer took one of those ten-milligram pills without being able to sit awhile in peace with my cold milk afterward.

Ritual. To replace habit with ritual was good. Everything a Eucharist. But still I hoped this baclofen I was taking would prove more than ritual.

Awaiting glance. I had been like that for years. The dread of eye contact. The dread of physical contact, of any physical intimacy. Somehow, as the years had passed, these had become anathema to me. But now it was over.

Then I thought of my eyes as they were now. I thought of the way Lorna looked into my eyes. I took a drink of milk. I lit a smoke. I thought of Lorna on the cross.

I called for the results of my blood tests. "I don't know how you did it," the croaker said over the telephone, "but your A1Hc is down to seven-point-six. It was ten-point-three last time."

A reading of seven-point-six on this glycohemoglobin test that measured the average level of sugar in the blood over the course of the previous three months was, I knew, only one-point-six percent over the upper end of the non-diabetic range. Even my diabetes was being cured, I thought, and not by any fucking hypocrite, Avandia-prescribing endocrinologist either. *How did I do it?* I felt like saying. *By turning into a fucking god, that's how.*

"Your vitamin D is low. I want you to take a thousand units a day."

"You've had me taking a thousand units a day for the past year," I said. "Take two thousand," he said.

I told him I would. And, like a fool, I probably would.

"And there's some occult blood in your stool."

"Where's it coming from?"

"The test can't show that."

"Is it red or black?"

"The test doesn't show that, either."

"It's probably my hemorrhoids. I've been bleeding out of my ass for the last forty years."

"I'd like you to come back in June for a colonoscopy so we can see what's what."

"Another one? I just had one last November."

"You haven't had a colonoscopy in two years," he said.

"It was last November. Remember, the prep didn't work, and I had to have it done twice."

"Right, we did it twice. But that was two years ago."

I wasn't going to argue with this guy. I wasn't going to tell him that I trusted my memory, not his. In any case, June was a way off, so I figured he didn't think it was anything serious. If he did, he would have wanted me to come in right away.

"And I don't know what this is," he said, "but your blood seems different."

"What do you mean?"

"Your blood test. All your blood. It doesn't really seem to be your blood type. It doesn't really seem to be any stable blood type."

"What do you mean?"

"Your blood type is A. But now it seems you've got some B glycoproteins mixed in with the A."

"What's that all about?"

"It's like you're an A becoming an AB."

"Does that happen a lot?"

"Well, it did somewhere along the line. First there was O. Then about twenty thousand years ago some people evolved into type A's. Then about ten thousand years later, other people evolved into B's. Then some A's and some B's mixed and eventually their glycoproteins merged and produced the last of the four blood types, AB."

"So it's a natural sort of thing?"

"It was natural over the course of twenty thousand years of procreation. Not spontaneously, not in a few months."

"So it has to be a mistake by the lab."

"We'll see."

"What's the difference between A and AB?"

"AB's a lot less common. Type O's called the universal donor. No matter what blood type, anybody can accept O."

"What do you mean, 'accept'?"

"A transfusion, say."

"And what's that have to do with type AB?"

"Well, AB is the universal acceptor. It accepts any and all of the four blood types."

"So that's not a bad thing?"

"I've just never seen anything like it before, an A developing AB characteristics. Never seen it, never read of it, never heard of it."

I knew it. All blood was mine. It was part of my rebirth. Twenty thousand years of spinning life cycles in the time it took to smoke a cigarette. Out of the cradle endlessly rocking. Every beat of my heart and pulse brought procreation, new life to a new me. Only lesser beings were born but once. Re-procreation. Was that a word? It was now. Talk about virgin birth. Talk about parthenogenesis. Talk about agamogenesis. Talk about fucking ham and eggs. I wanted Lorna on that cross right now, that Virgin Mary juice of hers drizzling to the floor. I wanted that fucking whip in my hand right fucking now.

There was a lot that the croaker had never seen, never read about, never heard about. A lot that the croaker did not know and never would. I told him I'd see him in a few months. Maybe I would, and then again maybe I wouldn't. I was pro-choice. My body, my bankroll. We'd see what Paeon advised. Otherwise happy fucking Passover and *a mise meshune.*

Inspiration came while I stroked my cock, ate almonds and cashews, and thought of Lorna spread-eagled on her cross.

I went to the hardware store on Chambers Street, then over to Weinstein & Holtzman on Park Row. I walked north, zigzagging in a wider and wider range, until, at a surplus joint on Sixth Avenue in the teens, I found what I wanted.

Heavy, rough three-quarter-inch raw-strand Manila rope. I bought seven yards and had it cut into five equal lengths of a little over four feet each. Enough of that cop shit, those cuffs and those leg irons, I thought. Tonight we were doing it the old-fashioned way.

I shelled and skinned a bunch of fava beans, the first of the season I had seen. This was always a time-consuming chore, a real pain in the ass, but it was worth it. I chopped up some pecorino Romano, put the pieces in a bowl with the fresh beans, poured in some olive oil, and ground in some black pepper. I cut into chunks what remained of the cheese, wrapped them in slices of tasso pork, and tossed them onto a paper plate. I sliced a red pear and put that on the plate as well. I took it all to the couch and feasted slowly. There might be a lot of hours, I figured, between now and that Shun Lee delivery that would come only after the crucifixion and the flogging and the wonders that followed.

It was still light out when I arrived at her place, but the dark soon set in, and that dim red glow from behind the black curtain became more pronounced. She made some coffee. She told me about her day, I told her about mine. She went off to her bedroom for a few minutes, then emerged before me in her see-through raincoat. In the room where the red light cast its hue, she began to fix the iron to her left ankle.

"No," I said, "wait."

She had seen the bulky plastic bag I had brought with me, eyeing it curiously but saying nothing. Now she watched as I withdrew the first length of rope from it. I hunkered down, wrapped it round the ankle she had been about to shackle, pulled tightly, knotted it, and with the two long end lengths, bound her leg with not much slack to the lower left lag of the cross. Removing a second length from the bag, I wrapped it round her other ankle, pulled tightly, knotted it, and with the two long end lengths, bound her leg with not much slack to the lower right lag of the cross. Then, with another length, and another, her wrists. I turned her head to the side and kissed her. Slipping my tongue from her mouth, I saw that it remained open. Her eyes were softly shut. I took a segment of the last length of rope between my hands and brought it taut to her open mouth, then wound the rope round her head so that a second thick mouthful of it further widened and filled that sweet open mouth. I tied the rope tightly at the nape of her neck. I stood back, looked at her, and stroked my cock. Her skin was already beginning to redden near where the harsh pricking bristles of the rope dug into her. This reddening was noticeable even in the diffuse red of this room. I stuck my hand under the raincoat and brought it to her cunt, to see if the rough piercing rope made her wet. I felt her moisture, wondered what of it came from anticipation and what of it came from the rope.

I took the blacksnake whip, encoiled it, held the coil between my hands. With fast hard movements, compressing the coil with a jerk of my hands and quickly jerking it wide again, I was able to produce a series of muted crackling sounds. From the swooning-ripe cries that barely escaped her rope-filled mouth, I knew that these sounds excited her. My first cast of the whip was tentative—I could not straightaway recapture the movements to which my previous wielding of this whip had led me—but it struck her, lightly, across her back with a soft smack of leather on vinyl, to which she seemed to react as if being teased by a touch of foreplay that, instead of pleasantly arousing her, brought her to the pitch of torment of overwhelming, unrelieved passion. Slowly it came back to me, the physics of it all, and, with increasing strength and accuracy, I gave it to her, harder and then harder, until her rainy juices trickled to the floor and her long, lithe limbs strained and shook, and her hair flung to and fro with the wild movements of her head.

I could see the faint markings on one of her buttocks and the back of one of her thighs where I had opened her skin on my prior night in this room. How wonderful it would be, how wonderful for both of us, I thought, if I could reopen those very same lash lines. I exposed her bare flesh as I previously had done, raising the little raincoat and bunching it above her hips. I aimed carefully, but the tip of the whip struck wide of those marks, slashing instead her other upper thigh. I fixed my eyes on the slash, which was like a thin crescent of color on her pale, pure flesh; and in an instant I saw the blood begin to flow.

Approaching her with my cock hard in my hand and my heart beating hard in my chest, I found myself wondering for the merest moment what type of blood it was that ran down the back of her thigh. Damn, the shit these croakers put in your head. Kneeling, I placed my tongue to the back of her knee, that bend so lovely and so soft where the blood was about to reach. I felt it meet my tongue, and I slowly raised my head, licking the ever-increasing flow of her blood, feeling the quivering of her hamstring muscles, until, as I clutched her other leg, my tongue came to the seeping crescent high on her thigh. With my mouth wide, I sucked and I drank and I closed my eyes and reveled until I could feel the blood descending in a thin stream to my chin. I braced myself, rose, and lay hard against the slight incline of her back. I thought of deflowering her like this, as she remained bound and defenseless on the cross beneath my weight. It could be beautiful. It could also destroy her. Beauty and destruction were often one in nature. The vast towering ocean waves of onrushing cataclysm, the wild rising flames of conflagration, the earth-shaking cracking open of the earth. The eye of the leopard. I stuck the fingers of one hand into her cunt, and with my other hand I greased my cock with her running blood. I brought the swollen blood-greased head of my cock to her ass, and I shoved myself into her, feeling the sudden severe spasm of her body and pulling back on the abrasive rope at the nape of her neck as I did so.

Just months before, my cock would have been too limp to slam and fill that cranny. But I was young again. More than that, I was an ithyphallic god, a force of flesh and of deeds, a bringer of fates. It felt great. I exploded inside her almost instantly.

We showered together. There was surprisingly little blood, but we lathered and rinsed each other slowly and luxuriously. I saw that there were tiny spots of blood on her lips, mostly at the corners of her lips, where the rough bristlings of the rope bit into her. She said little, and in an untelling voice. But then she hugged me closely as the warm water fell upon us. The lingering human weakness within me had brought me unease and doubt about what I had done to her. The tender clinging closeness of her hug showed me that my lingering human weakness must be left behind. A god can do no wrong, no matter what he does. I had not done anything to her. I had done something for her.

We shampooed each other. The back of her neck, beneath where her hair fell, looked sore and raw, and there were a few tiny spots of red there as well. We dried each other with the same plush towel. I wished I had pajamas to get into. It was not warm enough for just my skivvies, and I did not want to dress again, though I did. I had not slept at the home of another for more than fifteen years, but I would have slept there on that night. The blessed serene drowsiness was coming upon me. When she emerged in her robe, with vitamin E on her lips, I took her mobile telephone from the couch, placed it in her hand, and had her order enough Chinese food for a small family of wolves.

In my blissful, becalmed state, I tasted and delighted in what I ate as others could not. To prolong and deepen my pleasure, I used chopsticks instead of a fork. We spoke comfortably, with slow ease, as we ate likewise and randomly from the various containers we shared. She said that she felt like hearing music that was very tranquil and very lovely, more so than anything she could think of. Arvo Pärt's *Alina* came to my mind, and I told myself that I must have her hear it when she spent the night at my place, and I knew that she would come, soon, to spend the night. There was no cross, but it was so very close to where she worked; and I wanted so very much to have her there, in my living room and in my bed.

She spoke a little about what was going on at her job these days, the stupidity of drawing up a detailed budget for a project that did not and never would have the money to remotely bring any meaning to it.

"Sounds like the government," I said.

"Sort of like working for the government, too," she said. "Especially these days. Imagine doing bookkeeping for dreams and lies. They don't teach that at business school." She chewed awhile, made a very satisfied little sound. "Though these days they probably should."

"Why didn't you become a model? You know you've got the looks for it."

"Too short a career span. Plus, regardless of looks, it's a long shot. There are a lot of models out there walking around broke and desperate for work who look just as good or better than the ones pulling down big money." She paused, and then spoke again as if sharing a secret. "Besides, to tell you the truth, I wanted to be an actress. I wanted to be a movie star. I went for an audition once, and I never went for another. I think what I really wanted was to escape from my life into a dreamland. It didn't work. It couldn't ever have worked. I didn't have it in me. Business school I had in me. Barely. And that just got me deeper into what I wanted to escape from."

I had heard her speak honestly before. Very honestly. But not with such nonchalance.

"It's like that obsession with the scars. It's like wanting an unblemished outside to hide the damage that's inside. Like hiding it might make it go away, like the one might cancel out the other. That's the thing about escaping into a fake world, the thing about keeping the poison in a pretty little cloisonné box. All the same thing." She looked at me. "If that makes any sense."

"It makes a lot of sense, what you're saying. It makes even more sense that you're seeing it," I said. "You have to know the prison before you can break out of it."

"That all I want to do. I mean, not know the prison. That hurts. What I mean is break out of it. Blow it up behind me. Be free."

"You will, baby. The way you're talking, the way you're doing. You will."

"I hope you're right," she said. "Sometimes I think I like to suffer."

"Well," I said, as lightly as I could, "there aren't too many girls I know who have their own crosses."

"Oh, that," she said, dismissing my words as if they had been said out of innocence or ignorance or both. "That's not what I'm talking about. That's not suffering to me. That's pleasure. It gets me off. We're all fucking perverts, if not in our own eyes, then in the eyes of the person next to us. So I'm a fucking pervert. What's that old Grateful Dead song? 'I'm a thief and I dig it.' Yeah, well, I'm a pervert and I dig it. We don't burn witches anymore. We burn perverts."

"I think that was the Band, 'I'm a thief and I dig it.' I forget what song."

"Remember that guy a few years ago? That guy who covered British royalty for CNN? That guy with the breathless gay, gay royal grin? He got busted one night at four in the morning in Central Park with a noose around his neck tied to his balls, a dildo in his trunk, and a bag of meth in his pocket? Remember him? I can't remember his name. Richard something, I think. But remember that?"

I did remember something like that a few years back. The guy she was talking about was back, covering royal gossip again for that stupid so-called news network. I had seen that oh-so-happy face of his the other day on one of the televisions behind the bar on Reade Street.

"Yeah," I said. "I remember that."

"He's my hero," she said.

"Why not?" I shrugged and smiled. "If you're going to have a hero, why not him? Better him than a bunch of asshole cops. Yeah, better him than the cops who busted him."

My words, which were sincere, seemed to make her happy, and she dug with glee into a container of lobster. It was good to see her like this.

"I still want to see you whip yourself," I said. "With that crop, like you told me about. I still want to see that."

"I'm feeling pretty mellow and blissed-out right now," she said. "Maybe next time."

"That's what you said last time."

"You've got to remember before we start getting it on, before you take the whip."

"But then I'd come and wouldn't feel like whipping you."

"You'd like to see it that much?"

"Yeah, I would."

Still chewing her lobster, she stood and went into the dim-glowing red of the other room. She came out with the crop. She removed her robe and placed it on a chair. She faced the wall opposite me, and, supporting herself against it with her left arm and outstretched hand, she reached round the shoulder of that supporting arm with the crop that was held by her right hand, caressing the area beneath her shoulder blade with the little leather loop at the tip of the crop. These caresses were slow and seductive.

As quietly as I intently unzipped my pants and drew out my cock, she must have heard it, for she then immediately stopped the caressing movements and struck herself hard with a strong fast flex of her wrist. There was a startling snapping sound, and I then knew why that little leather loop at the rat-tail end of the whip was called a popper. She did it again. Then again. I watched her back flush as she thrashed. She turned her head as far as she could over her right shoulder to watch the self-lashing, the cracking of the whip on her own back.

"You're naked," I said. My cock was in my hand, which I began to move faster. "What about the scars?"

"Fuck the scars," she said. It was a sort of low, loud whisper that emerged from heavy, quickening breath.

I saw the scar on her thigh where I had opened her. I looked at all of her. I watched and heard the raising and striking of the crop, faster and faster, harder and harder, as her breathing likewise grew faster and faster, harder and harder. I went into the other room, got the biggest of the whips. I approached her from the right, out of range of the cropping. My cock was still hard, and I took it in my hand again as I worked the thick leather handle of the big whip into her cunt. There was a gasp, a final violent snap of the crop, and she loosened and seemed as if about to fall just as the whip handle fell from her unclenched cunt and my semen struck the salved scar on her thigh. Moving my hand back and forth, I spread the semen with the softening head of my cock over the scar and the surrounding area of her thigh, feeling the smooth oiled flesh, the smooth and warmer bare flesh. There was a single drop of blood beading on her back. I sucked it into my mouth. An even smaller droplet followed. I placed two semen-smeared fingers to it, then placed the fingers to her lips, which opened to take the fingers into it and suck them clean.

I washed and dried my hands, rubbed lotion on her back. She wanted to kiss me. My semen, her blood, her saliva. Fuck it, why not? She moved her tongue on mine, slowly withdrew it, and our lips met gently. As she put on her robe, I kissed the slight rise of her sweet small breast.

She looked to me like a tall, thin sylvan deity. A hamadryad, a wood nymph, a beautiful maiden and indwelling spirit of the trees. I thought of the frail tawny oak leaf that had appeared to me with the last breath of winter, the first breath of spring, the oak leaf I had imagined drifting over the sea waves of time, thousands of years, from ancient grove to the here and now of my windowsill. Balanos. Yes, maybe Balanos, hamadryad of the oak. Daughter, one of eight, of Hamadryas, the holy mother whose name was given to the hamadryas baboon of Asia Minor. The spirits of the wood nymphs were said by many to inhabit individual trees, and when a tree died or was killed, so was the nymph-spirit that lived in it. I thought of the mystical exquisiteness of the petrified blue handle of the big knife.

Dead monkeys. Dead oaks. Dead virgin nymphs.

But now was a time for life, a time for life ever new. I helped her on with her robe. We returned to the Chinese food, as if to a movable feast that awaited us at every pause for rest on an enchanted journey. My lassitude was wondrous. Every bite of food, though no longer hot, was sublime with orchestrally nuanced satisfaction, and the presence and soft sleepy voice of Lorna beside me enwrapped that sublimity in pure and peaceful happiness.

I was falling asleep. She invited me to spend the night. But I needed to fall full into this alluring sleep in my own bed, in the smoky air of the endless breath, my own breath, where for so long I had lived as if dead and where I now lived as if entering true life for the first time. Words passed through my mind as I held her and kissed her good-bye: "We are the breakers of our own hearts." But I was too tired to say them, and they probably needed not to be said, for I felt that she was very near to knowing this herself. Words did come from my mouth, but they were only three and whispered: "I love you."

I whispered those words again as sleep overtook me in my bed, but I did not know to whom or to what I whispered them.

THE CROAKER WHO RELUCTANTLY GAVE ME THE BACLOFEN had given me a prescription for forty-five ten-milligram pills. The prescription, which could be refilled only twice, stated that I was to take half a tablet three times a day for thirty days. And that is what I had been doing.

Dr. Ameisen had called from Paris some days ago and left a message for me saying that he was calling only to see how I was doing with the baclofen. His compassion impressed me greatly. I knew how busy he was, and while there was not a penny to be made from me, he showed more concern for me than the doctors who were shaking me down without barely bothering to know me. I had meant to call him back, but it was always too late in the day when I thought of doing so, and with the six-hour time difference, I didn't want to bother him at night. It was early afternoon when I dialed his number, and I heard his voice.

"I've been taking the baclofen for about two weeks now, maybe a little longer," I told him.

"And how do you feel?"

I told him that I felt no different.

"You still experience desires to drink? You don't feel less anxiety?"

"I feel no difference," I repeated. I was not about to tell him of the increasing sense of well-being that my new life was bringing me. I was not about to talk about this with any doctor. Though

I knew of no reason not to, I felt that there might be a reason of which I was not aware, or that a reason for regretting my honesty might arise in the future. So I remained guarded. I answered Olivier's questions only so far as they related to my alcoholism and my yearning to be rid of it.

"How much are you taking?"

"Five milligrams three times a day. Fifteen milligrams a day."

"No, no, no," he said. "That is what you're supposed to take for only the first day or so. Fifteen milligrams a day can have no effect on anyone. As I explained in my book, you should have increased the dose to thirty milligrams a day after the first day or so. And if thirty doesn't work, you increase again."

He went on to express exasperated disappointment that my doctor had not read or prescribed according to the case studies, medical papers, and abstracts reproduced in his book's appendix.

I told him that I would immediately stop splitting pills and increase the dosage from five to ten milligrams three times a day, but each of the two refills of forty-five tablets would then last me only fifteen days, or altogether only a month, even if I did not need to increase the dosage again; and I had doubts that the doctor would give me more plentiful prescriptions with more plentiful refills.

"Ask him to cite one single incidence of reported side effects from baclofen at higher dosages. He will not be able to do so, because there is none."

"But what if he refuses to increase the prescription? How will I get what I need without going through a lot of trouble?"

"If you were in Paris, I could treat you. A lot of doctors here could. The amount of baclofen being prescribed has risen greatly in Europe and it continues to rise. But in America there is ignorance and resistance."

The hydra of addiction was big business, big money. Baclofen was not.

"I'll start taking the ten milligrams three times a day," I said. "If this doctor won't give me what I need, I'll get new doctors."

"Increase the dosage," he said, "then in a few days let me know how you feel."

Again he impressed me. If other doctors even bothered to ask you about the effects of a medication that you had recently begun taking, they waited until your next paying visit.

I made up my mind to visit the nearby storefront Hindoo croaker, let him stick his finger up my ass, and see how he sat with giving me the sort of baclofen prescription I needed, as well as the Valium. And I would take a stroll through Chinatown to see how I fared with the doctors there.

And, yeah, I would schedule that colonoscopy with my internist. That would be a good opportunity to get things settled with him, one way or the other.

What, really, was this thing with the Valium anyway? The more I thought about it, the less sense it made. I was convinced that I felt no different, no better and no worse, with it or without it, before or after taking it. Wouldn't the glass of cold milk, without the Valium, suffice as ritual enough?

My friend Peter Wolf had pulled into town from Boston for a few days, and we rendezvoused at the bar on Reade Street. I had my container of coffee, he had a cup of tea. It struck me that, though neither of us was drinking, our talk was no different than if we had swilled so much jive-ass small-batch whiskey that we could no longer tell the difference between it and Old Crow and were still at it hard and heavy.

We went on and on about just about all there was to go on and on about, from rereading Faulkner's "A Rose for Emily" to Indian casinos to whether there was a feminine form of the word "Messiah" to the difference between how Bob Dylan played harmonica in the key of G by simply using a G harmonica but the old blues guys played in the key of G by cross-playing a C harmonica in the second position. At one point we landed on my affinity for Valium.

I was surprised to hear Pete say that he experienced unpleasant aftereffects from Valium, though I had heard this from others. Entering medicine-man mode, we discussed how Valium differed from Xanax. Pete believed that while both drugs were similar, the anxiety-quelling properties of Xanax were greater than those of Valium, which worked more as a muscle relaxant.

Our pharmacology was good. I trusted it. I figured that, after living with them for so many years, we knew more about our own bodies and brains than any croaker who got his knowledge from book learning.

I felt good after whiling away the afternoon with Wolf. Our talk was always good medicine. On top of still feeling the effects of my night with Lorna, and looking forward to my night, just hours away, with Melissa, I didn't need anything to relax my mind or body. I poured myself a glass of cold milk, took nothing with it, closed my eyes, and wandered.

Lorna. My willowy breeze. My darling sapling. What day was this? I had forgotten Palm Sunday. I had forgotten the full moon. The pear trees across from the bar on Reade Street were lush with white blossoms. Lorna. When was Easter? My willowy breeze, my darling sapling.

Lorna. I saw her cropping herself, sucking the blood and semen from my fingers. Rod of life and Lamb of God.

Beautiful hamadryad. The tree must not die, lest the spirit of the nymph die too.

The barracks. Those long, low two-family dwellings of white-washed wood and shingled roofing, built after the war in rows on every overgrown, weed-ridden, rat-ridden, debris-ridden vacant lot to provide cheap housing for the doomed, downtrodden victorious of god-knew-what from god-knew-where. At last we had people that we could look down upon. He lives in the barracks, our parents would say. The barracks all looked alike. Though they were newly constructed, by the time the curse of memory came to my childhood, they were all grayed, peeling, rotting, with roof shingles missing or hanging lopsided by single rusty nails.

The daughter of a family in one of those barracks was as healthy and as happy and as pretty a little thing as you could ever imagine. Her name was Karen and she was the first girl I kissed. We were three or four years old, all bundled up, sitting on a little sled on a snow-covered sidewalk, and for many years I had a photograph of this first kiss, one of those small old black-and-white pictures with the serrated white borders; and this always led me to believe that we were coaxed into this kiss by whoever it was who took the picture.

But most of the barracks-dwellers were not nice. They were bestial white trash from parts unknown, and they knew they were not wanted in the neighborhood.

The worst of them were the Fudgies. They lived a few blocks away. Their real name was something like LaForge or LaFurge, some fancy-sounding French shit, but if they were of distant French origin, they must have been some kind of homunculi descended from the first scumbag ever thrown into the Seine. Nobody called them the LaForges or whatever it was. Everybody called them the Fudgies.

The Fudgie I hated most of all was about twelve or thirteen when I was about four or five. Most of the Fudgies were ragpickers. I guess that with enough of them picking through garbage and selling what of it they could, they managed to put Fudgie food on the table to keep them going. The specialty of this particular Fudgie, the one I hated most, was old newspapers. He'd skulk around dragging this beat-up old red kiddie cart full of bundles of newspapers that always seemed befouled and soggy. Maybe they just seemed that way because they had come to be in the possession of a Fudgie. One day he was standing on the pavement chucking rocks up into the branch of a tree.

"What you doin'?" I asked him.

He looked down at me. "What's it look like I'm doin'?"

I looked up into the tree toward where he was throwing the stones. I saw a little bird nest.

"Got it!" he cried.

A little sparrow egg with a little baby sparrow splattered onto the street.

I was horrified. Growing up in an urban stinkhole, I was mesmerized and thrilled by every glimpse of nature that I came upon. A cocoon, a caterpillar, a monarch butterfly, a big black-winged butterfly, fireflies, a praying mantis, once even a walking stick, a bright red cardinal, a blue jay, a big strange-looking beetle, fat green tomato hornworms that found their way to every tomato plant that every old Italian woman planted in every available patch of earth, dandelions in the cracks of sidewalks and curbs, and every tree in every season. These were the beguiling beloved visitors from an enchanted world, a counter-world that I knew to be out there, that I spent hours lying on my back on pavements looking up at white clouds in blue skies envisioning and dreaming of escaping to. Now that even these little glimpses were no more to be glimpsed, I wondered what city children dreamt of escaping to that was not more dead and dire than where they already were.

That little splatter of egg and sparrow horrified me, and it angered me. If this Fudgie had not been more than twice my size and twice my age, I would have attacked him with intent to maim or kill. All the cursed lives of all the cursed Fudgies were as nothing compared to the life of the baby sparrow he had taken. I wanted to see a street splattered with Fudgies. They were a blight, and I hoped that they would die and go to hell. Especially this one. Maybe this is when I began to lose belief in God. How could God let the sparrow die and the Fudgie live? God was a Fudgie. Death to the Fudgies, and death to Him.

So I did not attack the Fudgie, as I should have, as I would have if God had not already poisoned me with fear and cowardice. Most likely I ran to my mother and cried, and tried without succeeding to tell why I was crying.

Not long after this, there he was again, with that rusted red kiddie wagon filled with newspapers, standing close to the same tree. In his hand was a big dirty butcher knife, with which he was stabbing into the tree with repeated downward thrusts. His face was contorted, which made him even more repulsive-looking than he already was. I saw that he had hacked through the bark and was now hacking with ugly grunts at the softer, milky inner cambium of the tree.

"What you doin'?" I asked him.

He looked down at me.

"I'm killin' this tree," he said.

I looked into the gaping splintered opening he was hacking with those violent downward thrusts of the butcher knife.

"Why you doin' that?" I asked him.

This time he didn't stop to look down at me.

"'Cause I want to," he said.

Twice my size, twice my age, and this time he had a butcher knife, too. Still, I should have attacked him. Still, I should have tried to gather up all that was within me and hack into him with his own stupid knife. But the fear with which that stupid spook-show God had poisoned me, that treacly blood of that sissy little Lamb, that coward Christ, was still in me. I probably ran again to my mother and cried, and tried without succeeding to explain what I was crying about.

Hubert Selby Jr. used to say that when he was a young man he had no choice but to believe in God, the old anthropomorphic God of his childhood. He had to, he said; and this was because the mad idea of grappling that fucking cocksucker of a God to the ground and fucking Him up the ass while beating Him—the *need* to do so—was all that was keeping him alive. God and the need to leave him raped and beaten on the ground were one. I loved Selby looking back and telling of this, and I understood what he was saying. But I myself had never felt anything of the kind. It was good enough for me to just turn my back on the whole cheap spook show and walk away. As far as I was concerned God and the Fudgies could go off together and fuck one another up the ass and procreate a new litter of Fudgies and true believers. They were one and the same. The Fudgies would inherit the earth, of which God was the rotten Jew landlord.

Years afterward, looking back at my later childhood and adolescence, I saw that most of the few acts of violence I committed were, no matter the victim, really directed at that Fudgie, who by then had vanished from the neighborhood but not from my mind. Maybe they were also directed a bit at that God who had vanished with him. Selby and I had a lot in common. Maybe more than I knew.

"Killin' this tree."

Beautiful hamadryad. The tree must not die, lest the spirit of the nymph die too.

Killing this tree.

Recalling his butcher knife, I thought of my own new magic-handled butcher knife: the gleam of its blade, the beauty of the petrified blue maple of its grip, imbued and imbrued with all the shades of all the skies of all the days and all the nights that ever were. A world apart, those butcher knives. A world apart.

I did not feel like getting up, but I did. I went into the kitchen, unfastened and opened the black case that lay on the counter, and stared awhile in the afternoon light at the magic handle and the gleaming blade.

Killing this tree.

Because I feel like it.

A world apart.

Killing this tree.

I nodded off, sitting upright on the couch. I dreamt that Lorna had a baby. A darling little baby girl that grew quickly into a darling little toddler. I cut her little throat and drank from her all her blood as she lay cradled silently in my arms. I was wakened by the doorbell.

Playing that night with some wide black silk ribbons that were in a box of gift wrapping I came across in a closet, Melissa and I discovered that we could control the flow of blood from her legs, increasing and decreasing it, by tying off one or two or more places on her thighs with these encircling ribbons, and could control it further and more subtly by tightening or loosening the ribbons in a variety of ways and to various degrees. A black-ribboned faucet-works of bloodletting.

We delighted for hours in our blood-play.

I untied all the ribbons and drank my fill, licking at her flesh between long, deep draughts. Warm and luscious, all of it: the soft, girlish flesh; the blood so fresh. My goddess lay beneath me and washed the blood from my lips with her tongue.

"But sweeter to live for ever; sweeter to live ever youthful like the Gods, who have ichor in their veins; ichor which gives life and youth and joy..."

Oh, so very, very much sweeter. So endlessly sweeter.

Casting aside a pillow and kneeling beside her, I wrapped my cock in her ponytail and began to slowly move my hand. I sensed her own hand in the dark between her legs. I clenched the fistful of her soft hair round my cock. I could now hear the motions of her hand on herself. The flounces of her body grew more intense, and I accelerated the thrusts of fists, hair, and cock until the tugging of her ponytail caused her head to jerk with the force of those thrusts; and her body arched in one great trembling, and we groaned with release together.

We lay there, close, like spent animal mates in a cave where the winds of the wild did not enter.

"I'm your whore," she whispered happily through lips that barely moved, "your dirty little whore."

Then something like the beginning of a faint laugh became and ended as a breath of sleep.

"No," I whispered, not knowing if her ears could hear me. "You're my goddess." A sound of contentment seemed to issue from her. "You're my beloved."

"Jst," I thought I heard her say, or try to say. But it was the exhalation of her breath alone that spoke. *"Jst."*

I was more than sated. I was glutted. My eyes were closed. I could not and I cared not to open them. And then I was fast asleep. If I dreamt, I remembered nothing. It was as if in the sheltering cave where we lay, so safely and so close, even dreams could not enter.

Sabled night became day. Melissa was already awake, showered, dressed, and drinking coffee when I woke, feeling like a great cat softly, slowly roused from rest by the fingers of the sun. Melissa was standing by the desk, holding her cup of coffee in two hands, looking down at the sheets of paper that lay there. I went to the kitchen and set some water to boil for my own coffee. She was still standing there, looking down. I kissed her neck. She did not respond.

"Where'd this come from?" she asked. Her voice was without its usual brightness.

I glanced down at the now familiar scrawled words—

Before that stirring I was a woman who spoke another tongue.

I was a leopard awaiting glance in bowering shade.

—and all the rest, without reading them. I don't even know why I glanced. Probably just to be sure which of the pieces of paper she was talking about.

"I wrote it," I said.

My voice possessed the brightness that was usually hers, the brightness hers now lacked. That spirit writing had no effect on me now. I felt only the effect of renewed life. I was sanguine and serene, at one with the morning and all that was good; vibrant with exuberance and strength.

"I don't remember writing it," I told her. "But I must have written it. I just found it there one morning. It's my handwriting. I just don't remember writing it. And I don't know what it means. It was very strange. One morning, there it was."

"When?" she asked.

"When what?" I was thinking about the water on the stove. I was thinking about how exquisite that cup of coffee would be.

"When did you write it?" There was an impatient urgency in her voice now. "When did you find it here?"

"I don't remember. A few months ago, something like that. Like I said, I just found it there one morning. It wasn't there and then it was. I must have written it in the middle of the night, then I must have forgotten about it; and then there it was."

"A few months ago?"

It was not impatient urgency that I heard in her voice. It was fear.

"Yeah, something like that."

"Before we met? After we met?"

"Right around then. Maybe a little before we met. Yeah. Maybe right before then. Why? What does it matter?"

Leaving her with my questions, I went into the kitchen and made my coffee. I sat down on the couch with it and lit a smoke. She had not moved from where she stood.

"And it doesn't mean anything to you? You don't know what it means?"

She spoke with her back to me. She looked great in her blue jeans.

"No, not really. Just crazy talk. Maybe it meant something to me when I wrote it. If it did, I forgot what it was, because it didn't mean anything by the time I found it there." I drank some coffee, drew some smoke. "Why?" I repeated. "What's the big deal?"

I looked out the window. Strange. It was getting dark. More rain? No. Very strange. It was dark as night.

I was shaken to see her turn. She was a leopard. On the floor, down on all fours, big and menacing. She opened her mouth wide, baring great sharp teeth, and with a deafening roar and claws extended, she leaped suddenly upon me and—it was all in a single fluid, terrifying instant, from her standing there to the wild killing weight upon me—I felt the claws and teeth sink into me and knew it was the end: the end of this single fluid, terrifying instant; the end of everything; and I screamed into the black of night but had no voice; and—

With a jolt, I woke in a cold sweat. I lay there, my eyes wide open, as my heartbeat settled.

I remembered nothing of what had horrified me so. I felt only good fortune and thanks that it had not been real. Then I felt only good. Yes, I was good. All was good. I could smell very clearly the scent of coffee.

Melissa was standing by the desk, a cup of coffee in two hands, looking down at the sheets of paper that lay there. I went to the kitchen and set some water to boil for my own coffee. She was still standing there, looking down. I kissed her neck. She did not respond.

"Where'd this come from?" she asked. Her voice was without its usual brightness.

I glanced down at the now familiar scrawled words—

> *Before that stirring I was a woman who spoke another tongue.*
> *I was a leopard awaiting glance in bowering shade.*

—and all the rest, without reading them. Yeah, yeah, enough already. I don't even know why I glanced. Probably just to be sure which of the pieces of paper she was talking about.

"I wrote it," I said.

My voice possessed the brightness that was usually hers, the brightness hers now lacked. That spirit writing had no effect on me now. I felt only the effect of renewed life. I was sanguine and serene, at one with the morning and all that was good; vibrant with exuberance and strength.

"I don't remember writing it," I told her. "But I must have written it. I just found it there one morning. It's my handwriting. I just don't remember writing it. And I don't know what it means. It was very strange. One morning, there it was."

This piece of paper, the words on it, which once frightened me, no longer did. Not now, not this morning.

"When?" she asked.

"When what?" I was thinking about the water on the stove. I was thinking about how exquisite that cup of coffee would be.

"When did you write it?" There was an impatient urgency in her voice now. "When did you find it here?"

"I don't remember. A few months ago, something like that. Like I said, I just found it there one morning. It wasn't there and then it was. I must have written it in the middle of the night, then I must have forgotten about it; and then there it was."

"A few months ago?"

It was not impatient urgency that I heard in her voice. It was fear.

"Yeah, something like that."

"Before we met? After we met?"

"Right around then. Maybe a little before we met. Yeah. Maybe right before then. Why? What does it matter?"

Leaving her with my questions, I went into the kitchen and made my coffee. I sat down on the couch with it and lit a smoke. She had not moved from where she stood.

With a wave of faintly disorienting presentiment, I felt as if I had been here before. Then I inwardly laughed at myself. Of course I had been here before, I told myself: I lived here.

"And it doesn't mean anything to you? You don't know what it means?"

She spoke with her back to me. She looked great in her blue jeans.

"No, not really. Just crazy talk. Maybe it meant something to me when I wrote it. If it did, I forgot what it was, because it didn't mean anything by the time I found it there." I drank some coffee, drew some smoke. "Why?" I repeated. "What's the big deal?"

No, not just been here before. Been here, in this very same moment, with this same cup of coffee and this same cigarette, in this same conversation.

I looked out the window. It appeared to be a lovely day. The sky was blue, the light of the sun was like that of soft-glowing hammered gold.

It was then that I remembered the dream that had wakened me with a current of panic.

Suddenly she moved. Putting down her cup of coffee near mine, she went to her big black shoulder bag.

"Because," she said. There was an edge of distress in her voice.

Digging into her bag, she took from it a small leather-bound journal and leafed through it in what appeared to be a great hurry for a minute or more. Then she stopped, stared down at one of its pages.

"Because," she said again. She brought the journal to me, held it out for me to take from her. As I did so, she pointed to one of the pages to which it lay open. "Here," she said. "Read this." The distress in her voice was more pronounced.

The entry was dated. As I began to read, she told me what I already knew by looking at the date: "That was about three weeks before I met you." She took her coffee and sat down beside me with a deep nervous breath as I read what was written:

"Weird dream. Couldn't move. Lost in the dark. Like a tunnel. Somebody spoke to me in a language I couldn't understand. He was dressed like an ancient Egyptian. Then I could understand him and I said something in the same language. Can't remember what we said. I had become somebody else. Then I wasn't anybody at all. I wasn't in the tunnel anymore. I was in a tree. High grass all around. I was a big leopard in a big tree. A lot of sun but a lot of shade. I felt sleepy. Where were my children? Then I was still a big leopard in a big tree but I was thinking like a human. I remembered kneeling by a river, a lake, an ocean, something, and praying. Then I was back in the tunnel again and I didn't know who or what I was. I began to move. I knew that if I moved I would get out of where I was. More like I was being moved. Very slowly. Floating very slowly. Toward some kind of light. And I was praying something again. Or chanting something. Or maybe just a voice inside me. I was moving so slowly I didn't have to breathe. I felt like I knew something that was more important than anything I knew. I forgot it but could remember it. Something about eternity. I understood eternity. Something like that. Can't remember. Then"—I turned the page—*"I felt something great start to embrace me. Like big arms or something. But soft. Like whatever I was float-*

ing in or through was comforting me. Then I felt the light would not be there and I wished I could get up. I wished I could get out of there because something I remembered about what I knew about eternity scared me. Something bad. Can't remember. Very weird dream. Didn't really turn into a nightmare but came close. Don't even know if I was really asleep or half asleep and just imagining. Weird!"

Then there were some mundane jottings about classes and clothes. I stared at what I had just read. Even in my state of well-being, grace, and strength I found it unsettling. I looked at her. I was at a loss for words. She apparently was too.

There had to be an explanation. I had written what I had written, what I must have written, and she had certainly written what she had written before each of us had known that the other existed. Yes, there had to be an explanation. But there was none.

"Are you sure you wrote what you did when you say you did?" she asked.

"I am very sure," I said. "And I'm very sure that I never saw what you wrote. The only time I ever looked into your bag was the time I wanted to see that Hesse book." Reverting to old habit, and also perhaps because of the unsettled abstraction I was experiencing, I said the name wrong. That did not matter. "And the only thing in that bag I ever snooped at was that suicide thing. That's the absolute truth. Even if I'm confused about when I wrote it— or, I should say, when it appeared on the desk that morning—I know there's no way it's connected to what you wrote."

"What do you mean: 'there's no way it's connected'?" Her voice rose. I realized too late that I had used the wrong words. "We had the same dream," she went on. "Or we experienced the same thing, the same vision, or whatever you want to call it. I wrote mine down in my journal. You, because you're some great fucking writer, wrote it down as some weird fucking poetry. But it's the same thing."

I said nothing. There was nothing I could say. I was about to say that I could not write as well as what was written on the sheet of paper on the desk, but I did not say it. I just sat there.

"This is *really* fucking weird," she said. "It gives me the creeps."

She took one of my cigarettes, put it in her mouth, and took a few drags before she spoke again:

"I mean, I don't believe in the supernatural or anything like that. At least I didn't think I did. But it's like..."

She obviously did not want to finish what she had begun to say. It was as if she did not want to hear herself say whatever it was she was thinking; as if giving voice to her feelings would make them more real, and as if she feared doing so. She finished smoking the cigarette in silence. Then very calmly she said:

"I think we're the same person." She took another cigarette and lit it. "The same soul. Whatever." She drew smoke, exhaled it. "I'm not talking about in any romantic sense. I'm talking about, like—boo! Two bodies, same person."

She looked to me, awaiting a response.

"Is that so bad?" I said.

"I don't know about 'bad,'" she said, her voice once again rising, "but it sure as hell scares the shit out of me." She inhaled. "It means that I'm talking to you but I'm really talking to myself. It means that I'm sleeping with you but I'm really sleeping alone. It means that you're sucking my blood but you're really sucking your own. No *way* I can get my mind around any of that."

As I listened to her, I felt that her thoughts were spinning dizzily out of control, that she was thinking herself into a kind of mental whiplash trauma. And as her thoughts spun more out of control, she expressed them more rapidly, skidding to a halt only to say:

"It means that when you die, that's when I die."

This was where I was impelled to speak. I knew that I was become a god, but I knew that I would remain always of partly human nature, mortality-bound, a demigod. I also knew that there was neither rhyme nor reason to whom and when death called. But I was more than forty years older than she, and I could not, would not have her believe that her life would end when mine ended.

"Now you're going crazy with this," I said. "Even if we are different parts of the same person, the same soul—not the same person, the same soul, as you're saying, but different parts of each other that we were lucky enough to find and reunite—we were born apart, at different times, in different places, and we'll die at different times. It's not like I was sitting around waiting for you to show up for forty years, and you didn't know I existed either. You're talking about some words on some paper, and you're getting all bent out of shape."

"I can't believe you." She slowly shook her head and dismally, hopelessly laughed. "You're sitting there with blood on your face, with a goddamn leopard skull on top of your television, and you're telling me that two people undergoing the same, experiencing the same, the same—the same whatever—at the same time without even knowing each other—you're telling me that this is normal."

"I didn't say that. What I said was—"

"Please go wash your face. Between you and that skull and all this leopard stuff—"

I got up, went and washed my face. She was right. It did look grisly.

"What I said was—" I did not know what I had meant to follow those words. I wished only that I had kept that piece of paper in the drawer. Not that it frightened me anymore. As I grew stronger and more serene, nothing did. But if I had kept it out of sight, she would not now know of my whatever-it-was—my experience, as she put it—and I would not know of hers. Ignorance was bliss. But we were in forfeit of that ignorance now. The strangeness of truth no longer surprised me or intimidated me. I wanted only to restore this morning to calm.

"Talk to me," she said.

"Do you believe in reincarnation?" I said.

"Right now I don't know what I believe in," she said.

"Well," I said, "a lot of the human population does. If you go outside of the big three Abrahamic religions—Judaism, Christianity, and Islam—reincarnation is central to all other major forms of religious belief. And even Sufi Muslims believe in it. Even those who dissociate themselves from religion foster ideas of it. The only religion, outside of ancient paganism, that ever struck me as being steeped in wisdom, rooted in it, is Ch'an Buddhism. 'When you meet the Buddha, kill the Buddha.' And you've got it there. They don't dwell on it, but it's there."

Did I know what I was talking about? Did it matter? What was that other one, that other great Ch'an proverb? There were a lot of them. "Those who seek for the Truth should realize that there is nothing to seek." A lot of them. "The teaching of the truth is not the truth." Yes, a lot of them. So let me speak of the truth.

"Maybe it's true. Maybe reincarnation is real. Maybe what a lot of people have always accepted is actually true. Maybe you and I crossed paths somehow before in different incarnations. Maybe what's so strange to us would be looked upon as completely natural by others. As a religious experience even. Maybe this shows us that reincarnation is real, and that sometimes we have obscure inklings of past lives."

"But the migration of souls isn't supposed to be the same funhouse for everybody. The Egyptian thing, the leopard—it's all the same for both of us."

She had me there. But what mattered to me was that she was becoming calm again, becoming her usual self again. Did I believe anything I had said? That was neither here nor there. All that mattered was that she, and this morning, were being restored and reclaimed.

"Do you know what really scares me?" she said, but she now spoke in a voice that was not scared. Serious, yes. Scared, no. "What really scares me is that this is the tunnel, this is the long dark passage. This is it now."

KEITH LOOKED GOOD. CLEAN, HALE, AND HAPPY. WE SAT in a back booth at the Minetta Tavern. I had known this joint now through three of its incarnations. I remembered the last days of the old place, which had been there since the late thirties. I remembered when Taka had it. My friend Cami and I had first encountered each other here in the days when Taka had it. I had just come back from Cyprus and my head was shaved. I was at the bar late one afternoon drinking a bottle of Amstel Light, which meant that I did not consider myself to be drinking at the time. And from out of nowhere came this big voluptuous redhead with a smile as open as the Colorado skies whence she had come, pointed at the bottle, told the bartender she'd have one of those, and introduced herself. We got to know each other pretty well. Even went to see the Doctor together one time. How many years had we known each other now? How many years since we met? Ten? Twelve? More? I couldn't remember. But she remained one of my most cherished friends. And now this new incarnation. It was the most upscale I had ever seen this place look. It was good that they had kept the old caricatures and stuff on the walls, retaining something of the spirit of the place going back more than seventy years.

"Maundy Thursday," said Keith offhandedly, as if about to begin a tale.

And so it was. Maundy Thursday. The Last Supper. We both studied the menu.

"Let's eat," I said, "for tomorrow the Crucifixion."

Keith ordered some ungodly-priced steak. I asked the waiter what made the Black Label Burger so different, at twenty-six bucks, from the Minetta Burger, priced at a mere seventeen bucks. When told that the twenty-six-dollar hamburger was made from a mix of dry-aged rib eye, skirt steak, short rib, and brisket, I went for it, along with an order of roasted bone marrow to start. To wash down the dead meat, a bottle of Chorey-les-Beaune 2006, a good red Burgundy that was better than a lot of the shit that glass-sniffing suckers paid ten or twenty times as much for.

Olivier had told me that one could drink while on baclofen, for one would then be drinking unbridled by the chemistry of craving and compulsion. Free of the snake in the alky's skull, so to speak. I had been taking thirty milligrams a day for a good time now. I was about to see if he was right, at least when it came to this alky's skull.

"To resurrection," I said, raising my glass.

"To resurrection," said Keith.

We talked about a lot of things. One night some years ago Keith had telescoped the history of rock 'n' roll into a rushing narrative that began with a certain classical composer, swept through the blues, the early years of rock 'n' roll, and ended with a crash in the midst of his own then-present circumstances. I had afterward forgotten the name of the classical composer, then thought I recalled it. Paganini. Seeking to confirm this with Keith, I had asked him if this was right. Confessing with a laugh that he himself had forgotten which composer he had been talk-ing about, it turned out that I remembered more of his narrative than he did. I had asked him several times since, and had long given up all hope that he would ever remember. Such a great and breakneck roller-coaster ride through time; and now with its starting point severed and forever lost to both the teller and the told. So the name of the forgotten composer had become a running joke of sorts.

"Heard any good Paganini lately?" I asked.

"I hear he's got a new one coming out."

"Speaking of new ones, did you ever finish that 'Just Because' thing?"

The last time I had seen him had been at a studio in the Flatiron district. "Just what the world needs," he had said with a laugh at himself. "Another song called 'Just Because.'" Sitting on a folding chair in the control room, in front of the control board, putting a pick in his mouth, then not removing it from his mouth as he played the electric guitar loudly over a loud playback of what he had previously recorded; the engineers, who had expected him to be in the empty studio that was prepared for him and not here in the control room, trying to record him on the fly, ending up with recurrent eruptions of distortion that bizarrely enhanced the noise of the guitar.

"One of these days," he said, "one of these days."

"What about the Hoagy Carmichael album? Are you ever going to decide it's done and release it?"

It was true. He must have been working on that album of Hoagy Carmichael songs for a dozen or more years now. It was great, what I had heard of it. But I was beginning to suspect that it might not ever see the light of day, that it would fall victim and be lost to some idea of impossible perfection that Keith had imposed on it.

"Why don't you write another book?" he flung back, as if to turn the tables on me.

"That's a good question."

He had a sly grin on his face that seemed to say: See, you already know the answers to what you're asking.

We raised our glasses again.

It was the best hamburger I ever fucking tasted. At least since that dive—what was the name of that place? May's?—on the outskirts of Tampa forty years ago, and I may have remembered that one only because I was starving at the time. It was the rib eye and the short rib fat that made it, I figured. If only all these fucking fancy-ass joints would stop serving the same bland shoestring French fries and start making some good old-fashioned steak fries again like they made in the best steak joints in France.

I was surprised a bit at how exceptionally delicious this hamburger tasted. The cheese and fruit I had eaten earlier in the day had none of the Eucharistic euphoria of taste that I had come to expect from the new wonders that enwrapped my senses. In fact, my serenity and my strength, as well as my heightened senses, had seemed to fade fast from me today. This struck me as very odd, especially as I had glutted myself for two nights in a row. Had what passed this morning with Melissa thrown me off more than I believed? Or was it something else? I had another sort of craving. After the last two nights, it made no sense.

Usually we ended up eating in a place that let us smoke. But this obviously wasn't going to be one of them, no matter how far in the back and hidden away from other customers we were, no matter who the fuck Keith was. We went outside to have a cigarette. Standing against the brick wall on the Minetta Street side of the corner, Keith watched a young man carrying a guitar case pass nearby on MacDougal Street.

"I wonder if that thing's empty," he mused.

We strolled a few steps down the street and turned in to Minetta Lane. Beyond the light that hung from the corner post, the short narrow passage that wound out of sight at the next bend was dark and quiet. Keith voiced a line of doo-wop into the night air, as if testing the acoustics.

"Did you ever drink blood?" I asked him.

"A bit here and there through the years, I imagine. Mostly my own. Swigging from crystal I'd cracked with my previous swig." He cast another line of doo-wop into the air, then looked me directly in the eyes. "Why?"

I looked directly back at him, in a way that said: You already know the answer to what you're asking.

He let the silence of my response pass before he spoke again.

"You'd better be careful, mate," he said, as if advising the devil on a chess move.

"In which way?"

"I've seen it. From what I saw, kicking it makes kicking smack look like a frolic in the daisies."

I laughed. "Why would anybody ever want to kick it?"

"I hope you never find out why," he said. "The few I knew who tried didn't really survive to tell me. But I saw them. I saw it."

"And what did you see?"

"The worst," he said.

"And what was that?"

He seemed to be measuring his words, thinking them out before saying them. This was not like him. His was an eloquence that usually flowed quite naturally.

A couple of tourists spotted him. The girl asked him if it was all right if the guy took his picture. Keith looked at the guy.

"You're the one with the camera," he said.

A few more people spotted him. We made our way back into the restaurant. A waiter poured the last of the wine into our glasses. Keith leaned forward.

"Here's the way it is," he said. The easygoing man I knew was gone. His familiar grin and laughter, and all the traits of his manner of talking, were not those of the man who leaned toward me with long fingers on the stem and foot of the wine-glass before him. "The way it is," he said, "is you've got to turn around now, while you still can. Go any further and there's no turning back."

"And what makes you think I still can turn back?" I asked him.

"You've still got those fucking pinwheels firing away in those fucking eyeballs of yours, that's what," he said. "Once those die out, you're done."

"And what were you talking about outside? What was that about 'the worst'?"

"I've seen it."

The thumb and one long finger of his other hand were now tapping a cigarette on the cloth-covered tabletop.

"I've seen men, what was left of them anyway, screaming for death."

The wine undrunk, the cigarette unsmoked, the words unsaid. The wine to soon be drunk, the cigarette to soon be smoked; the words to soon be said.

"I've seen things *come out of them.*"

He said these last four words in a slow spondaic cadence.

"What do you mean: 'come out of them'?" I asked. "What sort of things?"

"I've seen it. Once in London. Once in Paris. And even I can barely believe it. That's why I've never spoken of it. No one would believe me. But you, mate—right now—are in a very good position to believe me.

"I don't know what it was that came out of them. I don't want to know what it was."

"And what about those 'things'?" I said. "Are they still around?"

"You know, I wonder about that at times. I do." He raised his glass by the stem, and a trace of that familiar grin returned. "Here's to some things remaining beyond our knowing."

I raised my glass to touch his.

"May you live forever," I said, "and may I never die."

We drank.

There was not a fiber of me that believed what he said. Not that he was speaking falsely. He was not. But he was confused in what he was talking about. He had to be. Whatever he had seen, he had seen. What he had understood it to be, or misunderstood it to be, well, that was a different matter. True, I wondered what he had seen, once in London, once in Paris. But I knew he could not have seen men who had become like gods. Only his words about the tides of color in my eyes, his seeming recognition—no, it was not possible.

I walked with him diagonally across the street to where his car and driver waited. He offered me a lift, but I told him that it felt like a nice night for a walk. Which it did.

As I stepped toward Sixth Avenue, his car pulled to a pause beside me, and I heard his voice through the open rear window:

"Don't forget what we said, hey?"

I turned left on Sixth, figuring I'd walk down to Circa Tabac, stop off awhile, then walk on home. I didn't want another drink. Maybe the baclofen was working. Maybe godlike men, by nature, were not drunkards. But I was restless. And there was the other craving, odd as it struck me to be in the wake of the previous two nights. So I would look and lust awhile. It would do me good. I put on my shades.

There was Lee.

"Nicky," he said.

"Lee," I said.

"What's up?" he said.

"I just ate the best hamburger I ever ate," I said.

"Tell me about it," he said.

So I told him about the hamburger. The bite of the fresh lemon in the club soda tasted good, refreshing. I lit a cigarette.

Looking into the plumes of smoke as they vanished into the air, I found myself to be thinking of my little ebony-handled knife, wishing I had it with me, feeling for the first time that it should be with me, that it belonged in my jacket pocket as much as money belonged in my trouser pocket, that I was as uncomfortable without it as I would be without money, even if I had no need to use that money.

Then I saw her. The hair was different, shorter. But it was her. Yes, the fair Sandrine, who liked to be raped after bathing in warm water and milk and brushing out her hair. She was with a girl, a comely dark-haired girl, who looked even younger than she.

I approached them. I wanted to see if this Sandrine remembered me. I had been with her twice. She had put magic in my hands and mouth on those winter nights. For me, there would be no forgetting her. But had she forgotten me?

"How have you been?" she asked. "It's been awhile."

"You cut your hair," I said.

There was distaste in me for myself when I said this. How could I stoop to such banal small talk? It had no place in my resurrected life. Gods had no need of this sort of thing, which defined the evasive, meaningless speech of men and women who lived dishonestly on a low plane. As I thought this, I smiled at the girl who was with her. Sandrine introduced us as I stole a glance at the attractive knees and lower thighs that peeked from under both their skirts. I wanted them, both of them, then and there.

"Marie and I grew up on the same street. She's in town for the week with her parents."

I said nothing. If I was not going to tell them that I wanted them, I would not resort to further small talk in place of telling them that I wanted them. I would be still unless spoken to. I wondered at how young this Marie looked. I wondered at how young and lovely Sandrine looked. I could almost remember the feel and taste of her. I wondered what the other one felt and tasted like. I imagined bringing my mouth to their bared knees. I imagined swiping the narrow sharp blade of the *tosu* across those knees as they sat there. I stood there smiling, unhearing of them as they spoke lightly to me, while I imagined these things. Then I felt Sandrine's touch.

"Nick's a writer," she said to her companion.

"Oh, great. How cool is that? Anything I would know?"

It was better that I was unhearing of them. It was better that it was not the vapors of their mind that I wanted.

"I doubt it," I said. "What's the last book you read?"

"Oh, um, stuff for school."

"Can you name the last book you read?"

"Oh, what's his name, the, um, the guy that wrote—"

"Maybe you could recommend something she should read," Sandrine suggested.

"Nah," I said. "It's bad for the eyes. Just keep doing what you're doing."

There was suddenly a scent in the air, tallowy and vaguely acerbic, like that of a candle being snuffed. It seemed very real and very disagreeable, as if the unseen vaporing wick of an unseen extinguished candle were being passed beneath my nostrils.

The scent subsided, then returned, more complex, more unpleasant. Singed hair, burnt flesh. The quenched candle. The smells of vile sacrifice.

"Are you all right?"

It was Sandrine. She sounded far away.

"Are you all right?"

Her again, sounding even farther away.

I excused myself, or thought I did. Unsteadily, I made my way to the men's room. The sickening commingled scents followed me. I sat down. Had the wine affected me? I had drunk so little, but it had been so long. Could the wine have acted adversely with the baclofen? It was not supposed to.

My head and heart throbbed. My left hand shook violently. Is this what a blood-pressure attack is like? I asked myself. Is this what a heart attack is like?

It was Melissa. Words without voice. The remains of a tenth-century temple to a goddess existed on the outskirts of a town in France. What goddess? A name that defied memory. It was made clear to me, then it was gone. The mythic one. She of the legends. Tenth century? Twelfth century? It was made clear to me, then it was gone. What town? It was made clear to me, then it was gone.

The moisture in the soil where the statue was found is good. The hydration capacity is something like fifty percent per square meter. Capacity? Pressure? Level? It was made clear to me, then it was gone. Fifty? How many? Percent? Units? It was made clear to me, even converted for me to fractional parts per square foot, then it was gone.

What did this mean? It meant that I must bring forth the words. I must set them down. The soil is good. The soil is moist. The soil can sustain much water, much nourishment. The soil can give much nourishment.

But the words come too fast. They come to me, then they are gone. I tell Melissa I must go before the words rush through me and flee me and are forever gone; for many words come, and from each of them pour many more, and from each of these, many more, and they spill through my grasp.

Words are set down, but then I cannot read them, or they are gone. To where? They are set down. I go out into the night on the outskirts of the town many times, and I encounter many strange people, all of whom seem to know me, and I see many strange things—why is the weight of the mere head of this serpent that has turned to stone so much heavier than the whole of this identical serpent that has turned to stone?—and these venturings calm me; and the cappuccino in this place is good, and the man who gives it to me smiles to me as if we have been friends for many years, though I do not recognize him; but I must return always to set down the words, the words that are from or about her, the mythic one, from or about she who is of the legends.

When I do return, I ask Melissa how long I have been gone, how long it has been since she has last heard from me. I cannot see her, she is not there, but she understands me, and she answers. "I do not know," she says. "Maybe a few hours, maybe a few years." This does not matter. All that matters is that the words are brought forth and set down.

I pray to a memory
I kneel before a weathered stele

All that matters is that the words are brought forth and set down: the words that are from or about she who is of the legends.

I utter the names of phantoms
I carry within me the soul of the savioress

And this time, how long into the night was I gone? A few hours, a few years.

I have written these words before. But now, from each of them, issue many more, and from each of these in turn, many more; and on.

And why is the weight of the mere head of this serpent that has turned to stone so much heavier than the whole of this identical serpent that has turned to stone? But I ask this only of myself, and there is no answer, as close as I can feel myself to be to one. Something to do with the insides of it.

How long had I been here? I felt like I was drenched in sweat. I rose, still unsteady, and left the men's room.

"Are you all right?"

Her again. The one called Sandrine. Why was she asking me this? These words, even her voice, were beginning to madden me. I needed air. Maybe a walk around the block. I left the bar.

I stood drinking water from the bottle that I kept at room temperature in the kitchen. I was feeling better. I seemed to remember taking a long hot shower when I got home. That must have done the trick. That and the sleep that followed it. How long had I slept? That didn't matter, I told myself. All that mattered was that I had rested. The water tasted good. I felt that I wanted to write, that I needed to write. It was still dark out. I went back to bed. The desire to reenter my dreams, whatever they may have been, was stronger than the desire to write.

When I woke again, the soft spring morning light was full. I was making coffee when the buzzer rang. I took my false teeth from the plastic cup in which they bathed, rinsed them under warm tap water, and stuck them in my mouth.

It was a couple of cops in cheap suits. The old cop looked like he was about ready for the glue factory. The young cop looked too young to not be wearing a uniform. He must've made detective the day before yesterday, I figured. Either that or he was on his way home from a wake. The young one asked me if I was who I am, and I said yeah. He nodded in a slow, dull way, as if to say, well, that's good, we're making progress here. I invited them in, leading them to the kitchen.

I looked from one to the other inquisitively. As I did so, I studied their faces briefly to see if I knew either of them from the bar on Reade Street, or from anywhere. The old cop looked some-how vaguely familiar but, no, I didn't know either of them. Coffee dripped down into the bit of half-and-half that was in the cup.

"We're talking to everybody who was at Circa Tabac at the time of the incident last night."

Again it was the young cop who spoke. He had his back to me. He was looking at the calendar on the wall. It was a calendar from Our Lady of Pompeii. Year after year, hanging from the same masonry nail, there was a calendar from the same church. A round-cornered rectangular window was die-cut at the centerfold of every month, so that, no matter what the pretty picture was for that month—right now it was Bartolomeo Schedoni, *The Three Marys at the Tomb*—the same ad for the Perazzo Funeral Home showed prominently through the window under it. I thought for a second about the time, years ago, when the old building where the Nucciarone Funeral Home was, on Sullivan Street, collapsed and Nucciarone and Perazzo merged. A lot of racketeers had been laid out in Nucciarone, and the joke was that whoever was laid out that day must've been really bad. Then I thought of how odd it was that this cop was standing there staring at a calendar on my kitchen wall. I turned to the old guy with an expression that asked what was with the young guy.

"Come on, let's get out of here," he said. It was the first he had spoken since they arrived. "I know this guy. He's all right."

He knew me? Why couldn't I place him?

"What time did you get there?" the young cop asked, his back still to me.

"I don't know."

I probably should have asked if they wanted coffee, but I didn't. They might've said yes.

"You don't know?"

"No, I don't know. I went out to dinner, then decided to drop in on my way home."

"Where'd you eat dinner?"

The old guy shook his head with slow, tired impatience.

"The Minetta Tavern," I said.

"Who with?"

"A friend."

"And what time did you leave Circa Tabac? Don't tell me. You don't know."

"Come on, Charlie," the old one said. "Let's go fight crime or something."

I didn't say anything. I just sipped my coffee and watched numb-nuts stare at my fucking calendar.

"Nice place," the old guy said.

"Thanks," I said.

Numb-nuts finally turned around. He seemed taken aback to see the two of us old guys leaning lackadaisically against the counter opposite him.

"You got the list?" my leaning-mate said to him. "Come on, check him off and let's get a move on."

I walked them to the door.

"Have a nice Good Friday," I said.

I could hear them exchanging words awhile in the hall outside my door. Then they were gone.

After finishing my coffee and a smoke, I was struck by a curious appetite. I poured a glass of buttermilk, added two raw eggs to it, and drank it down. I realized then how good I felt.

What remained of the morning was spent writing. The words came more easily, more naturally than I remembered them ever coming. It was usually a torturous process, and had grown more so, not less so, through the years.

"The past is a very bad place," I wrote. "It is not good to go there. Not alone. Not like this."

What these words meant was clear to me, and at the same

time unclear. Which part of the past? I wondered as I followed their inner sound, their call to me to come forth and be put down. Or should I have asked: which past, or which pasts?

The words that pursued these words did not speak to any of my questions, nor did they make anything more clear or less clear. I knew only that they sang to me, that their song was mine, and that they must be given form, metered to and arranged on the page in a way that captured and conveyed the sound and colors of their spell.

For the first time in my life, I felt that I had written the truth, without the artifice of veil or illusion to conceal and protect me, the writer, from the reader. Was this because I knew that I would not have these words go beyond me? Because I was the reader, the only reader, as well as the writer? Because there was no need to conceal or protect myself from the truth of myself? But did I know and understand the truth of myself so well? Could anyone know himself so well as to separate the veils and phantoms of a lifetime from the hidden truths they obscured? Maybe I should repeat only that *I felt* that I had written the truth. That I felt as if the distance among the three of us—me, the writer, and the reader—had been closed, if only because I was all three.

These thoughts brought to mind the old cop, who, though he was here not two hours ago, seemed now to be of the remote past. "I know this guy," he had said. "He's all right." But I did not know him; he seemed only vaguely familiar, or not at all. What had he meant? Did he really think he knew me, and that I was all right? Was the distance among the four of us—me, the writer, the reader, and the old cop—one and the same, and ultimately unknowable? Were we all just our own old cops? Was I thinking of innumerable distances, ever in flux, as if they were a single shared and common distance?

That much had not changed. The words loosened some of the old knots in my mind while tying new ones.

If I wanted to eat on Easter, I had better shop now. The way they crowded the stores, you would think these rich creeps ate only on holidays. Melissa was on her way to Minnesota for the school break, to visit her parents. Maybe Lorna didn't want to be alone. Maybe she'd be in the mood to come by for some high holy pig meat. In any case, I would go shopping today. But first a glass of cold milk and a Valium.

I looked through the surface of what I had written. It was good stuff. But was it fact or was it fiction? Or had it not yet settled on either, and did that yet remain to be established? Or was it neither, but a tone poem whose key I alone possessed, to turn and unlock in words to come? Had I misplaced the key, or was it still not mine to turn? Did I even know where in these words the keyhole was? Or was it not in them at all, but in words to follow?

When I began writing a book—and I felt no doubt that this was to be a book—I habitually returned, as if by instinct, to read in one of the same three works: Flaubert's final *Three Tales,* Henry James's "The Lesson of the Master," or Beckett's "The End." Through the years I had come to view the first of these as deeply flawed, but I returned to it nonetheless as often as I returned to either of the others. Maybe this was because it served as a warning sign for the hidden hazards that lay ahead, on ground that, no matter how well traveled, remained ever treacherous. But this time I felt myself drawn to none of these works; not for warning, not for reinforcement, not for encouragement. Instead, looking for *The Meditations* of Marcus Aurelius but not finding it, I drew down a Bible. Sticking from its pages as a bookmark was on old hundred-dollar bill, from the years before the fur was censored from Ben Franklin's collar. I moved the bill to the opening pages of the book of Ecclesiastes, and I placed the Bible by my bed.

Later that afternoon, after returning from shopping, I brewed a hot dandelion-root drink, put on the second movement of

Respighi's *The Pines of Rome,* and relaxed. A certain feeling of unease came over me as the music played.

The shadows of early evening fell. I threw on my jacket and walked north, to Circa Tabac.

There was Lee. We were almost alone in the place.

"Nicky," he said.

"Lee," I said.

"What's up?" he said.

"I had visitors this morning," I said.

"The cops?"

"Yeah, thanks to you."

"Christ, that was something, huh?"

"What was something? What was this 'incident' they were talking about?"

"You didn't hear? Those chicks. Right around the corner from here."

"What chicks?"

"Those two chicks you were talking to. You left, and they left about ten minutes later. You didn't hear? They found them with their throats slashed. Right around the corner here."

He gestured in the general direction of Thompson Street. I was looking at him, but my mind was on what I was feeling in the inner right breast pocket of my jacket as I leaned to the back of the barstool beside him. Last night I had found myself thinking of my little ebony-handled knife, wishing it were with me, feeling for the first time that it should be with me. It was with me last night, I now knew, as it had been with me on the previous several nights when I had ventured out. The only thing different last night was that I had carried it in my right rather than my left breast pocket. Not sensing it where it had been, I had felt that I was without it.

I went into the men's room and locked the latch. I pulled the thin sharp blade from its narrow snakewood scabbard and looked at what I knew I would see. The blood had been dry for some time and was like a black crust over the blade. I remembered now: standing in the darkened doorway, taking the air, when they happened by. I heard the steps of the younger one first, in her high heels. She was a stepper, all right. Then I heard the voice of Sandrine, and she said it again:

"Are you all right?"

I would have to destroy the sheath as well as the knife. There was probably as much identifiable dried blood in it as there was on the knife. I hated to see this lovely little knife and its lovely little scabbard go. I felt that I was not alone in the men's room. I knew that there was no camera. Then I remembered. *Why is the weight of the mere head of this serpent that has turned to stone so much heavier than the whole of this identical serpent that has turned to stone?* I put the knife back in my pocket and noticed then that there was dried blood on my jacket as well. Had I walked home with blood on my face? Had I made my way across the bright Canal Street crossing like that? Had my jacket been draped like this, with the bloodstained knife in its pocket, on the same chair in the kitchen this morning, while those two cops stood near to it? I shook my head.

"I keep thinking about that hamburger you told me about," Lee said.

"I tell you, it was good."

He lit a cigarette. I lit a cigarette. I asked him if he had talked to the same two cops, young numb-nuts and glue factory. He laughed a little.

"I'm sorry about that. I was just trying to do the right thing. I mean, those poor fucking girls. Jesus."

"Yeah, you're right. Those poor girls."

He asked me if I wanted a drink. I took a club soda with a piece of lemon.

235

"You working on another book?"

"How'd you know?"

"You're not drinking."

What about my saliva? What about my DNA? No. They wouldn't check the cut marks for that. They'd check elsewhere, if at all.

"Both dead, huh, just like that?"

"Yeah. One of them was dead when they found them. The other hung on awhile. She was in shock. Then she went. Yeah, just like that."

I felt bad for Sandrine and the other kid. A part of me felt detached and different from whoever it was, whatever it was, that had taken their lives. Maybe that was why I could not clearly remember it. Because it was not me, not really. But it was to me that Sandrine had come. It was to me that Sandrine, who had given me my first taste of blood, had given her last.

In bed that night, I read slowly the words of the Preacher, the son of David, king in Jerusalem: "And I gave my heart to know wisdom, and to know madness and folly. I perceived that this also is vexation of spirit.

"For in much wisdom is much grief: and he that increaseth knowledge increaseth sorrow."

As I drifted off, I felt that I was about to leave a part of myself behind. Which part was it? The part of me that seemed detached and different? The good part? The bad part? The old part? The new part? Were the pieces of myself that easily divisible? The days and the nights would tell. Yes, I thought, the days and the nights would tell. I sensed a smile on my face, and I did not question it, but merely took it, as with any smile, to be a good sign. I did not consider that I might not sense this same smile again. I did not consider that it might be a smile of parting.

Easter passed. I neglected to call Lorna, and I was relieved that Melissa was away. I wanted to be alone, to enjoy my pork roast in quiet solitary peace.

There was a feeling of being in limbo. I drifted not only to and from sleep, but through my days and nights as well. I was aware of undergoing a metamorphosis of sorts, but I knew not from what to what this change was taking me.

Slowly I began to feel that I was being brought from a new dimension of being to yet a newer, higher dimension. I was wary of it at first, but ultimately I knew I could do nothing but surrender to it.

For a few days I did not write. This was usual for me. Whenever I succeeded in driving down the first stake of a new book, I took a break. In the past, I drank. But now I did not. It was with a degree of disappointment that I did not attribute this to the baclofen, for I did not experience any of the attendant changes that baclofen was supposed to have effected in me. There was no quelling of the nerves, no banishing of anxiety, no newfound calm. Not from the baclofen anyway. Maybe my own answer had lain elsewhere, and I had already found it there: in the same broached source of other wonders.

Or maybe I was not drinking simply because this felt like no other book on which I had ever set course. I thought of the book that lay ahead as a ghost-book, as something beyond a book, though I could not explain this to myself or to anyone else. And there was no need to. Aura and resonance transcend meaning and saying. Some things can not be captured and conveyed.

In a few days' time, when I resumed writing, first in the mornings, then in the mornings and again in the evenings, increasingly into the late hours of the night or early hours of the next day, it was with a feeling, again and again, of going to meet the ghost. And soon the ghost became to me the Holy Ghost. Not the Holy Ghost of Saint Paul, not the Holy Ghost of any other; but my own Holy Ghost. And I felt as if I were entering a church. Not a sanctified place, but a sacred place. Sacred to gods or demons or both, I did not know. Sometimes it felt that this church was within me. Sometimes it felt far from me, in the dark woods of my soul's traveling. Always it felt that I belonged there.

There were no cravings. I took this to be good. A sign of freedom. On May Eve, Walpurgisnacht, I lit a candle, a nice beeswax taper glommed from the emporium of high-born junk food and ecologically friendly toilet paper. On the first morning of May, I opened a bottle of good Margaux and drank two glasses with a big plate of soft-scrambled eggs and blood sausage.

I wanted to be alone. But I began to wonder why I hadn't heard from Melissa or Lorna. Had they forgotten about me? I wanted to be alone, not forgotten. I began to feel a jealous anger well up in me. I imagined the worst things, and I flung the worst curses against them. These outbursts of senseless wrath incited by imagined wrongs were not like me. Of course, I had in my younger years experienced the insecurities and angers of jealousy, just as I had occasionally heard the hissings of ethnic intolerance; but I had known these follies only in the way that they are endemic to the species, and had for the most part seen through them and outgrown them. Even in my younger and more foolish years, I had never felt the likes of the sudden fast-rising wrath I lately had been subject to. It was as if, in my new life, the last remnants of old failings had been sloughed off only to be replaced by new failings. It was as if some seething vengeance or fury were trying to force its escape from me through any means, any fissure possible. In fact, these were not fits of temper that I felt. They were more like the spontaneous turmoilings of an unfamiliar presence seeking vent. I wondered if what I had done in the doorway was but a lashing forth by this presence as well. It must have been, for it was not I. It could not have been I.

W HEN MELISSA CALLED, IT WAS NOT TO TELL ME THAT she loved me and she missed me. She said those things. But I could tell that she was calling about something else.

"Do you know what 'prions' are?" she asked.

"How do you spell that?" I asked.

She spelled it. And within an hour she was sitting beside me.

"'Prion' is a rearrangement of the initial letters of '*protein-aceous in*fectious particle.' Actually"—she paused—"why would they do it *that* way? Anyway, prions can be transmitted by drinking blood," she said matter-of-factly.

Her father. Of course. Her father was a medical researcher, and she had been home to visit him.

Prions. As she spoke I could not help recalling the night she expounded on Cologne and haunches and *Keulen*. I had learned later that *Keulen* was the Dutch name for Cologne, not an old German name as she had said.

"What, did you show him where I bit you, too?" I said.

"Oh, hush. He thought my curiosity was purely scientific. These guys can't even unscramble words." She looked down at her notes. "*Prion.* It should be *pro-in.*"

Like father, like daughter, I thought.

"I was amazed at what you *can't* get from drinking blood. You can't get blood diseases. You can't get leukemia. You can't get AIDS, because HIV can't be transmitted that way, unless maybe if you have lesions in the mucous membranes of your mouth, your esophagus, or your stomach. Your immune system would take care of the leukemia. Your stomach acids would kill the HIV and just about anything else." She looked impressed. "Ingested blood will be digested blood. Simple as that. It's not the same as a transfusion. The blood type doesn't matter. Look at a steak." She read directly from her notes: "A steak is merely cooked muscle with various amounts of blood. We do it all the time." She paused. "But there are certain parasites that the acids can't kill—and prions. They pass right through the acids and penetrate through the stomach into the system."

"But what are prions?"

"They don't seem to be so sure about that yet."

"What is it with these guys? They misname something, *then* figure out what it is?"

"They're these little virus-like particles. They're still sort of hypothetical. They seem to agree on scrapie. They think that's caused by prions, but only sheep and goats get that. Mad cow disease, that's another one. Anyway, prions cause fatal neurological diseases. And maybe other things. They just haven't figured it all out yet."

She put aside her notes.

"Anyway," she said, "here's the thing. Whatever these prions and parasites are, I don't want any. The same goes for HIV and whatever else, which I have more of a chance of getting from them going directly into my bloodstream from your mouth than you do from them entering your stomach.

"What I'm saying is, I don't know who else you're fooling around with like this. I like to think you're not. But—"

"Well, you're right. I'm not."

I don't know why I said that. I should have just kept my mouth shut.

"OK, you're not. But let's say you are, or you might. If you're not going to worry about yourself, think about me. And you should worry about yourself. Parasites. Prions. God only knows what they are."

What she told me served only to reinforce what I believed: that science as yet knew nothing. The croaker had said that my diabetes was improving, that my blood type seemed to be changing. These were impossibilities. Yet they seemed to be true.

"It's crazy," she said. "According to science, I have a better chance of getting sick from you drinking my blood than you have from drinking it."

She wanted me to be faithful to her. And so, after all that, in her own way, she was really telling me that she loved me and missed me. That old black magic. The prion of love.

The cravings had ebbed, and this, I felt, was good. But as I sat beside Melissa, I realized that my sexuality, my desire for physical intimacy of any kind, had dwindled as well.

Maybe it was over, I told myself. And in a way this was a comforting thought. I did not want to relinquish my new life and all that it had brought me. But what it had brought me in recent days scared me more than a little, and there were times when I would have reembraced and reclaimed the solitary misery of my old life if I could. If I was becoming a god, then that god in turn was becoming something I did not know. There was a darkness and a stillness in the air. It was like the darkness and the stillness when I encountered the dead monkeys. Yes, maybe it was over, all of it: from the dead monkeys to my resurrection to the doorway in the black of night to the presentiment of the darkness and stillness in the air now before me.

Melissa touched my hand, and I withdrew it. She touched my neck and I turned away.

"Have you thought any more about those leopards?" she asked.

I looked at her. She was smiling.

"No," I lied. "Have you?"

"Yes," she said. "And I've come to the conclusion that I'm insane. Or maybe we both are. Simple as that."

Her words were heard by me, but I was not listening. The whole business of that all-but-forgotten morning, the business of crossed lives and leopard souls was a minor key in the background now.

If I were going to tell anyone that I killed the two girls, it would be Melissa. And a part of me did feel a need to confess, and to expiate my guilt. But I would not. I knew in that instant, I would not. No, I told myself. It was done, and it was not really me. To say it was me would not quite be the truth.

Did I any longer know the truth? I was not sure. I was not sure of anything anymore: of what was real and what was not. All I knew for sure was the terrible feeling that I had passed through a state of bliss and was coming out the other side.

We fell to sleep that night slowly, silently, her arm lightly around me. I had a troubling dream. There was nothing odd in this. Most of my dreams, if not all of them, were troubling. I had come to learn that this was common to almost everyone. The good-night lovers' wish of "sweet dreams" was sardonic. But of this particular dream I could remember nothing.

I gently removed her arm from me and quietly went to make a cup of coffee. The morning light was still a mere insinuation. I returned softly to the bedroom and looked down at her. Her sleeping face to me, her raised right arm beneath her head, her left arm lying on her body, unseen beneath the bedclothes, the delicate protuberance of her hand resting on her crotch. She lay like the *Sleeping Venus,* but more lovely, and immersed in shadows that seemed to have grown and darkened and deepened in the more than five hundred years since Giorgione, as death neared, had labored with his brush to perfect the encroaching shadows of his painting.

I stood awhile. Her beauty mesmerized me. It was then, suddenly, that I realized that I hated her.

PALE LIGHT CAME SLOWLY AS I SAT ALONE WITH MY COFFEE. I did not delve into my feelings or my mind. I had no inclination to do so, and I knew that there was no real understanding to be had by such delvings.

The Ch'an Buddhists had known the truth. Thought was the great curse. Only when the mind was free of it could the power of no-thought bring the burning flame of being. Those who seek truth should realize that there is nothing to seek.

Faustus dismissed all Christian theology with the words: "What doctrine call you this? / *Che sera sera,* / 'What will be shall be?' Divinity, adieu!"

Yes, I reflected, before there was Doris Day, there was Faustus. And before there was Faustus, there were the Ch'an masters who knew that what Faust sought did not exist.

The coffee grew cold in my cup, and I drank the last of it and just sat there.

I had killed. I had killed without even really knowing it. I felt no remorse. Maybe a cheap metaphysical Hallmark sympathy card cast to the wind with scant emotional postage; nothing more. There was no sin in killing. Like the rest of the Ten Commandments, it was merely a reflection of man's fearful desire to protect himself by transferring to the supreme authority of an imagined God decrees against those things that man feared—being murdered; being robbed; having his wife fuck around; and so on—that consigned them to the realm of "sin" and the punishment of eternal damnation, the *"Che sera sera"* that Marlowe put in the mouth of his Faustus.

There was no morality. There was no sin. There was only fear.

Given the chance of returning to the moments before I had killed, would I do it again? But there was no going back. Never.

All I knew at this moment was that my abhorrence for the woman in my bed was so intense that I could easily kill her— were she not in my bed, in my home; were it not that there were others who had seen us together, who suspected or knew that we were lovers.

Thou shalt not get caught. The unwritten commandment, the palimpsest on the unseen side of the tablet. Again, there was only fear.

Then she was standing before me, in my robe, smiling with eyes still adrift with sleep. She was no longer the beautiful girl who had sated my cravings, the goddess whom I had loved. She was a detested creature, alien to me.

"Get that off," I told her, gesturing to my robe. "Put your own shit on. Then get the fuck out of here. I don't want to see you ever again."

She looked at me, stunned, the sleep gone from her eyes, her jaw lowered, slowly, remotely, as if it were a motion apart from her brain signals, beyond her consciousness.

"What?" she demanded. She had heard and comprehended my words and their stern seriousness. Her question was not a question. It was a delayed articulation of shock. She stared into my eyes. I do not know what she saw. Her stare did not waver, as if she were intent on discerning another to emerge through my eyes. Then she turned away and began to sob.

"Turn off the waterworks, baby, they don't move me no more."

I knew her sobbing was an overture to anger, and I would

have none of it. I went to the basket of umbrellas in the nook beside my stacked washing machine and dryer, near my front door. There it was, among the umbrellas, seventeen inches of pure heavy iron: a twelve-inch length of black iron pipe connected firmly by an inch-and-a-half Ward-threaded black iron coupling to another three and a half inches of black iron pipe affixed to a blunt black iron cap. An inch in diameter, the four base inches of the pipe were wrapped tight in McMaster-Carr grip tape for a perfect grasp. It was good to have friends who were plumbers and boiler men.

I raised it out, wrapped my hand fast around the grip, went back to where she stood, swung it sideways, and rapped her in the ass with just enough force for the iron cap to send a deep, long-lasting, and painful bruise through the fat of her buttock.

As I did this, she shrieked, flinched, and struck out all at once. Thus one of her flailing forearms was also none the better for the blow.

"You're crazy," she exclaimed in a high, panicky voice as she cowered away from me. "You sick fucking monster! You *really are* crazy." She placed her hand where she had been struck. Her face was contorted with wincing and crying and who knew what else. She ran to the bedroom. Shit, I thought suddenly, what if she knows where the gun is? But I did not hear the closet being opened. I glimpsed her pulling off my robe and throwing it to the bed, then gathering up her clothes.

I sat there, the pipe in one hand, a cigarette in the other. It hit me. This bitch is going to make a report at the First Precinct. I took a drag. So what if she did? I had asked her to leave. She had refused. That made her a trespasser. And besides, she'd never get a hospital report of any use out of this. A bruise on her ass, maybe her forearm; no big deal. Shit, a bruise on her ass. The fucking cops would spit out their coffee trying not to laugh. And if she pulled down her britches for the doctor, how would she ever explain away the telltale signs of our blood-play? Nah, fuck it, she wasn't going anywhere, except away from here. Still, I figured, it would be best to disassemble the pipe in my hand and put the two lengths and the connector in different places. I would ditch the cap that had left its mark on her ass. I could always pick up another at the hardware store for a couple of bucks, maybe less.

Then something else came to mind, but I was quickly reassured to see that her bag, as usual, was on the easy chair across from the couch where I was sitting. I peeked in, and there it was: that gizmo of hers, that smartphone, or handheld device, or whatever the fuck they called it. Good. That meant she wasn't in the bathroom or crouched in a far corner of the bedroom melodramatically whisper-calling or e-mailing or texting or tweeting or twittering or Facebooking or pressing little red all-points bulletin buttons or whatever the hell else these people did.

She stood before me, and she no longer showed any fear. She turned, shouldered her bag, then turned to once again stare into my eyes.

"I'll always love you," she said. She said it as one might say words over the dead.

Sarah fucking Bernhardt.

She forgot to fake a limp until she was almost halfway to the door. Then she was gone.

I poured a glass of cold milk and took a Valium. I breathed deeply. My pulse was calm. My mind was as placid with no-thought as ever I had known it to be.

Melissa had meant the world to me. I had come to hate the world. In casting her away, I had cast away the world that I despised. I felt free. I felt great.

Yes, fuck the living. Fuck the dead. Fuck the world and all that lies beyond.

I RAISED MY GLASS IN SALUTE TO MYSELF, TO THE VINDICATION of my hatred and my freedom. But there should be a different glass in my hand, with something different in that glass.

There was no shaving, no showering, no brushing of my hair or of my remaining teeth. I pulled on some clothes, stuck my cheap plastic choppers into my mouth. I had been advised by Olivier to take my doses of baclofen even if I were to drink. But I took no baclofen, and I left my morning diabetes medications, my glyburide and my metformin tablets, in their vials in my medicine cabinet. I had no time for these things. I wanted to get drunk. Now. Right now. I patted my pockets for money, cigarettes, keys. I slammed the door shut behind me.

The first thing I did when stepping forth into the world, which until this morning had bound me, was to spit with loud, thick vehemence on the pavement.

It was not yet half past nine, and the bar on Reade Street was still rather empty, the way I liked it.

When I was a little kid on my way to school at half past eight in the morning, I used to walk by joints like this, look in, and think: who are those guys? Now I was one of them.

I slapped a few twenties down and ordered a pint of Guinness and a double shot of Jameson. I drank the whiskey in two swallows, the Guinness in three, then I ordered more. I drank them and ordered more again. I stalked outdoors to spit again, loud and thick, and to smoke a cigarette. I watched the island-nigger nannies waddle by pushing white yuppie brats in three-grand prams and strollers. I'd rather have them as neighbors than the mothers of the brats they pushed. I flicked my cigarette butt in the direction of a passing twin stroller, then reentered the bar and drank more. I pushed the emptied rocks glass into the bar gutter and drank only Guinness.

A few city workers, a few union slobs wandered in. They watched, or stared at, the news on one of the three television sets behind the bar as they drank. They were like a bunch of old ladies lost in their soap operas. Whenever the satellite reception went on the blink, they grew nervous, unbearably alone with nothing but themselves, their dull empty lives, their dull empty talk, their dull empty laughter so like the sounds of cows at slaughter.

I glanced at the television screen nearest me. In these joints these days, it could not be avoided. In these joints these days, television had the attributes of the Judeo-Christian God: omnipresent, omnipotent, omniscient. That glance upon the face of Yahweh-Yeshua brought me something most unexpected, something I had never before seen. It was a commercial for Barnes & Noble, the bookseller whose corporation had come to represent something like a monopoly of bookstores. I liked Len Riggio, the chairman of Barnes & Noble. He was a good guy. But I had watched through the years as Barnes & Noble grew from a single store in New York to an immense chain that operated throughout the country. And as it grew, independent bookstores vanished and its own stores gave over more and more space to cafés, magazines, newspapers, comic books, children's books, CDs, DVDs, calendars, games, gifts, and greeting cards instead of books. And what books they did sell became increasingly of a timely and crass commercial nature. *Buddhism for Dummies, How to Get a Job You'll Love,* and ghostwritten celebrity autobiographies came to be more easily found than books by William Faulkner, Thomas Mann, or living writers of worth.

So here I was looking at a Barnes & Noble commercial. I had never thought I would see the day when a bookseller advertised on television. But how disheartening it was. It was not a commercial for books. It was a commercial for the latest model of the Barnes & Noble electronic-book reader, the Nook. Worse, there seemed to be little to do with reading or books, even e-books, in this commercial for the new Nook e-reader. Rather, its flashy gimmicks were to be set forth as its selling points. Its VividView color touchscreen, its Internet-browsing, e-mail, instant-messaging, flash-chat, flash-video, and game-playing functions; its access to high-definition movies, television shows, and music. As for reading matter, it could be downloaded via iPod, iPad, iPhone, Black-Berry, or Android smartphone, as well as a PC or Mac.

This was literacy as she now stood, or, more like it, as she now lay in the gutter. The last thing I wanted to do was think. But I am no fucking Ch'an master, and this stupid fucking commercial on this stupid fucking television pushed me to it.

I went back a long way with my friend and editor Michael Pietsch, the executive vice president and publisher of Little, Brown. We began working together in 1983, when he was with Scribner. I can still see and remember the feeling of those old Scribner offices, with their somber, age-rich wainscot paneling and creaking floors and books and books and books. Charles Scribner III could still be seen on occasion ambling about, pausing a moment here or there as if remembering it as the spot where, as a boy, he had seen his father conversing casually with Hemingway and now whimsically expected to hear the voices of the conversation resume. Those offices were in the grand old Scribner Building, on Fifth Avenue, on whose ground floor was the grand old Scribner Bookstore, which would close a few years later, losing out to the Barnes & Noble store across the street.

Through all the years that followed, as Michael ascended and I did whatever the hell anybody wants to say that I did, I have been proud to say that he is my editor. I loved our lunches together, talking about literature and the colors and music of words. But lately even Michael's talk wandered to the dystopia of electronic books.

The new, top-of-the-line Nook tablet cost $249, with, if one desired, a Saffiano leather cover available for $89. The top-of-the-line Kindle DX cost $379, with an optional Cole Haan hand-stained pebble-grain leather sleeve available for $119.99. The Kindle Prime membership fee was $79 a year. It was easy to see where Barnes & Noble, Amazon, and other e-book merchants were making their money, but what about the publishers? And fuck the publishers, what about the writers?

I thought of some of the books in my library. The five vellum-bound volumes of the eighteenth-century Zatta edition of Dante with its magnificent copperplate engravings. The first printed edition, from 1576, of Dante's *Vita Nuova*. The 1948 first printing of *The Cantos,* inscribed by Ezra Pound to himself while in the bughouse at Saint Elizabeths. The first edition of Lampedusa's *Il Gattopardo.* The signed and numbered limited edition of Faulkner's *The Wild Palms.* The twenty volumes of the hand-bound-in-leather second edition of *The Oxford English Dictionary,* their blue goatskin covers gilt-stamped, their pages gilt-edged. And so many more: so beautiful to have, to behold, to feel, to read.

These were books, the writer's words dignified and framed in ink and paper, leather and boards, not pieces of cheap plastic shit. I had been lucky to make it all these years to the end of publishing, the end of books, the end of literacy. I look forward to the day when I can put the piece of cheap plastic shit, the computer on which I now write these words with my right index finger, into a big black garbage bag, haul it down to the street, and smash it to the gutter with all my might.

I drank more. But wasn't I writing another book? That thing with the fucking leopard in the tree? The miller and the whatever? Yet another exorcism performed by the possessed upon himself, yet another telling to myself that after this the demons would be gone from me, yet another discovery that once they had been brought forth from me, I would find only deeper, darker demons that had lain beneath them? Yes, I seemed to sense, there were pages awaiting me at home. Pages with things on them that no black iron pipe could kill. But the demons and I would sit together now and drink.

Another double Jameson now to go with the Guinness. I gazed through the window. There was a lot of good-looking leg passing by out there. What a drag it was that rape involved so much exertion. Just to get some broad to be still while you jerked off on her calf or had her suck your cock without being properly introduced.

"So where you been hiding?" the bartender said. He must have figured that I had drunk enough to no longer want to be left alone. He was wrong.

"What do you mean?" I said. "I was here just the other day."

"You haven't been here in months."

The old guy was losing it. This was too much. First that commercial, now him. I looked at him and he looked at me. I pushed my empty glasses toward him. He poured more whiskey into the rocks glass, fetched a fresh pint glass, and drew another Guinness.

"I swear, Nick, I haven't seen you since the spring."

"You better lay off that Johnnie Walker before he tips his hat to you and walks off the label. This *is* the spring."

"Well, then, if you're right, the calendar's wrong."

I shook my head, looked away from him, nonplussed. I drank down some of the whiskey, drank down some of the stout.

The bartender leaned against the cash register, as if trying to determine if I was pulling his leg. Then he let out one of those high sheela-na-gig tee-hee-hee's of his.

"Hey, Charlie," he called out to one of the union flotskies. "What month is it?"

"What *month* is it?" Charlie called back. "Last time I looked, it was September."

The bartender looked to me, nodded in self-satisfied verification, then let out another little tee-hee-hee.

One of the drunken civil servants had a folded newspaper at his elbow. I put on my eyeglasses, went to it, squinted down at the date.

By now I had drunk too much to be rattled, but I was rattled. I could not remember the summer, not a single bead of sweat of it. Nothing.

When had I hit Melissa in the ass with that pipe? Hours ago, this morning? Or could it have been months ago?

I could not have gone unknowing through the summer. I could not have forgotten it. I mean, it was still the summer, there were a few more days of it left, and I was aware of this day, this moment. So what had happened? I was aware of this morning, of the hatred that had taken me. But, again, had that really been *this* morning? The lights still worked. That meant that I had paid my bills, that I had been conscious and functional. Then I realized that it didn't: I approximated and paid all my monthly bills for each coming year in advance every January. I felt my face. There wasn't much of a beard. I had shaved at some point recently. I saw in the mirror behind the bar that my hair was somewhat shaggy. I felt weak. I looked bad. But I must have eaten in recent days. Then again, I had once, years ago, gone three months just drinking and not eating. The doctor in the hospital where I ended up told me this was impossible. But I knew it was very possible because it was the truth. Now, however, I had been taking my baclofen and not really drinking much at all. Or had I been?

It was just a matter of relaxing and remembering, I told myself. But I could not relax and I could not remember.

After a few more drinks, I was not relaxed, but I was drunk and did not give a fuck about anything. And I remembered. Nothing that had to do with this season or that. But I remembered: images and things and feelings, barely discernible but recognizable, flowing out of time through my memory, or what I believed to be my memory, in the slow river of dark night that was my mind, or what was left of it.

That thing with the monkeys. Those monkeys, those dead monkeys.

The taste of Sandrine's blood, the taste of all their blood. Endeared and estranged, asphodels that bloomed in the night.

The taste of that croissant, the caress of that breeze, the heavenly corn silk and persimmon flesh of her pussy.

"Oh. Melissa. I don't really know her. She seems like a nice kid."

"Thenceforth evil became my good."

The woman who spoke another tongue, the leopard who awaited glance in bowering shade.

"For in much wisdom is much grief: and he that increaseth knowledge increaseth sorrow."

"It was the look in my father's eyes."

A doorway on Thompson Street.

"I know this guy. He's all right."

All that matters is that the words are brought forth and set down: the words that are from or about she who is of the legends.

I loved her. I wanted to have her for whatever remained to me of forever.

The oak leaf on the sill.

Maybe it was over, I told myself.

It was then, suddenly, that I realized that I hated her.

I had thought it was the drawing of the blood. Then I knew it was the blood itself that was the essence of the transformation. Then I knew there was no transformation.

"I've seen things *come out of them*."

Blood and spicy V8 juice.

The long dark passage without breath, the dark passage longer than life.

And I will never forget this. Or will I? All the brain-mold and deathless water bugs of memory that we cannot rid ourselves of, all the seemingly meaningless detritus that has bored into our minds and remains there, no matter how much we would extract it. Remembrance is a derelict, wretched, and infested broom closet in which almost all that is worth remembering, almost all that we wish we could recall, is lost and irretrievable amid the haunted litter of what we wish we could forget. The brain is not, as they would have us believe, a miraculously complex machine. It is a junkyard, a dangerous dumping ground of rusted ills; and what we regard as reason and intelligence are nothing but the diseased rats that dart and scramble through it: the crumbled plaster of things past turned to asphyxiating dust, stirred by the dead air of our inward stirrings. The mind is a lugubrious, malfunctioning instrument of self-torment, fear, and ghosts. Brilliance and beauty are but the flames of the mind that demolishes itself, the fire of arson in the junkyard. And memory is a killing thing, chewed upon and consumed by the rats, but rarely scorched by the fire that drives out the rats.

My eyes were shut. There was a sudden phosphorescence.

"If you can comprehend it, it is not God." Augustine, no?

And the human mind, which summoned that God into a lie of being, can never and will never understand itself. And whence this arrogance from brain to mind? The brain was just another organ, prone to if not defined outright by illness and disease. The heart, the liver, the prostate, the brain: one or more of them would get you in the end.

Well, I was still here. At least I believed I was, and that was good enough.

All of the lust and blood, Melissa and Lorna and the rest.

The cravings had ebbed, and this, I remembered, felt good. The dwindling of it all, my sexuality, my desire for physical intimacy of any kind.

Was a lingering of that lust still there?

There were cunts and there were pussies. Anatomically, I mean. Most women had cunts. Ugly jagged-purfled necrotic folds of livid flesh and tissue to which one all but had to close one's eyes. They had come to repulse me to the point where I would not enter into them, could not enter into them. But some young ladies had pussies. Alluring bivalves of pink, puffy vibrant flesh that were a pleasure to behold and to smoothly, lubriciously, sweetly enter. Behind my closed eyes I saw Melissa anointing with the chrism of her pussy the stiletto heel of her shoe, then slowly sliding it into herself. But now—for how long had it been so?—even pussy repelled me. What waited hidden within seemed to be not beautiful sacrament but something disgusting, unclean, and dangerous. And now I felt the same about a kiss, a caress, a touch. It was all repellent to me.

Even the bloodlust, the desire for new life, seemed to have left me. To recall the taste of blood was to be taken with repulsion. I no longer wanted to merge with those who possessed the youth that I had lost, the youth that, however fleetingly, I believed I had regained.

Awaiting glance. I had been like that for years. The dread of eye contact. The dread of physical contact, of any physical intimacy. Somehow, as the years had passed, these had become anathema to me. But now it was over. What was over? Something. Yes, something was over. Or was something just beginning?

Was I here? Was I really here? I did not even feel the hate of this morning—or whenever.

Why had I so intensely wanted a knife with a leopard-bone handle?

The theory of solipsism had now found a place in quantum physics. As the theory has it, only one mind exists, and all that seems to be reality is only a dream transpiring in that one solitary mind. The identity of the dreamer, of course, could never be known.

Was I the dreamer or the dreamt?

But that shit made no sense. Maybe I was going mad. Or maybe I was mad.

The shadows of early dusk were here. I staggered home. I felt the shadows to be those of another life than mine. The few blocks of my staggering seemed endless.

I saw that my kitchen was a cluttered mess of stinking empty bottles. Beer bottles and wine bottles. Vodka bottles. Whiskey bottles. A grain alcohol bottle. Even my glass jug of snake sake, with the dead snake coiled at the bottom, was opened, half empty, part of the snake protruding desiccated above the liquor that was left in the bottle. There was a pizza box, with a few slices of pizza still in it, lying on the floor.

Who had done this? Had Melissa done this in revenge? I could not remember if she had a set of keys or not. But no, who would conceive of doing something like this? I rushed about, banging here and there, looking for further signs of intrusion. I lunged to the drawer in the bedroom dresser where Melissa had kept her hosiery and fancy high heels. They were all still there. I gathered up some shoes and pantyhose and held them close to me. They were better than her—they were her—and they were still here.

I made it to the couch and collapsed. I tried to light a cigarette, but I could not. I wanted water desperately, but I could not get up. I coughed from deep within and thought I saw something like a rat, but vaporous, shoot from my mouth and scurry wildly away.

Lorna screamed from her cross.

I slept—it was a thousand years—then woke in darkness to see if morning had broken. But all was black, and I could not raise myself to go down again to self-annihilation. I felt that I had reached the depths of direst hell.

Then I felt someone sitting beside me.

WHO THE FUCK WAS THIS? HAD I BROUGHT SOME BUM home from the bar? It was a guy, not a broad. And I did not know him. I was pretty sure I did not know him.

He wasn't a queer: he was at the far end of the couch. He wasn't a thief: I had been unconscious, and he was still here. I had done this on rare occasions in the past, brought drunken souls home with me when I could barely get home myself. What had been the plan? We would listen to music and drink more? We would not be alone? Who knows? All I thought was, oh, God, not again.

I saw that somehow I had got my shoes off, and I looked down at my feet.

"Nice socks," he said. "Lisle?"

"Sea Island."

He seemed mildly impressed. He bent to see if there was skin showing between the upper cuff ribbing of the sock and the frayed blue jean hem of the raised leg, resting on the knee of my other leg, that was aimed toward him.

"Over-the-calf?" he asked.

"Mid-calf," I said.

He leaned back, then spoke as if pondering aloud. "Lisle," he said, "Sea Island, and cashmere. The only things a man should let touch his skin." I saw then that he was smoking an English Oval, and I watched him tap ashes from its end into the ashtray that was on the couch between us. I still had a lot of difficulty lighting a cigarette. He graciously withdrew a lustrous gold lighter from a pocket and lit it for me.

"Tell me," he said, "are you a Zimmerli man as well?"

I nodded, and he in turn nodded approval and reiterated, more softly, more reflectively, what he had said about the only things that a man should allow to touch his skin.

I was seized again by a hideous cough and saw, or thought I saw, another hideous, vaporous rat-haint rush from my mouth to the floor and flee, black on black, into the darkness.

"Pesky little things, those, hey?" he said lightly, a faint smile on his face. Then he resumed speaking of fine cottons. "Not many men go the tad extra for the Sea Island. After all, unless one has a good maid to wash and dry them with the proper care, what can one do but throw them away after a wearing or two? The essence of their delicate luxuriousness is lost to the washing machine, or even to slapdash hand-washing.

"But, then again, it's just like life, isn't it? Live it once and throw it away." He blew a smoke ring. "And those who don't even live it but merely throw it away almost invariably wear bad, cheap socks, to which they cling."

"What kind of socks do *you* wear?" I asked, for want of anything else to say.

"Handwoven Carstarphen. The only truly pure Sea Island cotton. It's the stuff Queen Elizabeth had her snot-rags made of. It was said those hankies were so light that they could float upon the air of the gentlest of breezes."

"Custom-made socks?"

"The toe seams, or rather the absence of them. A few other minor details." He extinguished his cigarette. "There's an old weaver in Kentucky. Exquisite."

"And you wear them once and throw them away?"

"Yes. Well, yes and no. I give them to storefront charities. I'm a great believer in charity.

"Should you like to feel them?"

"No."

He withdrew another English Oval from a lustrous gold cigarette case, lit it with his lustrous gold lighter.

"Those people who throw away their lives and cling to their cheap socks have no understanding of charity," he went on. "They are overall a curious lot.

"They all fear death, but they want to hurry and cast away the time remaining between now and the grave. 'I can't wait till this day's over,' they say. 'I wish this week would end,' they say. 'I can't wait until next month,' they say. All of life they will ever know lies in the moment; all of infinity they will ever know lies in the present breath that they are granted. But they, who would think us crazy for throwing away socks, throw away everything in their rush to obliterate their lives and be devoured all the sooner by their greatest fear. The end and its grave-mold. Their beginning is their end: a brief, nervous twitch of panic and dread, and nothing more."

As he spoke, I shut one eye to banish my diplopia, and I studied him, as best I could, in the dim night light that entered through the windows into the darkness of the room. He was clean-shaven, his sparse black hair streaked with gray or silver. His height, as he sat there, was indeterminate, as was his age, though he was definitely on the older side, perhaps a few years older than I. The cast of his face, which was a bit jowly, seemed to shift from grave nobility to innocent pleasance to a faraway, disincarnate gaze to complete nonchalance. His nose was rather thin, with nostrils that flared somewhat. He was dressed moderately, a bit conservatively, a bit shabbily and carelessly. From what he had said, if he was to be believed, his underwear and socks were probably more extravagantly costly than his outer wardrobe, though for all I knew, his shirt, white with blue pinstripes, may have been of handwoven Carstarphen as well. His eyes had a soft clear gleam. And he was sober, while even I could hear the thick slur in my attempts at speech. Most of the time, I could when very drunk speak with a precision and lucidity of articulation that belied my state and affected relative sobriety. It was a gift that served me well. But I was beyond that now. Why was he here?

I felt that I must summon the power to raise myself. I braced my effort with the arm of the couch. I stood. I fell. My balance was shot. This was a bad sign. It could mean that I had no electrolytes left. This was how I had ended up in the hospital the last time. I had never heard of electrolytes before then. I tried to get up from the floor but I did not have the strength. The stranger assisted me, helped me lurch unsteadily to the kitchen. I put a handful of vitamin capsules into my mouth—electrolytes—and washed them down with a long draught of water, what seemed like an endless draught of water. Dehydration. I needed to stave it off. I needed to live. I forgot completely about my diabetes medication, forgot completely the last time I had taken any.

When I took the container of Centrum Silver from the refrigerator, I saw and smelled the foul remains of partially eaten, partially unrecognizable things. It was amazing what a greasy lamb gyro looked like after enough time: part rock, part unspeakable laboratory experiment.

Gasping after almost a liter of water, I stood on my own legs, leaning on the countertop. The stranger aided my return to the couch, where I lit my own cigarette and took a deep drag.

"What say we raise a glass to ourselves?" he said. "I saw that bottle of Tignanello in there was still half full and recorked. Or perhaps a nice bourbon and branch? That bottle of Booker's still had a lot in it as well."

"Bourbon and branch," I said. Then I heard him opening the kitchen cupboards looking for the glassware. He poured, first the Booker's, then a bit of water. He set one drink on the little table near me, the other on the little table near him.

I saw then that what I had taken to be shabby corduroy pants were in fact corduroy of pure silk, soft and comfortable as soft and comfortable could be. I had seen and felt a pair once at a store in Milan, once at a store in London. His well-worn shoes, however, were plain and brown, with a vaguely pedorthic look, not unlike the SAS shoes I bought from the Eneslow Foot Comfort Center store. Though I had no doubt that his were more comfortable and custom-made of some rare and supple leather.

What the fuck was with this guy? He saw, he knew, that I was on the verge of going under, and he was not even loaded; yet here he was pressing more drink on me.

I took an unsteady sip. It livened me a little. I took another. There was in me not the least concern for what I said, or tried to say, so I turned to him and said:

"Who are you?"

He took a good swallow, lit a cigarette, laid back his head, and laughed.

"I mean, you gotta excuse me," I said, "I'm sorta fucked-up and all, but—"

"Here we are. We've known each other all these years. And you ask me who I am?"

"Where do we know each other from? I mean, like I said, I'm pretty fucked-up. I think I been blackin' out, gettin' everything all fucked-up lately. From the bar? Is that where we know each other from? The bar?"

"Yes, from the bar." He laughed again, and now there was something ominous in his laugh. "We know each other from the bar. We know each other from here, from there. We know each other from everywhere. Years and years and years. Everywhere."

I pressed the palm of my hand to my forehead. I drank. I pressed the cool glass to my forehead. I drank.

"Do you like *The Music Man*?" he asked.

I looked at him strangely. "I like that song 'Trouble.' I like that song."

"Ah, yes, perhaps one of the great Robert Preston's finest performances." He sipped, smiled. "I do a damned good Professor Hill myself." He leapt suddenly to his feet and stood before me. He began to sing in the stentorian speech-like cadences of "Ya Got Trouble," gesticulating with arch fervency as had Robert Preston in the picture. He was performing, not for me, but merely performing.

> *What would you rather do with your tongue?*
> *Would you rather lick a woman's flesh*
> *   or talk to her?*
> *Or are you one of those,*
> *   further doomed,*
> *   lost and undone,*
> *Torn between the two;*
> *   one who would do both,*
> *   or would rather the one,*
> *   whichever,*
> *   but settles, or would settle,*
> *   for the other?*
> *Tell me: which are you?*
> *   Psychiatry,*
> *   psychology,*
> *   therapy,*
> *   psychopharmacology—*

You don't need them; just come to me, And tell me:
which are you? And I'll tell you all about yourself,
parse your soul,
cauterize the hole,
set you right,
set you free.
And the best part is, I charge only
fifty bucks a pop;
Seventy-five for the bald
or broken of heart.
So tell me—cash on the barrelhead, pal—
which are you?

He seemed not at all taxed, not the least out of breath, after this exuberant routine. He merely resumed his seat and took a sip.

"Music by the great Meredith Wilson," he said, "lyrics by *moi*. Not bad, hey?" He lit a cigarette, smiled. "Or perhaps it's just the Irish in me." He took a deep drag, took another sip, followed by a sound of savorsome appreciation. "Have you a ditty of your own you should like to entertain us with? Come now. Conviviality is not a solitary affair but a feast of folly to be shared." Then his voice turned cold, cruel, and deprecating: "But you'd probably just fall down."

I drank, emptying the glass.

"May I replenish that for you?" His voice was again calm, measured, amiable.

I gave him the glass. He took it into the kitchen with his own, came back with two fresh and full drinks. He raised his to mine and said, *"Ave, Caesar, morituri te salutamus."* Then he smiled with a whisper of a laugh and drank. I nodded the best I could: Hail, Caesar, we who are about to die salute you. I drank. There was silence. He seemed to be almost inaudibly humming to himself something like ancient Ambrosian plainsong.

I coughed forth another of those rat-like shadow-things. I drank more.

"Who are you?" I tried again.

He stopped humming, if indeed he had been humming.

"Who am I?" He laid back his head again, laughed low and sardonically. "Who am I?" He fell quiet. "Who do you think I am?"

"I think you're the fucking Devil," I spat out.

He fell quiet again. "And your better half, too," he said decisively.

"And you're here to claim my soul, or buy it, or some such shit." I laughed, somewhere inside me, I laughed. It was a laughter most strange and unhealthy and indefinable.

"Buy your soul?" His voice rose. "I'm no fucking two-bit schlockmeister," he said with some indignation. "And how, in any case, does one purchase or lay claim to what was born forth and rendered to him?" He blew a smoke ring, opened his mouth wider, and one of those shadow-vermin leapt from it, through the vanishing ring of smoke, and made off like the others. "Souls?" Again he laid back his head and this time snorted a more forlorn sort of laugh.

I lugubriously composed words, lugubriously enunciated them. It was like moving heavy stones.

"So, my friend from here and there and everywhere, my friend of many and many years, Devil mine, grant me four and twenty years more, to live in voluptuous happiness. Surely that is yours to spare and give me."

"I would," he said pensively. "But it is not what you want. It is not life or happiness that you wish. It is death that you crave. Look at yourself, look into yourself. It is death that you pursue. You are not one of those, the great common multitude who rush to obliterate their lives, whose beginning is their end: a brief, nervous twitch of panic and dread between cunt and grave, and nothing more. But so much of you has been self-killed. You have been your own attrition. This is why I say I am your better half. I am what of you has endured. I am what of you stays you from the grave. But if truth be told, you seek death, not the years of life and happiness for which you petition me. It is death that you love. I feel that to keep you from it would be to deny you the true desire in you that goes unuttered."

"Is that why you force drink upon me now? To kill me?" I could feel the anger in the moved stones of my own voice.

"I force no drinks on you. I merely serve you. I give you only what you want."

"Then give me the four and twenty years more. If not of happiness, then of misery; of this."

"I feel that what remains of you, the you that is apart from me, can take care of that." He sipped. "But you can forget about those four and twenty years." He sipped again, then lit a smoke. "You will write three more books, and then you will die. Then to your true love you will go."

"And what if I do not write three books more? I've had it with that, anyway. I don't want to write three books more."

"Then you will die anyway."

"When? Not tonight?"

"Is that disappointment or relief, eagerness or fear? No, not tonight."

My glass was empty again. His was still almost half full. He asked politely, "Should you like another?"

I wanted to say no, but I was not strong enough to say no. I took the drink he brought, and I drank from it.

"Yes," he said. "Nice socks. Very nice socks indeed."

"So tell me. Is there a soul?"

He began to say something, then hesitated with an "oh," then laughed a slight laugh. "Excuse me. I had mentioned socks, and I thought for a moment that you were asking if a sock had a sole, which of course it does, so I was thrown off for a second. You were talking about the other kind, that breath-of-life thing, mortal to some ways of thinking, immortal to others." He shrugged. "I know only the wisdom that you have forgotten, or that you still retain. Plus a few things I've picked up on my own. Ways of thinking. Thought. The root of all evil."

"Picked up on your own? If you're my better half, how do you pick up things on your own, without my picking them up?"

"Because I'm not only your better half. I'm the better half of everything, all that was and all that is, and all that ever shall be."

"You talk more like God than the Devil."

"You can call me that, too. I don't mind it at all."

"I thought the Devil would be good for more than some imitation of Robert Preston in *The Music Man*."

"Ah, another sucker for conjuring tricks."

He began to sing to the melody of a vaguely familiar Irish air:

> *Oh, make me a pentacle on your floor, Gertie,*
> *Oh, do me wicked black magic galore, Gertie...*

An unlit cigarette hung from my mouth, and from the side of his own mouth there shot a laser-like blaze of fire that halted at the tip of that cigarette. I drew smoke. After this unsettling ignivomous feat, he drew a cigarette from his golden case, placed it between his lips, and lit it casually with his golden lighter.

"How about a clandestine jaunt, in the blink of an eye, to the pope's privy chamber? We shall be quite unseen, I assure you. And I can also assure you of some vintages in the papal wine vault that few have ever tasted."

I felt all strength ebbing from me. No. Worse. I felt all life ebbing from me.

"Oh, well," he sighed. "World-weary indeed is he who declines that one."

My head was lowered, and I peered to him. I tried to say something, not even knowing what I was trying to say.

"The puking sphinx," he said. "Remember that one?"

More than forty years ago, the poet Ed Sanders had shown me an old engraving of one of the most bizarre and arresting images I ever saw: a frontal view of an open-mouthed vomiting sphinx. It made quite an impression on me, as it had on him, and seemed to bespeak all manner of lost, unspeakable mystical powers and arcane, unknowable meaning. Just a few years ago, never having forgotten that image or the impression it made on me, I asked Ed where he had got it, where it had come from. He remembered it well, too, but could recall only that it must have come from an old volume that he no longer possessed and whose title and any other details were lost to him as well. Yes, that old engraving seemed to reveal all while revealing nothing. The puking sphinx.

"I could take you there," he said, "there and back, in a blink as well, to confront that wondrous thing, and not as an engraved image, but to see and touch and feel in the reality of this very moment."

How could he even know of this?

"But that would, I must admit, be rather a cheap shot, for what you took to be the engraved image of a puking sphinx was indeed merely an engraved image of one of the four water-spouting sphinxes sculpted in 1858 at the lower basin of the Fontaine du Palmier in Paris. It was an old engraving of one of those sphinxes you saw. The etched spewing water was to your eyes a spewing of a different sort. And from there grew the great mystical icon that has captivated you for all your adult life. Folly, fancy, and falsehood. But, nonetheless, I could take you there. If we're lucky—six hours later, daylight there now—the fountain will be working and the water will be spouting."

I shook my head as rapidly as I could, as if to clear it. It made me dizzy and nauseous. I drank. I leaned forward and labored to work my feet back into shoes.

"And where to now?" he said. "To bottomless perdition, there to dwell?" He took a sip. "Or there perchance to die?"

I had got my shoes on, and it was taking all my concentration to try to tie them. I was panting with the effort. His words broke my concentration, flustered me, angered me with frustration.

"Look," I said, "you only want to give me what I want? Gimme ten kilos of gold. Twenty-four karat, triple nine-point-nine."

"Credit Suisse or Johnson Matthey?"

"I don't care."

I returned to my shoelace, but was distracted by the grotesque bulging of his neck. The first of ten heavy kilograms of gold hit the floor with a loud slam.

"If I were a prick," he said, "I would have shit them out." He rubbed his neck and coughed modestly, then took a sip. I stared at the gold. My shoelaces were tied.

"Thank you," I said.

"Think nothing of it," he said. "'Tis something, nothing; 'twas mine, 'tis his, and has been slave to thousands."

"All the same, thank you. Not a bad pastime, sitting around spitting up gold."

"Oh," he said lackadaisically, "never cared much for it myself." He began to softly sing "The Best Things in Life Are Free."

"Buddy DeSylva, Lew Brown, that other fellow—what was his name?—Ray Henderson. Nineteen twenty-seven. Everybody and his mother recorded that one. What a bundle they must have made with it.

"That DeSylva was something, all right. He also made a

bundle with 'Wishing Will Make It So.' And they call the blues the Devil's music." He sang again, softly.

The best lies in life seem true...

I stood unsteadily. Looking down at the gold bars on the floor made me feel better. I coughed out one of those rat-things, a small one. I wiped my mouth.

"It's good to see you smile," he said.

"I feel good," I said.

"I'd hate to see you feel bad."

He cast his own eyes to the gold on the floor. "So," he said, "off to the melter for the gelt through your swarthy-complected inter-mediary, is that it? And so it is that Jew and Christian and Muslim become one, brought together by greed and stealth. Selah, selah.

"Shall we have one for the road?"

He brought more drinks.

"What's the difference between Satan and the Devil?" I asked.

"Words, words. Nothing but words. The former, as you should know, is a word rooted commonly in Hebrew, Greek, and Latin. The latter, in Greek and Latin alone."

He took a sip, lit a cigarette, went on.

"You really are a fool for words. Immersed as you are in the wisdom of Ch'an, you seem to hew your way through it, embracing what you wish, discarding what you wish. You bear close the wisdom regarding the foolishness of thought, but not the wisdom that follows close after: 'How can one obtain truth through words?' I am not really criticizing you, for, to the best of my knowledge, no one has had the wisdom to counter this wisdom by asking what it is if not just another bunch of words." He raised his glass. "Thoughts. Words. Hang them and fuck them. Let's just drink."

"Save me," I heard myself say.

"Save you?"

"Yeah. Save me. Enough of this. I want to go back to where I was. I don't want to go through the hell of life again just so that I can return to the wonder of those butterflies, those fireflies, that one lone blue jay, the magic in the clouds, the sense of illimitableness that only a child could know. Just take me back to where I was not so very long ago, when serenity and rebirth were in my grasp. No, don't take me back there. Bring that back to me, in this here and now."

"Serenity and rebirth were in your grasp? Nothing was in your grasp but a whip handle and the haunches and loins and thighs of females as lost to themselves as you were to yourself." He ruminated, snorted. "Drinking their blood to gain their youth. From what comic book did you get that ridiculous African ritual notion from?"

"It was real. For a while I was well, better than—"

Then, again, cutting me off this time, that lilting voice of his, which now was maddening to me:

Just keep on wishing and care will go . . .

I cut him off in turn. "You know I'm telling you the truth," I declared. "You know it was real. How can you say it's not happiness that I wanted, that it's not happiness that I want still?"

"Because you can't lie to me. You can lie to yourself, but you can't lie to *all* of yourself."

"Save me."

"Save you from what? Long ago ere this you would have slain yourself had not the sweet pleasures I gave you conquered deep despair."

He kicked at one of the bars of gold on the floor.

"You unappreciative prick," he said. "Though your brain can barely function, you gather the poetic bullshit to slur of butterflies and blue jays and magic clouds and happiness. You beg for salvation, and the while all you crave is gold and self-annihilation— a most odd combination as I see it. As the universal proverb has it, there are no pockets in a shroud. And you hardly need money to hasten your self-annihilation. There's no more smack about the place, but you've still got all that good old crushable oxycodone and a bag of insulin syringes right there on the shelf. And there's all that liquor still there waiting to be drunk. And all those other pills and shit you've got tucked away."

"Let's get out of here," I said.

"What you want to do can be done here. Besides, there are others out there." He cleared his throat. The pitch of his voice changed slightly as he delivered the quotation: "'I've always been interested in people, but I've never liked them.' That quite fits your own feelings, doesn't it?"

"Yeah, I know that one. Henry James. Or was it Somerset Maugham?"

"No evidence that either of them ever said it. I'm the one who said it, whispered it long ago to a barkeep in Trafalgar Square. If either of them said it, they got it from that barkeep. A moment of weary discontent, of wanting to turn my back on and turn away from it all. A moment such as this." He sighed. "But such is not one of the conjuring tricks allowed me. One might say that Nature casts her lots." He sighed again. "And you want four and twenty more years of this. Why not four and twenty thousand more years? Fool. If I had my druthers, if I had the powers of a storm god of olden myth, I'd blow it all asunder this very moment." Then a nuance of cheer entered his voice. "Or after the next drink, in any case."

I belched and sneezed in sickly counterpoint. Some sort of

bitter bile-like substance rose like a burning in my gut, and ran from my nostrils and gurgled from my mouth onto the front of my shirt. I held my stomach, for there seemed to be a pool of churning acid within it. With my free hand, I wiped at the slobber from my nose, lips, and chin. My body was rejecting and expelling the whiskey. Or maybe, worse, it was the water. I needed to switch to beer, to see if that would stay down. The rising acid in my gut would not subside. I felt my stomach constrict and convulse. Tremors ran through me.

"Well, pal o' mine," said he, "if we're to venture forth into society, no matter how low, I suggest you don a bib and diaper and try a change of trousers. Besotted, piss-sodden, befouled, and adrool. Thou biddest thyself adieu." He tsk-tsked as he beheld me.

I tried to speak, to force words through the rising bilious tide of acid that would have swallowed them in its undertow. Only guttural sounds and a spittle of vocules came out.

With two shaking hands I raised the near-empty glass to my mouth and tried to swallow. Sour saburral vomit spewed from my mouth and nostrils.

"Ah, in sooth, the puking sphinx!" he commented with a celebratory note in his voice.

"Gimme a beer," I demanded, wheezing. Words after all had come.

He rose, returned with a cold bottle of Asahi Super Dry, put it in my outstretched quivering hand. It felt good against the skin of my sweating palm and fingers.

"Enjoy it," he said. "It's the last one."

I pursed my lips and sipped tentatively. I belched deeply. It stayed down. The last one. I didn't ask myself how one who could emit gold kilos couldn't cough up a cold bottle of beer or two. I just opened my mouth wider and drank more freely. I belched, and my whole body shook when I did so—but the beer stayed down. I inhaled slightly—I could not take a deep breath—and lit a cigarette.

"Gimme Lorna."

"Oh," he said dismissively, "why her? Lorna. That boring crucified bitch in her peek-a-boo slicker. She ought to put a poor box at her door."

"Lorna," I said. "She would help me."

He waved his hand, with a more decisive, albeit silent, dismissiveness.

"Though I must say," he reflected calmly, "I did rather enjoy that night with the stun gun."

Yes, that night. It was her idea. I never asked her where she'd got the damned thing. A slim sort of two-pronged thing. At barely five inches it was mostly all handle, and weighed less than a pound. I had never held one in my hand before. It was black plastic with z-force sm and a lightning bolt and 100,000v printed on it, and it felt like a remote control, a small one, with most of its slight weight coming from the single nine-volt battery within it. She herself had no experience with one, either. She said she had been told that this was one of the lowest-powered stun guns available; that even the three-hundred-thousand-volt model was considered a lightweight. A hundred thousand volts didn't seem so weak to me, I said. But she just smiled, said "come on," and told me what she wanted; and it sounded good to me.

After our usual routine, as she began to climax spread-eagled on her cross, I stroked her sopping cunt with the plaited leather stock of the whip, hooped the whip over her head, placed a thick length of it in her open, eager mouth, which jerked forward for it. I stepped back, watching her head move to the sounds of her breathing deeply as she chewed and tongued the whip; seeing her sweet bared buttocks clench and unclench beneath the raised and bunched raincoat; watching and hearing it intensify.

I switched off the safety on the stun gun and when I heard the garbled feral scream "Now!" from round the whip in her mouth, I swooped my hand fast and stuck the two contact probes of the damned thing upward directly to her pussy for barely a second. She was praying for a clit-hit, and maybe she got one. The whip fell from her mouth and she screamed again as the jolt hit her, sending her body into a seizure of sorts before she passed out.

It was, she said later, cradled in my arms, the most unbelievable orgasm she ever felt. She offered to shoot me in the cock as I came in her face, but I demurred and ultimately declined. With the safety switched back on, she fell softly asleep sucking it like a beloved childhood thing.

"Yes, quite an evening, that," he said with a smile.

"Lorna," I said.

"Oh, enough of that. And why is it that you can only reach out for another person when you can barely reach out for another drink? What do you fear?"

"Death," I said, wandering back to his earlier words.

"Oh, that old farthing fuck-all of endless drivel. No. What are you really afraid of? Answer that in truth and we shall celebrate it, and you will be saved."

I drank the last of the beer. My mind was blank. There was nothing in me. Nothing but weakness, sickness, dread, and desperation. And together they were a black emptiness. Nothing. I could not answer him. All I could say was "No more beer?"

He sighed deeply, gravely, a bit whimsically.

"No," he said. "No more beer."

I stood on faltering legs. I did not wash and I did not change into clean clothes. I had not the strength, nor the care. In the taxi, we said almost nothing. I could see his reflection in the window through which I stared with blurred vision. Sitting next to me, he seemed to evanesce and materialize, evanesce and materialize, in a vague pattern of arrhythmic pulsations, now weak, now fast and hard, weak again, again fast and hard. I could hear them inside my ears, coming from within. By the time I realized these arrhythmic pulsations to be those of my own heartbeat, I could no longer see him beside me.

Propping myself on the corner barstool and staring into nothingness, I felt like a skull, a corpse, but anxious not to be taken, not to be recognized as such.

"Oh, no, not you again."

It was good, reassuring to hear Lee's laughter.

"Gin and tonic?" the bartender asked with an inscrutable grin. I wanted to say no, just a Guinness, but the words were too hard, too slow coming out.

"You're getting as bad as our friend, what's-his-name, there," Lee smiled. He drew nearer, took a whiff of me. "Worse." He laughed. "Maybe I should open up a funeral parlor upstairs. Catch 'em comin' and goin'." He laughed again.

I raised the glass. The place grew suddenly dark. This sent an enfilade through the arrhythmia of my heart. Everything became even darker and began to fade. The glass fell from my hand and spilled and shattered on the floor. A deafening skirl seemed to burst outward through my eardrums. Then, with my heart seeming about to burst as well, I tried to stand, and I fell crashing to the floor, feeling blackness overtake me as I fell.

I was dead.

THE LONG DARK PASSAGE, THE DARK PASSAGE LONGER THAN life. It could have been forever. It was only three days. When I first came to, I had no idea where I was. All I could remember was that I, whoever I was, had slept the deepest, most sublime sleep I had ever slept, and, for the first time, with dreams that were sweet and rapturous. That night-world teacup carnival ride in which those old men gaily relived the memories of the smut of their pasts—not erotica, nothing so cheap or stupid as that—in Fellini's strange, funny, and frightening *City of Women*. Or could that slowly swirling rising and falling teacup ride have been from another Fellini picture? No, it must have been *La Città delle Donne*. The colors were so lush. No matter: I had been there, dreaming without a care with the other old dreamers in the dream of that midnight dreamland ride of dreams, weaving round and round, reliving the luscious moments of life that were now alive again in dreams truer than any truth from which they had been born.

I remembered little else of what I dreamt. I felt more rested and more replenished than any sleep had ever left me feeling. This was short-lived, as I soon became aware that I was physically restrained. My wrists and elbows were bound to the side rails of the bed in which I lay. In time someone stood over me.

"You were in a coma for three days," he told me. "Every once in awhile you seemed about to come out of it. You were still out of it, still unconscious, when that happened, but whenever it did, you pulled the IV catheters out of your arms. We had to strap you down to keep you from doing that. Your life signs were pretty bad there for a while. It didn't seem that you were going to come out of that coma. And when it did, you yanked out the tubes that were keeping you alive. You're a lucky man."

"And what's in those tubes?"

"Saline solution and glucose."

I didn't ask. All I said was, "Well, I guess we can unstrap me now."

He left. Apparently it was beneath him to perform a menial task such as removing lengths of white tape. A black orderly came in a few minutes later and freed me.

"Welcome back, buddy," he said. "Where you been? Anywhere interestin'?"

I managed a worn-out laugh. He put to my mouth a straw that protruded from the sealed plastic lid of a plastic container.

"Here you go," he said. "This Bud's for you." He waited for me to take the straw between my lips. "Can you get that down?" It was water, and I got it down. "Man, you might be havin' yourself a reg'lar dinner in bed tonight."

I liked this guy better than the other guy.

In time the IV catheters were removed from my arms. They shot me up with something, then something else again, then yet again something else.

I was weak as hell, and disoriented. I could barely make it to the toilet to piss. But there was no delirium tremens. It was amazing. What was that shit they had shot me up with? They told me one was an anti-seizure drug. They told me the name of it, but I forgot. They would not tell me what the other drugs were, but I figured they had something to do with how all those alky and dope-addicted doctors made it to the office in the morning and they didn't want to reveal these remedies to common drunks or junkies like me.

The strawberry Jell-O that night was so good I asked for more, and they gave it to me. There were three other guys in the room with me, in various stages of getting well or croaking; it was hard to tell which. One guy introduced himself to me from his bed across the room. He lowered the sheet and cover, then peeled back a big patch of rubber from his abdomen, revealing a hole of sorts from which bubbles of shit emerged.

"Think I'm gonna die?" he asked me. He looked dead already.

"No, man," I said. "No way. You'll be out of here before you know it."

That seemed to cheer him a bit. But where was here? I did not even know what hospital I was in. All I knew was that, wherever I was, I wanted to get out.

Except for trips to the toilet, I lay in bed for three days. The shots came to an end. My blood was monitored regularly, insulin was delivered. In one of those trips to the toilet, I noticed with clear eyes how absolutely disgusting I was. My inner thighs, crotch, and ass were crusted thick with dried shit. There was a bath-and-shower room in the hall for ambulatory patients. I shaved, showered, and washed my hair under the watch of an orderly. I rubbed myself dry with a clean towel, put on a fresh Hospitex robe, combed my hair, and cleaned my nails. I asked for fresh bedding for my bed, and after some discussion, it was agreed that the bed rails could be removed as well.

And yet they kept me there another three days, performing every medical test on me that they could come up with, to wring every dollar from me that they could. For some of these tests I had to fast for a day in preparation. They found some sort of mushroom farm inside my throat, and only after further costly tests—it seemed, according to them, that this gullet fungus was often a symptom of AIDS or some such thing—only then, after there was no more money to be made from probing this anomaly, did a senior doctor appear to dismiss it all to a doctor within my earshot with the words: "Oh, he's been using his esophagus for nothing but drinking and smoking for so long; that's all that is."

The ophthalmologist had a pleasant disposition, and, with an ulterior motive, I began making small talk with him as he examined me. I told him of a cousin—less suspect as a subterfuge for oneself, I figured, than the invented generic friend—who had perfect vision but whose eyes seemed to change colors often and with great rapidity.

"Sounds like some kind of iridial anisochromia," he said abstractedly, intent on my own eyes. "It has to do with the flow of blood in the back of the eye, with the pigmented tissue in the eye, the density of cells in the iris. All sorts of things. Sometimes it passes, brought on by stress or sudden changes to metabolic balances. People who have permanently multicolored eyes—central heterochromia—are called cat-eyed."

Fucking Keith. Fucking me, staring into the mirror, going around in those dark shades.

The second or third time blood was drawn from me, I asked what type of blood I had. The guy said, "You don't know your blood type? You should." He looked down at my chart. "You're type A."

No mention of B glycoproteins, no mention of anything. Fucking labs.

Once the croakers were done with me, the head-case guys took over. The first of them asked me a series of questions, sort of like a test of some kind. One of the questions was "What does the phrase 'you can't teach an old dog new tricks' mean to you?" I knew how to play these guys.

"It's like what Aristotle said: 'You can't pour water into a full pitcher.' If a person refuses to empty his mind of long-held beliefs, he can accept no new, different, and better beliefs or ways of thinking and behaving. They will just overflow and be lost."

Aristotle had said no such thing. It was an impromptu paraphrase of some Zen jive about only an empty mind being ready and prepared to accept new wisdom. I think the Zen saying employed a full teacup—oh, that ride, that beautiful ride and that beautiful coma and its beautiful dreamy sleep—rather than a full pitcher. But in rendering the adage of the doctor's question in a more eloquent way and attributing it to Aristotle, I accomplished several things. I showed him, through my sham interpretation, that I was aware of the importance, even the need, of accepting change. I showed him that I was familiar with Aristotle, one of the pillars of Western learning, on which his own education had been based, and was therefore a man to be distinguished from the usual grist of his mill. (Assuming that he had never read Aristotle was a very safe shot; and even if he had tried to read him, he would have thought, without daring to reveal it, that he had missed or forgotten this pitcher business. In getting him to accept this phony Aristotelian syllogism, I gained the upper hand. To attribute it truthfully, to Zen, would have led him to suspect me of being a bit "off," especially as he was of neither Japanese nor Chinese descent.) In sum, I showed him—or, rather, gave him the quite convincing impression—that I was sane and fully equipped to see and correct the wrongfulness of my ways.

This doctor was followed only minutes later by another man in a white smock. He proceeded to ask me the very same questions that the previous crackpot had asked me. A check for consistency, for stability of mind. He was a diminutive Filipino.

"Are you an intern here?" I asked with feigned interest and kindness after the first question I had been asked was repeated by him. I smiled gently.

He said that, yes, he was.

"Oh," I said with subdued mock surprise, "that's why you're asking me the same questions the doctor just asked me. This must be part of your training. Well, he already has the answers that I gave. But if this is a matter of comparing your notes to his, I'll be happy to repeat my answers for you."

He thanked me, and I went through that rigmarole with false patience, false good cheer, and just a tad of added explication here and there as if to help him out in view of his lesser experience and erudition than the previous quack.

After lunch I called my friend Frankie. His was the only telephone number I remembered other than my own. I told him where I was, asked him to bring me a new pair of pants, a new pair of socks, a new shirt, a pack of Parliaments, a box of Nico-Derm patches, a pack of lined index cards, and a pen. While I was on the phone, they wheeled out the corpse of the guy who had asked me if I thought he was going to live.

That afternoon they took me to the office of the chief nut-cracker. He had you at a disadvantage right there: him sitting there in his impeccable white shirt and asshole Hermès necktie beneath what seemed to be a formal, custom-tailored, impeccable white smock, and you in a cheap chair across the desk from him in a flimsy cotton hospital gown that barely covered your balls and kept slipping from your shoulder as he held forth with an air of superiority.

"When you were brought here," he began, his eyes rising from the clipboard chart before him to look perfunctorily into my own eyes, "you were suffering from severe alcohol poisoning, malnutrition, dehydration, and other life-threatening conditions that brought about a state of coma. You also upon entering exhibited all the symptoms of what is called a schizophreniform disorder. It may also have been what is called a brief psychotic disorder. The difference between the two is one of duration. A brief psychotic disorder lasts from a day to a month. Schizophreniform disorder lasts from a month to six months. Both are serious and, combined with periods of alcoholic drinking or other forms of substance abuse, can deter the natural remittance of these disorders and result in what we call substance-induced psychotic disorder or even full-blown schizophrenia and psychosis." He looked perfunctorily again into my eyes and said, "You, my friend, have been playing with fire." A blasé theatricality in his voice led me to believe that this was one of his standard lines. "If there is a next time, the fire will win."

But, ah, the sweet sleep, the sweet dream, the sweet teacup ride! As I thought of these things, I presented the figure of one who heeded and hung on his every word.

Frankie, as I knew he would, came through for me. I wrote on the first of the index cards, in the best penmanship I could: "What a fool. All these years. All this wasted time." On other cards I wrote a lot of toned-down versions of half-remembered lines from Milton—notes for my new book, I would say, if asked. I placed two of the nicotine patches on my upper arms, left the opened box conspicuously on the bed, then went into the toilet for a smoke. A couple of nurses smelled it, but the opened box of nicotine patches on the bed worked well.

"At least he's trying," I heard one of the nurses say to the other.

I trashed my old puke-stained, shit-stained, piss-stained pants and shirt and stinking socks. The pants, shirt, and socks Frankie had brought me waited neatly in the narrow little locker near my bed.

The valedictory address came the next morning.

"I hope you know," the young doctor said, "that if you take another drink, the next ride you take after that will be with a sheet over your head."

I did my best to assure him with my facial expression and a slight, repentant nod that I was well aware of this. It had to have been almost thirty years since I had first heard that line of shit.

"I strongly advise that you go to A.A. and get yourself a sponsor," he said.

"I've already called someone about that," I lied.

"You might also look into Silver Hills. It's only about an hour or so from here, in New Canaan. I can't speak highly enough of it."

"Do you have a brochure or something?" I asked with convincing interest and sincerity, with just the right hint of trepidation in my voice.

"I'll look. If not, you can just call there." He wrote down the name and location on one of my index cards. "You can find it on the Internet, too."

I sat on the edge of the bed silently, as if waiting for, even hoping for, him to say more. Then I said simply, quietly, "Thank you, Doctor."

"Remember," he said, "when the going gets tough, the tough get going. But you can't do it alone."

Fucking punk. What was he, half my age? What did he know from tough.

When he stood to leave, I stood. I thanked him again, put out my hand to shake his.

I got dressed, signed my extortion papers, and got out of there, grinning, lighting a smoke, free under the crisp blue sky in the breezy morning air. De day ob jubilee!

Autumn was here. The first sough of its lovely diapason wove through all that was. Exundant, glorious autumn. My season.

The last time I had escaped from one of these joints, it was a balmy summer night. I had jumped into a taxi, lowered the window all the way as the cabbie sped off with the fat guy in the toupee singing "New York, New York" loud and clear through the cab's speakers. I had him take me straightaway to the bar.

But this time was going to be different. I walked awhile, a good while, slow and easy. Then I got a cab to take me home. Yes, this time it was going to be different, very different.

WHEN I GOT HOME, THE FIRST THING I DID WAS TO fetch a thirty-gallon black plastic garbage bag from the cabinet under the kitchen island, swing wide the refrigerator door, and empty all the rotten, spoiled, and soured food from it into the bag. Without shutting the refrigerator, I opened the kitchen window to let in good air. I then went about, gathering up and tossing into the bag the mess of bottles, empty and dregful alike, and bottle caps and wadded paper napkins and such that were scattered, alone and in clusters, throughout the room. It was a shame to see the remains of that dead snake go.

I hauled the big, heavy bag out of the apartment to the disposal chute in the outer hall, pulled down the chute door, forced and maneuvered its weighty bulk through the disposal opening, and heard the bagged bottles bang and crash with loud noise in their five-flight fall to the basement. I never recycled garbage. Even if it didn't all end up in the same landfill, I still wouldn't do it. This world was shot, irremediably so. Recycling garbage was like flicking lint from the collar of a stiff as he lay in his coffin.

Back in the kitchen, I set the dirty glasses and silverware that were lying round into the sink to soak in hot soapy water. I dipped a sponge into the water and scrubbed the stains from the floor, counters, and tabletop. I went into the living room, took the over-flowing ashtrays and emptied them into the toilet and flushed, then left them to soak with the glasses in the sink. With a wet paper towel I cleaned the surfaces of the small tables at either end of the couch and some stains of unknown origin on the floor.

There were clothes strewn about. After going through their pockets, I tossed them in a heap into the washing machine. I threw back the sheet and light cover on the bed, opened wide the bedroom window. I poured bleach down the toilets, into the sinks. Then I slammed shut the refrigerator door. I left and bought fresh milk, eggs, butter, bread, some cold cuts, and some fruit. I boosted only a single but expensive bar of pure handmade bath soap.

The washed clothes were in the dryer, the cleaned, rinsed glasses were set on paper towels. I went to the telephone. Twenty-seven messages awaited me. I erased them all without listening to any of them. I went to the computer. There were at least a hundred e-mails in the in-box. I deleted them all without looking at them. Both of these acts felt very freeing.

I finished drying one of the ashtrays by hand. I poured cold, fresh milk into a sparkling clean glass, set them on the end table at my side of the couch. I washed down ten milligrams of baclofen, ten milligrams of Valium with big slugs of cool water, sat down wearily, lit a smoke, took a sip of milk, and sighed wearily. It was a most pleasant weariness.

Some of the erased messages must have been calls of care and concern from Lorna. Maybe there was among them even a plea or two to come back to me from Melissa.

This may not have been true, not any of it. But it made me feel good to believe that it was.

I called Frankie, let him know I was all right and thanked him for being a friend in need. We laughed about doctors and hospitals and illness and age. When I hung up, and then shut off the phone, I took to wondering what others might be thinking had become of me. Maybe they thought I was dead or lay dying in some unknown place. Whether or not this was true, it too made me feel good somehow to believe it was.

Back in my own bed, in my own exorcised home, I slept long and well, and rose early the next day. I went out, bought buttermilk at a corner store, moved on to Whole Foods for more provisions: a big thick boneless rib eye steak, baking spuds, onions, strawberries, coffee, a pint of half-and-half. I was now adept at boosting from the butcher counter. After the meat was wrapped and price-stickered, I merely rounded an aisle and slipped it in a jacket pocket. On my way out, I slipped a sixteen-ounce container of Hemp Pro 70 protein-and-omega-3 into my bag. The stuff went for $24.99, but it was good—even better when free—and I liked to mix a big, heaping tablespoon of it into my buttermilk in the morning. Walking home, I bought bottled water and cigarettes at the same corner store where I had bought the buttermilk.

After putting everything away, I turned on the phone, called Elena, my cleaning lady of almost thirty years, and arranged to have her come by in a few days. Then I shut off the phone again.

I took my vitamins, my supplements, my baclofen, drank down a big glass of buttermilk and hemp protein. I put on some Bach cello suites, took a Valium, and poured myself a glass of cold milk. It was quiet outside. There was only the Bach. I sat and lit a cigarette. I felt great, calm, free.

There was a cigarette butt on the floor, where my fortune in gold bullion had lain. How this butt had escaped my previous notice I did not know. I rose, picked it up, and went to the kitchen to throw it in the trash. Sure enough, it was an English Oval butt. I had already found the English Oval pack in a pocket of the dirty clothes I had laundered. There were still a few cigarettes left in the pack, which I had set near the ashtray on the end table. How had I come to have a pack of English Ovals? I must have got them from the array of cigarettes on display for sale at Circa Tabac. I hadn't smoked one for so many years that I had forgotten what they tasted like, though not what they looked like: sort of as if someone had sat on them. Maybe I had wanted to take another shot at figuring out why Frank Costello had been so enamored of them. I knew that they were looked on as quite elegant in Costello's heyday. But I did not know if they were still made of the same tobacco, or if they had ever even been English. I knew that their maker, Philip Morris, had started out as a tobacconist in nineteenth-century London, but I also knew that Philip Morris had moved to America in the early twentieth century. And I knew that, whatever they tasted like back in the 1930s, 1940s, and 1950s, Costello smoked between two and three packs of them every day.

I lit one, which was probably quite stale by now, inhaled, and sought not to figure out what Frank Costello had liked about them, but thought only of what he had said about there being only so many bullets in the gun. How true, I told myself, how true. And mine, like his when he said those words, were used up. Or were they?

My eyes closed, and I wandered. He was right, of course. I was afraid. Not foremost and above all of death. But something. Knowing this did not affect the loveliness of my mood. I pondered it as I pondered the silent mystery of clouds in the sky. No, not death. But something. For a very many years I had fancied myself, and been fancied by others, fearless.

Those years were behind me now. And in my acknowledging and searching for the fear within me, however unknown its nature, and doing so in serene, unflinching calm, perhaps the fancy of fearlessness was drifting cloud-like to the reality of fearlessness. Or, cloud-like, to nothing at all.

THERE WAS RISOTTO WITH MARROW ON THE MENU, BUT THE waiter said they were out of marrow.

This sent us to studying anew the menus we had pushed aside. The waiter made several suggestions as we did so, but waiters seemed always to suggest what the kitchen was trying to be rid of. We each ordered a dry-aged young Hereford sirloin steak for two, telling the waiter that we wanted them burnt on the outside and very rare on the inside. Spuds with some kind of fancy name, peas with same. I told Keith I wasn't drinking. "Well, I am," he said, sipping his Campari and soda and looking over the wine list.

"Remember the last time we had dinner," I said, "I asked you if you'd ever drunk blood?"

"Yes." He laughed. "And how is the old vein-broaching business these days?"

"You were all, like, oh, God, no, don't go there. You said you could tell by my eyes that I was headed for trouble."

"As I recollect, you seemed half insane. Looked it, too, if you don't mind my saying. 'Barney Google with the Goo-Goo-Googly Eyes.'" He indecisively ordered a bottle of some grand cru or other. "My grandmother Emily used to love that song."

He palpated the cork, took a snort of the wine, knocked off the taste in the glass, nodded, and the sommelier decanted and poured.

"I thought it was the dope or the booze that was dragging you down by the yoke. Believe me, mate, you were not you."

"And what was all that about seeing things coming out of people?"

"What?" He laughed. Then: "Oh, that. I did at one time or another. I saw things come out of people. I didn't say that things came out of them. I said that *I* saw things come out of them."

"And you said it led to their death."

"Well, hell, look, they are now pushing up daffodils, but my seeing things coming out of them had nothing to do with it."

This was somewhat like getting him to try to remember what he had said about Paganini, or whoever it was.

"Did you ever hear of Magnan's sign?" he asked. "It's a type of—what the fuck do they bloody call it?—some sort of, some kind of paraphasia, or paraesthesia, or para-something-or-other where you feel things moving under your skin or coming through your skin or whatever. It's mostly an end-of-the-line coke thing."

"Never heard of it."

"Well, maybe I had a spot or two of it in reverse, seeing it in others rather than myself. Or maybe their ranting about what they felt under their skin and saw coming through it made me, in whatever state I may have been in at the time, see it too. Worms, I think it might have been, or little baby snakes, some such nonsense."

The steaks arrived, and the spuds and peas with the fancy names.

"That was the first song I ever learned to play properly, drop-down, on guitar: 'Cocaine.' I learned it from an album, ten-inch album, that Jack Elliott put out in England in 1958 or so. I learned that in the john of my art school. It was so pretty. I had no idea what cocaine was. I just surmised it was some weirdo grown-up perversion. I really didn't know what it was. I didn't know what cocaine was."

He burst out in laughter, shook his head, cut off a piece of steak, swabbed it in the blood that ran from it.

"I don't use cocaine," I said. "The only times I ever did, it was to help me stay awake to drink more. Never really saw much in it."

"You never had the good stuff, the real Bolivian marching powder."

We chewed awhile in quiet.

"Anyway, all the same shit," he said. "Smack, coke"—he gestured with his fork to the glass of Médoc before him—"booze. All the same."

"Well, all I know is I wasn't fucked-up that night."

"You'd checked your mind in the cloakroom of a place you couldn't remember." He laughed.

Schizophreniform disorder. Drive-by psychosis. Magnan's sign.

"I saw ghost-rats, shadow-rats come out of me," I said.

"Worms, rats, snakes, belching frogs. Whatever. We could start a zoo of empty cages and terrariums. People have paid more to see less."

"You had me going that night," I told him.

"Ah, you know me. Preaching is the one thing I've never been accused of. But I wanted to give you a kick, a gentle kick, in the right direction." He ate some of the spuds with the fancy name. "Right direction," he repeated. "Sometimes I wonder what direction that might be."

I finished my peas with the fancy name. I always dispose first of what I like least.

"Anyway," he said, "I'll take you any way I can get you, but I prefer you like this. Nobody at this table is getting any younger. And you've got that diabetes thing, like my old man, Bert." His tone lightened. "He looked just like Popeye, old Bert did."

I asked him how the Hoagy Carmichael album was coming

along. He looked at me as if he suspected that I was trying to give him a dig, which I was.

"We will sell no wine before its time."

He told me that he didn't even have a record label these days. Then we were on to the evaporation of the recording business, and the publishing business, the downloading from the ether of both music and books, all executed with the suckers' shibboleth of "back money."

We were lucky, we reflected, to have grown up as boys in a world full of magic vinyl and cheap paperbacks all about and waiting to be discovered for a few coins. The best stuff was happened upon by accident. Discovery after discovery in the oddest of bins in the oddest of shops. But now the age of discovery was over. All were reduced to industrially bred cows at the same trough of the same slop.

Suddenly we realized that we had not taken a cigarette break.

"If only our forgetfulness could have gone on forever," he said as we made our way out of the restaurant into the street.

I asked him if he knew whether or not English Ovals had originated in England.

"Oh, those things. The ones that come pre-sat-upon. I've no idea. I don't much remember seeing them around there when I was coming up."

We stood silently smoking awhile.

"Why do you ask?" he said.

"I don't know. Maybe because lately I've been concerned inexplicably with meaningless things. With questions whose answers have no meaning. I don't know."

We smoked awhile more in silence.

"It's all meaningless," he said. "And it all has meaning."

I looked at him, flicking my butt toward the gutter.

"And I have not the least fucking idea why I said that," he said, laughing, "or whatever it could possibly mean."

He flicked his butt. We returned slowly to the restaurant. As we did so, he glanced at the night sky and sang a few lines.

Barney Google tried to enter paradise,
Saint Peter saw his face, he said "Go to the other place."

The sky above the spiritless electric haze of this island of dead souls was about as black as it ever got. It was good to imagine that someday black night would reclaim it, and the firmament would again be one of stars near and far.

YES, AUTUMN WAS MY SEASON. IT WAS WHEN I FELT WHAT was beyond the power to express. Part of that feeling was a minor-key fugue of deep, delicious melancholy that filled me and swept me into myself and the billowing swift-moving clouds at once. With every bright leaf I saw drift away in its death, borne by a breeze or a gust, the feeling grew deeper, and the melancholy became more exquisite than ecstasy: an inspiration, a truth of sadness and joy dancing gently together in a way that almost brought to the eyes the tears, so unknown and so longed for, of happiness and sorrow commingled.

I had once articulated this autumn spell as best I could, looking back on other autumns. I remembered recalling in it the autumn of my mother's death, the autumn I shared with the love of my life, the autumn I lost her, or drove her from me—autumns and autumns, when times were good and when times were bad, but, no matter what, that same autumn spell cast its magic.

This had been written down in one of my notebooks or diaries, and I now set about searching for it. While, after many hours, these words were not to be found, I remained convinced that I still had them, somewhere. What I did find was a darkly revealing shock. As I went through the pages of decades of disparate notes, I saw that they possessed what my labors of long composition, my books, very often lacked: a theme. I had in fact some time ago consciously forsaken and denounced the frill of theme as almost as silly a writerly pretense as symbolism. Yet here, scribbled amid the omniana of these ruled and unruled pages, spanning from the 1970s to the 1990s, I encountered what struck me increasingly as not only a theme, but the theme of my being.

In the oldest of the notebooks were the ancient Greek words for "poet of savagery" (αγριοποιος) and "beyond even the gods' ability to express" (αθεστος). There was the orphaned phrase "Louise, in the darkness of her desire." In notebooks that followed came—and I here set them down chronologically, be they notes intended for envisioned novels, diary entries, or personal secrecies:

> *I think these things—they plague me—awful dark moistures of past dreadful deeds or sins—and then somehow find myself smiling in the dark, my mind one way, my heart another...rapacity...fill mouth with water before blowing brains out...Face down, legs apart—wide, unmoving. In sleep you are a stranger. By some unbeing river in a dream you might meet me, slaughter me, and move on. I stare at you, kneel by you, by the bed, and masturbate. I rise, wipe the sperm from my hand, and sleep myself, by some river you do not know...*
>
> *She made him jealous, made him want to kill her, and he did...deathward...*quattuor novissima—*the last four things...Hamlet's resolution to 'speak daggers'—III.ii.387...*
>
> *Her blood so sweet...*Illaque favente dolore—*fondling me in sorrow...*Vera incessu patuit dea—*she walked in the manner of a goddess...*ψυχοδλεθρος—*the death of the soul...Indo-European* ne, *the primeval grunt of negativity, negation;* nek, *destroy* → *Greek* nekros, *dead body, and* nux, *night, Latin* nox, *Italian* notturno, *Germanic* night...Indo-European leuk, *shining* → *Sanskrit*

loka, *open space, the universe, Greek* leuko, *Latin* lux, Lucifer, *Germanic* light... *Death is this night's light... I used to drink and fuck. What do I do now? I write: I used to drink and fuck... I am going mad, or growing sane, in the dullest, the deadliest of ways... "fucked girls and fat leopards"—Pound, Canto XXXIX... Pound re nuclear bomb / nuclear holocaust: "Step on it" (1946, St. Elizabeths)... the leopard alone removes the hide from the carcass of its prey... caress the dead... something in the blood... the blood of black night...*

There is a sadness within me as vast and as deadly as the Eocene dusk... He had never fallen for her, not really. It was better that way. He would've ended up hating her, loving her, one of those things... I wish I had a mother... To be like the leopard, to devour, to lay open the heart and drink the blood of beauty. To move with that blood flowing in the veins, unseen, like leopard or like wild dog, predator... May the leopard within become a creature of grace w/ no need again... "that which we are, we are"—Tennyson, Ulysses... *"Whatever you is, be that"—Lightnin' Hopkins...*

I have come from Mastema, have come from the quiet well of your fear. Enter me... When I drew the blade across her throat it was not only the blood of her extinction that flowed forth but also that of any love I might henceforth know... There is no love in my heart. There is nothing in my heart.

Words come to me from an ancient stillness, from nowhere... and to know that there is no love in one's heart is to know love itself. And so—delendum est—I await the breath from the mouth of the Other... What cunt of you gods did rhythm my life w/ ink so black to leave me here to die alone?... umbrosus et immensus... *"Fear stops men."—Homer... the demon confessor...*

I await the savioress. I await deliverance. I cannot dwell here, in the dark of me, alone. A dark enshrouded in dark. A man can rip out his own liver, but not his own brain, not his mind.

The first time I saw her, I wanted to rape her. Not have sex with her, not make love to her: rape her. Maybe you can understand this. Why have I written that last line? There is no you. No one will ever see this. I am the you to whom I write. I am you. The only you. And of course I can understand this. I—you—of course we understand it...

*I wanted to know. But I did not want to know what I ended up knowing...*in hora mortis...odium Dei...*What Hesiod knew of neuroscience we have yet to learn...."Thomas Cantipratensis, a Dominican of the thirteenth century, beheld the Devil in the form of a priest, who was exhibiting himself in a most indecent attitude."—Arturo Graf,* Il Diavolo *(1889), English translation (1931), p. 35. Term "altar boy" not known until 1772...*

"Ye are of your father the Devil, and the lusts of your father ye will do. He was a murderer from the beginning..."—John 8:44... "Good and evil things fall without discrimination upon those who are good and those who are evil."—Marcus Aurelius, Meditations...

Heel in 🜨*, ottobre 17...*

Let those who care for me, and those who do not care for me, die. Let those who share these breezes perish... On a night such as this, I arm myself against love and disbelieve in all that has inspired and brought me breath. I prepare to go down... I had delivered myself. I was to know my fate...

1/16/94. Twenty-five years, a quarter of a century ago, I fucked her, came in her cunt, her mouth, her ass. Today, on the phone, sitting here watching Dallas not beat the spread,

Houston not beat anything, on this freezing day, coldest since 1893, she somewhere in Pennsylvania, not far from Valley Forge, said she's a grandmother; he's the joy of her life. How strange and how long the years. It's as if that quarter century, what began w/ her, ended w/ Linda. That quarter century is over. Do I have another left to live? It is time to seize the years, these years, these moments—time to draw new blood, new life, new cunt into these days to mingle with, to temper, and to lighten the company of ghosts...

This last entry, this reflection and resolution of long ago, had been written, I could tell from its date, in my old poky flat in the Village, not long before I moved to my present place. But I had moved so little, inwardly, since that reflection and resolution of long ago.

I discontinued my search. I was unsettled to see my inner life so unchanged through all these years, from what was written in the oldest, leather-bound sketchbook, from the early 1970s, to the smaller notebook of the 1990s, to this very day, many years after abandoning the recording of such things. I had traveled the world, experienced much, learned much, done much, escaped death and the death-in-life of the workaday world. But I had not changed through all these years. These volumes of words to and of and by myself, from the earliest to the last of them, no matter how impressionistically, attested to this undeniably. They revealed my insides when they were written, and they revealed my insides today.

From the first diary entry to the last—I had stopped some years before the end of the century—the sporadic accounts of the days of my life reeked of booze and sex and desolation and little else. There were names of people that I no longer even faintly recognized. Many dated entries bore only the word DRUNK, noted after the end of this bender or that in a devastating succession of them. The sex grew more sparse as the entries neared their end, but not the drunkenness and not the desolation.

What I read obliterated the search for my lost eloquence on the nuanced elusive magic of the fall. It all but obliterated that sense of magic itself.

All that blood. All that loneliness, no matter the laughter and companionship of the barroom scrouge, no matter the rare, loving women or all the others who held me close night after night, swooning in or accommodating me as I discharged my desperation into them. The leopards. All that death and all that dark. And, like a haunted rustling through it all, the fear.

I must change. Once and for all. For real. I must. But this realization, this resolution, seemed heartbreakingly futile in light, or in the darkness, of all that lay before me, the testament of my years, the seeming proof, in these pages and in me now, that I was ever thus, and thus I would ever be.

Could what I had written have been less of errant memoir, notation, and contemplation, but rather a foresight into what was to follow? Not a capturing of this moment or that, but more the annals of a foredooming, a capturing of the inevitable moments of here and now?

I saw the blood on the razor-like Japanese killing blade. I saw the leopard awaiting glance. I saw myself laying the whip hard to Lorna on her makeshift cross. I saw myself as I had been the other night, making love to the hosiery and high heels that Melissa had left behind, fucking them and with a wicked sigh telling myself afterward that it was better that way, for there was no one there, no one near, when the lovemaking was done. My preferred company—what had I called it?—"the company of ghosts." Happily ever after, with a bunch of pantyhose and a few high heels, watching the shadows fall, seeing them grow darker every time they fell.

Where were they now: Lorna, Melissa, the others? They were here, with me. Ghosts.

His words whispered again through the air. Loath as I was to return to that night, I heard them. They were without voice.

"And why is it that you can only reach out for another person when you can barely reach out for another drink? What do you fear?"

I said aloud, with a bit of false roguish sarcasm, as if to banish the questions without voice:

"Ah, yes: To be, or not to be."

But the questions, which I had unintentionally but very justly equated with Hamlet's question, still whispered soundlessly in the air. For me—maybe for everyone—the questions came down to the same fear. There could be no life where fear lurked.

Enough of this. It occurred to me that I wanted to smoke a bit of pot. This was something I only very rarely did; but I recently had been given a small amount of good Hawaiian buds by a dealer—he was the only dealer I knew who could get real Hawaiian marijuana, as well as Nepalese hashish, these days—in the hope that I would lay out a few grand for more when the soon-coming harvest season arrived. I hated to roll joints. I used a little corncob pipe, which I stuffed and puffed away at. Fuck those journals. Fuck fear. Fuck everything. I felt like watching an old movie. But a good one or a bad one? As I coughed and tapped the pipe empty into the kitchen sink, I deliberated as to which would be more entertaining.

I washed down a Valium with water and took to the couch with a glass of cold goat milk.

It was then that it hit me, in a most undramatic manner. I was roaming back in time, back to a time in my life before there was a word that I could read or write, before even the alphabet was known to me. My mother and father had gone to a picture show or a nightclub or something, and they had left me in the good care of my grandmother, whom I loved dearly, from earliest and all but unremembered childhood until now, almost forty years after her death. She could not read or write either, not even in her native Italian; so we made a good pair. As that night progressed, I became aware that it was getting quite late. This led to the unshakeable conviction that my mother and father were not coming back. They had run off, fled from me, left me with my father's mother, and would never return and were gone from me forever. They had abandoned me. My grandmother assured me in her best broken English that this was absolutely not true. I cried and yowled so wildly and ceaselessly in my imagined abandonment that my grandmother's daughter, my aunt Dora, who knew how to use a telephone, was pressed upon by her mother to call the theater or nightclub or wherever it was that my mother and father were, and get my mother to the phone to reassure me that she loved me and was coming back in a little while. Words, lies, not to be believed or trusted. In the end, they left wherever they were and returned to me. As well as I could remember, it was the first night out they had taken for themselves; and I ruined it for them. I don't know where this overwhelming, all-consuming fear of being abandoned came from. Could one be born with the sprouting seed of such a fear? All I know is that, from that night on, though there was no more crying, no more yowling, the fear of abandonment was in me like a growing, stifling vine.

I did not recognize it as such. I did not recognize it as I drove away every woman who loved me, before she had a chance to abandon me. I did not recognize it as I went about allowing no one to get close to me, not really close, lest she betray and abandon me. All my life, I did not recognize or sense this great fear of abandonment at work. I was not aware of its dominion over me.

I saw myself rising in blind, senseless wrath, rapping Melissa on the ass with that length of pipe, telling her to get out. She could never abandon me, then. It was my way.

Where was she now? And Lorna, who might have enjoyed the smack of the pipe on her ass, whom I simply cast aside, not remembering when or how; but now knowing why.

In driving away love and intimacy—drunkenness and sex took their place—I had inflicted on myself and perpetuated and nourished my own fear. I lived in self-imposed abandonment. I had chosen to live, or exist, in fear. I had not only surrendered to it; I had enslaved myself to it. And I never suspected it, choosing instead to be a noble creature, a lone leopard who needed nothing or no one, except as prey. No, I really never knew it.

Until this moment, on this holy autumn night.

LIKE ALMOST ALL REVELATIONS, THIS PARTING OF THE clouds of unknowing, this brilliant forthshining fear-of-abandonment illumination, was little more than pure bullshit.

Better it would have been to watch that old movie, good or bad. That was all reefer was really good for: making you stupid enough to enjoy that which was stupid.

I had recalled a meaningless childhood incident, nothing more than that, and invested it with meaning. It was not the luminous insight into the origin of what imbued my life. It was not the sagacious guide to understanding my past, my ways, my nature, and my life that I had taken it to be. I had in my head composed my own personal Book of Revelation; and like that Revelation of Saint John the Divine, it made not one fucking bit of sense. The book of the Seven Seals held not wisdom but folly. Rimbaud did not go nearly far enough when he said that everything we are taught is a lie, a farce. *"Tout ce que nous croyons que nous savons est farce,"* not *"Tout ce qu'on nous enseigne est farce,"* would have been more like it: Everything we think we know is a lie.

This statement has nothing to do with Epimenides, nothing to do with Eubulides, nothing to do with paradox. It is the simple truth. It was true when the first thought entered and skewed the brain of *Homo habilis,* and it has been true ever since. Look at what we call ourselves, in the idiotic arrogance of what we think we know! *Homo sapiens*—wise, or knowing, man! The self-anointed crown of evolution, and, no less, self-proclaimed to have been created in the very image of the God of his own idiotic imagination. Yes, everything we think we know is a lie. *Ipso facto.* Everything.

I did not drive people from me to preclude or prevent them from abandoning me. I simply didn't want them around me for long. If you take a good look at yourself, you'll understand why.

It was never I who in my years cried out in any tongue: *lama sabachthani?* It was never I who in my years crooned the theme song from *High Noon*. No, anybody who needs another person in a lasting way is just lacking.

I recall a night in a bar on the Lower East Side. Me, my friend Frankie, and the woman whom at the time I was living with. It was the dead of winter, snowing hard. I don't remember what it was that I said to her—the woman with whom I was living—but it must have been so grossly insulting that she stood, announced that she was through with me, and that was that. She was not at all drunk, and I had never known her to react so resolutely to my verbal abuse. She buttoned her coat, drew her scarf close, put on her woolen hat, and strode out through the door.

"You might want to go out there, catch up with her and apologize," Frankie said.

"Ah," I said, "she'll be back in five minutes. And if not, fuck her."

Frankie looked at me, shook his head, laughed low, and said:

"You're probably the most self-sufficient son-of-a-bitch I ever knew."

He was right. Where was my fear of abandonment then? There was none. Not then, not on any of the occasions when those I loved walked out on me, with or without being confronted by what some might call my "bad side." I had never really been shaken up by abandonment. It had only brought me closer to myself, and to a feeling of gratitude that there was a me to be close to. Why had I so foolishly, in my Revelation of Saint Nick the Divine, dwelt only on those I had cast away, and not those who had cast me away? It was as I jokingly told people when they brought up the subject of cohabitation:

"I can't even live with myself, but I do retain visitation rights."

I wanted to be alone, except for when I didn't want to be alone. And I wanted it my way on both counts. I wanted it as I wanted it whenever I wanted it. Of course, this was something far easier said than done. Hence the pangs of loneliness, hence the desire to be rid of, or to be got rid of by, whoever breathed on me when I wanted to breathe alone.

But I could handle it. One day I might wake in the middle of the night and wring my hands in loss and in longing for Melissa. At the moment, however, I was happier to have her silent nylons and shoes than to have her.

At the computer, I went to the Internet and searched under the words "pantyhose encasement." Ninety-nine bucks and eighty cents later, I had ordered three DVDs. Their titles were straightforward: *Sexy Seamless Hardcore Pantyhose Action, Pantyhose Multilayer Fetish Sex,* and *Sexy Lesbian Pantyhose Fetish Sex.*

I was set. While at the computer, I went to my iTunes thing and put on Tony Bennett's recording of "This Is All I Ask," a song that my buddy Pete Wolf had turned me on to one day when we were talking about getting old. I turned up the volume and went to take some baclofen and pour a glass of cold goat milk.

Beautiful girls, walk a little slower
When you walk by me . . .

It was superbly autumnal: the music, the milk, the relishing of having escaped false revelation; all of it.

More music, less sublimely melancholic, far less; but no less superbly autumnal.

> *Ain't gonna be no wedding, baby,*
> *No vows beneath no trees.*
> *Truth be told, little girl,*
> *I'm in love just with your knees.*
> *Gimme your knees,*
> *Your knees is all I need.*
> *Gimme your knees;*
> *On thy patella shall I feed.*

I was dancing slowly round the room, alone and smiling, with no feeling or pity for those who were not. My own Parousia was here!

May every altar boy kneel with open mouth before every priest!

May Satan take every soul and fetch me pastrami from the Second Avenue Deli!

Fuck the second fucking coming of the king of the kikes! Multilayer pantyhose sex was coming!

All that was holy, let it be holy still. Holy, holy, holy!

> *Well, God gave you them knees*
> *To give 'em unto me;*
> *I'll grease them up good and set you free.*
> *Might work my way*
>
> *Up or down a foot or so;*

There just ain't no tellin'
Which way Old Nick will go.
So take off them britches,
And set right in this chair;
I'm gonna finish this cigarette,
Then, baby, I'll be right there...

And, yes, I was right here. And, yes, damn it all and fuck it all, I was set.

THE HUNTER'S MOON, THE BLOOD MOON AS SOME CALL IT, the full moon of the month of my birth, passed.

It was the most distant, the farthest full moon of the year, and therefore seemed to shun the lower heavens and the eyes of those who gazed.

I spent my birthday alone, as I wanted to spend it, in the quiet heart of autumn. I had not had a drink in quite awhile, and I did not want to drink on this day. But I was looking forward to a glass or two of good—I mean really good—single-vineyard champagne to go with the Muscovy drake I was going to roast, pancetta-larded, garlic-larded, with quartered spuds, which never tasted better than when set to cook in duck fat. So I had blown about a grand on a bottle of Krug Clos du Mesnil 1995. It would be something of a waste, as I would not drink the whole bottle, and the rest could not be kept in the refrigerator, no matter how well-stoppered, for any length of time. But it was what I wanted to taste with my fine, greasy duck.

This was not a surreptitious alcoholic craving. Alcoholics who like the taste of the booze and beer they drink are rare. Almost all of them hate it, no matter what they say to the contrary. They endure the taste for the sake of the effect. They will endure anything, down to the ruination and forsaking of their very lives, out of their enslavement to that effect. I wanted nothing to do with the once dear oblivion that drink had brought me.

The idea of the taste of it repulsed me. I wanted only the taste of a bit of fine champagne.

I felt the same about blood. The very idea of the taste of it repulsed me.

Could the effect of the baclofen be psychosomatic? I did not know. In the past, I had been administered all sorts of drugs that I was told would work on my brain chemistry and banish darkness and depression. Never had I felt any effect whatsoever. So I figured I was not much susceptible to the so-called power of suggestion. I had not been in touch with Olivier in a long time, so had not discussed any of this with him.

Maybe the change I seemed to be undergoing had nothing to do with pills. Maybe the baclofen had simply become a part of my routine, like the Valium I took with the milk, the Valium that made me feel nothing but which I continued to take, always with cold milk, more as a ritual than anything else. There were those who told me that a mere five milligrams of Valium all but knocked them out. The ten milligrams I took at least three times a day did nothing but subtly enhance the milk breaks I took. Milk and cookies. Milk and Valium. But I continued to take the baclofen. If it was not really helping, it surely was not hurting.

There was no baclofen, no nothing, for bloodlust. Maybe because there was no bloodlust, but just an insane desire to steal back what had been lost: the florescence and wonders of youth and strength and life and love. If ever I had fallen for the power of suggestion, I had done so then: acting, seeing, feeling a madness beyond that of Ponce de León's, and maybe even Alexander the Great's, belief in and search for the Fountain of Youth. I had actually seen, or believed I had seen, the marasmus of my flesh relenting, reversing. I had tasted and experienced anew, as if relishing all about me for the first time. It was like the guy said: "what fools these mortals be!"

Ponce de León was about sixty when he kicked. Alexander was thirty-two. At least I had beaten those fools out.

I still have six of the volumes of the American Artists edition of *The Complete Works of Mark Twain*. They must be all but a hundred years old by now. They were, as inscribed in one of them, the "Property of Ernest Tosches," a great-uncle of mine who did not read. These were the books with which my mother introduced me to the idea of literature, reading to me from them before I myself could read. All I remember is asking her to begin over and over again with the sixth chapter of *Huckleberry Finn*, "Pap Struggles with the Death Angel," because it had the word "damn" in it and I liked to hear this curse word, and there was something even better about hearing her read it to me. I've kept these books out of the childhood associations they hold for me: my great-uncle (the oldest member of my family to have been born here rather than in Italy), the vaguely remembered voice of my mother, and the books themselves, and her reading them to me, having been my introduction to what I later learned was called literature.

I stopped right there. Yes, these beat-up old books held a certain sentimental value. But my later love of words was, as much as in them, rooted elsewhere. I could just as easily trace my scurrilous and dirty mouth to my mother's repeated reading to me of that chapter I so liked solely for its cussing. Wordsworth was full of shit: the child was not the father to the man. The child was just a child, a stupid fucking kid.

As it turned out, I never came to care much for Mark Twain. But I did like a few of the things he said. In his autobiography, he said something about there being more satisfaction to be had from a single wicked deed, if it was truly heartfelt, than in all the kind deeds in the world. And as pertains to this business of my particular madness and the sought-after Fountain of Youth, he is supposed to have said that life would be infinitely happier if we could only be born at the age of eighty and gradually approach the age of eighteen or so.

The champagne was good, and so was the duck, and the blood that trickled out when I tore the limbs from its body.

But I didn't want more champagne than the two flutes I'd had. And I sure didn't want any blood.

THE FULL BEAVER MOON CAME, THE BEAVER MOON WENT. The last of the leaves, golden yellow in the brilliant beauty of their death, fell and were swept from the trees. The lackeys of business proprietors and luxury-priced dwelling-coops were made to brush them away with brooms, blow them away with handheld electric leaf blowers, treating the leafy colors on the pavements and in the gutters as if they were trash, as if they were litter, as if they were an unsightly intrusion in this played-out neighborhood where great old trees were few and unsightly intruders crowded the streets in ever-increasing numbers.

Then came the cold moon, the last full moon of the year, the moon of long nights, as it was also known. This autumn, my season, would soon be no more. Winter was on its way, drawing closer every day. The sun began to hide, and with it all else.

As the days of autumn dwindled, I spent a lot of time on the bench outside the joint on Reade Street. I wanted as much of what remained of my season as I could get. I wanted to fill my lungs, heart, and spirit with it.

By some blessing of nature, I began to rise earlier and earlier, until I woke daily with the dawn. Down the block from the bar and the bench, there was a New York Sports Club. I passed it almost every day, shaking my head as I saw all those unsightly intruders on window display as they trotted, going nowhere, on treadmills facing the street. But downstairs, unseen, where the yuppie window vermin in their designer athletic fashions rarely ventured, there was a real gym with real gym equipment. I hadn't worked out in years, not since I quit going to La Palestra uptown. The gym on Reade Street involved no subway rides; it was just a few minutes' walk away. Sure, it was less fancy, less exclusive than the joint uptown, but it was a gym all the same, with the same fucking equipment. And it opened every weekday morning at just about the time I was waking up. I joined up and began to work out there early every morning after taking what medications and supplements I needed to take, drinking my pint of buttermilk and hemp protein, taking my first Valium of the day, and sitting with my first glass of cold milk and a few cigarettes. After a couple of weeks of this, hitting the gym more mornings than not, I began to regain strength in my decrepit carcass. I looked as I had looked—or had imagined that I looked—months before, when I had believed that the blood of virgins and their reasonable fac-similes had brought me new life. I emerged on those mornings from the gym, after awhile in the steam room, a good shave and shower, hot water followed by cold, and a change of clothes, full of energy and life. I picked up a coffee or cappuccino, sat with it and my cigarettes on the bench—on some mornings the bar was not even open yet—and breathed out my energy and breathed in the sweet calm of autumn's long farewell.

On that bench, I fell into reveries, feeling at times like one of the old men in Fellini's teacup. Not long after my birthday, I came to see that the darkness within me was not, and never had been, a curse from which I suffered. I was born into darkness, literally—uttering my birth cry a moment before the stroke of nine in the dark of night, in a hospital in downtown Newark that no longer exists—and by the cast die of something that might be called fate. I could live with that. In fact, I could not live without it. To deny the darkness, to seek escape from it, would be to deny and seek escape from myself. I must not do that. I must not do what most do, deny and seek escape from themselves. To betray one's nature is to be betrayed in turn. What was in me embraced itself, and I smiled and breathed very deeply.

I came also to see, with a lighter and more wistful smile, that as the years flowed by, I had come to take after my grandmother in so far as religion was concerned. Born in Abruzzi in 1896—her birth certificate described her mother as a *contadina,* a peasant; her father a *mugnaio,* a miller; the both of them *analfabeta,* illiterate—she came here as a stowaway early in the last century. She was a woman full of life and love and laughter. Overflowing with them. She could also be a formidable character at times. She once dispatched a nigger punk who tried to steal her purse while she was waiting for a bus on Broad Street in Newark, on her way home from the doll-eyeball factory where she worked. "God-a-dam, you little tootsie sumabitch bastid!" she had said as she struck him, favoring as always the epithet "tootsie" to the down-and-dirty *tizzun',* whence it derived. She was also an ardent and accomplished shoplifter, methodically having obtained by theft over time complete settings for six of fake Tang dynasty chinaware from the Canton restaurant. As I grew up, my father and I took turns going to fetch her and get her out of Dutch every time she got caught loading her big purse at Bamberger's.

She would have told you she was a Roman Catholic. She had rosary beads, and there were a few crucifixes around. I recall her on a few occasions going to church with some kind of doily on her head. I remember her, when I was small, lying beside me telling me the story of the little manger scene that was set up under the tree. I don't know where she got it from, but it was a lot better than the one in the Gospel of Matthew. In her version, one of the three wise men who held forth a box was, I think, bearing *"a piz"* from Ilvento's Pizzeria on West Side Avenue. And the black wise man was, of course, an endearing "little tootsie" who had happened along.

She probably even believed she was a Roman Catholic. But what she really was, deeply and devoutly, was a superstitionist. For her, opening an umbrella indoors or placing a hat on a bed were to be avoided more, and held as more dangerous, than any sin that might send one's soul to hell. There were countless other taboos. And I suspect that the rosary beads and crucifixes were essentially apotropaic charms, like the amulet she wore to avert and protect her from the evil eye.

And I had become quite a superstitionist myself. Though not quite as devout as she was, perhaps because I was not and could not be as well versed in the hermeneutic ideology as she. But while I knew it all to be utter nonsense, I was a practicing superstitionist all the same, down to spilled salt and walking under ladders.

Much of the pleasure of getting old is in outliving one's enemies. There were two—one was a magazine editor, the other a book editor—whom I wanted to help along. A friend had worked on a movie crew down in the Louisiana bayous. She brought me back three voodoo dolls. Two of them were obviously of the kind foisted off on tourists and other suckers. But the third, oh, the third of them! Fashioned round two cruciform twigs, and menacingly nasty to behold, it had been made by a true believer whose trade lay in the mist between priestess and medicaster.

After deciding which editor I wanted to see go first, I had spent a very long time trying to obtain something—a hair, a used tissue, a discarded Band-Aid, anything—that possessed a trace of the DNA of this particular person. This was now done, and it had been placed in a small black envelope and affixed to the doll with a map pin. The first of the longer, death-inducing needles had now been inserted remordently into the stuffed body of the doll.

So far, I had heard nothing of the editor's demise, but time would tell. Look at the multitudes who went to churches and temples. My superstitionism made as much sense as the far more ridiculous twaddle they called religion. At least my gods were real.

Those risings at dawn, those early mornings at the gym. That bench, those lingering autumn breezes that wrought joy through melancholy.

One day, savoring every breath, I strolled home to find that my pantyhose-encasement DVDs had at last arrived. I readied some of Melissa's hosiery and one of her red-soled high heels, placing them on the cushion next to where I sat. I slipped *Pantyhose Multilayer Fetish Sex* into the player, but, shutting off the machine, did not play it then. I was simply preparing for later, for the dark. Just to imagine it! Not just pantyhose, but layers of it, to further separate one from the flesh under it while at the same time intensifying the sheer salacious seductiveness of lust most thrillsome; and should one care to delve the flesh within, a rending of all that luscious nylon was only a brute ripping or a stroke of a number-nine single-edge razor blade away. My love life was full.

I had it all, motherfucker, I had it all. Yes, my gods were real.

On my way to buy some goat milk and steal a rib eye steak, I sang aloud, plangent and uncaring, the opening lines—the only lines I could remember—of "I Ain't Got Nobody," and I grinned like a fool at those who looked at me sideways or were taken aback as I passed.

THE APPROACH OF WINTER WAS GENTLE AS THE MOON OF long nights waned. With my blood flowing warm and well from the gym, with my paper cup of hot coffee and my smokes, my mind yet wandered comfortably as I sat in the mornings on that bench feeling the coming of whatever warmth the day would know.

The fear that I had tried so much to plumb, classify, and understand, I now saw, was but a chimera. What fear there was in me was of that chimera. I had sought its origin in my past, but its origin, like that of the origin of this universe in which I, and everybody else, was but a meaningless, fleeting, passing note of nothingness, was not knowable. Theory was the mother of stupidity. Fearlessness and fear were one. One rid oneself of the chimera; one simply *was*. It did not pay to fear any more than it did to worry. Almost all, if not all, of what we feared, like almost all, if not all, that we worried about, never in our lives came to be. A brave man dies only once, a coward dies a thousand times, sacrificing a piece of himself to feed the chimera every time he does.

The chimera lived on booze, too. Booze was a great fear maker. When I ducked into the bar with my coffee every now and then, to escape a sudden biting chill, I looked around, I listened, and I knew that. I didn't even need to look around, to listen. The place could just as well have been empty. Merely looking into myself, seeing myself at the bar with my booze and my beer, I knew it.

Yes, booze was the fear maker, the drainer and destroyer of one's self and one's life. I had surrendered these things, my self and my life, to it. I was a fool, a fool more foolish than most. I loved my life now, every breath of it. I enjoyed thieving more than ever before. And the biggest thievery, the stealing back of my own self and life, I enjoyed most of all.

The booze, the blood, the desperation. I'd had my fill. I had survived on the surface of the earth for a long time now. Before long, with good fortune, I would be twice the age that Alexander the Great had reached. He was a character who had always intrigued me, conquering the world so young, going down so young, so fast, with a golden drinking goblet of fear in his hand. I once had wanted to write the story of his last night on this earth that he conquered, this former private student of Aristotle, this young man so wise beyond his years, who would vanquish the world, but whom in the end drink conquered. What did *he* fear? What was his unknown, unknowable chimera?

Suetonius tells of Julius Caesar standing before a statue of Alexander, sighing to reflect that however long he lived, he would be as nothing to the shadow of that man. The next night, he woke shaken and shocked by a dream of raping his own mother. His soothsayers shored him, telling him that this dream augured great things. It meant, they told him, that he would conquer the world.

What had been Alexander's dream? These were things that fascinated and beguiled me. This was why I had wanted to make a tale of history and dreams, of fucking one's mother and all of the world, of demons and of drink. But who would want it? In this age, Alexander and Aristotle meant nothing. They were nobodies, except perhaps in name, who had never even texted or tweeted. Alexander the Great? Aristotle? No market value. Hoi polloi twaddle, the milk toast slurry and fodder of which best-sellers were made—now we were talking. Would Alexander have even cared to conquer this world?

He had conquered the world, but not himself. That's what I wanted to do: subdue and possess the world that was in myself.

Part of this, I knew, was inseparable from ridding my life of the bourne stones of its freedom. True, I was freer than most; but I was not as free as I could be.

Soon I would get a driver's license. I had never had one. This would give me the freedom to travel alone to an idyllic little town I had come across in the middle of deep-wooded nowhere in eastern Pennsylvania. The grandiose, delusional expectations of youth were behind me now, and all I really yearned for was a few years of peace and quiet and solitude at the end of the road, a little place with a hammock strung between two great old trees in the breezes of being. A driver's license would allow me the means to get there when I wanted. It would demolish one of the bourne stones of my freedom. Whether I could yet cut the umbilical cord that held me to the corpse of this city was something that remained to be seen, and it had to do with an even greater bourne stone. But in the desire for freedom there was strength. I entertained traveling back and forth between here and there for a while. Whether I could afford both my Manhattan place and my little place with a hammock also remained to be seen, but this was a matter of hard reality, not desire and strength. We would see.

And I knew that I had to turn my back and walk away from this business of writing. It was not what it once had been. No matter what publishers claimed, the racket was now only a vestigial withering on the much bigger dying racket of conglomerated business itself. And freedom of speech was dying, and literacy was dying, and reading was dying.

Just as important, I no longer felt a need to assert my own

existence by communicating to others. And on the occasions when I did, I felt there was no one out there at the other end.

Only an utter fool would rather express himself than simply be himself. To live was a beautiful thing. To write about it was a labor. And the pay had given way to pay cuts.

Writing was not an act of the imagination or, may the Devil take me for even using the word, creativity. (How I cringed when people used the word "creative" in referring to me in my presence. I knew then and there that they did not know what work was. I knew then and there that they lived in a dream world. Often they themselves were make-believe "artists," living the "creative" life under the shelter of trust funds, inheritances, or family money of some kind. Often they were trying to imply an intimacy that did not, could not exist with me or what I did.) There was absolutely nothing to be romanticized in what I did. If flower garlands of words and phantoms of imagery had come to me in visions, so had some of the stupidest fucking ideas I have ever had: ideas that landed me in jail, emergency rooms, or hock.

No. The seduction of writing in one's impressionable years could prove fatal in one's later years.

In the folly and self-torture of trying to say what cannot be said lies nothing but ruin. This is why the greatest of writers have in the end always forsaken words for silence. As George Steiner said: "The true masters are those who relinquish their vocation." In this regard, he mentions Tolstoy. I would summon Dante, Rimbaud, Pound, Beckett. It was Rimbaud who saw the light earliest, quitting the racket six days before his twenty-first birthday, to run guns and coffee in Africa. But it was Pound who put it best, after fifty-seven years' work on his *Cantos:*

"I have tried to write Paradise / Do not move / Let the wind speak / that is paradise."

Yes, the greatest of writers have always forsaken words to

embrace and cede to the more expressive powers of silence. I was not great, but in an age bereft of any greatness whatsoever, I could pass for it.

So why go on writing? It was no longer a means to freedom. It was barely anymore even a means to make a buck. It just stole your real life and immured you in a sort of counter-life, neither here nor there. There were no holy words, no words that bore wisdom. Holiness and wisdom belonged to silence alone. To believe otherwise was vain arrogance; and worse, to know this and to persevere in the exaltation of words was to become the cheap carny barker of lies peddled as truth—a degradation and a wrongfulness, and nothing more.

IT WAS AN OVERCAST MORNING OF DRIZZLING RAIN. COOL, BUT not cold. To me it was a lovely morning, except for the humidity, which I could always feel throughout my system, from my nasal passages to my guts, like a malaise.

The diminutive Ecuadorian drudge who tended to the upkeep of the joint had not yet arrived. The retractable dark green awning above the bench had not been lowered, and the bench was wet and getting wetter in the drizzling rain. I went into the bar, got the long, unwieldy awning crank from the barroom corner where it leaned, extending from the floor almost to the ceiling, brought it outside, raised its hooked end, finally engaged the small hoop of the rig, and cranked down the awning to keep the rain from the bench.

I returned the crank to its corner in the bar and looked about for a newspaper to place on the bench under my ass. I found a copy of the *Post*, and as I was about to lay it on the wet bench I saw its headline: BADGE BETRAYED. I never read newspapers. They were bad for you. But occasionally I was drawn to one of their tawdry front pages. Both the *News* and the *Post* had grown almost unbearable in their use of worse and worse puns. It was the old-fashioned Dick Tracy sort of headlines, the feigned public-spirited cries of outrage and shock, that I liked. So I stood there in the light rain to check out the story.

"A veteran NYPD officer assembled an 'army' of his fellow

not-so-Finest," the two-page spread began. The cop had "boasted to an FBI informant" that he could pull together the perfect "crew" for any crime. The army had been branching out from smuggling guns and cigarettes and slot machines to offering violence for a price. "We got cops with vests and guns," the veteran officer had told the fed. "I'm setting up a good army here. A good f—kin' army." There was a bunch of pictures. The guy who shot his mouth off to the informant, several of his "army" members. My eyes passed over the pictures, returned very suddenly to one of them. And I heard his voice:

"I know this guy. He's all right."

Those two cops that morning last spring. Numb-nuts and glue factory. It was glue factory. Good old glue factory.

I had wondered a lot about that strange visit from those cops. I had wondered even more about the events of the night before. Had I really slashed those girls' throats? All I remembered was a dim, indistinct flickering in the blackness of what could have been a dream. But I had seen the blood. On the blade of that knife. On me. Or had I only imagined seeing it?

I had wondered about the old cop in my kitchen with his moronic young acolyte. He seemed so intent, old glue factory did, on simply writing me off as innocent and getting the hell out of there. It left me wondering, and I had been wondering ever since.

He, not I, was the killer, I told myself at times. He was, I told myself at other times, a secret brother, a fellow blood drinker, who somehow recognized me as one, and who understood.

When I wondered, my mind went everywhere. Now, as I put the paper on the bench and sat on it, I told myself that he was likely far more concerned with unloading his latest shipment of assault rifles than with any kind of pain-in-the-ass cop work.

Sitting on that paper, the awning overhead, sipping coffee and smoking a cigarette, looking into the foggy drizzle that seemed to quiet the street, I wondered again if I had really killed those girls that night in that doorway. I recalled my last words with the Japanese guy at the store, just a few blocks from here, where I had bought that knife. My last words to him were about the long knife with the leopard-bone handle that I wanted to have made. He told me that the knife master had spoken with several of the great craftsmen in Japan. Using leopard bone was totally against the law, he reported; it could not even be obtained in Japan. One of the craftsmen could make for me a *higonokami*— a folding knife—with a handle of ivory, maple, and ebony. I could also have a *tanto,* a dagger, with a handle of ivory, persimmon, and white sharkskin. I could, if I wanted, have a *higonokami* made entirely of silver. I asked the guy to thank the knife master for me, but also tell him that he should trouble himself no further. "The special knife," I told him, "can only be made of leopard bone."

I still didn't know why I wanted this thing, this "special knife" with a leopard-bone handle. Why did anyone want anything he didn't need?

As I sat there, I tried to remember what those two girls looked like. I stared into the diffuse mist of silent rain, trying to bring forth their faces.

In that diffuse mist under a sky that showed nothing but a gathering of heavy gray clouds, there were here and there the odd faint twinklings of the slight refractions of stray half-light passing through the raindrops.

If I had in fact killed them, I should at least have the memory of having done so. This at least should be mine. The feel of their warm flesh in the springtime night, the drawing of the blade across that flesh, the terror in their eyes, their blood in my mouth. These things, the memory of them; they should at least be mine. If one was to be a killer, then the memory of killing should be his. What was it to be a killer who had not even the pleasure of—

It was there and then that I caught myself and turned away from wondering. I gave myself to, became lost in, the semitransparent windblown veil of the muted light-falling rain. I did not feel so good. It was the weather. The humidity.

I T WAS NOT WITHOUT FEAR, OR FEARLESSNESS, THAT I DECIDED to call Melissa and Lorna. I wanted to know. Whatever it was, if anything, that I was to know, I wanted to know it.

This would have been a lot easier, a hell of a lot easier, if I had a few drinks under my belt. The booze would bring forth my words with ease and without anxiety. But those days were over, the days of the slaking silver tongue. The booze was behind me. I took some baclofen, some Valium, poured a glass of cold milk, turned on the telephone, and dialed Lorna's number. Truth be told, I had a premonition. A bad one. I had the eerie feeling that Lorna was dead. This Venus born from a sea of gloom, this night flower whose wails of ecstasy sounded so much like cries of suicide, or of one being murdered. She was dead and was no more. I was almost sure of this as I listened to the phone ring once, twice, three times. I should be doing this in the light of morning, I told myself, not now, when all was dark. I was about to end the call when I heard her voice.

"Hey, stranger," I said. "It's me."

There was a pause, as if she did not recognize my voice. Then she spoke. There seemed in her a mixture of curiosity, surprise, and concern. The emotion that lay under these things was unreadable.

"What happened to you? It was like you vanished. One day you were there, and then you weren't."

It made me breathe easier to know that she was all right, or at least that she was still there, still alive.

"I was sick, baby. I got sick, really sick. I ended up in the hospital for a while. I'm just now starting to feel better."

There was another pause. I could hear her breathe. I felt that there was anger in her, but that she could not speak it after what I had said. It was good to know that I could still cast my cape of deceit over the cheap prop of the truth on its worn little pedestal.

"God." She sighed. "I don't know how many messages I left, how many times I called you."

"I haven't listened to any messages. They told me just to rest, to take it easy. But I had to call you." I took a swig of milk. "I had to call you."

"Can I bring you anything?"

"I'm OK." I tried to sound as weak and sickly as I could, and I hated myself as I did so. "I'd love to see you, though." Why did I say that? Why?

"You sure you don't need anything?"

Why had it taken her so long to answer the phone? Was she in the middle of prodding that stun-gun gizmo into her own crotch?

"I just needed to hear your voice and know you were all right."

And to know that you were not dead. To know that you had not killed yourself, and that I had not killed you, and that you do not want to kill me.

"Do you remember the last time we saw each other?" I asked her.

"Yes," she said. For a moment I grew tense, as if she would say no more. "I knew something was wrong then. I knew you'd been drinking. A lot. I was going to ask you to leave, but I was worried about your diabetes. With the drinking and all. I asked you about it and you waved it away. I should've done something, but I didn't."

"How long ago was that?"

"I don't know. A couple months ago." Again, her breath, nothing but her breath. "Maybe more. Then you weren't there. I didn't know what to think. The worst things went through my mind." Then a moment of further silence. "But you're going to be OK, right?"

It was hard to tell if this was an *addio senza rancore* or an utterance of heartfelt concern, a caress of undiminished closeness. Yes, I assured her, I was going to be all right. I tried to temper my best weak and sickly voice with something like an aspiration of strength.

"I love you," I said, cursing myself as I said it.

Then there was just the sound of our breathing together. At last I heard what I wanted to hear.

"I love you, too."

For some reason, a reason I did not seek, that made me feel better, made me feel happy that I had called her.

"Maybe in a few days?" I said. I thought of her, and of that haunted flat of hers and that curtained room with its dim red glow, and her cross and her whips and her stun gun and her blood and her cries. I wanted nothing to do with those things. Nothing. "Maybe for breakfast or something," I said.

"That sounds great," she said. The unreadable emotion that lay under her voice was gone. These were plain and simple words of plain and simple happiness.

"And now I'm going to drag myself off to bed again," I lied. "I'm really glad I talked to you," I said in all truth. "Really glad."

I heard her kiss the phone, then I like a fool kissed my phone as well, and then slowly ended the call.

Calling Melissa required a fresh glass of milk and a fresh cigarette. I sipped, smoked, and dialed.

"Hey, baby," I said, humbly but nonchalantly.

I heard her breathe. It sounded nothing like Lorna's breath had sounded. Nothing at all like it.

"Fuck you," she said. And that was that.

I faltered for a moment with the phone dead in my hand before shutting it off. Then I merely smiled and slowly shook my head. Well, I told myself, she was certainly all right. No doubt about that.

And so I knew. Whatever it was, whatever it meant, I knew it. I sat in the dark and savored my cold milk and my smoke.

IDECIDED THAT EVENING THAT MY LAZARUS ACT AT CIRCA Tabac was long overdue. I went for a haircut, shave, and manicure, then went home, took a long hot bath, put on a custommade Stefano Ricci black-on-black silk shirt and a beautiful gray custom-made chalk-striped suit of Dormeuil pashmina. I pulled on new black lisle socks, freshly buffed crocodile shoes. I put on my cashmere-lined python-skin duster with the dark mink collar, my Lock & Co. midnight-blue homburg, and I went out into the night.

"Gimme a club soda with lemon," I said. "The bartender reached instinctively for a wedge of lime. I caught him and repeated the word "lemon."

Lee was at the other end of the bar. I smiled at him, let him be. I knew that he would sooner rather than later use me as an excuse to get away from whoever was bending his ear.

It had been a long time, I reflected. A long time without a drink. I did not know exactly how long. But a long time. The club soda, effervescent with the tang of the lemon, was refreshing. It was good. I *was* changing, goddamn it, and I felt great.

The talk of those in their cups could be overheard. One spoke of the fine line between good and evil.

People were always talking about the fine line between this and that. The fine line between genius and madness. The fine line between love and hate. The fine line between pleasure and pain. But where were these and all the other fine lines to be discerned?

The truth was that there were no such fine lines. They did not exist. There was not the least, most translucent filament of a line between the one and the other. It was as impossible to see where love became hate, where genius became madness, and so on, as it was to distinguish where red became orange or green became blue on the spectrum.

There was a certain sense of dejected festivity in the air. The little tootsie with the pizza was coming.

Already I had begun to receive invitations to Christmas celebrations. I merely threw them into the trash, along with most of the seasonal cards that arrived.

It was my editor Michael who told me of the card that Evelyn Waugh had concocted to send in response to most of those who wrote to him, asking him to do this or that, inviting him here or there: "Mr. Evelyn Waugh deeply regrets that he is unable to do what is so kindly proposed." A bit archly polite perhaps, but oh so wonderful a stroke.

"Hey," said Lee when he worked his way down to me. "You're looking pretty damn good there for a corpse."

"Hell, man, you know me. Best-dressed cat in the boneyard."

So much for the thin line between life and death.

"You hear about the Jewish dilemma?" he asked. I'd heard this one before, but not from a Jew, and he was a Jew, so I shook my head.

"Free ham."

I laughed. He laughed. He asked me what I was drinking. I told him it was vodka and soda. He called the bartender, who was nearby, and told him he'd have the same. Only then did I tell him what was really in my glass.

"Put some vodka in mine," he told the bartender.

I loved this guy. So much in common. So much apart. Yet together, we always let all the birds fly free from the cage. We talked a good long time. We laughed a good long time. We sloughed the layers of secrets from us and came away clean with new skin.

"You know," he said to me at one point, referring obliquely to the night the ambulance took me from here, and probably to a lot of other nights as well, "with you it's not the booze and drugs that worry me. It's the diabetes." Then, as if intuiting that I wanted him to change the subject, he asked me if I was at work on something new.

"Nah. In fact, I'm thinking of quitting the racket."

"You could never stop writing," he said. His words made me think of something else Michael had told me: "You're only happy when you're writing." I wondered if they were right, the both of them.

"Besides," Lee said, "it's all a fucking racket. All of it. Everything."

I told him about my plan to get a driver's license, my dream of a little place with a hammock, far away from it all.

He laughed. I grew defensive for a moment, then reminded myself that it was him.

"Yeah." I laughed a little as well. "I guess dreaming's a racket, too."

"Well, dream on. It's how I make my money."

We laughed a little together then. Yeah, I thought, the fine line between this racket and the next. The endless fine lines that simply weren't there in the infinite wheel of suckers' rackets that constituted the racket of being. World without end. Amen.

Afterwards I went over to the Lakeside, then later dropped in at Reade Street.

Yeah. The dirty unshaven drunk slobbering on his dirty shirt, shaking in his dirty stinking pants. Or he who stood before them now. Which would they remember? Both perhaps. But if so, it would be the power of transformation that they remembered most of all. And the embodiment of that power would be me.

Yeah. I showed them all what change looked like. Showed them all what they could never look like, change or no change.

AT HOME THAT WEEKEND, I WATCHED TEN THOUSAND bucks I'd bet on the Raiders against the Packers plunge down the shitter. Eleven grand with the vig. Eleven fucking grand. I would have done better to lay three grand straight across on a horse. Even if I had lost, I would have saved two grand, and the whole thing would've been over in minutes rather than hours. Jesus fucking Christ. I was insane.

I poured a glass of cold goat milk, took two ten-milligram Valiums, and sat there. The thought of fucking Melissa's clothes passed through my mind. It might bring some sort of release, I told myself. But fuck it, I concluded. I was even mad at her pantyhose and shoes. I felt like killing somebody.

THE LONGEST NIGHT PASSED, AND THE SUN BEGAN ITS northward ascent in the sky. The winter solstice. The witches' Sabbath of the Yule.

I mulled over my Christmas feast to come. I craved lasagne with a nice cool salad of iceberg lettuce, cucumber, radishes, and mint with a dressing of unpressed, unfiltered olive oil, Regina red wine vinegar, and garlic. Yes, that is what I wanted, but I did not feel like putting in the work to make the lasagne. Feast days were for feasting, not for work. I had turned down the few invitations that I had got to join others. That was work of a different kind—beholden socializing—and without even my lasagne as a payoff. I would get a kurobuta pork roast from Lobel's, put it in the oven with some stock, spuds, onions, and parsnips. I'd have it with applesauce and garlic sauerkraut. And I would make the salad that I would have made to go with the lasagne. That would be work enough.

The more I thought about it, the more I looked forward to that salad. I had been having a lot of dry-mouthed thirst lately. There was something about the idea of the chilled cucumber slices and fresh mint, the cool iceberg lettuce hearts and oil-rich dressing that promised to quench this thirst where water failed.

I wanted another glass or two of good champagne. But I had ended up pouring half of the last bottle down the drain, which had resulted in a tab of about five hundred bucks each for the two glasses I had drunk. There was no way I would ever get to keep this joint and have a little place with a hammock in the hills if I kept up that sort of shit.

Then again, as a great man once said, what the fuck.

O N CHRISTMAS EVE MORNING I LISTENED TO WQXR, the classical station, as I sat with my cold milk and Valium. I heard something about a belief that Paganini had made a deal with the Devil. I heard something about the blood of Christ, something about eternal life. I made a mental note to watch *Abbott and Costello Go to Mars* that night. I felt loneliness go through me like a breath that had nothing to do with breathing. I saw those who had beckoned me to follow them down side paths that led away from loneliness. I wondered what those remembered beautiful faces looked like now after the passing of the years. I wondered what horrors, what miseries, what more doleful loneliness had lain hidden in wait at the end of those side paths. Or could it have been happiness?

I bundled up and walked against the cold wind down to Reade Street. It was Saturday, and I was hoping that the usual small weekend gathering would be there: Andy, Jim. Bill, Dewi, and the one or two or three others who constituted our convocation of kindred buddies. Maybe Musial would be there. Maybe even Bix, who was boycotting the joint in a one-man war of pique, would be stirred by some Christ-hating sort of Christmas spirit to put in a surprise appearance. It was a good bunch. Some of us drank, some of us didn't, some of us went back and forth.

There was no one there when I got there. It was early, not quite eleven yet. It was too cold to sit outside on the bench for any good length of time, so I took my coffee inside, made some small talk with the bartender, and gazed out through the window. I asked myself why I had never called Lorna back, never had that breakfast with her.

One of the neighborhood girls passed by. I knew her father and remembered her when she was just a toddler. I had no idea how old she was now. Not quite twenty, I would say. Maybe eighteen, nineteen, or so. Dumb as dishwater, but, God, she was beautiful.

She too was bundled up against the cold. All you could see, besides her pretty face and soft windblown hair, was the nakedness of her knees between the bottom of her coat and her boot tops. It was all I could do to stay on that bar chair. I wanted to rush out, to watch the bend of those knees from behind as she continued down the street. But if I moved, I would miss what of those knees and what of her face were now mine to see if for only an instant more.

In that instant, I imagined her wiping blood with her soft, pale hand from the vermilion corner of her lips. I imagined her knees suddenly lacerated as if slashed by an eidolon of the wicked wind.

Then she was gone, and I shook it all away.

I HAD NOT SEEN HIM IN A LONG TIME, A VERY LONG TIME. Now, two or three days after Christmas, I stood near the bench smoking a cigarette with one gloved hand and holding a paper cup of hot coffee with the other.

Him again. That pain-in-the-ass fucking stumblebum. He paused and looked my way, stood there, drunk and weaving, looking like shit.

He took a slug from the pint he was carrying. His bleary eyes roamed round him, then returned to me.

"You know what I mean," he rasped in a low and broken voice. "We were there. We know."

He wove closer with that pint in his hand, grinned that big, drunken grin of his, baring those dirty gums and few dirty teeth of that mouth that was even worse than mine.

I placed my cup of coffee carefully down upon the bench. My right hand was now free, and I hauled off and punched him square in the face.

He fell backwards, hit his head on the pavement. His pint lay broken in a small pool of whiskey. There was blood running from his nose. He raised his head slightly, laid a dirty hand to the back of it, then stared at the blood that covered his hand.

"Why'd you do that?" he asked, looking up, not at me but toward me.

"Because I felt like it," I said.

I stood for a moment in the early quiet, looking down at that pain-in-the-ass fucking bum lying there with his shattered bottle and his silenced bullshit. He seemed unable to get up. I enjoyed watching him try. My hand ached as I retrieved my coffee from the bench. I took the coffee back into the bar.

"That was a good one," grinned the bartender, who had as yet only one customer, some guy down the far end, lost in his beer.

"Fuckin' pain in the ass," I said.

"Ought to roll him out of the way from out front of the place."

"Ah, he'll manage to get rid of himself. Look at him. He's already up on his fuckin' knees."

Then, sure enough, with the help of the bench, he was on his feet and somewhat upright again. He rubbed the back of his head, at the hair that was matted with blood, gazed at the broken pint bottle, and staggered off.

The bartender called out for the little Hispanic lackey, had him sweep up the broken glass and throw a bucket of hot water on the spilt whiskey and blood.

Yeah, he was gone, all right. And so were those fucking dead monkeys.

"Goddamn dead fuckin' monkeys!" I heard myself yell out. The lone drunk at the far end of the bar stirred, nodded besottedly as if in sullen agreement. The bartender laughed. This whole fucking world was nuts.

My breath eased as I finished my coffee and wondered whether that was the last punch I would ever throw.

I decided to get another coffee from the corner store across the street. I asked the bartender if he wanted a cup of tea, and this idea brightened his morning all the more.

I T OCCURRED TO ME THAT I COULD GO TO A MEETING, THAT maybe I should go to a meeting. It was well over ninety days since I had last been drunk, and, in A.A., ninety days of sobriety is, for reasons unknown, considered a milestone, a big deal. When the chairperson asked at the beginning of the meeting if there was anyone present today who was celebrating ninety days, I could raise my hand and everyone would applaud. The thought made me cringe. Then I told myself I didn't have to raise my hand. For one thing, I had more than ninety days, so I wasn't actually celebrating ninety days today. For another, and more important, there wasn't a single fucking thing I had to do if I didn't want to. Drunk or sober, I had never gone in for that A.A. prima donna shit. I didn't need any drama queen applause. I didn't want any. Not for being drunk, not for being sober. If it helped some people get sober and stay sober, fine. But it was the sort of shit that drove me to drink.

There was a lot to be said for the inspiring strength that could be felt in a roomful of people at a good meeting. And there was a lot to be said for the unbearable bullshit in a roomful of people at a bad meeting. It was said that it took only two people to constitute a meeting. I had found some of the most honest and fortifying of meetings to be of this kind.

So, hell, why not a meeting of one? I was not opposed to applauding myself in unostentatious privacy.

It was true. I was not a good A.A. member. I was not a good member of anything, really, not even of the human race—and I say this with a sense of pride. I saw the twelve steps not as a sacred path to enlightenment but, all in all, as a load of churchy bullshit concocted by a few characters who were as wrong as they were right. I saw the twelve steps as leading nowhere and to nothing. It was change that I wanted, for myself and for anyone I might help along the way. I wanted life. I wanted freedom, not congregationalism.

I would rather lie far from the church, not sit in it. Lie far from it on the sweet-smelling grass, communing with that higher power that was within me and the sky above.

Hear ye, hear ye! This meeting is hereby called to order!

Hi, my name's Nick and I'm an alcoholic.

We will now pass the basket.

This meeting is hereby adjourned.

THEY SAY THAT NEAR THE END, NOT LONG BEFORE HIS death at the age of forty-three, Guy de Maupassant felt and saw his melting, dissolving brain flowing from his nostrils. He hallucinated, saw ghosts. Before he was put in a straitjacket, he declared himself to be suffering from "sheer madness."

So much for the popular saying that tells us that if we think we're crazy, we're not. Then again, maybe Maupassant's brains really were running out of his nose.

Maupassant's story "The Diary of a Madman," as it is called in English, is no longer available these days except as a Kindle e-book, an MP3 download, or an iPad app. To use the title of one of his final tales: *"Qui Sait?"*—"Who Knows?"

I had never felt that my brains were oozing out of my nose. I had never been put into a straitjacket. I had never purchased an e-book or an app.

Was I sane? Why did I so often suspect myself of being insane? Was it actually my brains that I had been blowing into my snot rag? Had anything I had written been turned into an iPad app behind my back? Who knows? More to the point: *qui se soucie?*—who cares?

It was true that I did not like the way I was thinking lately. But it was also true that I did not like a lot of the ragged, old, awkward winter clothes I was wearing lately. I would go to Modell's, buy some new winter things to wear. I would go uptown to Orvis, get one of those shearling-lined ox hide leather coats, a nice warm cashmere turtleneck sweater and nice warm cashmere watch cap to match. And I would get some new thoughts, some new ways of thinking. Easy to find, in me, in the sky. And a lot cheaper than shearling, ox hide, and cashmere. Free, in fact. Yeah. That was all there was to it. All new shit. From brain to britches, britches to brains: all new shit. Hell, it was all the same. What shall it profit a man if he shall gain his own soul and lose out on a new set of Duofold thermal underwear and Wigwam socks?

The wisdom to know the difference? Fuck it. There was none. No wisdom. No difference. No acceptance. Let others weigh what could not be weighed in scales that did not exist. Let others compromise and fiddle-faddle with the fate they toyed with like a trifle in their idle hands. There was only change.

The festerings of the brain that we call thoughts could be cast away and forgotten as easily as old clothes.

Swift and resolute action leads to success; self-doubt is a prelude to disaster. He who hesitates is lost.

CHANGE. HOW WAS I GOING TO CHANGE? HOW, AT MY age, after all these years, was I going to change? Heraclitus said that it is through change that things find repose. It was best perhaps to just let it happen. There had been no struggle as far as turning away from booze was concerned. It had happened, and that was all there was to it. All I had done was to not question it, to just let it happen. And that was change of the highest order. A change that, try and struggle as I might, I had not been able to achieve in the almost fifty years of my drinking life. Change. Repose.

I moved aside on my bedside table the book I was then rereading—Henry Miller's *A Devil in Paradise,* a wonderful book if ever there was one—and placed nearer to the bed, beneath the lamp, Philip Wheelwright's *Heraclitus.* Though more than half a century old, it was the most perceptive, erudite, and valuable presentation of the fragments of the philosopher, and probably always would be.

Heraclitus speaks to us from more than two thousand five hundred years ago. This is just a breath away really when you consider that almost two million years lay between the first hammer stone that man fashioned and the first bronze spike to be driven in by a hammer. And the hammer and nails of the philosopher's words remain today as uniquely indestructible as when he spoke them, in the fifth century B.C. All was change. You could stand in the same spot by a river and stick your foot repeatedly into the water. Yet, as he said, you could not step into the same river twice, for as the river flowed, its water was thus in its flux never the same.

"Nature loves to hide," says another of his fragments. In this fragment, Wheelwright finds much about nature concealing herself "beneath vague indications and dark hints." There is, he says in his reading of this fragment, "a hidden attunement in nature, the discovery of which is far more deeply rewarding than the mere observation of surface patterns." For me, this was as true of our own natures as of the vaster nature of which we are a part.

Change. The hidden and its vague dark hints. Discovery. Repose. Reward.

One fragment states simply: "I have searched myself."

The like of this has been uttered so many countless times, dragged through the dirt and dust of lies by so many countless voices. But he is the only one who I feel is to be believed, who I feel to be wholly honest, wholly truthful in saying this.

Yes, just a breath away. I used to dream of sitting with him and speaking with him. Now I did sit with him and speak with him. On a bench, beneath the sky.

I wanted so much to give him the Wheelwright book, that he might tell me what he himself thought of it. But, of course, I could not. He could read only Greek, and while there were words and phrases of Greek to be found in it, the book was written in English, a far cry from the Ionian dialect in which he had written the great lost work from which most of the surviving fragments derived. And, of course, there was no physical hand into which to place the book, or any book, or any thing. Nor were there eyes to read it.

The other morning, on that bench, I saw a large gaping of raw wood on the trunk of the great old pear tree across the street. The big long bough that had arched almost all the way across the street had been torn from it and lay in the gutter. It had to be twenty feet long. A fucking truck, a big ugly reckless fucking van, must have crashed into that bough. I cursed the unknown truck. I wished upon the unknown driver a violent, painful, and very imminent death. He had destroyed beauty, of which there was so little left to destroy. And for nothing. The bough of the tree, the bough of beauty, lay ravaged and dead. It should instead be the ravager who lay dead and mutilated in the gutter. Or crucified on the desecrated trunk of that tree.

Staring at the open wound of that dismembered tree, I asked Heraclitus: "Where is the repose in this change?"

"Change comes by chance, not the will of gods or men. Change can never be brought about or averted. Chance is the master of all. Yes, change brings repose. It also brings strife, which is the essence of nature. Repose is strife slowed, or, at best, a respite from strife; but never a lasting escape from it. What has befallen this tree, and your love for it, is but one infinitesimal particle of water in the immeasurable sea of flux. And from that immeasurable sea of flux, the constant strife of nature, between the hot and the cold, the dry and the moist, the constant frothy waves of chance bring constant change, and in that change there is repose."

He seemed to sense that I did not quite follow him, and he resumed:

"For is there not repose in knowing that without constant flux, the endless strife of nature, sometimes witnessed by us but for the most part hidden from us, the vast universe, the world in which we live, would cease to exist?"

There followed one of those lingering moments, like a long breath, when he seemed to leave me but did not.

"Homer was wrong in saying, 'Would that strife might perish

from amongst gods and men.' If that were ever to be, all things would come to an end."

Then, as if in the afterthought of inner searching, he softly said, "No, change does not always bring repose to each and all. My own death brought none to me, even as I knew it to be but one infinitesimal particle of water in the immeasurable sea of flux. No. Death brings no repose. Knowing that might bring some repose as you look upon that tree, which, though smitten by strife, still lives. As do you still live."

When we spoke, he answered silently. But what he said was always clear in its wordless eloquence.

I never contradicted him or argued with him. Even when he silently whispered to me that I should take a drink, or do worse; even then I just sat and let his silent suggestions pass without question.

There were times when I found myself speaking aloud to him, casually gesticulating as I did so. I always caught myself when this happened. But sometimes it took me longer than other times to realize what I was doing.

One morning, something very strange happened. I was sitting with him when I heard one of two passers-by say something about "her clitoris." It seemed such an odd phrase to overhear, yet I was certain that I had heard it.

Then, almost instantly, it hit me that she had not said "her clitoris," but instead was mispronouncing the name of Heraclitus. She knew, I told myself. She did not know the proper pronunciation of his name—or maybe she did, and I had simply misheard her—but, in any case, she knew. She knew who was there, unseen, beside me.

I should have taken a few steps after the two women, and, excusing myself for the intrusion, asked the one I had overheard if she had spoken his name. I did not do this, but I should have. She had nice legs, too.

He himself may have heard her as well, for it was not long after this that he suggested we remove ourselves to a different bench. I had become so habituated to this bench that for a moment I hesitated. A block north, we entered little Duane Park. Walking slowly and looking round at the barren winter trees, we chose a bench, a good one, beneath one tree and facing another. It also faced a sign that, in three languages, forbade smoking. I took to aiming my cigarette butts at the sign when I flicked them.

A different bench. The notions of change and repose were in the drifting of the fallen leaves in our path.

Then one morning he was not there. And I somehow knew that he was not to return. He had moved on.

ON NEW YEAR'S EVE, I MADE *ARAGOSTA AL SALMORIGLIO,* broccoli with anchovy and garlic sauce, and thick-cut French fries. And, fool that I was, I blew almost another grand on another bottle of that Clos du Mesnil 1995. Money down the drain, almost literally. But fuck it. The year past had been the most diabolically fucked-up year in my life. I would toast its end with the champagne I chose.

The broiled lobster came out beautifully. I had watched it closely and pulled out the pan the very moment that the olive oil in the *salmoriglio* sauce set it aflame, placed the hunks of sizzling hot lobster, still moist and tender on the inside, into a bowl, and poured over them more *salmoriglio,* which I had reserved and only very, very slightly chilled.

It was *un pasto ambrosiaco,* a meal fit for the gods—of which I was one, was I not?

I should have got myself a cake or a pie or something, too, I thought with some regret. I had been good, all too good, these last few months as far as my diabetes was concerned. But one could not live in deprivation. That was not living. Fuck my diabetes. It had fucked me.

A banana cake from Billy's. An apple pie, or a pecan pie, from that little joint on Chambers Street. A half-dozen cannoli from— oh, fuck, I didn't even know who made good cannoli anymore. And ice cream. And fresh whipped cream. But what had I got?

Fruit. A fucking pear. Some blue goat cheese, a stick of finocchiona. Not even a few sweet figs or dates. Oh, well, maybe it was better in the end to ring out the old year and ring in the new salubriously.

New year? Who the fuck knew what year it was, anyway? According to the old Roman calendar, we were now in the year two thousand and fifty-something. The sixth-century abbot who, through his interpretation of a fairy tale, decided to split everything into B.C. and A.D., reckoned the year preceding what he, and we after him, call A.D. 1 to have been the first year of his snappy new Christian calendar, rendering the year called A.D. 1 to have been not the first but the second year, thus throwing us all off by a year ever since. To further confound matters, the hypothetical Jesus could not have been born in the year the abbot set forth. Historical research into New Testament "evidence" reveals that he would have to have been born a few years earlier. So A.D. 1, or the abbot's zero year, would really have been more in the range of 4 to 7 B.C. We were off on all counts.

And then you had the Chinks, who were in the year four thousand seven hundred–something, and the Jews, who were a little further on in years than the Chinese. According to some of our Muslim brothers, we were now only in the year fourteen thirty–something; and one of a confusing variety of Indian calendars has us well past our four millionth year.

As for the custom of the first of January marking the start of the new year, this was not widely accepted even throughout Europe until the seventeenth century, with Italy and England holding out until the middle of the eighteenth century.

So what the fuck was it, and why was I celebrating it? Without banana cake and ice cream, no less? This whole fucking world was crazy. Its brains were running out of its nose.

Lingering with my second champagne, I drew from a desk

drawer the slim bundle of papers on which I had written during the four seasons past. I sat with the last of that second champagne, my cuttings of pear, cheese, and finocchiona, and I began to peruse those writings.

There were not many sheets and scraps, and of what was written on them, not much made sense.

Several of the scraps presented words that found their place in my memory as well: notes about the taste of blood, with adjectives and similes and such crossed out, one after another, deemed insufficient, inadequate; a shopping list with "dated after 4/10" underlined in parentheses after the item "goat milk"; a poem of sorts that remained untitled:

> *It is the gods, the nine of them,*
> *whose names we have forgotten*
> *that we must love and fear,*
> *for they are within us, seeking light*
> *in the darkness where we do not look,*
> *where the dead parts of us lie.*

One piece of paper contained no writing at all, just the impression of a cute lipsticked kiss. After a moment, seeing the color to be not red but a reddish dark brown, I realized that it was not lipstick but dried blood.

Hadn't I started work on a new book this past year? Or had I just thought that I was beginning work on a new book? Was there any way in hell that I possibly could have considered what was on any of these papers to be even the germ, the seed, let alone the worded opening breath of a book, however inchoate?

Yes, not one of the most diabolically fucked-up years in my life, but the most diabolically fucked-up year in my life.

Something that struck me was the disregard for grammar and

syntax in much of what was here. Even in my most hurried notes, I usually gave more care to these things than to the legibility of what was being scrawled for my own eventual decipherment. And there were pages here where my illegibility was so daunting that, after some effort, I merely turned them aside with a shake of the head.

Then there was a page on which I had very neatly printed with an unwavering hand these words alone:

YOU WILL DIE VERY SOON

IN THE MORNING LIGHT, THOSE WORDS NO LONGER GAVE ME pause. They meant nothing to me, for I knew them to be the words of a madman. That I was that madman meant nothing either. I was at repose with myself, as the old ghost might say.

And besides, it was true. I was very soon to die. As are we all.

What did give me pause was that, looking back on all those crossed-out adjectives, similes, and such with which I had tried to capture in words the taste of my fair maidens' blood, I now, in the calm, quiet morning, found myself trying to recall and summon that taste with all the power of my physical senses.

And more than just the taste, but the feeling it brought with it, too.

But try as I might, I could not. I entertained the notion of renewing and refreshing my memory.

No. Nature may love to hide beneath vague indications and dark hints. But I must not further hide the hidden. I must allow my own nature no longer to cast or to hide or abide in vague indications or dark hints. I must not betray myself.

THE WOLF MOON SIGHED FULL IN THE DARK EASTERN SKY. In the night's breath just before dawn, under the sea-goat of Babylon, she could be seen with her consorts, godly Saturn and the blue giant Spica.

I saw them in the cold black before morning light, on my way to the gym. The one thing the gym lacked was a heavy bag. On some mornings, I went instead with my old sparring gloves to the old boxing gym, a few blocks farther south, on Park Place. I loved striking out at the heavy bag. Ducking, circling, left, right; hitting, hitting, hitting, and hitting, hitting, hitting again; harder, harder, harder, and harder, harder, harder again.

The winds grew ever more bitter, the whistlings of their siren songs ever more strange, more rapturous in their deceit. Soon the Year of the Dragon would begin.

I did not call it that. I called it the year of the nine gods, because these gods whose names I did not know were now no longer to be loved and now no longer to be feared. They were to be slain. For I myself had looked within me, and I myself had found and let loose the light, had found and given light to the dead parts of me.

The change in the winds was as nothing compared to the change in me, and the songs of their sirens were as nothing compared to the songs with which I lulled myself to sleep, and the Year of the Dragon was as nothing compared to the seasons I claim for and unto myself. May the slaughter of the gods begin.

THIS WAS IT. I WAS WARM IN MY FINE NEW COTTON LONG johns, flannel-lined britches, thermal socks, my cashmere sweater and watch cap, shearling coat, and lightweight Sorel Avalanche Trail boots. Warm with barely cooked soft-scrambled eggs and good hot coffee going down my gullet. Warm in the repose of the infinite change whirling round and through me as I sat on my new bench watching the world shiver past, fleeing from nowhere to nowhere.

I was warm and I was ready. I was ready to cut through the nylon again. Ready to cut the past to shreds and leave it for the hungry wild dogs that roam that netherworld of nonexistence, that wasteland of the past. Ready to look on and howl with those dogs as they devoured those shreds, then cut those wild dogs to ribbons as well. Ready to cut away all the residue of bullshit and lies, mine and the world's, that so stubbornly clung to me and in me. Ready to cut myself free, once and for all, of the whole fucking world of bullshit and lies, which is the only fucking world we have beyond ourselves. I was ready to cut into a good big greasy slab of swine. I was ready to cut the throat of anything called God and all the fools that knelt before it. I was ready.

The new bench the spook Heraclitus had led me to was a big part of it. Not only a great change in itself, but a change that brought with it more change. The few buddies I had who congregated at the bench in front of the bar rarely ventured to these benches, just a block away, in little Duane Park. That brought more solitude, more repose. And there was a change in pussy as well. There were new legs galore, legs that would rather walk the path through the trees than pass by the bar on their way from nowhere to nowhere. Even the sky seemed to change as seen through the branches of trees so nearby, so much closer.

As I closed my eyes, smiled, and raised my face to the sun of the new sky, I could almost see the rushing blood of the slaughter of the gods. There were whisperings in the wind. They were hard to make out at first. But in time they grew clear.

The first of the whisperings that I was able to grasp came to me in a voice that I recognized. It was the voice of a young woman I remembered from somewhere. Slowly I became aware of whose voice it was. Yes. Her. But her name eluded me. I had forgotten it, yet it seemed to lie so tantalizingly, so frustratingly, in the periphery of vague memory. Yes. It was her. Sandrine. The redhead who liked to be raped after bathing in warm water and milk and brushing out her hair. Yes, of course, Sandrine, the first of those whose blood I had tasted. Sandrine, who, with her young friend Marie, had met her end in a doorway on Thompson Street on a cool spring night.

She whispered nothing of her death, nothing of her young friend Marie, nothing of Thompson Street, nothing of blood or of flesh. But she did speak of some sort of doorway, some sort of entranceway, which may have been of this world, or the world within, or some kind of otherworld.

"You were there," she whispered to me, "but you did not enter. You did not go beyond where you had been led. You did not go to what awaited you, to what you did not and do not know. You did not enter."

None of the other voices was recognizable, except for my own, which at times seemed to be whispering to me from outside myself. But most of the voices, like Sandrine's, spoke in a cryptic way, like seers, soothsayers, or the deranged. It was all rather peaceful, like playing with the pieces of a puzzle: pieces of a mystery that the voices brought to me.

Then one day, that peacefulness was gone. There was, as always before, but a single whispering. But all of a sudden it was joined by a multitude of others, speaking all at once, and all these whisperings became a babel of screams that rose to a maddening pitch.

I jolted up from the bench, and as my heart pounded and my legs quaked, I tried to concentrate on the sounds of the cars, trucks, and people nearby.

The babel of voices in my head subsided, but I feared they might return. I walked slowly away, and it was awhile before my heart beat quietly again and my legs regained equilibrium.

I could not remember anything of what these whispering, shrieking voices said. I did not want to.

As I walked, I tried to con myself into believing that all of this was the whispers and cries of a book gestating within me, calling out to me to be written. But I wasn't buying any of it. This had nothing to do with words destined for paper. It was something else, completely different; something I had never before known.

Why was I walking, in a roundabout way, to the bar? It was, I told myself, because I needed to hear familiar voices talking the same old familiar bullshit. Real voices.

Then again, were they not all real? The ones from which I had fled, and the ones to which I was fleeing?

I shot the shit awhile with a buddy of mine. We both fell silent after a few minutes, then I thought he was resuming our wayward conversation.

"What did you say?" I asked him, raising the brim of my wool cap from my ear and leaning a bit toward him.

"I didn't say anything," he said.

Sweet, fair Venus came forth from the waves of clouds that were like froth in the cold night sky.

Myrtle of the sun god. Lover. Purifier. Seducer of slayers, born of severed cock.

THE VOICES WENT AWAY FOR A FEW DAYS, THEN LATE ONE night as I lay in bed, I heard Sandrine whispering for me to rise. A soft, lone whispering that brought no alarm or unease. I found it in fact to be rather soothing, and rather welcome: an emollient of sorts, an opiate tincture for my troubled mind. The return of a familiar.

She whispered that I tarried, that I must be on with it. She whispered that I knew this. She whispered that the turmoil of voices that had beset me were all merely trying to tell me this, and that among the assailing voices had been my own, descending upon me with the others, telling myself what the others, and she herself, had been trying to tell me.

The manner in which she spoke was different from what it once had been, in life. Her voice, too, had about it a more dulcet tone. I felt it to be somehow beatific. The voice of Sandrine, yes, but the voice of Fra Angelico's *Angel of the Annunciation,* too.

I asked her about this business of tarrying, this business of getting on with it. She whispered to me words that were my own:

"To betray one's nature is to be betrayed in turn."

And then she whispered more:

"The entranceway. You must pass through it. You await yourself on the other side.

"There, as one, you will find change. There, as one, you will find repose. True change. True repose."

I saw things in my mind: abominable, unutterable, and worse.

She was in me, seeking revenge, seducing me to wreak it for her upon myself.

Fra Angelico's angel was tempera and gold leaf on a piece of poplar wood. And it was sometimes better not to look too closely at such things. Had not art restorers recently uncovered the image of Satan lurking in the hallowed clouds of a fresco by Giotto in the Basilica of Saint Francis in Assisi?

No, this was no Annunciation of any kind at all. It was a trap, a damnation, a snare.

"Trust me, my love. Trust me."

I could feel myself glaring. I stood and paced forward on the floor, my forefinger extending and waving in anger at her who was not there.

"Trust you!" I growled aloud. "Trust you!" I cocked my head to one side, menacingly. "You fucking bitch. You dirty rotten little fucking bitch. I killed you once, I'll kill you again."

"Yes, my love, yes."

If only she were really there. If only I could kill her again. Oh, how I wanted to kill her again. And again. Kill her over and over, again and again, forever and forever.

"Yes, my love, yes. Now, my love, now."

There were knives everywhere, all sorts of knives. The Walther in the closet. The capped black iron pipe. Oh, Christ, how I wanted to kill her again, fuck her corpse, jerk off on her dead fucking face, then kill her again; murder and desecrate her again and again as she said those words through a bruised and swollen mouthful of blood, broken teeth, and ebbing breath:

"Yes, my love, yes. Now, my love, now."

I took a step back, took a few breaths, each calmer than the last.

"I put you here," I said, tapping my head and lowering my

voice, to her, who did not stand before me and was not to be seen. "I put you here, and I can take you out of here."

I felt suddenly strong, not with anger but simply stronger, as if with the weightless armor of tranquility.

"For no one has power over me."

There was something then like the trace of a whisper—no more, probably, than the cold wind entering through the slight opening of the kitchen window—and then there was nothing but the familiar and faint shrill ringing in my left ear.

That was the end of the whisperings, the end of the voices. But the things that I had seen in my mind, abominable, unutterable, and worse, they stayed with me.

THEY WERE SCENES OF RAPE AND TORTURE AND BUTCHERING, and of things far more horrid, things on which I will not dwell lest they become further embedded in my mind. I walked down the street, and with the merest of glances at them, set people afire, caused them to clutch their hearts and drop dead with a scream, made little schoolgirls to tear away their skirts and blouses and masturbate in a frenzy, shattered windows here, brought about terrible crashes there. It was all so horrifyingly delicious, especially those visions of which I cannot tell. And I was immune to all consequence. It was my own world, the world of these visions, a world of crime without punishment.

At times I yearned for it to be real. At times I wished to banish it all from my mind. At times I merely wondered at the darkness of an imagination given more to seeking beauty in the sky.

I brewed some coffee, stuck another pin in the voodoo doll, and reflected that this day belonged to me, and that it would bring whatever I willed it to bring, if only within myself.

From the window I saw, like cockroaches down in the street, hurrying little figures of hurrying little people, flinching and cowering in the cold and the wind. This made the hot coffee taste and feel even better. I looked at my thick leather and shearling coat draped over the chair.

At the bar I sat with another coffee, in a paper cup, from the corner store across the street. Candlemas was only a few weeks off. On the television set above the bar, I noticed a commercial for what seemed to be a Christian dating service called Christian Mingle. The ichthus, the Jesus fish, was part of its logo. I thought of Lorna on her cross, scaring away whatever kind of suitors she might find through Christian Mingle. I wondered if anybody ever got raped and strangled through Christian Mingle. I thought of the origin of the Jesus fish thing. It was a stupid fucking acrostic in which the five letters of the ancient Greek word for "fish," pronounced *ichthus,* were taken in order to stand for the first letters of the five words in the Greek phrase "Jesus Christ, God's Son, Savior." A stupid fucking acrostic. The goddamn Church made the Word Jumble look high-class, if not downright divinely inspired, by comparison. Fucking mah-jongg mackerel.

No, it would probably be impossible to get away with it, raping and strangling one of these Christian Mingle cunts. Ah, but what a sweet thought.

THERE HAD TO BE A WAY OUT. OR A WAY IN. OR A WAY. I WAS free, but I was lost. There was something beautiful in this. But something scary, too, when it began to get dark.

I CALLED BENNET, MY ACCOUNTANT, AND ASKED HIM WHAT HE thought my annual living expenses would be if I had little or no income. I also asked him what I would get in social security payments if I began to take them now.

I called Greg, my lawyer, and asked him what the statute of limitations was on bank robbery.

My accountant responded by saying it all depended on which Nick I was taking about: the Nick who had once lavished away eighty grand in a week, or the Nick who had calculated that he was now spending eight grand a year on coffee and cigarettes, and reacted with the shocked resolution that measures must be taken to reduce this sum. The fact that both Nicks always stopped to stoop and pick up pennies in the street—not only, as I saw it, a habit of perspicacious economic prudence, but also damned good physical exercise as well—signified nothing to him.

My lawyer said: five years, if no killing was involved. He also advised me not to get any ideas.

Of course, I had already considered several possibilities. I could live lavishly for a year or so, then sell my apartment for a million bucks or so and be the wealthiest homeless guy around. I could take what I had, less a few hundred grand for a private plane to London, and try to double it at the blackjack tables at the Ritz Club. But every time I pondered this particular idea, I saw myself sitting weeping on the edge of a bed in a three-grand-a-night hotel suite. And there was always the prospect of selling my apartment, getting that imagined little place with a hammock in the sticks for a quarter of what I would get for my place, and pocketing the rest for living out the rest of my allotted days at a far lower cost, but in comfort. But this would mean cutting the umbilical cord without any period of acclimation to new surroundings, which I might end up hating, and which in any case would seem to irrevocably seal the fate of solitude and loneliness. I couldn't see, in such a place, the occasional nine stone of sweet young gal-meat on nights of need, let alone love that might be mine to have and to hold, in my small town in the sticks.

For some years, a certain middlebrow magazine paid what amounted to my monthly bills for the privilege of using my name on its masthead. Then, when hard times hit, this stipend was annulled. I guess the alter rebbe of whose Philistine empire the magazine was a part felt the economic squeeze. It must be a terrible thing to be in one's eighties and have only ten or twenty billion dollars left to live on for the remainder of one's life. Perhaps the next time I ran into him, I should ask him if he needed a few bucks.

I had my name removed from the masthead. Without the few grand each month for doing nothing, I surely did not want to be incriminated, no matter how fancifully, as a contributing editor of a rag that now encouraged, or at least condoned, language such as "adorkable" and "tweepulsive" on its website. It had never been a literary magazine, but it had been minimally literate. Now it was merely another celebrity-gossip rag for housewives on the racks at supermarket checkout lines.

I have here, in fine ink, a handwritten letter from a dozen years ago and more, from the rebbe's lapdog, saying of one of the pieces I wrote: "It is, quite simply, a masterpiece. The best thing I will ever have published, in fact. I cannot thank you enough."

And these hollow men were indistinguishable from so many other dishonorable hollow men who had come to define this fallen, shoddy racket.

There were mornings when I wondered whose death would bring a sweeter smile of fleeting pleasure: the monkey-faced one or the pig-faced other; this lying dolt or that one. Oh, the ways of idle musing. Oh, the ways of this world.

In the same box of correspondence where this letter lay, I also came across many letters from a young lady whom I had known and cherished:

"Because of you, joints loosen," began one of these, then went on:

"I want leather shoes with high high heels. I want patent leather gloves that go past my elbows. I'm kneeling over you, lying on your back. Your neck is exposed. Your head is tilted back off the edge of the bed. The hairs of my cunt graze your neck. My left fist is in your mouth. My right hand is in your hair, pulling. Give me your neck. You feel my cunt on your chin. I feel your hand on the back of my thigh, through my stockings. Ultra ultra sheers.

"I take my fist from your mouth, leaving one finger in to pull your mouth to my tit. I leave it in while you suck and bite. My finger and your tongue roll around each other. My knuckle pushes hard against your teeth."—I had real ones then.—*"The ones in the back. Hard. My right hand stops pulling your hair to hold your neck so you can fuck my tit (I think this is possible) with your mouth without distraction. Suck, baby. Suck. Bite. Draw milk.*

"I let your head down gently. I take my finger from your mouth. I turn around and now you feel my tits and patent leather around your dick. My nipples brush your balls. Your fingers are in my cunt, moving in and out in the same rhythm my hands move up and down, tighter and tighter around your dick. I place the tip of my heel between your lips. Your left hand grabs my hair. It's in a ponytail, high and tight. Grab it. Pull. Wrap it around your wrist. I arch my back. My nipples are so hard. I pull against you. I want your

cock down my throat. As I lower my mouth, as you slide down my tongue, my heel slides down yours. Suck, baby. Suck. Bite. Draw blood.

"Don't let go of my hair. Keep pulling. Harder. Harder. Push my head down. Harder. Harder. Don't stop fucking me with those fingers. Don't stop. Fuck. Fuck. Don't stop coming, baby, don't stop…"

That letter is dated October 20, 1996. Another letter from her, this one handwritten on lined yellow paper, from a few weeks later:

"Oh Nick, I love you more than I have ever loved. You, Nick, you. Not an image of 'man' or of 'Nick' but small shards you let out that I glimpsed— Oh Nick, I love you so and your love"—and here there is a verb that I have trouble reading; it begins with an *h*, almost surely ends with a *t*, but, I told myself, it cannot be "hurt," it must be something else—"deep."

I should have looked further, to see what the next letter from her was like, to see if there was a next letter. All I know is that we were together again about six or so years later, but I don't know for how long.

Did what she described in her letter of October 20, 1996, ever happen? I do not know. I can't even remember having received a letter like this from her. I know we had a lot of wondrous strange nights together. She was, somewhere in me and under these stars, one of the loves of my life.

There was an accordion file and five thick archival boxes of correspondence in my bedroom closet, all of which, along with the rest of my papers and notebooks and manuscripts, were set to be sold later this year to a university library. If I had forgotten this letter, as I had, I could surely forget anything. Maybe I should cull some of this stuff before it got hauled away.

The letter made me miss her and want her again very badly. It even made me think of calling her. If only I could hear her voice saying what she said in that letter.

Talk about change.

From praise for "a masterpiece" that was "the best thing I will ever have published," and for which I could not be thanked enough, to being treated like a nigger slave. It was, as his website might have it, downright "tweepulsive." People told me that I should be careful, that I should not burn my bridges behind me. I told them all the same thing, which was the truth: I've always loved the smell of gasoline.

From the love and wanton luscious desires of a lithe young beauty who walked and talked like a poem to nothing, to staring at a piece of paper and trying to remember.

Change. Yes, things had changed. And, yes, there was no way out. I could not step into that same river again. How many rivers had I stepped into, feeling it all to be the same river?

"Suck, baby. Suck. Bite. Draw blood."

I got up, went to the drawer that held Melissa's hosiery and shoes, took it all my arms, brought it to the garbage chute in the hall, and dumped it.

"I cannot thank you enough."

I tore the fatuous flattering letter to shreds and flushed them down the toilet, where such words belonged.

Who was on a thousand-dollar bill?

"Draw blood."

Grover Cleveland.

Was it she with her rosy golden youth who had put this blood quest into my mind?

The only president to serve two nonconsecutive terms.

Could it be that I had drawn her blood, then forgotten about it?

And the ten-grand note? What about the ten-grand note?

Impossible. I would have remembered.

Chase. Samuel P. Chase. He was on the ten-grand note. They stopped making them both, the grand and the ten grand—and the five hundred and the five grand—all of them; they stopped making them all in 1946.

But how I wished she were here now.

No, not Samuel. I always got that wrong, his first name. Then again, what did it matter?

She mattered.

Love and loneliness, loneliness and love. How many times had these dice been cast throughout my life? How many testaments of endless love, how many vagrancies of the heart, lay forgotten in those boxes in my closet? When would I come to see that these things were, like breath itself, merely the inhalations and exhalations of my life, and, like breath, not to be dwelt on.

But I had seen it. I had seen it and forgotten it. A memory came to me.

Club de l'Aviation, avenue des Champs Elysées, Paris, December 2002, the middle of black night. I sit at the blackjack table with my beloved friend Héloïse because my hotel room is haunted, the hotel is haunted, all of Paris is haunted, as my heart is broken. Love has sly-rapped me yet again.

But you would never know this. For I have lived long enough to learn that all things pass, and that after every suffering, the gods have blest me with a happiness that I had never known. And so I smile and I laugh and I speak like a holy fool.

An elderly woman at the table begins to cough her brains out. She seems to go into apoplexy. She seems about to croak.

With a raised arm, the floor man in his tuxedo who has paused at our table calmly calls out with a smile: *"Cigarettes pour madame!"*

A fresh pack of cigarettes arrives. The floor man opens the pack with alacrity and graciously offers it to madame, who, with what seems like her final act in life, places one of them between her lips and extends it to the waiting flame of the floor man's lighter. She draws deeply. The coughing and hacking of what seemed to be her death throes cease with a spasmodic breath of resuscitation.

It is good to know that madame is well.

The game resumes. Madame is dealt two aces, splits them, draws two face cards.

The floor man congratulates her and moves on.

It is good to smoke. It is good to drink. It is good to gamble. It is good to laugh. It is good to hold a kindred spirit close, in suffering or happiness, in the middle of the night. It is good to live.

How could I have forgotten, until now, the memory of that long-ago night and its dissolute magic?

Love and loneliness, loneliness and love. Flush times and lean times, lean times and flush times. Where would the dice upon their final toss come to rest?

As the demon barker said: *"Ev'rybody wins at Skill-o!"* The parting words of the god who fled.

It was getting late. Not just this night. All of it. There was no moon, and the ever-flowing, ever-changing river lay in darkness. I had little time to linger. Fuck lost love and fuck all those who would trespass against me. Maybe there was to be no more money. Maybe there was to be no more love. What was it all anyway? The one nothing more than ever more devalued paper scrip, the other just a temporary calmative for desperation.

And yet I craved them. But what I craved above all in this world of lies, this world of strife, as the old spook called it, was repose. If I could not summon gold from the maw of the Devil; if I could not summon her who had taken my cock into the exquisite passioning of her warm, wet mouth—and, yes, the sweetest girls always gave the best head—her who implored me to clutch and to bite; I could at least leave behind me all that was done and forever gone, and summon the strength to embrace change as I had embraced her.

Let there be no more lamentations, self-mourning, and woe. Enough of hollow or treacherous praise, of words of love, or of this bitch or that bitch crying that I drank too much.

It was all the same, and it meant nothing. I could give myself all the praise, love, and reproach that I needed. There was no need to seek it elsewhere. If it came, it came. If I chose to take it, I would take it with a laugh, and I would not take it as praise or as blandishment, as love or as desperation, as reproach or as madness.

This memory, the feeling evoked by this memory, by all memory, echoed through me.

It was good to drink; it was good to gamble, good to laugh; good to hold close a kindred spirit, even if it was yourself, in suffering or happiness, in the middle of the night or fulgent day. It was good to live.

I need not seek. I would simply take what came; take it as a breeze of change that might, if only for a breath, bring repose.

After all, as I had told myself, I was to die very soon. Old leopards, I liked to say, doddered on because they never really knew how old they were. But it was a good thing that I was not a leopard, because, even if unknown to them, their lives in fact rarely lasted more than seventeen years.

Christ, I had barely got going by the time I hit seventeen. Beautiful to behold, the leopards, and to sense, or to imagine sensing, their spirit within. But, no, I was not one of them, and I was damned glad that I was not. They didn't have a name for cats like me.

I T WENT BACK TO WHEN I WAS AN ADOLESCENT, ABOUT THE age at which some leopards die.

My left eardrum was punctured with a thin pointed stick by a five-buck doctor seeking to pierce an abscess that he said might prove fatal if it got to my brain.

He succeeded in piercing the abscess. Pus drained from my ear for a week.

But the damage to the eardrum left me with the shrill ringing in my ear that never went away and made the experience of silence impossible.

In later years, I had far more costly doctors examine my bad ear thoroughly. After a battery of tests, it was concluded that my condition, to which a fancy name was now given, could not be alleviated. When blocked, even by a pillow, it was worse, almost maddening. This is why I always slept on my right side, never my left.

That night, after coming across the letters and looking at my life through enhanced eyes, I lingered awhile, then went to bed.

It took me a few minutes to realize it, but the shrill ringing had become something like the sound of a rushing freshet.

Almost peaceful, almost lulling, after what I had heard within my damaged ear for the past fifty years or so.

"The river," I murmured to myself as I fell asleep, "the river."

I felt a smile on my face. I could not remember the last time I fell asleep with a smile on my face.

When I woke the next morning, the shrill ringing was still gone. I could still hear the soft-running river. It was like a miracle, the inflection, the modulation of the sound in my inner ear.

I told myself that it was nothing more than a miraculous respite, a passing blessing. But the banshee stayed away. The river kept flowing.

WHEN I WENT OUT INTO THE DAY THAT MORNING, I felt beautifully alone and beautifully oh so not alone as I walked through a world that forthshone amid the world of lies.

With every breath I took, I was aware of stepping into a new river of infinite possibilities.

I was free. Free of it all, even as I walked in the midst of it all.

What had been, had been. What would be—fuck it. What was, at this very breath, was all that mattered.

I was answerable to, responsible to, myself alone. Well, all right, myself and the law. But fuck the law. Fuck those who imposed it. Fuck those who enforced it. Fuck those who abided by it.

As I sipped my coffee from a paper cup, I realized that I had never done it before. You can't sip the same coffee twice. If you are free, you can't do anything twice. You can't take the same breath twice.

And I was free. Now and forever.

I was free to drink again, free to kill again, free to write again.

It could never be the same drink, the same killing, the same book.

But did I want to do these things, any of them? Was the desire to do what I had done, no matter how different the outcome, in the breeze of this breath? Or were these mere wisps of mere velleity?

Would these things, any of them, bring me repose?

Was it for me to know, or even to ask?

As one of the Gnostic tractates had it: "What is the light? And what is the darkness?" These words, written near the end of the second century or early in the third, survive in the Coptic fragments of what is known as the Testimony of Truth, a forbidden sacred text that tells the story of the Garden of Eden through the eyes of the serpent.

I slowly sipped the last of my coffee and luxuriated in my freedom.

My freedom to drink, to draw blood, to write again.

Could I think of nothing else that lay in the limitless vast of freedom?

Yes. Food. There was always the delight of food.

My feeling of exhilaration and elation seemed to fade for a moment. It returned, then seemed to fade again.

Could they really be right after all? Michael, in saying that I was happy only when I was writing; Lee, in saying that I could never stop writing?

Maybe I should write another book, just one more. It was a freeing thing, to write. And a freeing thing seemed to befit a free man.

I had no real desire to drink.

I had no real desire to draw blood from young flesh, let alone to kill. Christ, with the deep periodontal pockets round the few remaining real teeth I had, I was lucky not to have got some kind of disease from one of those girls' blood.

Had my lust-driven desire for rejuvenescence, which brought me madness instead, been a manifestation of sickness of mind or soul or body? I did not know, I never would; and I did not care.

The Apophthegmata Patrum, the sixth-century Sayings of the Desert Fathers, tells of a monk who cherished the memory of a very beautiful woman. When he heard that she was dead, he went and dipped his robe into her decomposed body, that he might live with this stench to help him fend off the constant thoughts of beauty that beset him.

Now *that,* set forth as an exemplum of holiness and piety, was sick indeed. It was beauty and its magic that I wanted, not the vile putrefying corpse of it to turn me away from it.

And what of my craving for booze? Would I ever truly understand it? The Bible itself, I told myself, had no shortage of bad things to say about this—more than enough to sanction it, in reverse, on principle alone.

But, no, the taste of booze and the taste of blood were right now both repellent. And yet I couldn't free my mind from the words in that letter:

"Suck, baby. Suck. Bite. Draw blood."

Nor, as I sat on that bench outside the bar, could I banish from my mind the distant sounds of all the laughter and oblivion of all the bars of my life.

But these things—blood, booze; even if my desire for them was not born of sickness—would they not in the end again lead me only to sickness, of mind and of body? Having found freedom, was I now not capable of halting myself in repose, before I lost control?

And didn't writing bring a sickness of mind and body as well? When writing, I forgot to eat, I forgot to take my pills and my insulin, or rather postponed eating, postponed my medications as I sat there for stretches of from ten to twenty hours, hunched over, smoking, trying with the index finger of my right hand to wrest something from nothing, to hammer through rock and dig through dirt to find a word that seemed not to exist until it was found, all to bring a sigh of power or poetry to a single phrase. And all in solitary confinement, with only yourself to tell whether or not you are lying in the gutter looking at the stars, or merely lying in the gutter, or are actually ready for a padded cell. And there is no fucking muse, that bullshit metaphorical bitch of those who speak of "creativity." There is no fucking muse.

And talk about a sickness of mind and body. After the last novel I wrote, I ended up in a medical gown at some joint called Regency Medical Imaging, on East Seventieth Street.

They put me in this big coffin-like thing. It was cold and dark in there, in that coffin-like thing.

In the enclosure encasing my head, there came a loud whirring clatter, and what sounded like a few small-caliber pistol shots. Then this hellacious noise like a jackhammer and a cement mixer going at once, all aimed at my skull.

Then there was stillness. And there was this nurse, or something, out there somewhere. Her voice was cool and calm.

Why did I remember it that way?

No, her voice wasn't cool and it wasn't calm. It was chilling, and without feeling. The gruesome voice of a monstrous maternity, a voice nectared with extreme unction.

"The next scan will be six minutes."

And it came again, longer, worse: that whir and clatter, those sharp firings, the jackhammer and the cement mixer. Then again the descent to immense sightless silence.

"Are you all right in there?"

Who's she talking to? She's talking to me obviously. But she couldn't hear me if I responded. She must know that. Who is she? Maybe she's—

"We're going to inject you now..."

That was just a few days after finishing the book. I was convinced I was suffering from a brain tumor. My doctor had assured me that I was not, but I was certain that I was, so, to ease my mind, he sent me to the cement mixer place.

But, God, I loved that book, even if it did take me awhile to recuperate from it. I still love it. If I hadn't written it, it never would have existed for me to love. Two people I didn't know later told me that it prevented them from committing suicide. I told them both the same thing: "There's always the money, but it's hearing something like that that makes all this typing worthwhile." And I meant it, too.

When I was young, I thought it would get easier. But as it turned out, each novel got harder. Maybe this was because, with each one, I was flaying a further layer from inside me, exposing yet another, deeper layer. Maybe this was what made it harder. When I was young and thought it would get easier—the days when I was thrilled to see my name or my picture on a book—I hid. I did not even dare to write in the first person. Then all that changed, and when it did, it reminded me of that sixteenth-century anatomical engraving by Amusco something-or-other, or something-or-other Amusco, the one of a guy stripped to his inner anatomy holding a knife in one hand and the drooping entirety of his body's own freshly removed skin in the other.

The special knife, I thought as I recalled this: the special knife. Maybe I needed to write. Maybe, even with all the illness it brought, it was the least destructive, least dangerous alternative that I had. And I should be thankful that I had it.

Every gift a curse, every curse a gift.

Did I really need or want anything anymore? Or did I just need to want, or want to need?

But what would I write about? While feeling strong and good and free, as long as I was set on doing nothing but living, I also felt spent, world-weary, and drained by the very strange events of the past year and their repercussions.

If I wrote another book, I could buy a bottle of *really, really* good champagne. A fucking magnum. Or I could just lie in my hammock and sip iced tea.

Electra and some boy-ass sittin' in a tree. Up popped the Devil, and the Devil was me...

Tea, tree, me. Free.

Perhaps I could write a very simple book, a book that involved neither self-torment nor the hammering and digging for words that were evocative of what was almost impossible to express. But even as I told myself this, I suspected that I could no more do this than could I write a best-seller. That was one gift that I had not been given as an alternative, though I did so want to write a very, very simple book. I was not there yet. I was happy on this day. I was free. But I was not all-powerful, as I sometimes told myself in my vanity, just as I sometimes vainly told myself that I had left all vanity behind.

How often had I thought and at times spoken of the elusive spell of words, of seeking and trying to capture the sounds and colors of that spell. And all the while, neuroscience has told us that neither colors nor sounds exist outside our brains. Words, the hues and the music of them, were magic.

And if the neuroscientists were right about Bach cello suites, about the suites of dawn and dusk, what then of light and dark, good and evil?

It was all a crapshoot, the toss of a penny found in the street. The spin of a wheel, the turn of a card. A Zoroastrian football game.

Yes, I said to myself yet again, free to drink, free to kill, free to write.

But did I want to do any of these things? Deep down, did I really want to? Did I have it in me, in the fullness of my new freedom, to merely and superlatively and sublimely just *live* and enjoy whatever came to me, from within, from the sky, from unforeseen chance and the change it brought?

As much as I craved that, it seemed somehow vaguely daunting. Maybe I was not there yet, either. Maybe I never would be.

Out of the blue, I remembered that I still had the address and telephone number of the girl who had written me that letter. Could she still be there after all these years? I very much doubted it. Besides, if I recalled correctly, she was about twenty years younger than I, which would put her in her forties by now.

I had better scratch her off the list of possible candidates to hold my hand as I lay dying, even though I had never thought of a hand in patent leather. That returned the list to a grand total of nobody.

As I finished my coffee and threw the paper cup into the gutter, those words went through my mind again like a broken record: free to drink, free to kill, free to write.

There must be countless other options. Why did I seem so enthralled by these three?

Why could I see into the sky and, at the same time, in a way, not see beyond my own right hand?

Then again, the sky didn't seem to have too many options, either.

With some disappointment, I realized that the shrill ringing had returned to my ear. It was inevitable, I told myself. I just sighed and let it settle back in. The return of the beloved.

A pretty girl passed. She smiled to me as if she knew me from somewhere. Maybe she did know me from somewhere. I smiled back. My eyes followed her as she continued down the street. I thought of what she might look like in the boots and gloves that what's-her-name described in her letter.

I had to admit that I never cared much for patent leather. I thought of a girl at the Lakeside one night, a girl in over-the-elbow gloves of black satin. I asked her where she had got them. Some store in midtown, she said, somewhere in the West Thirties. They were really a lot cheaper than they looked, she said; maybe eighteen bucks. Why, she asked; did I want to buy them from her? Just the right one, I told her. She could keep the left, I would give her twelve bucks just for the right. What was a single glove good for? she asked with a bemused grin. You'd be surprised, I told her, you'd be surprised.

Yeah, fuck patent leather, at least when it came to gloves. Satin was the ticket.

My eyes drifted to the sky.

If only it were a recording rather than a letter. I think I still had some pictures of her stashed somewhere. Good pictures.

Big billowing white clouds moved fast across the sky from over the river.

The cold wind that moved the clouds stirred and rustled through the winter branches and the few dried remaining leaves that clung to them.

Free to—

"Enough already, I get it," I said aloud.

I walked freely through the door, freely laid a twenty on the bar, and freely ordered a drink.

"What's new?" the bartender asked.

Such talk, I figured, came from wandering back and forth all day beneath three television sets that foddered the sparse, wretched herd with the ongoing sham of the most trusted name in news.

I glanced at one of the screens, was mildly pleased to see that the stock market was taking another dive and that the children of Shem were still blowing one another to hell.

"Nothing at all," said I.

There was a smile on my face. I could feel it.

This smile, it seemed, was for me, and for the billowing sky, for chance and for change, for all that lay behind and all that lay ahead, and for this moment in which I found myself still breathing in this very strange and unforeseeable accident of blood and stars called life. "Nothing at all."

ABOUT THE AUTHOR

Nick Tosches lives in New York City and is uniquely acquainted with the half-lit world in which his tale is set.